Beyond This
Moment

**Center Point
Large Print**

**This Large Print Book carries the
Seal of Approval of N.A.V.H.**

BEYOND THIS MOMENT

TIMBER RIDGE REFLECTIONS

TAMERA ALEXANDER

CENTER POINT PUBLISHING

THORNDIKE, MAINE

This Center Point Large Print edition
is published in the year 2009 by arrangement with
Bethany House Publishers,
a division of Baker Book Group.

Scripture quotations are from
the King James Version of the Bible.

The text of this Large Print edition is unabridged.
In other aspects, this book may vary
from the original edition.
Printed in the United States of America.
Set in 16-point Times New Roman type.

ISBN: 978-1-60285-456-7

Library of Congress Cataloging-in-Publication Data

Alexander, Tamera.
  Beyond this moment / Tamera Alexander.
    p. cm. -- (Timber Ridge reflections)
  ISBN 978-1-60285-456-7 (library binding : alk. paper)
  1. Women teachers--Fiction. 2. Self-actualization (Psychology)--Fiction.
  3. Colorado--History--19th century--Fiction. 4. Large type books. I. Title. II. Series.

PS3601.L3563B49 2009b
813'.6--dc22

2009003317

To my editor, Karen Schurrer.
Your laughter is a cup of cold water
to this thirsty soul, and your gift with words,
a blessing to me.

Search me, O God, and know my heart:
try me, and know my thoughts:
And see if there be any wicked way in me,
and lead me in the way everlasting.
PSALM 139:23–24

1

SULFUR FALLS, COLORADO TERRITORY
JULY 26, 1876

Molly Ellen Whitcomb stepped from the train onto the station platform in Sulfur Falls and paused, unsure of where to go and what to do next—in so many ways. The train whistle sounded, its shrill blast echoing off the station walls and bouncing down the crowded open-air corridor. The engine belched a steady stream of smoke and soot, and from somewhere behind her, the distinct clearing of a throat urged her forward. Each step was heavy, coerced, a reminder of what had brought her to this place. And of just how far she'd fallen.

Holding tight to the worn periodical tucked under her arm, she followed the flow of disembarking passengers and allowed herself to be swept along with the tide. Her arrival to Sulfur Falls was premature, four days earlier than planned. She'd wired the mayor of Timber Ridge to let him know of the change, but the clerk informed her the telegraph lines were down due to heavy rains.

Peering up into steely skies, she rubbed the ache in her lower back, doubting that status had changed.

To the west, still streaked with vestiges of winter, the lofty peaks of the Rocky Mountains reigned high above the rustic cattle town. She'd seen pictures of the mountains before, and while the gray-toned images were impressive, renderings on paper paled when standing in the shadow of their truer splendor. She almost felt as though she should curtsey out of respect—until a breeze stirred. Then she grimaced.

Her stomach reacted to the smell, and she put a hand to her nose. The stench of manure hung heavy, and trash scuttled along the station platform and edges of the street. When the steward in Denver had told her yesterday that Sulfur Falls marked the end of the line, he hadn't been exaggerating. The train track literally came to an abrupt stop a hundred yards past the depot before looping back to join the main line.

"Trunks can be fetched down line, ma'am! At the end, to your left."

With sparing breaths, Molly looked up to see a steward motioning her forward.

He eyed the periodical under her arm. "Want me to dispose of that for you, ma'am?"

She tightened her grip. "No, I'll keep it, tha—" The gratitude died on her lips. The man had already looked away.

She moved in the direction he'd pointed—until a storefront across the street caught her eye. The wooden shingle hanging above the shop door swayed in the breeze, as though beckoning. And with the soft flutter of a moth's wing, a possibility brushed the edge of her thoughts.

She hesitated, then stepped to one side of the platform to let others pass.

The idea forming in her mind went against every scruple she held, and against the integrity she'd sought so earnestly to pass along to her former students at Franklin College in Athens, Georgia.

Scruples. Integrity. Honesty.

"Two wrongs don't make a right, Miss Cassidy," she'd lectured a female student last fall who'd been caught cheating and tried to lie her way out of it.

Molly stared at the wooden shingle, knowing that was what she would be attempting to do if she acted on her impulse—trying to make two wrongs equal a right.

Her body flushed hot and cold as she recalled being ushered into the college president's office early one morning only three short weeks ago, before first-hour classes convened. Her dismissal from Franklin College had been swift and humiliating, on so many levels. What she'd done was wrong. She knew that. That was never in question. Yet the punishment seemed so severe, and she'd protested—at first.

But when President Northrop conveyed his intentions should she refuse to resign her position and leave the college, she'd acquiesced.

Immediately. He'd found the one weakness in her armor and had quashed her with it.

His "strong suggestion" that she take this particular teaching position and start over again had only been made more so by his refusal to provide a letter of recommendation for any other, including any school she'd suggested back east. And without a letter of recommendation, no reputable college or school would give her a second glance.

Taking a steadying breath, she smoothed a lace-gloved hand over her blue jacquard vest. She'd worked hard to earn her doctorate, to garner the revered title of *Professor*, same as her father, and to make a forward stride for women in academia. And had lost it all in a single act.

In the end, President Northrop had won—as men in authority always did. Because here she was, a world away from civilization and proper society, with everything she'd worked to achieve . . . stripped bare.

Her decision made, Molly made a beeline for the storefront.

She glanced around to see if anyone was watching her, then caught herself and choked back a bitter laugh. No one knew her in this town. Not a single solitary soul. A more remote location for her new "teaching opportunity" could not have been found. Not unless the Alaskan Wilderness had been an option. If it had, she was certain she would have been stepping from a train onto a vast frozen tundra about now.

Meanwhile, back at Franklin College, Professor Jeremy Fowler had been given a strong reprimand, a renewed professorship—and was sending out wedding invitations. But without her name on them. She swallowed the bitter taint on her tongue. She should have been accustomed to the unequal standards by now, but she wasn't.

Eyes downcast, she waited for a carriage to pass, then started across the street.

"Beg your pardon, ma'am, but trunks are claimed on down the way there."

She turned to tell the steward she was only running a quick errand, but it wasn't the steward addressing her this time. Judging from the man's rain-slicked duster and weathered wide-brimmed hat, he wasn't employed by the railroad. And she was certain she'd never seen him before. She would have remembered if she had.

Handsome hardly began to describe him— which, at one time, might have been enough to pique her interest. Not anymore.

The man's expression seemed open and honest, especially his smile. "I noticed you getting off the train just now, and . . . well, ma'am, this part of town isn't the friendliest. Just wanted to make sure you knew where you were going. 'Cause if you don't, sweet lass"—a twinkle lit his eyes as he slipped into a flawless Scottish brogue—"you might soon be findin' yourself somewhere you're not wantin' to be." Laughing softly, he gave the brim of his worn cowboy hat a tug. "That advice comes free, compliments of my grandfather, Ian Fletcher McGuiggan, God rest his soul. He used to tell me that every time I stepped foot out the door."

Molly could spot a flirt as fast as she could a roach on a wall. Being a professor of Romance Languages, as they were often called, tended to attract men of that persuasion. But there was nothing flirtatious in this man's manner. Quite the opposite. Sincerity punctuated his tone, as did familiar Southern roots.

"It sounds as if your grandfather was a very wise man, sir."

"He was that. Ornery as the day was long, but you'd be hard-pressed to find a kinder, gentler soul who ever walked this earth."

It took Molly a second to realize she was smiling. Then another to realize the response was genuine this time, not the brittle fabrication she'd forced in recent weeks.

Judging from this stranger's accent, she guessed him to be from Tennessee. Or South Carolina, perhaps. Definitely educated. He'd been out of the South for a while, telling by the gentler drawl. But he certainly had his grandfather's brogue mastered.

His expression turned wistful. "Not a day goes by that I don't think about him."

"And wish he were still here with you," Molly added, sensing what he hadn't said.

"Yes, ma'am." He tilted his head. "I take it you had a grandfather of similar character?"

"A father, actually . . . God rest him." And not a day had gone by that she hadn't wished he were still with her. Yet, at the same time, for the past few weeks she'd thanked God daily that he wasn't. Her punishment was great enough without being made to live it through her father's eyes.

"My condolences to you, ma'am." He removed his hat, and his voice went soft. "Was his passing recent?"

"A year ago . . . yesterday. He'd been ill, so I knew his time was close. At least I had an opportunity to say good-bye," she whispered, struck by the intimacy of their exchange. And in the train depot of a forgotten little town in the Colorado Territory, no less. Her father had said that their good-byes weren't forever, that they were only for now. But at times they certainly felt more final than temporary.

The man stared, saying nothing, and she waited for a feeling of awkwardness to set in at the lengthening silence. But it didn't. The oddest sense of ease flowed between them, and something told her such a situation wasn't an unusual occurrence for him—this tendency not to fill every moment with words, despite his having approached her first.

She hadn't expected such chivalry so far west,

especially considering some of the brutish men she'd met on her two-week journey.

"Well . . ." He returned his hat to his head, and his coat shifted in the process, revealing a badge pinned to his vest beneath. "My apologies if I've kept you from your business, ma'am. Good day to you, and I hope you find Sulfur Falls to your liking."

It was on the tip of her tongue to ask him what he knew of Timber Ridge, but seeing the badge was enough to silence that urge. She wanted nothing to do with another man in authority, however genuine and kindhearted he seemed. "Good day, sir. And thank you again for your concern."

Avoiding the muck and mire as best she could, Molly continued on across the street, resisting the nudge to glance back at the lawman. A cargo wagon barreled down the street, and the driver, his whiskered cheeks bulging, showed no sign of stopping. Giving him a hard stare, Molly paused in the middle of the street until he passed. Uncouth rabble . . .

The main thoroughfare was scarred and deeply rutted. It made for interesting walking, especially in her heeled boots.

A rather large and odorous *deposit* loomed in her path, and she managed a quick side step to avoid it. From the plentitude of droppings, it looked as though a herd of cattle had been driven straight down the center of Main Street. *Unbelievable.*

Thankful to have reached the boardwalk unscathed by man or beast, she climbed the stairs and cut a path down the uneven plank walkway, apprehension nipping her heels. Standing in front of the shop door, she pulled her father's pocket watch from her reticule. The stage for Timber Ridge was scheduled to leave within the half hour, and she still needed to facilitate the transfer of her luggage. So little time.

Gathering her flagging nerve, she opened the door.

A gentleman stood behind the counter sorting through a drawer. Not until Molly saw him did she realize how much she wished a woman were there to assist her with her purchase. An image of her father rose in equal measure with the voice of reluctance within, and her stomach knotted tight. *"Well done, Dr. Whitcomb,"* her father had whispered as she'd paused beside him on the stage, diploma in hand. *"A father could not be prouder of his daughter."*

That had been four years ago, and still the words, and the memory, resonated within her. Yet for an altogether different reason now. Knowing what her father's opinion of her recent choices would have been made her question what she was about to do. But knowing what her future held if she *didn't* carry through with this decision silenced the voice of hesitation.

The store clerk looked up. "Good afternoon, ma'am. How may I help you today?"

She glanced at the clock on the wall behind him. Best get directly to the point. "I'm interested in—" she took a deep breath—"purchasing a ring."

"Ah . . ." The man's expression brightened. "You've come to the right place, then, madam. Brentons' offers the finest collection of rings in all of Sulfur Falls."

Molly tried to look impressed.

He eyed her. "Let me guess. . . . Your taste runs more toward . . . rubies."

She shook her head, trying to find the right words. Her request was going to be harder to say aloud than she'd thought. "What I'm interested in is—"

"No, no!" He smiled. "Don't tell me." He gave his chin a thoughtful rub. "Sapphires," he said, expression hopeful.

He seemed a nice enough man and she hated to dash his hopes, but she could feel the seconds ticking. "No, sir. Those stones are lovely, I'm sure. However, I have something more specific in mind. And I'm pressed for time, so if you'll allow me to—"

"Diamonds!" He beamed. "I should have known. Come, follow me! We have a handsome assortment of them right over here."

The stagnant air inside the store grew thicker as Molly formed her next sentence. "I'm not looking for a ring with a stone, sir. I'm looking for something much . . ." She swallowed, hearing the jingle of his keys. "Simpler."

16

Bending to unlock one of the cases, he stilled, then slowly straightened. "Oh . . . I see." He gave a soft chuckle. "Let's go about this a different way, then, madam. Why don't you describe the type of ring you're looking for, and I'll show you what we have in that style."

Her mouth felt as if it were stuffed with cotton picked fresh from the bole, and she bit the side of her tongue, just a little, in order to trigger the mouth's natural response—a trick an elder professor had passed along moments before she walked in to teach her first college-level course. "What I'm looking for is a wed—" Her voice broke. She couldn't say it. But she had to.

She couldn't bring herself to look the salesman in the eye. *Lord, please forgive me. Again.* "I'd like to look at your wedding bands, sir. Nothing ornate. Your most simple band will do."

He stared. "I see," he whispered, doubt filtering through his expression. He glanced past her. "Will your . . . husband be joining you today? To help make this purchase?" He said it almost hopefully, as if wanting to give her the benefit of the doubt.

"He will not," she answered softly.

The salesman gave her an appraising look before walking to a case at the back of the store. "We customarily have an assortment of silver and gold bands, but the only silver bands I have right now have stones mounted in them. So singling out the *cheapest* bands we have—"

Did she imagine his emphasis on that word when he looked up at her?

"—you have two choices." He laid two rings before her, his manner becoming a touch brusque.

Eager to finish, she picked up the ring on the right. It was lovely. Shiny gold with delicate etchings that gave the finish a brushed look. "What's the cost of this one, please?"

He told her, and she tried not to put the ring back too quickly. Three months of her new salary as a schoolteacher! She picked up the ring on the left. It had a sheen but lacked the artistry and depth of color. "What about this one?"

He didn't answer immediately. "That one is . . . four dollars."

Well, that definitely suited her budget better. She held it at varying angles. "Why is this one so much less expensive?"

"Because it's not pure gold. It's only brass with a thin gold coating."

She inspected the ring more closely, then pulled off her gloves and slipped it on the fourth finger of her left hand. A perfect fit, as though it had been specially made, waiting for her. Running the scenario through her mind again one last time, and arriving at the same conclusion as before, she knew she had no choice. "I'll take it, thank you." She quickly counted out the bills, laid them on the counter, and turned to leave.

"Not to belabor the point, ma'am. But you do realize that the ring you've bought is not real?"

Molly paused at the door, her hand on the latch, his words lingering in the silence as their meaning took deeper hold, along with the weight of her choice. She didn't look back as she opened the door. "Yes, sir. I'm fully aware of that fact."

2

By the time Molly reached the station depot where the baggage had been unloaded, only her trunks remained. Winded, she handed her baggage tickets to the young steward standing watch.

"I wondered who all this belonged to." He checked the stubs affixed to each of the trunks. "All accounted for. You sure don't travel light, do you, ma'am?"

His youthful grin reminded her of the steward in Atlanta who'd said much the same thing. "I'm a professor. Most of these are filled with books and curriculum." Though she doubted there would be much call for teaching Italian, French, or Spanish—her areas of linguistic study—in a back-woods mountain town. Especially when she would be teaching children, something she hadn't done in years. And that she hadn't enjoyed the first time around. "Where might I find the stage for Timber Ridge?"

He motioned to a stagecoach at the far end of the

boardwalk. "But he's about to pull out, ma'am." He glanced at her luggage. "I don't think he's got room enough for all this, anyway. We have us a hotel down there a ways. Four rooms total. If you hurry, maybe you can—"

Molly pressed some coins into his hand. "Would you please catch the driver of that stage before he leaves? And ask if he has room for another passenger?" She had no intention of staying in Sulfur Falls for the night. "And determine how many of these trunks he can accommodate."

The steward tipped his hat. "Will do, Mrs. . . ."

Seeing him glance at the ring on her left hand, Molly's mind raced. The town council in Timber Ridge—the board who had hired her—already knew her last name. No need in muddying the already murky waters. "It's Mrs. Whitcomb. *Professor*—" She stopped herself. No longer teaching college, she couldn't exactly continue using that title. But she *did* still have her doctorate. "*Dr.* Molly Whitcomb, actually," she said, hoping the steward would address her in that fashion.

"Will do, Mrs. Whitcomb." The young man sprinted down the boardwalk.

Minutes later, Molly found herself seated inside the stagecoach with a rather girthsome gentleman occupying the opposite bench. Grateful to be spared the experience of spending a night in Sulfur Falls, she situated her satchel—the single piece of luggage the driver, a Mr. Lewis, had said he could accommodate—on the seat beside her. The rest of her belongings would be shipped by wagon, as the steward had suggested, to arrive in a day or two. She hoped. But at least she had some toiletries, and the periodical she'd purchased at the train station in Atlanta.

She opened the dog-eared magazine to the marked page. Having read the article countless times, she practically knew it by heart and hoped for the chance to meet the woman who had—

Catching a whiff of something, she stole a glance at the man across from her. His mouth hung open, and his eyes were half closed. She guessed him to be asleep. Either that or "sleeping one off," as she'd heard said.

"I'm tellin' you, I'm not takin' on any more luggage! I'm loaded as heavy as I can manage for this trip."

Hearing the driver's voice, Molly peered out the window, wanting to make sure he wasn't referring to her trunks. She spotted Mr. Lewis—and a gentleman speaking to him.

The gentleman, well dressed in a suit and top hat, faced Mr. Lewis, his feet firmly planted. "You're a good man, Mr. Lewis, and a wise one. I appreciate your attention to detail. But you know as well as I that two more trunks won't make that much difference. Not with your fine animals in the harness."

"I'm tellin' you, I can't do it! The roads are soft with recent rains, and I won't risk gettin' bogged down again on the side of a cliff. Took me half a day to dig out last time."

Bogged down again? *On the side of a cliff!* Molly's interest in the conversation was piqued.

"Again, Mr. Lewis, I trust your instincts and experience beyond measure. However, I'm none too eager to part with the contents of these trunks and am therefore willing"—the man reached inside his suit—"to pay an additional fee for my passage on your stage this afternoon."

"I told you, Tolliver, I'm not—"

Lewis fell silent, and Molly strained to see what the man held out to him. *Whatever it is, Mr. Lewis, don't take it. Don't let yourself be—*

Her eyes went wide at the stack of bills, and her jaw slipped open as she counted along with the driver. For that amount of money, she would've dragged the trunks up the mountain herself!

Lewis eyed the taller man as he fingered the bills. Then he stuffed them into his vest pocket. "If my rig gets stuck, Tolliver, you'll be the first to get out and start diggin'!"

Tolliver bowed. "And I'll do it gladly. Thank you, Mr. Lewis." He turned and Molly averted her gaze, but not before he'd caught her staring.

He opened the door, briefly assessed the seating arrangement, and looked in her direction. "Dear lady, would you be so kind?"

Already retrieving her satchel, Molly scooted to the far side of the cushioned bench. He climbed in and claimed the space beside her, placing the fine leather case in his grip on the floor at his feet. He took up well more than half the space, though not without excuse. He was a broad-shouldered man and muscular.

Molly shot a glance at their traveling partner seated opposite them, only to find his eyes still closed and his chin slumped forward on his chest. His soft snores grew steadily louder.

"Brandon Tolliver, madam."

As was customary, she offered her hand. "Dr. Molly Whitcomb."

He brushed a kiss across her fingertips, his expression registering surprise. And—if she wasn't mistaken—a spark of recognition, though that was impossible.

"Doctor?" He held her hand longer than decorum allowed. "I'm duly impressed."

His tone, however, said quite the opposite, as did his smirk, and Molly returned her hand to her lap, feeling pretentious now for introducing herself that way. But the title was hard earned, and people thought nothing of it when a male colleague introduced himself in that manner. "If that's truly the case, Mr. Tolliver, then I fear your respect is too easily won." She smiled to soften the barb.

He pressed closer on the seat. "Respect? I never said anything about respect, my dear woman. But admiration, on the other hand"—his gaze took in more than her face, and more than a gentleman's should—"is another issue entirely. Has anyone ever told you, you're much too pretty to be a schoolteacher?"

Molly did a pitiful job of masking her surprise. "How did you know—"

He laughed. "There was an article about you in the newspaper, *Dr.* Whitcomb. Woman professor comes west to teach children," he said, punctuating each word with a gesture and with counterfeit enthusiasm. "I believe that's how the headline read. But never did I dream that a college professor could be so—"

He paused, and Molly trailed his focus to her left hand resting on the satchel in her lap.

He slowly straightened. *"Mrs.* Doctor Molly Whitcomb?" His eyes narrowed. "A married woman who's maintained her independence . . . that's something one doesn't see very often. And something that wasn't included in that newspaper article." He huffed a laugh. "The town council must be more open-minded than I thought."

"You got enough room in there, Mrs. Whitcomb?"

Welcoming the interruption in conversation, Molly directed her attention to Mr. Lewis, who stood peering in the window. "Yes, sir. I'm fine, thank you."

"All righty, then, we'll get under way." The stage leaned to one side as Mr. Lewis climbed to the driver's perch, and Molly held on as the coach jerked into motion.

The clomp of horse hooves and the squeak of the stage—along with cavernous snores from their traveling partner—drowned out any chance of normal conversation. She was careful not to look in Brandon Tolliver's direction again, having no desire to continue their dialogue.

What he'd said had caught her attention, though—about the newspaper article not including that she was married, and about the town council being more open-minded than he'd thought. Perhaps her solution wasn't the best idea after all. But what could she do now? Any chance of turning back, either literally or figuratively, was gone.

She felt Tolliver looking at her, but he didn't pursue conversation.

Grateful for the time to sort her thoughts, Molly scanned the article in the magazine, familiar now with its contents, and compared the author's descriptions of these mountains to the scenery outside her window. Both were breathtaking. Elizabeth Westbrook Ranslett, the author of the article and—according to the note at the end—the editor of the *Timber Ridge Reporter*, painted word pictures with such authenticity and beauty that Molly felt as if she were seeing the surrounding scenery for the second time, instead of her first.

Enjoying the cool breeze on her face, she slipped the magazine into her satchel and settled back into the seat.

Evergreen trees of all shapes and sizes populated

the mountainside, and she took a deep breath, relishing the pungent, incongruous scent of Christmas in summer. The higher the stage climbed, the cooler the temperature grew, and the more vibrant the air. The waning afternoon sun seemed to race toward the western peaks, its light filtering through dingy gray storm clouds and bathing the vista in a silvery veil.

As she'd ridden the train west and watched these mountains rise from the dusty floor of the plains, their magnificence had been undeniable. Their rugged beauty had beckoned, but it also held warning. And she experienced that warning again as her gaze skimmed over the edge of the cliff, plunged downward into the chasm, and then rose with determination to the jagged peaks still ribboned with snow.

Stark and pristine in its beauty, the rugged land she passed through was every bit as wild and untamed—and awe-inspiring—as the article in the periodical professed it to be.

She'd heard people speak of the western territories before but had never paid much attention, until recently. They said life out west was different, that things were possible here that weren't back east. She prayed that was true.

Facing the back of the coach, she wished again that the opposite bench had been available when she'd boarded. She never traveled well when facing backward, even under ordinary circumstances, and was feeling more than a touch queasy with all the bouncing around. Not to mention she feared sliding from her seat at any moment.

With concern, she watched as the road narrowed and finally thinned to a few scant feet of earth jutting from the side of the mountain. Perhaps she should have inquired how long Mr. Lewis had been driving the stage. Odd what trust she'd placed in a man she didn't even know.

Mindful of the sleeping passenger across from her, Molly discreetly braced her feet against the opposite cushioned bench and held tight to the satchel in her lap.

The bruised sky soon delivered on its threat and a light rain began to fall.

Within minutes, it became a downpour, and she and Mr. Tolliver worked quickly to lower the curtains on the coach windows. Once tied down, the heavy fabric kept out most of the rain, as well as the light. The air quickly grew musty and thick in the enclosed space. The stage jostled and jolted beneath them, and Molly gripped the door, trying to exercise enough discipline not to peek through the crack in the curtains on her side to where the edge of the road abruptly ended.

Thunder rumbled over the mountains, and she held her breath each time until the noise passed. Its reverberation echoed inside her chest.

Tolliver leaned close. "Don't be alarmed, ma'am," he said, half yelling. "We're used to this.

Storms pass quickly up here. And Lewis has been driving these mountain roads all his life."

Wishing she were comforted, Molly raised her voice to be heard over the wind and rain. "Thank you . . . Mr. Tolliver." Her fingers ached from holding so tightly to the door and her satchel, and she clenched her jaw to keep her teeth from rattling.

A loud cough contributed to the thunder overhead, followed by a gravelly snore. She stared across from her, disbelieving. How could their traveling partner sleep through this!

Oh, God, why did I agree to come here? Why hadn't she stayed in Georgia? She still had the family home her father had left to her. She could have found another job doing something—*anything*—and tried to make a new life there. But as soon as those thoughts came, so did their impossibility. She would never have been able to start over there. Not with Jeremy getting married and her watching it all unfold while sidestepping inquiries about her sudden dismissal from Franklin College.

The stage hit a bump and Molly flew off the seat.

Screaming, she grappled for a hold and came down hard on the bench. The coach shuddered as though sharing her terror, and Tolliver swore beside her.

A high-pitched scream split the air, only this time it didn't come from her.

Another scream followed, and another. Primal,

elongated squeals that sent chills down her spine. Realization knifed through her. It was the horses! Something was happening to the horses—

Without warning, the coach shimmied to one side and slid to a stop.

Relieved, cautious, Molly let out a held breath as the gentleman across from her sat upright. He belched, and the stench of stale bourbon soured the closed compartment. With surprising quickness, he stood, and his head met the ceiling with a loud *thwack*. Swaying, he sank back down, his head lolling. Molly found herself praying he wouldn't be sick.

The coach began moving again. But . . . it wasn't its usual forward motion. Gone was the bumping and bouncing. Maybe the road had smoothed out. Or perhaps—

Then she felt it, and her insides melted. Something was terribly wrong. They were moving, but downhill! Sliding . . .

Tolliver's arm came around behind her, and she thought he meant to shield her, but he braced himself instead. She did likewise and watched the large man across from them slump to one side.

Thunder roiled overhead, and everything took on a slower motion.

Mr. Lewis yelled something from the driver's seat. To them? To the horses? Whatever he shouted was lost in the confusion and noise. A loud *crack*—and the world spun.

Molly slammed against the side of the coach and pain exploded in her shoulder. Tolliver landed against her with a grunt. He shifted and groaned beside her. She waited for him to move, but he didn't. Another hard jolt whipped them backward, and her head smacked the wood paneling behind the seat. Pain fanned out across the back of her head as something landed on top of her, knocking the air from her lungs, pinning her down.

She tried to move but couldn't.

Arching her back, she fought to get a decent breath as lights danced before her eyes. The rancid smell of soured bourbon told her what—or who—was on top of her. She tried to push him off, but it was no use.

Then everything went strangely still. And silent.

She glanced beside her. "Mr. Tolliver?" she said, nudging him. "Mr. Tolliver!" His head slipped forward, and she fought a rising tide of panic. Blood marred the right side of his face. Tears rising in her throat, she shook the man on top of her. "Sir?" She shook him harder. *"Sir!"*

He didn't respond. Didn't move. But he shared every putrid exhale.

The walls closed in around her. She needed air! She had to have air!

Blindly groping along the door panel, she finally located the latch. And pulled.

Nothing.

Teeth gritted, she tried again, harder this time,

putting her weight against it, but the latch wouldn't budge. Her fingers brushed against one of the leather ties that held the curtain in place, and frantic, she worked at it until the loop slipped free. Feeling a trickle of relief, she pushed the curtain aside and took in a deep breath—that never reached her lungs.

The ravine opened below like a hungry mouth gaping wide.

Molly tried to scream, but the sound lodged like a fist at the base of her throat. For a brief, agonizing instant, she imagined what it was going to feel like as she plummeted downward and her body hit the jagged rocks far below.

With renewed motivation, she fought to move beneath the weight pinning her down—and felt the stagecoach shift. A chill crept through her. She began to tremble. Her jaw shook. And every thought fled except one.

She was going to die on the side of this mountain—she and her unborn child—and she wasn't ready yet.

3

Mindful of how the road narrowed along this stretch, James McPherson nudged his horse closer to the mountain, his earlier run-in with Brandon Tolliver in Sulfur Falls still wearing on him. He pulled his Stetson lower over his eyes, a shield from the drizzle. Judging from the clearing in the clouds overhead, it looked like the worst of the storm had moved past. Unusual amount of rain for this time of year.

He'd tried to get Tolliver to see reason, but the man could be downright obstinate when he wanted to be. James smiled. Not that *he'd* ever been accused of being obstinate. As sheriff of Timber Ridge, he was all for progress and growth, but the safety of the people was at the center of every decision he made. Both for the folks who'd lived in Timber Ridge since the town was founded, and for newcomers who seemed to be arriving in droves every day.

Construction of Tolliver's Colorado Hot Springs Resort was providing much-needed jobs, especially since the Shady Susan silver mine had all but stopped producing. Miners were looking for work until a new mine struck it big, and Tolliver's venture was giving the town's economy a boost. James shifted in the saddle. But the construction of the new resort was also causing all sorts of problems between locals and immigrants. Every day, tensions escalated. Locals accused "foreigners" of taking jobs they considered rightfully belonged to them, while—

James's thoughts fell away as he rounded the corner. He struggled to make sense of the scene before him.

At first he thought the rain and afternoon

shadows were playing tricks on him. But when he heard a woman scream, he knew what he was seeing was real. He jumped from his horse and grabbed the coiled rope looped around the saddle horn.

The switchback trail was saturated from the rains, and twice he slipped as he clambered uphill. He recognized the coach as belonging to Lewis, but the scene was surreal. The stage lay on its side, hugging the rocky edge of the cliff, partially suspended over the ravine. The team of horses—frenzied and wild-eyed—was still harnessed, and each time the animals strained forward in the mud and then let up, the stage edged closer to the drop-off, threatening to take the animals with it.

James slogged through the mud and gripped the harness of the lead mare. He whispered low, trying to hold her steady.

"Lewis!" he called, searching for any sign of his friend. He'd just seen Lewis in Sulfur Falls not an hour ago, and the man had only one passenger then—Charlie Daggett, a local from Timber Ridge. But judging from the woman's scream, Lewis had apparently picked up a second.

Peering down, James saw that the wooden tongue securing the harnesses to the stage was split down the middle. Meaning it wouldn't hold much longer. Worse, it also meant there was no way to use the horses to pull the coach free of danger.

Mindful of the slippery slope, he moved closer to

the underside of the carriage, eyeing the distance from the stage to a stand of aspen anchored between boulders across the road. He heard something and stilled. It sounded like a woman crying.

He took a step closer. "Hello! Are you all right in there?"

The crying quieted. *"Please . . ."* Another soft sob. "C-can you h-help us?"

Moved by the pleading quality in her voice, James wondered if she had any idea how dire the situation was. "That's exactly what I aim to do, ma'am. The most important thing for now is to stay absolutely still. Do you hear me? Don't move and don't try to climb out."

"I won't." She sniffed. "I c-can't move."

Quickly sizing up his options, and considering how badly she might be hurt, he looped one end of the rope through a brace on the backside of the carriage body and tied it tight. "I'm working to get the stage secured, then I'm going to get you both out of there, all right?"

Silence.

"All right. B-but . . . there are three of us."

Three? James winced, already having estimated the time and care it would take to get Charlie Daggett out. He was no small man. But *three* people? "Are the other two men?"

"Yes."

He wondered why the men weren't speaking. "Are they hurt?" Not waiting for her to answer, he backed his way across the muddy path, mindful of his footing, to loop the other end of the rope around a clump of aspen. It wouldn't hold the weight of the stage if gravity took over, but it would buy him some time.

"Yes . . . and no," she finally said. "One man has a gash on his head. He was knocked out when the stage flipped. The other man . . . he doesn't seem to be hurt. But he's passed out too. From . . . too much liquor."

James easily guessed which man was the latter. Charlie Daggett was a regular in the Timber Ridge saloons. A quiet fellow who kept to himself, Daggett drank too much, but even well soused he possessed the strength of three men. If the town had a workday, he always showed up ready to pitch in. And despite Charlie's reputation for the bottle, James had never had to arrest him, or even issue a reprimand.

With the rope secured around the aspen, James tied an extra knot. "Who's the man that's hurt?"

"A Mr. Brandon Tolliver."

James sighed. *This just keeps getting better and better.* Walking back, he removed his hat and duster and tossed them on a nearby boulder. At least the woman's voice was sounding stronger. Good. She'd need every bit of courage she could muster to get out of this mess.

The horses surged forward again, whinnying and pawing at the soggy ground, causing the stage to creak and rock from side to side. The woman screamed, and James grabbed hold of the rear coach wheel, watching the already taut rope strain tighter against the weight.

But the rope held. For the time being.

Choosing the largest boulder he could manage, he hefted it, back muscles straining, and deposited it by the stage to use as a makeshift stair. He had a plan. He just prayed it would work, and prayed that the hundred things that could go wrong wouldn't.

He raked a hand through his hair. "What's your name, ma'am?"

"Molly." Timidity softened her voice and gave it a little-girl quality.

She'd only told him her first name, as though they were just kids. But she was probably scared witless, with good reason. "Well, Molly, my name is James, and I'm looking forward to officially making your acquaintance in a few minutes. But for now, the best thing you can do is to stay still. Okay?"

"Okay," she said after a moment.

James was looking around for something else to use as a rope when a rustling down the trail drew his attention. A hand slowly emerged through the brush. *Lewis!* James ran to meet him and pulled him clear of the ledge.

Lewis held his head, panting. "I came to and . . . heard your voice, Sheriff. I thought we were done for."

Knowing that might yet describe the fate of those

in the coach, James kept his voice low. "Are you fit to help with the horses? We need to get them unhitched."

Lewis hobbled to standing, his left pant leg torn and bloodied. "You just tell me what you want done and I'll do it."

James squeezed his shoulder and relayed his plan. Lewis stared for a few seconds, and James sensed he might offer up argument, but the man turned and set to work.

Minutes later, with the horses unhitched and tethered across the road, James tested the slipknot in the lasso he'd fashioned from one of the reins. It should work well enough. Molly hadn't said anything else, but he sensed she was waiting for him to tell her what would happen next.

Murmurs came from within the carriage, and he saw it begin to sway.

"Molly, don't move! All of you, stay still!" he shouted, steadying the coach as best he could with Lewis's help. "Tolliver? Daggett? Can you hear me?"

The men answered in unison.

"We're going to get you all out of there, but it's going to take working together. I've done some figuring on this, and . . . Molly?"

"Yes?"

"We're going to get you out first."

"I . . . I don't think that will work, James," she answered.

"Why not?" He stepped up onto the rock and tried to peer through the opening above the door, but the curtain was tied shut from the inside.

"Cuz I'm layin' on top of her, Sheriff."

Recognizing Daggett's voice and the predicament inside the stage, James exhaled. The woman was pinned beneath Charlie Daggett? God help them. . . . "Which one of you is closest to the door?"

"That'd be me, Sheriff." A hand appeared through a slit in the curtained window.

James wished there were a way to get Molly out first, but apparently there wasn't. "All right, then, Tolliver. Looks like you're up. As carefully as you can, see if you can get that door open. And try not to move too much."

Tolliver untied the curtain from the window, and his head slowly appeared through the opening. The stage shifted beneath him. The man's customary smirk was noticeably absent as he worked at the latch. The door finally gave, and he eased it back against the side of the carriage.

James tossed up the rope. "Slip it over your upper body and we'll steady you as you climb out. And remember . . . move slowly."

Tolliver did as instructed. The man was agile and fit and climbed out with little trouble. James steadied the coach as Tolliver eased himself over the side.

Gaining his footing, Tolliver removed the rope

and eyed James for a second, no doubt recalling their argument that afternoon in Sulfur Falls. "Thank you, Sheriff." He held out his hand. "Much appreciated."

"You're welcome, Tolliver." James quickly shook his hand, then refocused on the carriage. "Okay, Molly. You're next." He didn't know what size a woman she was but felt safe in betting she wasn't the likes of Charlie Daggett. "Daggett, I want you to raise up nice and slow, and keep your weight to *this* side of the carriage. Not toward the ravine." Daggett wasn't slow-witted, but James wasn't taking any chances. "You understand what I'm saying to you?"

He waited, hearing murmurs coming from inside.

"Yes, sir, Sheriff McPherson," Daggett finally answered. "I understand. Me and Miss Molly, we got it worked out between us."

Hoping they did, James tossed the rope up again, and seconds later, a pile of blond curls appeared through the doorway. He blinked to make sure he was seeing right. It was *her*! The woman he'd spoken with in Sulfur Falls. Their eyes connected and her expression mirrored similar surprise and recognition.

"I'm ready . . . Sheriff McPherson," she said, her voice higher pitched than before.

Wishing she'd stuck with his first name, James began pulling her up as she climbed through the door, watchful of where the coach was on the cliff. Judging from the resistance on the rope, she didn't weigh much. "You're doing real well, Molly," he said, seeing the fear in her eyes. "Just come on the rest of the way."

Halfway out, one knee on the carriage, she tossed him a weak smile . . . then stopped, frowning at the reticule on her arm. "It's caught on the door hinge." She braced herself, tugged it free, and started to climb again. But then she turned and glanced behind her.

"No, Molly. Don't look back!"

She slipped. Screaming, she slid back inside the opening. But not far. James held the rope taut as the carriage rocked from side to side. Lewis and Tolliver anchored the rope behind him.

"Look at me, Molly," he said, his breath coming heavy, more from fear than from supporting her slight weight. "Look at me!"

She did. Fear widened her eyes.

"Don't look behind you. Just concentrate on coming to me. We've got you, and we're not going to let you fall."

She finally offered a tentative nod and managed to climb through the doorway again, James anchoring the rope. As she slid over the side, he caught her at the waist and lowered her down.

Hands on his shoulders, she tightened her grip. "Thank you, Sheriff."

Smiling, he removed the rope from around her.

"You're most welcome, Molly." She stepped to the side as he widened the loop in the rope, then tossed it back inside the open doorway. No sign of Charlie yet. "You 'bout ready in there, Daggett?"

"Yes, sir, I reckon I am. But I don't think I'm gonna fit through that door as easy as she did."

Humor laced Daggett's tone, and James found himself admiring the man's calm. "You got into that carriage and we're going to get you out. Do you have the rope around you yet?"

Daggett answered with a tug.

"All right, then. Stand up, slow and easy. We'll hold you steady." James shot a look behind him and saw Lewis dig in his heels. Tolliver stood behind him at the ready. And at the end of the rope—God bless the woman—stood Molly, white-knuckled, bent at the knee, ready to pull.

The carriage creaked beneath Daggett's weight. His head appeared through the doorway and his massive shoulders filled the portal. He angled sideways and lifted one arm through at a time, but after several tries at hoisting his body through—the stage inching dangerously closer to the cliff each time—shades of acceptance darkened his eyes.

"It don't look like I'm gonna fit through here, Sheriff. Not without me givin' it my full strength. And if I do that, I'm afraid I'll—"

"Yeah . . . me too, Daggett." James blew out a breath. He had no doubt Charlie had the strength to heave himself through, especially with them pulling. What he hadn't counted on was gravity working against them so much. Going through a coach door sideways, with the stage right side up, was one thing. Climbing up and out while it balanced on a cliff was another.

But he wasn't going to lose this man. Not after coming so far. He tried to think of another idea and couldn't. "Listen, let's try it again. Except this time, on the count of three"—James glanced behind him—"we're all going to pull . . . *hard*. And, Daggett, I want you to suck in that gut of yours and push through there like a case of fine Irish whiskey depends on it!"

A smile ghosted Daggett's face. "Yes, sir, Sheriff."

Gripping the rope tighter, James said a quick prayer. "One . . . two . . . *three!*"

They pulled, and Daggett—red-faced, neck muscles bulging—finally managed to push through the door, looking like a prize-winning calf two months overdue. Panting, he paused on the upturned side of the carriage, a big smile lighting his face. Just as the stage began to tip back toward the ravine.

Daggett's face went white.

"Hold the rope!" James yelled, realizing what was happening. The weight of the luggage was pulling the stage over the cliff. He hoisted himself up beside Daggett, heart pumping.

"What're you doin', Sheriff?" Daggett shouted.

But as the coach steadied, Daggett gave a quick nod, seeming to understand.

James stretched out, pulse racing, and strained to reach the ropes that tied the luggage on. In the space of a second, an image flashed through his mind . . . that of sharpening this knife two nights ago with his younger nephew, Kurt, on the front porch. He sure wanted to see that little guy again, and his older nephew, Mitch. Emotion tightened his throat. Death had never felt so close. He was ready to die and meet his Creator. That wasn't a question, and it was strangely reassuring to know that. But he still had things he wanted to get done. People he needed—and wanted—to take care of. But God knew all that. *Don't you, Lord . . .*

He slid the knife beneath the rope. "When I cut this, Charlie"—his breath would hardly come— "we're going to shift back toward the road, but we won't have long. You're going to have to—"

"I know what I gotta do, Sheriff. And I'll do it! I make my oath on it."

With a single cut, James sliced the rope and sent the luggage plummeting. As gravity dictated and as he'd banked on, the stage shifted back toward the mountain. Only not as far as he'd estimated. Or for as long. He scrambled back, trying to make it in time. But momentum stalled as the stage angled back toward the mountain for the final time.

He saw Lewis and Tolliver straining to hold on to the rope and felt Charlie Daggett's grip go viselike around his wrist. But nowhere—nowhere—did he see Molly.

And oddly enough, hers was the face he would've liked to have seen again. Just one last time.

4

Molly dug in her heels and pulled hard on the mare's harness. "Come on, girl! Move!" she screamed, but the animal was slow to obey. Overlong reins trailed the muddy ground. Lewis and Tolliver yelled, and Molly turned to see the stagecoach dipping back toward the mountain.

Fear spurred her courage, and she swung onto the horse and gripped the harness—in time to see the stage slide off into the ravine. She sank her heels into the mare's flank.

It wasn't but twenty feet to where Lewis and Tolliver stood, gripping the rope, their bodies braced against the weight of Charlie Daggett— who lay hanging off the edge of the cliff, belly down, holding on to James McPherson one-handed.

Growling as he tried, Charlie strained to pull him up but couldn't.

"Hold on, Charlie!" Molly slid from the mare and led her as close to the cliff and to Charlie Daggett as the animal would go.

The horse reared, but Molly's instincts kicked in,

sharpened by years of riding, and she held her steady.

"Mr. Lewis!" she called, and found him already there.

"Daggett! Grab hold of this!" Lewis yelled, tossing him the rein.

His shirt slick with sweat, Daggett reached for the rein behind him, finally grabbing hold. With surprising speed, he looped it around his thick wrist. One, two, three times. Then Lewis smacked the mare's rear, and the animal dug a slow path up the incline, protesting the load.

Unable to see James's face, Molly kept her attention glued to the wrist locked tight in Charlie Daggett's grip. Inch by inch, the mare pulled Charlie forward. But not until James lay on the ground beside him, panting and laughing, did Molly allow herself to breathe.

The men's whoops and hollers carried over the canyon and echoed back. And though she shared their relief, she couldn't share their laughter. Her legs barely supporting her, she turned away, not wanting them to see her tears.

The reality of what had almost happened to her—to them all—left her bone-chilled and shaking. She'd thought her life was over. Staring down into that ravine had been the closest to death she'd ever come, and she despised how it had felt, and the dark disturbing restlessness it awakened inside her. That throbbed in her bones even now.

45

Tears slid down her cheeks. She tried to gain her breath. Death was a thief, an intruder. Unwelcome and abrupt. And that it would seek her—and nearly find her—out here . . .

She shivered, numb inside, recalling the undeniable knowledge that she hadn't been ready to meet her Maker face-to-face. That she still wasn't. And what of the child in her belly?

Renewed guilt and shame washed over her as thoughts of Jeremy Fowler forced themselves back in. Following their one—and only—night together, his affections for her had cooled. And that was putting it mildly. Devastated, humiliated, she'd done her best to continue instructing her classes, but it had become increasingly difficult to concentrate, and her teaching had suffered.

One morning in early July, President Northrop had summoned her to his office to discuss her poor performance and to question her propriety on the *rumor* that her reputation had been sullied. She'd asked him to reveal his source, but he'd refused. Days later, when she'd read in the newspaper about Jeremy's engagement to Maria Elena Patterson, daughter of the college's largest donor, she'd found her question answered. And later that week when another article reported a record donation to Franklin College by Jeremy's future father-in-law, her humiliation had been complete.

By then, she knew she was with child, and though that didn't ease the betrayal, it had made her leaving her hometown more palatable. In the article that announced the donation, President Northrop had been quoted as saying, "This generous gift from the Patterson family marks an important day in the history of Franklin College, and its bright and promising future."

Molly drew in a shaky breath. And it had marked the end of hers.

She twisted the wedding band on her left hand. It looked so odd and out of place, with good reason. She'd been so foolish, so trusting. And she was paying the price.

She glanced back at the men and saw James standing, brushing off his clothes. She'd recognized his last name when Charlie had used it earlier, from a telegram she'd received, confirming receipt of President Northrop's letter of recommendation.

In his letter, President Northrop had stated one of the reasons for her resigning her professorship was because she wanted to see the western frontier before it was tamed and settled and vanished into history. Such foolishness . . .

But apparently, the council in Timber Ridge had believed it. Because in the same telegram, which came from a Sheriff McPherson, they'd offered her the job. Turning away, Molly clenched her hands tight to ease their shaking. The teaching position had been hers for the taking. And, in his own way, Northrop had made sure she'd taken it. She'd accepted, via telegram, and was scheduled to sign the contract upon her arrival.

"Molly?"

Hearing James's voice behind her, she patted her cheeks and put on a brave face before turning.

Dirt smeared his chin and forehead, only adding to his rugged appeal. "Are you all right?"

She nodded, noting how kind a look was in his eyes and how striking their blue. "I'm fine, Sheriff McPherson."

A smile tipped one side of his mouth, giving him a boyish look. "If it's all the same to you, ma'am, I'd prefer we stick with our given names."

She nodded. "I'm fine . . . James," she said softly.

He looked her over. "You're sure you're not hurt?"

"My nerves are a bit worse for the wear." She touched the back of her head, coercing a smile. "And my head promises to remind me of this tomorrow, but I'm fine." Or would be. She motioned beyond him. "You were quite . . . heroic just now."

He raked a hand through his hair. "You wouldn't be saying that if you could've felt my heart pounding. I saw that ravine rushing up to meet me and—" He blew out a breath, grinning. "Let's just say my thoughts weren't all that brave."

She laughed softly. Courageous *and* humble. That was a combination she didn't come across often.

He stared at her for a moment—that same patient, assessing look he'd given her in town earlier, and she did nothing to dissuade him. "You showed a lot of gumption just now, Molly. I hope you'll take this the right way, but . . . I'm real impressed by how you did."

Her emotions threatened to surface again, but Molly held them under. From the corner of her eye, she saw Tolliver approaching.

"Say, Sheriff . . ." Tolliver moved in close. The gash on his forehead was crusted in blood, and his shirt was stained with it. He briefly glanced over his shoulder at Lewis and Daggett. "What do you aim to do about all that luggage you just sent over the edge?"

The warmth in James's eyes cooled. "That I just sent over the edge? You mean, to save a man's life?"

Tolliver stiffened, and Molly sensed something pass between the two men. Something beyond what had just happened.

"I'm not saying what you did wasn't justified, Sheriff, on some level. I'm simply asking what you intend to do about it."

"I intend to leave that luggage right where it is, Tolliver. At the bottom of the ravine, at least for now. Unless you want to scramble on down there before nightfall and haul it up."

Tolliver's smile was a tight curve. "You're right, of course, Sheriff. It'll be dark soon. I'll drop by your office this week and we can discuss it then." False gentility shaded his tone. He turned in her direction. "It's been a pleasure to make your acquaintance, ma'am. Though I wish it had been under different circumstances, *Dr.* Whitcomb." He said it with a raised brow, as though they shared some private joke.

Molly refrained from offering her hand as she'd done before, glad to see him walk away. She recalled the image of him looking down at her and Charlie Daggett one last time before he climbed out of the carriage. It was a look that said, "Better you than me." The more she observed Brandon Tolliver, the less she liked him.

"*Dr. Whitcomb?* From Athens, Georgia?"

James's question pulled her back, and Molly nodded. "Yes. I'm the new—"

"Schoolteacher in Timber Ridge." He eyed her. "I sent you a telegram."

"Yes, you did."

That same wry smile eased up one corner of his mouth. "Seems fate gave us a jump on introductions back in Sulfur Falls."

"Yes, I think it did. It's nice to finally make your acquaintance, James." She offered a slight curtsey. "My instructions were to stop by your office when I arrived in town."

"Yes, ma'am. And, actually, I planned to meet your train in Sulfur Falls. But you're a few days ahead of schedule."

She nodded, trying not to stare at the pieces of sagebrush in his hair. "I sent a wire yesterday morning, but—"

"The telegraph's down due to rain." He smiled again. "Unfortunately, that happens a lot up here. We've got men out there right now trying to fix it. The folks of Timber Ridge are eager for your arrival, ma'am."

"And I'm looking forward to meeting the people of Timber Ridge," she countered, feeling a check in her spirit. Earlier during the day that statement would have been false. But in light of what had just happened, and now that the numbness was fading, life suddenly seemed more precious. Even hers.

She caught the sideways look James was giving her. "What?" She looked down, smoothing a hand over her skirt. "Is something wrong?"

He shook his head. "No, ma'am. Nothing's wrong. It's just that the letter of recommendation and the telegram said *Dr.* Whitcomb. And you're not exactly what comes to mind when I picture a female college professor."

Responding to his grin, she raised a brow, inviting him to explain.

He shrugged. "Let's just say you're a mite more . . . *stylish* than most of us had envisioned. In a good way, though," he added quickly. His gaze took in her vest and lace jabot. "Don't hear me complaining. You're just not what I was expecting, that's all."

His comment was an honest one, and while she sensed approval in his demeanor, Molly also felt a prick of guilt, considering the underlying truth of his statement.

"Sheriff, we're ready to head on, if you are." Lewis approached, leading two horses. "It'll be dark soon." He glanced toward the ledge where the carriage had gone over, defeat lining his features. "I'll come back tomorrow, see what can be salvaged from the wreckage. For what it's worth, Sheriff, you did the right thing . . . cutting that luggage loose. However much it's gonna cost me."

James put his hand on Lewis's shoulder, and Molly was struck by how natural a gesture it seemed coming from him. Even though, judging from appearances, Lewis was the older man.

"How heavy was that carriage loaded, Lewis?" James's gaze was steady.

"Too heavy, Sheriff." Lewis looked away. "I already had a full load when Tolliv—" He shook his head and glanced back to where Tolliver and Daggett sat astride the other two horses. "In the end, sir, it was my fault. And I'm sorry." He looked at Molly. "I ask your pardon, ma'am, for puttin' you in danger like I did. For puttin' us all in danger. It was foolish and it won't happen again."

Molly nodded her acceptance of his apology, finding words unfitting for the moment. She thought of her satchel and its contents at the bottom of the ravine—some clothing and personal items, the magazine she'd saved. But the loss paled when compared to what it could have been, and she was glad now that her trunks hadn't been on board.

Lewis gestured. "One of the mares has a bruised fetlock and ain't fit to ride. I'm wondering if Mrs. Whitcomb here might ride with you, sir?"

James's gaze swung from Lewis back to her. "*Mrs.* Whitcomb?" His eyes clouded. "You're *married,* ma'am?"

Molly froze inside. She briefly looked down at the ring on her left hand, then found James doing the same. And she glimpsed herself through his eyes—hardly acting the part of a grieving widow—and the open, attentive quality she'd considered so attractive in the man suddenly set her ill at ease.

Her guard rose. "Yes, I . . . I mean, no, I'm not . . ." She couldn't maintain his gaze, nor that of Mr. Lewis. "Actually, Sheriff, I'm a . . . recent widow." She barely managed the words, and they sounded false, even to her. *Oh, God, please help me. . . .*

But realizing what she was asking God to help her do, Molly knew she was on her own.

5

Molly took a deep breath and made herself look at James. And this time, she saw the entire town council of Timber Ridge staring back through his eyes, and the messy slate of her life waiting to be wiped clean and rewritten. She hoped the anguish she felt in that moment—over the illegitimate child she carried and the fabrication she was weaving—would somehow be mistaken for the sorrow of a woman in mourning, instead of the guilt and shame of a fallen woman.

"A recent widow?" James repeated, the disbelief in his voice cementing her where she stood. "But the advertisement we posted in the papers back east, the one you answered"—unwavering conviction steeled his voice—"stated that applicants were to be unmarried. It's a requirement of the job. And one that was spelled out quite clearly, as I remember."

Molly's remaining confidence buckled at the authority in his voice. She would've sworn the laces on her corset cinched themselves tighter. Part of her wanted to start hiking back down the mountain right then. But where would she go, other than back to what she'd just left? And that wasn't an option. She had no income, no prospects for a job—other than as schoolteacher in Timber Ridge.

Catching herself fidgeting with her skirt, she

coerced her hands back to her sides, relieved to see that Brandon Tolliver and Charlie Daggett didn't seem to be listening. Her voice shrank in volume along with her courage. "I *am* unmarried, Sheriff. Again, I mean. My . . . husband," she forced out, barely able to breathe, "died about three months ago."

She bowed her head to avoid their scrutiny, aware that the action would likely be construed as grief, which served her purpose while also feeding her guilt.

The silence lengthened.

"I'm sorry, ma'am," James offered softly. "Please accept my condolences. I truly regret your loss."

"Me too, Mrs. Whitcomb." Lewis ducked his head.

The sincerity in their eyes triggered a weight in the pit of her stomach, so heavy and dense she thought she might be ill. Orchestrating a lie was one thing. Lying to someone's face was another. She could only nod her thanks.

Sensing James wanted to speak at greater length on this topic, she waited. The intensity in his gaze heightened, and she wondered if he wasn't considering escorting her back to Sulfur Falls and putting her on the first train headed back east. If he chose to, there would be nothing she could do about it. And there was a part of her that wouldn't blame him in the least. It was what she deserved.

"Lewis, in answer to your question . . . Mrs. Whitcomb is welcome to ride with me."

Mrs. Whitcomb. He'd said it politely, not a trace of sarcasm in his voice. But it was a reversal toward formality, which was best under the circumstances, she knew.

Not relishing the prospect of riding with him as much as she might have before, Molly took a breath. "Thank you, Sheriff."

He stared at her for a beat. "We're down this way."

She followed, pausing as he retrieved his coat and hat, and accepted his help onto the horse, riding forward as he indicated. She carefully arranged her skirt over her legs as he eased into the saddle behind her. He reached around her for the reins, and she found herself watching his hands— so different from Jeremy Fowler's. James's hands were large and tanned, rough from work, and he held the reins with an ease that bespoke years in the saddle.

They rode in silence for a while behind the other men, and though she could have been imagining it, she felt James watching her. The change in his demeanor was almost palpable. Normally, she was confrontational by nature, willing to address a difference of opinion with a colleague in the hope of reaching common ground. But James McPherson was not a colleague, and they were not merely having a difference of opinion. Her marital status

in relation to this job was of much greater consequence than she'd imagined, and a subject she
wished to avoid. Especially with him.

"May I ask you a question, Mrs. Whitcomb?"

"Yes, of course." Her voice came out smaller
than she'd intended.

"With your husband passing so recently, are you
not still in mourning for him?"

Molly cringed, hearing his real question. "Yes, I
am." She glanced at her vest and skirt. "And I'm
sure you're wondering why I'm dressed this way."

"That question had crossed my mind. Yes,
ma'am."

She fixed her attention on the violet and pink
hues of twilight hazing the western horizon and
worked to keep her answer rooted in truth. "The
black dress I was wearing became soiled on the
trip here, and this was the only outfit I had available to wear." Which was true—except . . . the
black dress she'd been wearing had been in
remembrance of the anniversary of her father's
passing, not that of her *late husband*. "I apologize.
I hadn't planned on meeting anyone from Timber
Ridge so soon. And, I assure you, as soon as my
trunks arrive, I'll choose more appropriate attire—
and most certainly before meeting with the town
council."

The silence stretched taut, and she resisted the
urge to look over her shoulder at him.

A cool wind swept over the trail, and the twisting

mountain road widened before them and rose at a steady, steep incline. The other men were a good distance ahead, taking the trail at a faster pace riding single. James tightened his grip on the reins, and the higher they climbed, the more difficult it became to resist leaning back into him.

Gradually, having no choice, she relaxed her weight against him, appreciating his warmth, and wondering if he was as aware of their closeness as she was. Though she'd been intimate with a man—once, and briefly—she still felt naïve when it came to understanding the opposite sex. But her limited experience told her he was as conscious of their bodies touching as was she.

"So your trunks weren't on the stage?" he asked.

"No. By the time I arrived, there wasn't any room. They're being shipped by wagon, to arrive in a day or two."

"If you're lucky. Shipments can take a mite longer getting up to Timber Ridge, depending on the weather and the mountains. It's an inconvenience, but—" He guided the horse up and over a ridge, and slowed at the highest point. "I think it's worth it . . . to be able to live in the middle of all this."

Molly looked out over the ridge and barely contained her gasp. She already considered the land beautiful, but this . . .

The sheer drop-off to their right swept downward for hundreds of feet before leveling into a sheltered, sequestered valley. Buildings and small dwellings dotted the landscape below, and in the pale light of approaching night, she viewed the layout of the town, the various roads spidering off and leading up into the mountains. She even glimpsed what appeared to be a waterfall in the distance. Not far beyond, two mountains stood out from among the others, nearly identical in appearance and height. And from this height, she could see peak after peak rising in blue-gray splendor, one after the other for miles, like jagged waves on a dusky ocean of rock and snow.

"So that's Timber Ridge?" she whispered.

"Yes, ma'am . . . that's it."

Pride deepened his voice, and she didn't fault him in the least. She pointed to the two mountain peaks she'd noticed earlier. "Those are beautiful."

"The Maroon Bells. Most folks around here call them the Twin Sisters."

Perhaps it was due to the long days of travel or the circumstances surrounding her coming west, but she had a hard time subduing the swell of emotion the mountains inspired. "How long have you lived here?"

"I came out shortly after the war. Never intended to stay." James nudged the horse and they began their steep downhill descent.

Fighting the sensation of falling, Molly searched for something to hold on to—when James slipped his right arm around her waist and held her secure against him.

"Is that better, ma'am?"

She'd read about higher altitude making it more difficult to breathe. But she knew better than to blame her reaction on the altitude. "Yes . . . thank you."

"Steep's not so bad when you're going up." His voice was soft in her ear. "But coming down can get prickly."

She warmed at his wording and grew more certain of his Tennessee heritage. "What made you stay?" she asked, still thinking about what he'd said previously.

"A whole lot of things. The South wasn't the same after the Federals got done with it, and neither was I. Most of my family was gone. There was nothing to keep me in Franklin anymore. And I wanted to see this land . . . before it was all settled and tamed. Before all this was gone."

President Northrop's words drifted back to her, and Molly couldn't help smiling. Could it be that what he'd fabricated in his letter of recommendation had actually helped secure her this position? Strange how things worked sometimes. . . .

As soon as they reached level ground, James withdrew his arm from around her waist. They caught up with Mr. Lewis, Brandon Tolliver, and Charlie Daggett in town in time to see Tolliver and Lewis going their own ways, Lewis leading the horses. But Charlie Daggett stood in the center of the street, waiting.

James reined in beside him. "Charlie? Everything okay?"

Charlie's eyes were earnest, full of a need to be understood. "What you did up there today, Sheriff . . . I'm much obliged to you. Can't think of one other person who woulda done that for me."

James sighed in a way that usually accompanied a smile. "I appreciate you, Charlie. And I appreciate what you contribute to our town. You always show up when something needs to be done, and you stay until the job is finished. You're someone a person can count on. Can't say that about a lot of folks."

Charlie Daggett's rough-bearded face softened beneath the praise. "Anything you need, Sheriff McPherson, you just ask and I'll be there. That goes for your sister, Miss Rachel, too." He doffed his hat. "G'night, Miss Molly. And my apologies again, ma'am, for landin' on you like I did."

Molly smiled. He'd already apologized earlier in the carriage. Four times. And had also told her she smelled nice—not a hard thing to do when a person was accustomed to the stench of days-old bourbon. "It was a pleasure to make your acquaintance, Mr. Daggett," she said, meaning every word.

The flicker of coal-burning lamps illuminated the thoroughfare, and James guided the horse through town, past a darkened general store, a telegraph and newspaper office, a land and title company, an attorney's office with an oversized shingle, and a modest-looking dress shop. More offices and retailers than she'd thought such a town would boast. A few of the buildings looked newly built, and several more were still in early stages of construction. Perhaps Timber Ridge wasn't exactly the end of the earth after all.

All of the retail businesses appeared to be closed, but the town was definitely not asleep. She peered down a side street to see several establishments on the far end—saloons, she assumed—all well lit and well frequented, by the looks of men coming and going. Raucous tunes and tinny piano chords being pounded out at a surprisingly hectic rhythm drifted toward them on the cool night air.

James gave the horse a nudge and they passed on by, but not before Molly saw Charlie Daggett disappear through one of the open doors. And seeing it disturbed her. Only not in the same way it would have before she'd been through their experience on the mountain. Earlier, he was just a drunkard. Now he was a man who drank too much but who had also valued her life above his own.

"I could take you to the boardinghouse, Mrs. Whitcomb, but if you're agreeable, I'd rather take you to my sister's for the night. Her ranch is only a short distance from here, and you'd be more comfortable there. She'll have some clothes and woman things you could borrow, I'm sure. I think you'll like Rachel too." His voice took on a smile. "The two of you should get along real well."

Knowing he was right on the borrowing of some "woman things," Molly welcomed the lighter turn in conversation. She glanced back at him. "Is your sister a very stylish woman, Sheriff? Is that why you think we'll get along?"

Shadows of night hid his eyes beneath the brim of his hat, but his mouth tipped the faintest bit on one side. "My sister certainly is stylish . . . or she used to be, anyway." His smile fell away. "But my thoughts were running more along the line that both of you are widows, Mrs. Whitcomb. I think you and Rachel will have an understanding of the heart right off."

Her face heating, Molly faced forward again. "I see," she whispered, wishing she could take back her foolish statement. This man's thoughts ran deeper than she'd credited him for, and he obviously cared deeply about his sister. "I'm sorry for your sister's loss. When did her husband pass on?"

"Thomas was killed twenty-one months, two weeks, and four days ago. I only know because Rachel reminded me this morning."

Heartsick regret settled inside Molly, not only for James's sister and her loss, but for her earlier callousness and insensitivity. She'd told him her own husband had passed on "about three months ago." She felt every bit like the imposter she was.

Something told her that posing as a "recent widow" was going to prove more difficult to carry off than she'd anticipated. Yet which would the people of Timber Ridge prefer in their new schoolteacher—a pregnant widow . . . or a woman pregnant without benefit of marriage?

Knowing the answer to that question—not only for the town council, but for Sheriff James McPherson—Molly twisted the wedding band on her left hand, telling herself again that she'd made the only choice available to her. "I'd appreciate staying with your sister, Sheriff McPherson. Thank you."

They rode on a while longer, crossing a ridge that overlooked the town. Molly saw the faint glow of the streetlamps dotting the main roads. It was beautiful, especially cradled between the mountains, and she could see why James had made this his home.

Minutes later, the darkened cabin came into view. It didn't look like anyone was awake, or even home, and she questioned the wisdom of riding this distance from town, in the dark, with a man she'd just met. Yet as soon as the thought came, everything she'd witnessed about James McPherson swiftly dismissed her doubts. From what she'd seen earlier, she would stake her life on his honesty and principles.

He wasn't the kind to ever knowingly do something wrong.

James helped her down from the horse, and moonlight lit their path. Molly wasn't certain of the time—she only knew she was more tired than she could ever remember being and that the lunch she'd eaten was long gone.

She followed him up the porch stairs. "I hope my arrival won't be an imposition for your sister."

"Rachel will welcome you like family, Mrs. Whitcomb. Which, in a sense, is what you are now. Out here, anyway."

"I'm not sure I follow you."

He paused, his hand on the latch. "One thing about living out here that's different from back east is that people have to depend on each other. You get to know folks real quick that way."

Under normal circumstances, Molly would have found that idea charming instead of intimidating. "I guess that makes Timber Ridge a close-knit community, and makes your job as sheriff a little easier. With everybody knowing each other."

"It does. But Timber Ridge is growing—faster than a lot of folks would like—and we've already lost some of that close-knit feel. Still, the people of this town are honest and decent, for the most part. We don't have many secrets among us." He lifted the latch, the silver light of night revealing his smile. "Or if we do, we don't keep them long."

Molly managed a nervous laugh and preceded him through the entryway.

"James, is that you?" a decidedly feminine voice called.

"Yep, sis, it's me. I've brought some company for the night."

A woman stepped into the hallway, her silhouette backlit by an oil lamp on a table behind her. Though Molly couldn't see the woman's face, she would've sworn she sensed her smiling.

"I've got our new schoolteacher with me. She arrived earlier than planned." He shot Molly a look that said so much. "We sort of *met* on the way up the mountain, near Devil's Gulch."

Devil's Gulch. Recalling the ravine, Molly considered that an apt name. Rachel drew closer and surprised Molly by grasping her hands.

"Miss Whitcomb, please forgive me for being so forward, but I can't tell you how much we've anticipated your arrival." She beamed, the Southern lilt of her voice as soft as her smile was bright. "And to have you in our home! All the parents and children in Timber Ridge are talking about you."

Uneasy beneath the attention and the prospect of being town *news*, Molly briefly bowed her head. "That's most generous of you, but I assure you I'm not worthy of such—"

"I'm not being generous at all. It's the truth! We're so honored that you would give up teaching college to come and teach our children. And here of . . . of all places." Rachel's voice broke, and she laughed. "I'm sorry. But this is such a pivotal time in our community, and in my family. Having a school, and a real teacher now . . ." She squeezed Molly's hands, shaking her head.

Overcome with emotion herself, but for different reasons, Molly found it difficult to speak, and she was grateful when James leaned over and gave his sister a hug.

"Rachel, I should've given you forewarning that I was bringing our new teacher home. That way you could've made her feel a little more welcome."

Smiling, Rachel swatted his arm. "Oh . . . stop it."

Molly looked between James and Rachel, wishing—not for the first time—that she hadn't been an only child. "Thank you for your kind welcome, Mrs.—" She realized she didn't know Rachel's last name.

"Boyd. Rachel Boyd," she said.

"Mrs. Boyd," Molly repeated. "You're very kind, and I appreciate your allowing me to stay in your home this evening."

"You're welcome to stay here as long as you like, Miss Whitcomb." Rachel glanced beyond her. "Do you have your luggage with you?"

"No, she doesn't." James removed his hat. "There's a bit of a story there, but first . . ."

Sensing what he was about to say, Molly looked away.

"As it turns out, Rachel," he said, his voice soft, "you and *Mrs.* Whitcomb have more in common than just your Southern heritage."

Frowning, Rachel looked from her brother to Molly again, her question clear.

"Mrs. Whitcomb lost her husband three months ago," he whispered.

Compassion filled Rachel's eyes, and Molly's mind scrambled. She was determined not to lie any more than she had to. But if they started asking questions about her husband—

"I'm so sorry. . . ." Rachel's arms came around her. "It does become more bearable, with time. I promise."

Molly gave herself to the embrace, feeling both comforted—and not, at the same time. "Thank you," she whispered, closing her eyes so as not to have to see James. "And I'm sorry about your husband."

Rachel nodded, then finally drew back. "Well—" She wiped her eyes, smiling. "Come with me, both of you. I've kept dinner warming on the stove, and there's plenty for two." She led the way to the kitchen and Molly followed.

James pulled out a chair for her, and when Rachel deposited a plate of roast beef, mashed potatoes, green beans, and butter-slathered corn bread before her, Molly felt as if she were six years old again, back at Grandma Willet's table. She inhaled the aromas, grateful to feel none of the nausea that had plagued her for the past several weeks. "Everything smells delicious."

"Rachel's a great cook." James draped a napkin across one leg.

Waving aside their compliments, Rachel joined them at the table. "The boys and I ate earlier. I've got two sons, Mrs. Whitcomb. You'll meet them tomorrow. Mitchell's nine, and—"

The scamper of footsteps filled the hallway, and two boys rushed around the corner, running head-long for James.

"Uncle James!" they yelled, and launched themselves onto his lap, their momentum threatening to send him and his chair toppling backward.

"Hey, boys!" James kept his balance and tousled a red mop of hair with each hand, laughing with them.

"Did you arrest any bad guys today, Uncle James?" the younger boy asked, his hair a brighter red than his older brother's.

James smiled, sneaking a tickle to each boy's tummy. "Not yet. But—" He looked in Molly's direction. "I did bring home your new teacher."

The boys stilled and turned their big blue eyes to her.

Molly actually felt herself blush. "Hello, boys."

Rachel's younger son scrunched up his face. "You don't look like a teacher."

"Kurt!" Rachel corrected, then softened it with a smile. "Mitchell, Kurt . . . may I present Mrs.

Whitcomb. And these, Mrs. Whitcomb"—she gestured, pride overshadowing her former embarrassment—"are my sons—Mitchell, who's nine, and Kurt, who's seven. They're very much looking forward to attending school."

If first impressions could be trusted, Molly guessed from Mitchell's observant nature that he would make an excellent student. However, the glint in the younger boy's eyes promised quite another challenge. "It's nice to meet you both, and I look forward to having you in class."

Rachel stood. "Okay, boys, back to bed. Let's go." She gathered them to her like a mother hen gathered her chicks. She glanced over her shoulder. "I'll be right back. You two go ahead and start eating."

The kitchen quieted immediately. Molly reached for her fork just as James reached out his hand. Realizing his intention, her face heated again. What must this man think of her?

"Shall we pray?" he asked softly.

"Yes, please," she whispered, and bowed her head.

His hand was warm and his grip gentle. And his touch had far more of an effect on her than it should have. Several seconds passed before Molly realized she wasn't even listening to his prayer.

She refocused her attention as he offered thanks for the food, for safety earlier during the day, and for her arrival in Timber Ridge. She placated the guilt the prayerful posture inspired by pledging to do all the good she could. She would truly make a difference in the children's lives; she would work harder than she'd ever worked in her life. And she would prove herself worthy of—

Feeling someone's stare, and hearing the silence, she slowly lifted her head.

"Amen . . . *again*." James smiled at her and gave her hand a gentle squeeze before letting go. "Unless you'd like to add something."

She hadn't blushed so much in years. "No, I think you covered everything." She reached for her fork and tucked her napkin in her lap.

"Mrs. Whitcomb."

She peered up.

"I was sincere when I gave thanks just now for God bringing you here. But I wouldn't be completely forthcoming if I didn't tell you that, while I don't personally have a problem with a widow being our teacher, there are some on the town council who will." His expression turned somber. "The mayor, for one. He's an influential man in this town, and . . . you haven't officially signed the contract yet."

Molly felt her jaw slip open. She'd come all this way for nothing? "But . . . I have the town council's offer. In the telegram. It's in my—" She gave a humorless laugh. "In my satchel. At the bottom of the ravine."

"I'm not saying that this job isn't yours, Mrs.

Whitcomb. All I'm saying is that you need to be prepared, in case there's some opposition."

"Opposition," she whispered, nodding. That was something to which she was accustomed. Still hungry, she found the food on her plate less appealing.

Rachel returned, and while they ate dinner James gave an account of how he'd found the stage flipped on its side, "hugging" the edge of the cliff, as he put it. Molly listened, only commenting occasionally, eating more than she thought she would and watching the brother and sister interact. The conversation stirred within her a longing for home, for her father, and for the life she'd thrown away so carelessly.

When it came time for bed, Rachel went to get her a nightgown. And after Molly made a visit to the privy outside, James showed her to a bedroom down the hallway. He set the oil lamp on a side table, and warm orange light haloed the modest room. The bed looked so inviting that Molly was tempted to crawl into it right then, until she realized that she was in *his* room.

"Sheriff McPherson, I can't take your bed. I can sleep on the couch in the—"

"Nonsense." He withdrew a shirt and pair of pants from a wardrobe. "I insist on it." And his smile said he would brook no argument. "I'm surprised you're still standing after all you've been through. I hope you get a good night's rest."

"Thank you, Sheriff."

He hesitated at the door. "One last thing . . ."

She read disquiet in his expression and shook her head. "If it's more 'opposition,' can we please wait and save it for morning? I'm not sure I can handle any more today." She smiled but was sincere in her request.

That same crooked grin tipped his mouth. "Actually, I was just wondering if you might consider moving back to a first-name basis. If . . . you'd be okay with that."

His unassuming manner was so refreshing. Yet keeping a certain distance between them would be best. For them both. But seeing the disappointment on his face . . .

"If you'd rather not, Mrs. Whitcomb, I—"

"Thank you for lending me your room, James. I appreciate it very much."

His smile slid back into place, and he stepped to one side to let Rachel through the doorway. "Well, all right, then. Good night to you both," he said softly.

Molly smiled, more certain than ever of his integrity.

"Good night, James." Rachel shook the nightgown and held it out. "You can borrow this for as long as you like. I have another. And if there's anything else you need, I'm just down the hall." She walked to the door and turned. "We're so glad you're here, Mrs. Whitcomb. You're an answer to so many prayers."

The compliment, well meant by Rachel, Molly knew, had the exact opposite effect. "Thank you. But, please, call me Molly."

"If you'll do likewise." With a soft smile, Rachel closed the door.

Molly changed into the nightgown, shivering by the time she was through. It was July but felt more like fall back home. She turned down the covers to find the indention from James's body still there in the feather mattress. She blew out the candle and carefully fit her body into the curve he'd left behind, and imagined being held. By him. Only not in the way she might have imagined if she'd met him months ago. She just wanted to feel safe again. Hidden and protected, guarded from the world. From choices she'd made. James McPherson seemed like the type of man capable of doing that—of protecting a woman, of making her feel safe.

She scrunched the covers closer beneath her chin. Why did that thought bring such melancholy?

She sought sleep, but each time she closed her eyes, the ravine rushed up to meet her. She turned onto her opposite side, sinking into the fluff of the feather mattress, and hugged the pillow tighter. It had a faint scent of bay rum and spice, and Molly breathed deep, finding the smell a comfort. She'd been so tired and grateful for the bed, she hadn't even asked him where he would sleep.

What would have happened if he hadn't come across them on that cliff . . . ?

She pulled the blanket closer beneath her chin and relived what it had felt like after he'd rescued them. She'd seen her life differently, and that difference—that sweet renewed appreciation—still pulsed steadily inside her. But somewhere above that gentle thrum, a bittersweet dissonance renewed the fear she'd felt when she'd stared down into Devil's Gulch, *knowing* she was about to die.

She hadn't yet made peace with what she'd done, or with the unwanted child in her womb. But even more, she hadn't made her peace with God.

But how did she go about doing that when she was choosing to live a lie? When she had no intention of telling the truth. Not when it would cost her the sum of everything she had left. No matter how little that was.

6

James paused in the hallway outside his bedroom door, listening for any sound that might indicate Molly was awake. He started to knock, then thought better of it. Best let her get some sleep after the long trip across country, not to mention yesterday's incident. She would need the rest.

School was set to start in a couple of weeks, and as Mayor Davenport made clear in the last town council meeting, the new teacher would be expected to visit every student and their parents in their homes before classes commenced. Not to mention accomplish a host of other tasks the council had assigned. But if anybody could handle it, he guessed Molly Whitcomb could.

Discovering she was a widow had been surprising. The correspondence had referred to her as Dr. Whitcomb, not Miss or Mrs. He'd just assumed she'd never been married, and he knew from the board's discussion that the other members had too. Mayor Davenport's reaction to the news promised to be nothing short of volatile.

Knowing Davenport, a former attorney, James was certain the man would likely push to advertise for a new teacher. But with school scheduled to begin so soon and Molly's outstanding qualifications, Davenport's success at doing that would be slim. And, as Molly had said, she did have grounds for defending her position. Because she was—for all practical purposes—*un*married.

He ran a hand through his hair, none too eager to referee this new development between council members. It had been hard enough to reach an agreement on a suitable candidate in the first place. Especially when Mayor Davenport's spinster sister from Denver had also applied for the position. James headed back to the kitchen.

In the end, he'd been the one to convince Mayor Davenport and the other board members that *Dr.*

Whitcomb, a woman with her doctorate in language studies, was the most qualified candidate. So now it would fall to him to be the one to explain if it turned out that she wasn't. That thought brought a troubled sigh.

Rachel stood by the stove, stirring a simmering pot of oatmeal. She added a dollop of butter and wiped her fingers on her apron. "She's still sleeping?"

"That's my guess. I don't hear anything."

"I'll check on her later. Don't worry. She did look tired last night, James," she said, her voice low. "And don't forget, the trip out here is wearing. Even by train. Add to that the drama of what happened with the stage. I wouldn't blame the woman if she slept for a week."

James retrieved five bowls from the kitchen cupboard and set them on the table. The images from yesterday were still fresh in his mind. How that coach had stayed on the cliff for as long as it had, he didn't know. Then again, he did. And he thanked God again for intervening.

Rachel set the pan to the side of the stove. "I'm surprised Molly didn't ask you right then and there to take her back to Sulfur Falls so she could catch the next train home."

"Molly, is it?" Smiling, James poured another cup of coffee and took a slow sip.

She gave him a look and handed him the jar of molasses. "I like her, James. She's nice, though

77

quieter than I was expecting. And prettier too." Raising a brow, she gave him a well-aimed grin.

Ignoring her teasing, James opened the jar and handed it back to her, then busied himself with gathering spoons and cups of milk for the boys. "She didn't seem too quiet at first but got more so the longer the day went. Which would fit with her being tired, I guess." Still, something about how Molly had bantered back and forth with him at first didn't sit right. Not that she'd done anything inappropriate. It just wasn't what he'd expect from a widow, especially one so recent.

"James."

He turned to find Rachel watching him.

"You're telling me—" she tiptoed over and peered down the hallway—"that you didn't notice how pretty she was?"

"I never said I didn't notice."

"But you didn't comment on it."

"You didn't ask for a comment."

Hands on her hips, Rachel playfully narrowed her eyes. "Well, I'm asking now."

He worked to hide his smile. "I still haven't heard a direct question."

"Did you or did you not, Sheriff McPherson, notice how pretty she is?"

"How pretty who is?"

He didn't even try to avoid her fist when she popped him a good one in the arm. "I noticed . . . all right? It'd be awfully hard not to. But don't let

your imagination go running off with you, okay?"
It was good to see Rachel smile these days, and he
did everything he could to make that happen.
She'd been so reserved following Thomas's death.

"My imagination's not running anywhere . . . for
now." Grinning, she turned on her heel and
sashayed back to the stove.

James took another swig of coffee, and the warm
brew burned a path all the way down. He wasn't
about to admit it, but he'd more than noticed Molly
Whitcomb.

Riding back into town with her last night had
been nothing short of an exercise in self-control.
The feel of her leaning back against him, her hair
smelling of some kind of flower he couldn't
remember but also couldn't forget. And of how his
arm had fit so well around her waist. He'd told
himself he was thinking of her safety. But, truth be
told, Molly Whitcomb's safety hadn't been the primary thought on his mind.

He noticed women on occasion. What man
didn't? But with discipline, he always guided his
focus back. Something not as easily done with Dr.
Molly Whitcomb.

He'd noticed her as soon as she'd stepped from
the train, and his attraction had been instant and
compelling. Not at all a common occurrence for
him, and not a welcome one either. Not in his line
of work. Not with a recent widow. And certainly
not with the town's new schoolteacher.

Rachel spooned oatmeal into their two bowls and joined him at the table. He'd offered thanks and whispered the final amen when it came to him. Thinking back to how Molly had bantered with him there at the first—it had been months after Rachel had buried Thomas before Rachel had felt spirited enough to joke with him, her own brother, like that.

And, as far as he knew, she had yet to speak at length with any man, much less spar with one. He unraveled that thought as they ate.

He'd never been married, had never even come close, but he'd known enough couples to realize there were all different kinds of marriages. Maybe Molly's had been more a marriage of necessity or convenience. Rather than of deep, abiding love—like Rachel and Thomas's had been. That would help explain things.

"This is good, Rach. Thanks."

Rachel looked at him and shook her head. "It's only oatmeal, James. Tonight I'll fix us a good dinner. Hopefully Molly can join us." She touched his arm. "Did you tell her about the cabin yet?"

He shook his head, speaking between bites. "I thought I'd let that be a surprise. It should be ready in another day or two, and she's welcome to stay on in my room until then. I actually enjoyed sleeping in the barn." He laughed softly. "Reminded me of when Daniel and I were boys and we'd sneak out to—"

Rachel's expression went blank.

Realizing what he'd done, James set down his spoon. "Rachel, I didn't mean to bring up—"

She shook her head, and though her eyes held warmth, they also held warning. "Don't . . ."

He stared at his bowl, letting a moment pass. He loved his sister, but he was weary of this foolishness.

Rachel cleared her throat. "Now, about this afternoon—" Deliberate cheerfulness tinged her voice. "I'll make sure Molly gets into town. The boys and I need to make a trip to the general store, anyway. Then I'll bring her by your office, and maybe we can go with you to show her the school and the cabin." She gestured to the pot of coffee on the hot pad between them. "Would you like some more?"

He recognized the evasive behavior, having witnessed it often enough. "Rachel, it's time for you to let this go," he whispered. His chest tightened as her fragile façade slipped from its place.

Tears rose to her eyes. "Don't, James . . . please."

He covered her hand on the table, keeping his voice low so the boys wouldn't hear down the hall. "This has gone on too long, Rachel. Daniel is not responsible for Thomas's death."

"I know you mean well, and you've been such a help to me and the boys since Thomas passed." She took a shallow breath. "I don't know what we would have done without you, but . . . you didn't know the situation like I did, James. You weren't

81

here. You didn't see how Mitch and Kurtie talked about Daniel in front of Thomas. How they idolized him." She pulled her hand away. "Daniel Ranslett might not have led Thomas out there to the woods that day, but he *is* responsible for what happened to him there. Whether you can accept that or not." She stared at her bowl for a moment, then stood. "And I'll thank you to not bring this up to me again in my home." She busied herself at the cupboard, her back to him.

My home. That last part brought James up short. He rose from the table and gently set his empty bowl in the tepid water of the washbasin. "Are you ready for me to move back into town, Rachel? Because if you are, just say the word. I don't want to get in your way here, and I certainly don't mean to overstay my welcome."

She bowed her head. Her shoulders began to shake. "No, I . . . I appreciate you moving in with us, and . . . I like you being here." Her voice quavered. "It's not that." She turned to face him, tears on her cheeks. "I only wish you'd believe my side of things instead of *his*."

"I do believe you, Rachel." James pulled her close for a hug. "But grief can make you do things, make you see things in a way that's not the truth, that's all. It feels like the truth because you're hurting so bad, and you'd do just about anything to make it stop."

He drew back and saw her struggle in her expression. She was still looking for the "why" behind her husband being taken from her and their boys. And as long as she was doing that, she'd never see beyond seeking to lay blame. And Daniel Ranslett was a convenient scapegoat.

He kissed the crown of her head. If he pushed her on this, she and Daniel might never mend their ways. Best stay out of things and let God work. That was a lesson their mother had taught him, among many. Their mother's life had been a series of sacrifices for her children, especially for him. Only he hadn't understood just how much she'd given until his father was on his deathbed.

That was one secret his father should have taken to his grave. And one James was determined to take to his. Not even Rachel knew.

He reached for his hat hanging on the back of the chair. "I'll look for you all in town this afternoon sometime. And would you mind making sure that she has—"

"I've already got a dress airing out for her," she said, reading his mind as she so often did. "And, James . . ."

He paused in the doorway.

"I know you didn't ask me, but if you were to . . ." She fingered the hem of her apron. "I'm not saying that she did this intentionally, but I can understand why she might not have wanted to reveal to the town council that she was married before. After Thomas died, I can't tell you how many times I wished I could just up and leave with the boys and start all over again. Someplace far away from all the reminders, from the looks people gave me in town when they thought I wasn't watching. I don't feel that way anymore, James. This is where Thomas wanted to raise our sons, and the memories are starting to be a comfort rather than a thorn. But still, I remember. So, please, let me say this without interruption."

She held up a hand, smiling, and looked so much like their mother in that moment that James couldn't have spoken if he'd wanted to.

"Don't judge Molly too harshly for wanting to try and start her life over again. I plan on doing everything I can to make her transition a good one, and I hope you will too."

Riding down the mountain into town, James sifted through what Rachel had said.

And by the time he reached his office, he'd determined to set aside his doubts about Molly Whitcomb and—if she did, in fact, get the job—to do as Rachel suggested and try his best to make her transition to Timber Ridge a good one.

On occasion, his intuition about people had been proven wrong. He reminded himself of that and chalked this up to being one of those times.

7

Molly slipped the last pearl button through the narrow slit in the high-neck collar and stepped back. She could only view the upper half of her reflection in the mirror mounted above James's dresser, but the dress Rachel had given her at breakfast—if one could still call the meal that, considering how late she'd slept—fit snug about her waist. But at least it fit.

She was sore from yesterday's "crash," as Rachel's younger son, Kurt, had referred to it, and her head ached, but the willow-bark tea Rachel had made was helping. Thankful the earlier bout of queasiness had passed, Molly smoothed a hand over her still-flat stomach, knowing it wouldn't be flat for much longer. What would she do then, once she started to show?

"We don't have many secrets among us," James had said last night. *"Or if we do, we don't keep them long."*

She searched her reflection in the mirror, able to see the deception so clearly in the dark half-moons beneath her eyes and in the tiny creases in her forehead that never seemed to smooth away. She looked as pale as she felt, and the black dress only washed out her already fair complexion and hair.

How far developed was the child inside her? Was it a boy or a girl? Did he or she have fingers and toes yet? During the night she'd awakened, and it had occurred to her that the trauma from yesterday might have affected the baby. She'd checked for bleeding then, and again this morning, but her concern proved unwarranted. The baby's life appeared to be unharmed—and still on course to change hers irrevocably.

And those were changes Molly didn't welcome. How could she? Knowing what was coming. And though she honestly didn't wish any harm to come to the child, she did wish it had never been conceived, which made her wonder again how Jeremy could ever have suggested what he did. She'd debated on whether or not to tell him about the baby. But finally, she'd decided she owed him that much, his being the father. His response had been chilling, and had shown what kind of man he really was. How could he begin to fathom putting an end to a child's life? She regretted its existence, but she could never follow through with what he'd suggested.

She pressed lightly on her abdomen. Could one so young and defenseless sense the depth of its mother's love and affection? For the child's sake, she hoped not.

Knowing Rachel and the boys were likely waiting on her to go into town, Molly threw the sheet over the bed and followed with the quilt. She hadn't said anything about it to Rachel, but she planned on moving to the boardinghouse today.

She appreciated Rachel's hospitality, and James's generosity in giving her his bed last night, but staying in the home of the most powerful authority in Timber Ridge, or one of them at least, was not where she wanted to be. Much less sleeping in the man's bed. She'd had her fill of men in authority and of their having influence over her life.

A knock sounded.

"Molly?" Rachel's voice carried through the closed bedroom door. "The boys and I will meet you by the wagon, all right?"

Molly opened the door. "Thank you for your patience, Rachel. I'm nearly ready." She smoothed a hand over the delicate lace-tiered skirt, sensing approval in Rachel's soft exhale. "Thank you again for being so generous with this."

"It's beautiful on you, and looks like it fits well."

"It does." And would, at least for a little while. "I'll take extra care with it, I promise. And I'll return it as soon as my trunks arrive."

"You can keep it for as long you need." Rachel's look grew reminiscent. "Come October, two years will have passed since my Thomas was killed. It's time for me to move on, I know. Some would say it's past time." Her fingers trailed the waistband of her dark blue skirt. "I started wearing colors again a month ago."

Molly hardly considered that dark a blue a "color" but said nothing.

"Out here, men and women tend not to wait as

long as they do back east before moving ahead with life and remarrying. It's not that people don't miss their loved ones. They do—it's just that, typically, there are no other family members. And there are children to be raised and ranches to be run." A fragile look crept in behind Rachel's eyes. "If not for James, I don't know what I would have done. Or would've had to do. He moved in right after and took over responsibilities I just couldn't handle at the time."

Molly imagined the number of men who must have lined up to court the beautiful young Widow Boyd, especially with a ranch as part of the deal. "I'm guessing you had plenty of eager suitors."

Rachel's cheeks pinkened. "Thomas hadn't been buried two months when they started calling on me. But having the sheriff for a big brother provided a strong deterrent." Her smile was sheepish.

"I can well imagine, having seen him in action yesterday. He can be quite . . . commanding." Which was all the more reason for her to be out of Rachel's house and on her own.

Rachel touched her arm. "Is your stomach still upset? Because if you need to see a doctor, we can stop by his office while we're in town."

"No, no, I'm fine now." Molly shook her head. When the bout of nausea had hit earlier, Rachel had insisted on accompanying her to the privy. "Too many trains and stagecoaches, I'm thinking." The last thing she needed was a visit to the town doctor. That was one person she wouldn't be able to fool for long.

Rachel motioned down the hallway. "Take your time, and come on out when you're ready."

Leaving the door ajar, Molly finished getting ready and worked the last few hairpins into place. Two books on James's dresser drew her attention, as they had last night, and told her something of the man who lived in this room. Her gaze went to the Bible with its cracked, worn leather binding, then to the thick volume entitled *Unchanging Laws of These United States*. Shreds of paper were tucked at odd angles every few pages.

Neither of the volumes was surprising, considering her initial impression of the man. She had a feeling that James McPherson on the outside was exactly who he was on the inside. She turned away from her reflection.

After putting the room to right, she joined Rachel and her sons out front, doing her best to avoid puddles from yesterday's rain. She gathered the full skirt of the black dress and climbed up to the bench seat. Rachel was busy doing something with the harnesses, and Molly admired her skill, which was far above her own. She knew how to harness a single mount but not a team. And she certainly didn't know how to hitch a wagon. Rachel seemed to know how to do it all.

With yesterday's accident still close in mind, Molly was none too eager to chance the winding mountain roads in a wagon or coach again. But like James, Rachel inspired trust, and Molly determined to sit back and not grip the seat—too tightly.

It had been dark when she and James arrived last night, so other than quick trips to and from the privy, she hadn't seen the land surrounding the homestead.

The cabin was ample size, and though it still fell within the parameters of "rustic," obvious care had been given to the finish work around the doors and windows. Southern influences abounded in the wide front porch and thick pine columns framing the front entrance. Studying the detailed workmanship, Molly caught a glimpse of the talented man and attentive husband Thomas Boyd must have been.

She breathed deeply the scent of evergreens and of something sweet she couldn't quite identify, surprised at how cool the air still was, and with August just around the corner. Rachel wasn't wearing a wrap, so Molly had hesitated asking for one. People probably grew accustomed to the chill in the mountain air much like they grew accustomed to the heavy days of summer back in Georgia. Only, the chilly temperature was a far more pleasant adjustment.

Rachel climbed up beside her and gathered the reins. Molly heard a sniffing sound to her left and turned.

Kurt was leaning close, smiling. He sniffed again. "You smell good, teacher."

"Kurt!" Rachel shot her younger son a reproving look. "It's not polite for a boy to comment on how a woman smells. And you need to address your new teacher as Mrs. Whitcomb."

Kurt's mouth pulled to one side. "Yes, ma'am," he said quietly, watching Molly with curiosity and not just a little mischief.

Still wary of the gleam in the boy's eyes, Molly gave her soon-to-be-student a hesitant smile. When sunlight hit the boy's red hair, the rays turned it an autumn blaze color, reminding her of fall in the Smoky Mountains.

Mitchell hunched over the back of the seat beside his brother. "Mama, can we go by Uncle James's office first?"

"We'll wait to go by Uncle James's office until a little later. First we're going to show Mrs. Whitcomb some of Timber Ridge and take her by the mercantile." Rachel gave the reins a whip and guided the wagon down the wide rain-rutted road. She glanced at Molly beside her. "That way you can pick up any incidentals you might need. Then we'll meet James and go see the school building, if you'd like."

"That sounds wonderful to me. Thank you. And if you have other errands you need to take care of, I'm happy to ride along."

With a nod, Rachel indicated for Molly to look

upward. At first Molly thought she was simply motioning to the mountains; then she spotted a hawk soaring above in the cloudless blue. The bird swayed from side to side, its wings seemingly motionless at this distance and its telling screech drifting downward.

They rounded a curve and Molly shielded her eyes from the sun, continuing to watch. "What must it be like to experience that kind of freedom? That kind of perspective on the world?"

Rachel sighed beside her. "I've often thought that very same thing. In early evening, I'll sit on the front porch and watch the elk and deer graze alongside the meadow. Life here can be hard, and painful at times. But there's also such beauty and joy to be found. And I've learned . . . in all my long years"—her expression hinted at humor—"that those things often go hand in hand."

Watching the hawk until it disappeared over a ridge, Molly prayed that what Rachel said was true. That along with the bad in her life, with all the mistakes she'd made, there might also come some good.

"Sheriff, you got a minute?"

James looked up from his paperwork to see one of his deputies. "Sure, Willis. Grab a chair." Dean Willis straddled the chair opposite his desk, and James checked his pocket watch. Rachel, Molly, and the boys were supposed to stop by sometime.

Rachel hadn't said exactly when, but he hoped they could have lunch together.

"Couple of things happened yesterday afternoon, Sheriff. We got another complaint from a worker out at the resort, and then there was a run-in over at Clara's Cafe." The deputy frowned, as if knowing James wouldn't like the news. "Between a group of miners and some of those . . . newcomers."

James leaned forward in his chair, suppressing a sigh. Willis always referred to the Italian immigrants as *newcomers*. Willis didn't harbor any prejudice, James knew. It was simply the deputy's way of making a distinction between the townsfolk and other groups of people new to Timber Ridge. "Does the complaint from Tolliver's place involve the same man from two weeks ago?"

Willis shook his head. "Different man, last name of Moretti. But the same complaint. Says the working conditions aren't safe. Want me to talk to Tolliver about it, sir?"

James considered his exchanges with Brandon Tolliver recently and shook his head. "No, I probably need to speak with him myself on this one. But do some checking around for me first. See what you can find out about the worker—what his specific complaint is, if it's founded. And if he and Tolliver have had words recently. But do it quietly, Willis, without an audience." James angled a look, making sure the younger man understood what he was saying.

Willis touched two fingers to his brow. "Understood, boss. And about the cafe . . . Workers from the resort, some newcom—" He paused. "Some Italian men stopped by to eat late yesterday. Clara said she was fine with serving them. You know Clara. If someone's hungry, she'll feed 'em."

James nodded.

"Anyway, Clara says she was serving them when some miners—she didn't recognize the men—walked up and told the fellows they had to leave. That their kind wasn't served there. Scuffle broke out, tables got overturned, and some dishes were broken. Clara doesn't care about the dishes, but she's afraid her regular patrons might start staying away if something like that happens again. I tried to track down the names of the miners, but people said they hadn't seen them before."

Sighing, James stood and walked to the front window. "Doesn't matter who they are." Used to be, he knew every face that passed on the board-walk outside, and the families that went along with them. But not anymore. "Finding those men isn't going to make this go away." He blew out a breath. "Make sure our office pays Clara back for the cost of anything she lost. I'll stop by there later to let her know we'll be keeping an eye out for her."

Once Willis had left, James started in on the paperwork covering his desk, the part of his job he liked least. But every few minutes, he found his attention returning to the window, and his thoughts returning to Molly Whitcomb.

Unbidden, a realization rose inside him, and he stared at the quill in his grip. Perhaps part of the reason he had doubts about her was due to his strong attraction to her. She carried herself with quiet grace and confidence, which only made the vulnerability she tried so hard to mask that much more intriguing.

He knew better than to encourage the thoughts he was entertaining. Nothing would, or could, come from them. Still, he would've sworn—based on a feeling he'd gotten from their first meeting in Sulfur Falls, and again on the cliff—that she'd felt a spark of something for him too.

Drawing his focus back, he pulled out a report from the territory's Governing Office in Denver. But after reading the first paragraph four times and still retaining nothing, he grabbed his hat and took the long way to Clara's Cafe, welcoming the chance to walk.

His thoughts returned to the two incidents Willis had reported. Timber Ridge was growing, changing, and not all for the better. It was his job to keep people safe, and yet each day he felt that responsibility moving further and further beyond his grasp.

He stopped by Mayor Davenport's office, but the man wasn't in. He rarely was.

"Would you like to leave him a message, Sheriff?" Davenport's secretary asked.

James declined. News of Molly Whitcomb's widow status was something he needed to tell the mayor in person.

He continued toward Clara's, as he did most days about this time. Making himself available to townsfolk helped keep his thumb on the pulse of Timber Ridge. He hadn't gone two blocks when he heard his name being called.

"Sheriff McPherson!" Mrs. Mattie Moorehead, wife to one of the more senior town council members, waved to him from across the street. "We have a question for you!"

James smiled to himself, already having a good idea as to what that question would be. Especially when he saw Mrs. Frances Hines following, hot on her sister's heels. "Yes, ma'am?" He acknowledged Mrs. Hines, who arrived three steps behind Mrs. Moorehead and slightly out of breath. "How are you two ladies today?"

"We're fine, Sheriff." Smiling between huffs, Mrs. Hines elbowed her way in front of her older sister and squeezed his arm affectionately. Both women were old enough to be his mother and had treated him like a son since the first day he'd taken office. "We're discussing whether my cherry pie would best be served at the upcoming—"

"Frances!" Mrs. Moorehead shot her sister a reproving look and took hold of James's other arm. "We were discussing whether my gingerbread cake"—her smile held as much confection as did her ribbon-winning dessert—"would be best for the upcoming celebration. Or whether the town might indeed prefer something with a little more . . . *tart* to it." Brow raised, the older sister gave the younger a dismissive glance.

Mrs. Hines pulled James closer. "My cherry pie is not tart, Mattie Moorehead! It's sweet and—"

"Gingerbread is far more fitting for the occasion, Frances. And you well know that it's . . ."

James looked between the two women. Seems the debate over which cake or pie would be the "official" dessert for the celebration of Colorado's statehood still wasn't settled. A celebration that would occur only if President Grant didn't veto the statehood bill as the presidents before him had.

Mayor Davenport had it on trusted authority that the territory's proposal to be granted statehood would pass this time, and the town had been planning the celebration for weeks. The entire community was expected to turn out for the event.

"Ladies . . ." He slipped an arm around each of their shoulders, immediately silencing their bickering. "I've had the privilege of tasting both of your desserts and believe I can state with full authority that both cherry and gingerbread would be well received. In fact," he continued, sensing Mrs. Moorehead's protest, "I believe they're both necessary in order to make this celebration complete."

The sisters stared up, attentive.

"After all, cherry pie is noted as having been one of President Washington's favorites."

Mrs. Hines beamed up at him.

"And President Lincoln enjoyed gingerbread better than most anything else."

Mrs. Moorehead squared her thin shoulders and managed a smile at her sister. "Well, I guess we *could* have both. And—" she sniffed—"I have the perfect lace tablecloth for the occasion."

"I have a lace tablecloth too, Mattie. One from Grandmother, and I—"

James made a hasty exit, leaving the ladies dickering over which cloth would be used. He continued on, mulling over the changes facing Timber Ridge.

Statehood had its advantages. But in his experience, whenever you gained something, you gave up something in return. It was that way with business, and with people.

"Sheriff McPherson!"

He spotted Dr. Brookston hailing him from a side street and slowed his pace. "How are you, Brookston?"

Rand Brookston ran to catch up with him. "I'm well. Doing better now that I've gotten this." He waved a sheet of paper.

Guessing what it was, James felt a sense of satisfaction.

"I'm sure I have you to thank for this, Sheriff."

"It was your plan, Doctor, and it's a good one. All I did was present it to the town council. They agreed with you and gave it full backing."

Brookston shook James's hand. "We both know the mayor wasn't too favorable toward the idea. It was due to your influence that this passed so quickly, and I appreciate your support. Improving the health of families in Timber Ridge is something I'm committed to, Sheriff. And mandating physical examinations for all the schoolchildren is an important first step in that."

"Well, you've got not only my support, but the town council's. And if there's anything else you need, let me know and I'll do my best to get it for you."

"I'd like to solicit the new teacher's support in this too—as soon as she gets into town."

James nodded. "I think that's a good idea, and she arrived yesterday. I'll encourage her to get in touch with you this week."

"Excellent." Brookston nodded. "I'd appreciate that. I've found it helps students feel more comfortable if their teacher takes the lead in getting her examination first. Especially since most of these children have never visited a doctor."

"I can't see why Dr. Whitcomb would have a problem with that. And I'll go you one further." James clapped Brookston on the shoulder, grateful the man had chosen to come to Timber Ridge a year ago. "If you need the sheriff to get his examination too, tell me where and when and I'll be there."

Brookston grinned. "How about next Tuesday morning at nine o'clock in my office?"

"Done." James laughed. "And I'll bring Mitchell and Kurt with me too."

"And, ah . . . what about their mother? She's been feeling well lately, I hope."

If James wasn't mistaken, he detected a note of interest in Rand Brookston's voice. One beyond a physician's normal curiosity. "She's doing very well. Thanks for asking."

Brookston fingered the black leather bag in his grip. "If she wanted to come along, that'd be fine too. Not for an examination, of course. But to accompany her sons. Unless she needed an examination, then I'd be happy to provide whatever care she requires."

James smiled. "I'll be sure and pass that along." He liked Brookston and would welcome the man's interest in his sister, if Rachel were open to it. But Brookston being a doctor wouldn't help his chances any. Quite the opposite, in fact. Which was odd, in one sense, given that their own father had been a physician.

As he continued down the boardwalk, James recognized the recurring direction of his thoughts and couldn't decide which bothered him more—the fact that he found himself so attracted to a woman who'd recently lost her husband, which just seemed wrong, or that, try as he might, he couldn't shake the feeling there was more to Dr. Molly Whitcomb than met the eye. Far more than she wanted him to see.

8

Molly stole glimpses beside her as Rachel negotiated the wagon's path through town. Rachel Boyd seemed the perfect blend of grace and beauty, ensconced in a spirit of steel. Rachel hadn't said how her husband, Thomas, had died, and Molly didn't feel at liberty to ask. But it was odd that both James and Rachel had used the phrase "was killed."

Just ahead, wagons clogged the main thoroughfare into town, many stuffed full with families and furniture, trunks and stoves, with chairs and barrels tied onto the sides.

"Each day it seems more families arrive," Rachel said softly, her brow furrowing.

"Is it mining that brings them here?"

"The lure of silver is part of it. That and Brandon Tolliver—you met him yesterday—who's building a resort on the outskirts of town. A hot springs resort. He's hiring immigrants to do the work."

From Rachel's tone, Molly sensed she didn't approve of Tolliver's actions. She'd read about the hot springs in this region and about their touted curatives. "Do you think the resort will be a good thing for Timber Ridge?"

"In the long run, yes." Rachel waved another wagon on through. "If the town—and my brother—can survive its being built."

None-too-subtle accusation colored Rachel's tone, and Molly decided not to delve any further.

The streets of Timber Ridge were bustling, and when men and women saw Rachel, they either tipped their hats or waved. But Molly noticed that when they spotted her, they stopped what they were doing and stared. Mothers whispered to children and the children's eyes grew round.

Rachel giggled. "Welcome to Timber Ridge, Molly. I'll give it until suppertime for the whole town to know you've arrived."

Molly did her best to smile and appear confident and teacherlike as they passed. And by the time they reached the end of the street, she'd counted fourteen children. All of them of school age. She realized then that she hadn't inquired as to how many children she would be teaching. Not that it would have had any bearing on the situation.

"There's Uncle James!" Kurt leaned over the seat, waving big as the world. "I see him! Uncle James!"

"Uncle James!" Mitchell called with no less enthusiasm.

Enjoying the boys' reactions, Molly spotted James down the street—speaking with a Negro gentleman. James shook the man's hand and smiled, and Molly couldn't help but have the same reaction, witnessing the exchange. That boded well for the direction of this town, and hopefully for the school.

There was no doubt how much Mitchell and Kurt adored their uncle, but it was the smile that lit James's face when he saw the boys that told her even more. As did the number of people who greeted James as he strode toward the wagon. Men and women alike, on the boardwalk and in the street. It soon became clear that James McPherson could no more choose not to lead than he could choose not to breathe.

"Hey, fellas!" James gave each boy's head a good rub. The brothers squirmed, but not out of his reach, Molly noticed. "Did you two get the stalls mucked this morning?"

"Yes, sir," they answered in unison.

"All right, then. You've earned this." Reaching into his pocket, James threw Rachel a wink. "You take this to Mr. Mullins"—he pressed a coin into Mitchell's hand, then one into Kurt's—"and ask him to give you each the biggest sugar stick in the store."

"Thanks, Uncle James!" Mitchell catapulted off the side of the wagon and headed down the board-walk. "Come on, Kurt!"

But Kurt lingered, edging closer to his uncle. "I used the pitchfork too, Uncle James, just like you showed me. Then I put it back on the hook."

"That's real good, son." James drew the boy close, and Kurt's little arms came around his neck. "You're a fine boy, you know that? And you're making a right fine rancher too. I'm sure your papa's mighty proud of you."

Beaming, Kurt nodded, his smile going a little wobbly.

James swung him over the side of the wagon, taking him extra high as he went, then patted the seat of the boy's pants. "Now run catch up with your brother, and make sure you choose the sugar stick you want."

"Yes, sir! Thank you, Uncle James!"

The boy flew down the street, his short legs taking him faster than Molly would've imagined. He was adorable, hungry for a man's attention, and missing his father. And her heart went out to him, despite his mischievous gleam.

James came around to her side of the wagon. "Good day, ladies." He touched the brim of his hat, his gaze taking in Molly. "You look nice this afternoon. And rested. I hope you slept well. The bed in that room's a touch on the soft side."

"I slept very well—after I stopped seeing the ravine every time I closed my eyes. Thank you, Sheriff." Despite their pact to use first names, Molly considered it best to keep some formality between them in public settings. She took his subtle smile as agreement. "My grandmother had a feather bed a lot like—"

"*Thief!* Get back here with that!" somebody yelled from down the street.

Heads turned and from her perch on the wagon seat, Molly spotted a thin dark-haired boy running pell-mell toward them, something tucked in the crook of his arm. Too late, the boy spied James and skidded, trying to alter his course.

James caught him easily and held him by the arm. "Whoa, there, son."

The boy wriggled in his grip, glancing back over his shoulder every few seconds. *"Per favore, signore, mi lasci andare! Un tipo mi sta inseguendo: é arrabbiato! Ha imbrogliato me e la mia famiglia."*

"Settle down," James said, his voice firm, his expression patient. "I'm not going to hurt you."

A crowd quickly formed in the street, but a large, burly gentleman shoved his way right past them, his features twisted in anger.

Molly got an inkling of why the boy was so frightened. This man was massive—and beyond livid.

"This little thief stole a loaf of bread from my store!" The man pointed, the muscles in his forearms bulging. "I saw him! And I got witnesses to prove it."

The crowd pressed closer. Some of them began siding with the man. "Bolden's right, Sheriff! These folks'll rob you blind if you let them." "They're only here for what they can get." "Our town would be better off without 'em!"

"Per favore, signore." Addressing James, the boy spoke quickly, voice pleading, his words tumbling out one atop the other. *Gli ho sbrigato le faccende di casa. Vi do la mia parola. Gli ho spazzato la veranda, buttato via la spazzatura. Chieda alla signora del negozio, ve lo riferirà. Lei mi ha visto! Quest'uomo aveva promesso di pagarmi ma poi non lo ha fatto. Ho solo preso un pezzo di pane e della carne per quello che mi deve!"*

The man named Bolden lunged forward as if to grab the boy by the scruff of the neck, but James blocked his effort. "Step back, Bolden. And everybody else just calm down."

Eyes narrowing, Bolden complied, his expression saying he didn't like being ordered around.

James pinned the boy with a look. "Can you understand what's being said to you right now, son?"

The boy looked at him, confusion written in his face.

Molly leaned forward in the wagon, unsure whether to intervene or keep quiet. Taking into account what James had told her last night about her not having signed a formal contract yet, she knew her standing with the town council was precarious. And she had no intention of further jeopardizing her position or future relationship with the board. She needed this job, however temporary it might be.

Still, something in the boy's manner inspired her belief in him and made her want to help him.

The boy slowly bowed his head and produced a package of what appeared to be salami from within his shirt, followed by a loaf of bread with two bites missing.

Bolden swore loudly. "See? I told you, Sheriff! These people are thieves by nature. Didn't I tell you that last week in the town council meeting?"

This man was on the town council? Molly leaned back in her seat. The last thing she needed was to get on the man's bad side.

The boy's dark eyes darted to and fro, looking for a way of escape. He was slight of build by nature and his olive complexion had a pasty undertone, but the thinness in his arms revealed the malnutrition. Watching him more closely, she realized he was older than she'd originally guessed him to be.

His lower lip began to tremble. He locked eyes with her, and Molly felt the pangs of his hunger in her own stomach.

James loosened his grip. "Bolden, have you ever seen this boy before?"

"I have not." Bolden eyed the boy with disgust. "But his kind keep hangin' around my store, probably robbing me blind and I just don't know it."

"Sheriff?" Surprised at hearing her own voice, Molly climbed down from the wagon. The weight of attention shifted to her, though none was heavier than the boy's. She gently touched his arm. *"Ora é tutto chiaro e se vuoi lo tradurrò allo Sceriffo McPherson. Lo sceriffo di Timber Ridge é un uomo buono e onesto, vedrai che ti tratterà giustamente."*

Tears sharpened the boy's dark eyes. *"G-grazie mille, signora, grazie."*

"Mrs. Whitcomb?" Frustration and disbelief weighted James's voice.

Molly read the surprise in his eyes. "Yes, Sheriff McPherson. I'm sorry for interrupting, but . . . I speak Italian, and I understood everything this young man just said." Bolden's dark glare communicated his displeasure. "I offered to interpret for him." She looked back to the boy. *"Come si chiama?"*

Ragged hope rose in his eyes. *"Mi chiamo . . . Angelo Giordano."*

"Angelo," she repeated softly. "I offered to interpret for Angelo and he accepted. If you'll allow me?" Awaiting James's response, she noticed Angelo edging closer to her.

James nodded. "Go ahead."

"Thank you, Sheriff." Counting the cost of what she was about to do, Molly found she had no choice. "Angelo says that he worked for this man. That he swept off the man's porch and hauled away his trash. He says for you to ask the *good woman* at the mercantile who will verify this. That she saw him do these things."

Bolden's expression turned stony, and Molly felt

her job slipping away. But she also felt something else—a protectiveness within her. And that protectiveness lit a spark deep inside.

She slipped an arm around Angelo's thin shoulders. "Angelo also said that Mr. Bolden promised to pay him and then didn't. And that he only took what was equal to what he was owed."

James's attention moved between the man and Angelo. "Bolden, is any of this sounding familiar? And think before you answer because I plan on confirming everything with Lyda Mullins."

Bolden's jaw hardened. "The boy might've done some work for me a time or two, but I had to fire him. He was lazy and wasn't gettin' his tasks seen to. Just like all his kind. I told you last week when we discussed how to—"

"That's enough!" James's tone was controlled but firm. "Go back to your shop, Bolden. I'll be over directly." His gaze swept the crowd. "And everybody else, go on about your business."

Bolden stared at the boy for a long moment, then at James, before muttering something and stalking away. The crowd began to disperse.

"Mrs. Whitcomb." James gave an exasperated sigh. "Would you please tell Angelo to be at my office at ten o'clock tomorrow morning to discuss what happened here today, and to talk with me about finding him a job. And that if he decides not to show up—I'll come looking for him, and I'll find him."

Molly relayed the message verbatim.

Angelo's head bobbed up and down. *"Si, si. Grazie, signore, grazie. Ci sarò. Vi do la mia parola."*

"He says he'll be there," Molly supplied. "He gives you his word, Sheriff."

Angelo held out the loaf of bread and meat to James, who shook his head and motioned for him to keep it. The boy dipped his head in Molly's direction. *"Lei e molto gentile, Signora . . . Whitcomb."* He pronounced her name with some uncertainty.

She nodded. *"Prego."* Then she patted his arm. *"Benvenuto."* She watched him until he reached the corner. He glanced back at her and smiled, tore off a piece of bread, and took off at a good clip.

"Well, that was mighty impressive, Molly," James said softly.

She turned back to find him watching her—Rachel too, from the wagon—and felt an unexpected sense of accomplishment. She lifted a shoulder and let it fall. "I'm glad I was able to help, but it's not that impressive. I simply have an ear for languages. I always have."

"Have you been to Europe?" Rachel asked.

Molly had been asked this question before, and each time she wished she could give a different answer. "No, I haven't. It was encouraged, of course, but . . ." She managed a carefree tone. "My schedule never allowed opportunity to travel like that." Nor did she have the funds. Her father's occupation as a college professor at Franklin College had meant stretching every dollar.

"So . . ." James shifted his weight. "Just how many languages do you know?"

Molly warmed at the admiration in his voice. "I speak Italian, Spanish, and French. Those are the languages I taught at the college in Georgia. I can read Portuguese and Romanian fairly well, but I'm not fluent in those languages by any means."

"That's a real disappointment." He made a *tsk*ing sound with his tongue, and the gleam in his eyes reminded Molly of Kurt.

"That's astounding." Rachel shook her head. "And to think, you're the woman who'll be teaching my boys. Speaking of—" She gathered the reins. "I need to catch up with them. Would you like to ride along, Molly?"

"I think I'll walk, if that's all right."

"I'll walk with you." James looked up at his sister. "How about we meet you there?"

Nodding, she released the brake, then glanced in the direction Bolden had gone. "Be careful with him, James," she whispered down.

He reached over and pinched the toe of her boot. "I'm always careful, Rach. And don't you worry about Bolden. He's harmless. A lot of boast and swagger, is all."

Rachel gave the reins a snap, her parting look saying she thought otherwise.

"Shall we walk, *Mrs. Whitcomb*?"

Hearing the formality of his tone, Molly half expected him to offer his arm. But he didn't.

She fell into step beside him, thinking of how he'd pinched the toe of Rachel's boot. It was such a sweet gesture. She appreciated how he had handled the situation with Angelo Giordano too—except one niggling doubt persisted. "How can you be so sure that Angelo will show up at your office tomorrow morning?"

Staring ahead, James smiled. "Don't worry. He'll show."

She said nothing but hoped for Angelo's sake that he was right.

James acknowledged a young woman passing by whose smile was shy but whose stare certainly wasn't. After walking several paces, Molly still sensed someone watching and chanced a look over her shoulder. The same young woman continued to stare, her attention fixed on James. And the man seemed oblivious to it. Or maybe he only pretended not to see.

Molly studied him, wondering why he'd never married.

Then again, she didn't know his history. Perhaps he had been married before. But something told her otherwise. He seemed as eligible as a man could be. Handsome, kind, obviously well liked by people in town—at least most people.

He turned to her. "I wouldn't have let the boy go if I didn't know he'd come back."

She decided to take the supportive route. "I hope you're right."

"I am," he said softly, with not a trace of arrogance. "You see, much like you've always had an ear for languages, I've always had a knack for reading people."

Molly started to bring up the woman they'd just passed on the street, but seeing James's serious expression and realizing what his "knack for reading people" might mean for her, she didn't. "So . . . you're saying you can tell when someone's telling the truth?" She hoped her question sounded more casual than it felt.

He paused on the side of the street. "It's more like I can tell whether someone's genuine or not. It's a sense I get right off about a person. And it's usually proven true, over time."

A cool wind of caution blew through her. His attention deepened, and it was all she could do to maintain his gaze. Nerves twisted her stomach. Did he know about her? Had he guessed her secret? The sick feeling inside her fanned out. Somewhere down deep, she'd known her chances of living out this ill-fated charade were slim. But how had he found out?

A blur of questions fired rapid speed through her mind. If James did know, it would be best to get it over with right now, before things went any further, though she would have preferred someplace more private for their confrontation.

She took a deep breath and tried not to stammer. "And just what sense have you gotten about me . . . James?" she said discreetly. "In the short time we've known each other."

He studied her. "Are you certain you want to know?"

The seriousness in his voice caused everything around them to fade. Any moment now her knees would give way, she was certain. She attempted a soft laugh. "Well, of course I want to know." Her effort at nonchalance failed miserably.

Staring down at her, he took his time in answering. "I see a woman standing before me—" His voice was soft. "A very talented woman who's been through a painful time in her life, and who's left that behind her. Or who's trying real hard to." The gentle lines that framed the corners of his eyes and mouth crinkled. "But she's also hiding something."

Molly told herself to keep breathing, and wondered if she would meet the wagon carrying her trunks up the mountain as she was sent packing back down.

"My guess is"—a gentleness no sheriff had a right to possess, especially one so handsome, softened his rugged features—"that you're hiding a similar hurt to the kind my sister has known. Only . . . different somehow. And you don't realize yet that you've come to the right place to start over again. It won't be easy, but you'll have friends to help you through this, if you're willing to let them."

Molly's throat tightened. If he only knew how willing she was for that to happen. But would these *new friends* accept her for who she was if they knew the truth? Which would reveal itself soon enough. Sooner than she would be ready.

"I could look down the street right now," he continued, "and point to person after person who came to Timber Ridge to begin again. Some came due to failed businesses back east or lives ruined by war. . . . People come west for all sorts of reasons."

Though she would have thought it impossible, the kindness in his eyes deepened.

"So if that's why you've come here, Molly, to start over again, then you're in good company."

She swallowed, both relieved and bewildered. He didn't know she was with child. But he did have insight into people. Into *her*. Which meant she would have to be careful with him.

After several beats, her heart considered returning to its normal rhythm. A wagon passed by on the street, and James urged her closer to the boardwalk. She'd long prided herself on being plainspoken, but this man's straightforward manner, and the honesty and gentleness with which he laid out the truth, was unnerving. And downright appealing.

"Are you always so direct, Sheriff?"

His smile came gradually. "You asked me a direct question, ma'am. And I make it a rule to always answer a direct question as honestly, and kindly, as I can."

He resumed their stroll, and Molly fell into step beside him again, considering that self-imposed *rule*. Never again would she ask James McPherson a question unless she truly wanted—and was prepared to accept—his answer.

9

Later that afternoon, Molly sat wedged between James and Rachel on the wagon seat, on their way to see the schoolhouse, the last stop on their brief tour of Timber Ridge. The boys sat behind them in the back, slurping on sugar sticks and laughing as they bumped along. A flicker of relief still wavered inside her knowing that James hadn't discovered her secret. But it wasn't empowerment she felt. Quite the opposite.

It was dread of people eventually discovering the truth. And of what it would cost them. Not just her. But them too.

She cringed when she thought of James or Rachel or cute little Emily Thompson, a student she'd been introduced to at the general store, learning about what she'd done. The people she'd met that afternoon, among them eager parents willing to entrust their children to her care, were already accepting her as their teacher and as part of this town.

She'd come to Timber Ridge with a pile of preconceptions about the community and its people. And though she wasn't willing to concede that all of her opinions were unfounded, the townspeople she'd met so far had given her cause to rethink most of them.

A name on a building they passed drew her attention. *Miss Ruby's Boardinghouse.* She remembered a boardinghouse being mentioned in a telegram and wondered why that wasn't being included on the tour. "Is that where I'll be living?"

She aimed her question at Rachel, who leaned forward and looked at her brother.

James gave something close to a nod, his focus remaining on the road. "That's where the town council planned you'd be living. Yes, ma'am."

Molly glanced behind them as they passed. The building looked nice enough. Nothing fancy, but clean. And, she hoped, absent of bugs, which hadn't described her overnight lodgings in Denver. She shuddered remembering.

Sensing an opening, she chose her words with care, not wanting to offend. "Perhaps we could stop by there on our way back through town, and I could speak with the proprietress about moving in today. That way I wouldn't be an imposition to either of you."

Rachel frowned. "You're not an imposition at all. And you're welcome to stay with us until your . . ." She paused. "Until your room is ready. Right, James?"

"That's right. Still . . ." He glanced down at Molly. "We want you to be comfortable. We'll see if we have time to stop by once we're done seeing the school."

Satisfied with his answer, Molly sat back. "How far is the walk from the boardinghouse to the schoolhouse?"

"About ten minutes or so." He glanced down at her heeled boots. "Give or take, depending on how fast you can walk in those fancy shoes of yours."

Jesting curled the flat edge of his voice, and Rachel and the boys giggled.

On a whim, Molly angled her left boot as though admiring it. "I'm flattered you've taken such a liking to my shoes, Sheriff. I've won many a footrace in these boots," she said, not having attempted such a girlish feat in years.

"Footrace?" Kurt's red head popped up over the back of the seat.

"You run footraces, Mrs. Whitcomb?" Mitchell appeared beside his brother.

Eyes widening, Molly heard James's quiet laughter beside her. "Well, no, boys. I was only—"

"That's something I'd sure like to see, ma'am." James did nothing to hide his smile this time.

"You running a footrace, and in those fancy boots, no less."

Hearing the boys laughing behind her, Molly couldn't prevent a grin. She eyed her shoes. How fast could she run in her heels if given proper motivation? It was on the tip of her tongue to challenge them to a race when she caught herself. How would that look? Timber Ridge's newly widowed schoolteacher running willy-nilly through a field.

She turned on the seat and briefly covered Kurt's little hand. "Maybe we can race sometime later, Kurt. Once . . . more time has passed."

"But I don't see how come teachers can't—"

"Kurt . . ." Rachel's voice adopted a motherly tone. "Remember what we talked about earlier."

The *clip-clop* of horses' hooves filled the silence.

Mitchell looked over at his brother. "Mrs. Whitcomb's husband died, and she's in mourning, like Mama was."

Kurt squinted. "That's how come she's wearing your dress?"

"Yes, that's right." Rachel gave Molly's arm a gentle squeeze. "Her trunks haven't arrived yet, so she's borrowing my dress."

Quiet settled over the wagon, and the humor there only moments before quickly evaporated. Molly ran a hand over the skirt of the black dress, regretting how she'd bantered back and forth so casually with James. Not that she'd been flirtatious. She'd simply been more . . . playful than was her custom with men. Part of her wanted to blame him for having this effect on her, but she knew better.

His friendliness, the way he made everyone feel so comfortable, drew something out in her. Something light and carefree and that made her feel so at ease—things she shouldn't be feeling right now.

They left the town behind, and the towering Maroon Bells steadily rose before them. The Twin Sisters stood sentinel over Timber Ridge and were even more impressive closer up. Timeless stone monuments vaulting up from the earth with a beauty so striking and unrelenting that Molly found it difficult to look away. If the schoolhouse was located nearby, coming to work every day would be a privilege.

A lake spread out at the foot of the mountains, tranquil and serene, its placid surface mirroring the highest peaks and the tufted clouds shrouding them. Molly angled her head sideways. The image on the water's surface was so pure, so clear, that if she hadn't known the truth, she would've had a hard time telling which was real and which was the reflection.

Glimpsing a building past the lake, she leaned forward on the seat. "Is that the school?"

"Yes, ma'am, it is." James guided the horses down a side road.

It wasn't as she'd imagined. The schoolhouse

wasn't rustic in the least. It was made from lumber, just like schoolhouses back east. Coats of white paint covered the walls and gleamed brightly in the afternoon sun. There was even a play area set off to the side, complete with a seesaw and a swing looped over a low-hanging limb.

As they drew closer, Molly saw a bell affixed to the side of the building by the double front doors, and already, she could imagine its clarion tone. "When was the school built?"

James looked over at her. "I thought you would've read that in the advertisement for the teaching position."

Molly had never seen the original advertisement, not that she could tell him that. "I'm afraid that part slipped my mind."

He gave her a look of amusement. "The building's new as of last fall. Mayor Davenport insisted on putting that in the advertisement. Said it would be an added incentive to applicants." He raised a brow. "I'll be sure and tell him it had a big influence on your decision to accept our offer."

Molly sought to cover the minor misstep with a teasing laugh. "Please don't tell the mayor any such thing. I'd like to stay on his good side. I guess the mention of the new building made less of an impression at the time than where Timber Ridge was located." Which was the truth. When President Northrop had first *suggested* her accepting this job in the Colorado Territory, all hope had drained from her as she'd pictured a community of mountain ruffians and illiterate children. She was grateful that wasn't proving to be the case.

James brought the wagon to a stop, and Mitchell and Kurt leapt from the back. The boys set off at a run with Rachel following them. Molly climbed from the wagon, surprised when she felt hands come about her waist, assisting her descent.

For an instant, she feared James might notice the slight thickening in her waistline, then realized how silly the thought was. "Thank you, James." Standing so close to him, she caught the scent of bay rum and spice. Same as was on his pillow.

"My pleasure, ma'am." He motioned for her to precede him up the path to the door.

She'd already begun preparing her lessons. The hours spent on the train coming west had allowed ample time for that—when she wasn't nauseated from the rocking motion. What she didn't know, and wouldn't until she met with each student, was where each boy and girl was in their studies. She stared at the building ahead. Teaching children in Timber Ridge was going to be a far different challenge from teaching at Franklin College. One for which she wasn't certain she was ready.

Rachel and the boys stood on the landing, all smiles, and Molly realized they were waiting for her to enter first. Reaching the top step, she bobbed a curtsey and opened the doors. She hadn't known what to expect, but nothing could have prepared her for what awaited inside.

Not one but two large chalkboards hung on the front wall. Rows of students' desks—she estimated thirty, at a glance—were lined up in neat rows across the width of the room. And upon each desk was a new slate and supply of chalk, along with one of various editions of *McGuffey's Readers*.

But what drew her attention most were the stocked bookshelves that ran the length of the back wall. Emotion tightened her throat. Even at Franklin College, a highly respected and accredited institution, the latest curriculum and ample supplies were not something easily acquired. That's why she'd brought so much with her, for fear there would be so little available here. "Where did all of this come from?"

"It's a long story." James came along beside her, hat in hand. "One of the women in town is the daughter of a U.S. senator. Her father pulled some strings and had all this sent out. I doubt there's another school in all the territories that's as well equipped as this one."

"Or back east," Molly added softly.

"When do you start teaching us, Mrs. Whitcomb?"

Molly turned to see Kurt peering up, his blue eyes inquisitive. "School begins in a little less than three weeks, is my understanding." She looked to James for confirmation, in case something had changed.

"Hardly more than two weeks, I'm afraid." He pulled a piece of paper from his vest pocket and handed it to her, apology lining his expression. "The town council met last week and came up with a list of items they'd like to see accomplished before school starts."

She unfolded the page and read the list, and worked to suppress her shock. They wanted her to accomplish the whole list in two weeks! But she'd always said she liked a challenge—and she needed this job. Feeling the pressure of everyone's attention, she summoned confidence she didn't feel. "I think all of this is very doable, Sheriff, and I look forward to getting started. Immediately!" She laughed to soften the exclamation.

"If the boys and I can help in any way"—Rachel stepped closer—"we'd be happy to."

"Thank you. I'd appreciate that."

Mitchell tugged on his mother's sleeve. "Can we play outside for a minute, Mama? *Please?* We'll play fast."

Rachel tousled the boys' hair. "Five minutes." She narrowed her eyes. "But the last one to the swing's a rotten egg!" Giggling, she raced them out the door.

Still absorbing her new surroundings, Molly walked toward the front of the room to the teacher's desk. *Her* desk. She ran a hand along the edge, noting that the desk differed from the others in the room. Stained a rich maple, it possessed a rustic elegance the others lacked. Careful attention had been given the delicate carvings on the drawer pulls and the beveled edges along the top. Someone had taken great pride in crafting it.

James's footfalls sounded behind her. "It's made from pine taken right off the mountain out back."

She opened one of the drawers. It pulled smoothly in her grip. "It's beautiful. So much nicer than anything I expected to find here." All of it was. The town of Timber Ridge, its people . . .

"I'm glad you're pleased with it, Molly."

Something in his tone brought her gaze up. "You sound surprised. As if you expected I wouldn't be." She huffed softly. "Why do people always assume that about me?" Too late she read his expression and realized she'd inadvertently invited his opinion about her character. Yet again.

His laughter was immediate. "I've seen that look before. Just last week, when I had a doe lined up down the barrel of my gun. She raised up and spotted me—" He shook his head. "And the look on her face said she wanted to be anywhere but where she was."

"You're comparing me to a doe you shot last week?"

He raised a hand. "I never said I shot her. I said I had her lined up in my sights."

"So you didn't shoot her?"

"No, ma'am. I didn't."

Though tempted to pursue that line of conversation, Molly decided to pick at another thread instead—one she'd run up against before—knowing he would answer honestly. "How is it that you've known me so short a time, yet already you assume I'm a woman who would be hard to please?"

This time he looked away first and developed a sudden interest in a book on her desk—*Little Women*. He picked it up and flipped through it. It was a favorite of hers, one she'd read numerous times.

Realizing he was stalling, Molly tilted her head to gain his attention, glad to be on the offensive with him for a change. "I can make the question more direct if you'd like, Sheriff."

That earned her a grin. "No need. I understood your question the first time. I'm just trying to think of a way to answer honestly that won't get me into further trouble." After a moment, he returned the book to her desk. "First off, I apologize for giving you the impression I thought you might be hard to please. It's just that, in my experience, women who come west, especially those coming from larger, more proper cities back east, tend to find life out here more . . . rustic than what they expected. Most don't take kindly to it. Some do, in time, but it takes them a while."

Molly found his statement fair, especially considering what he knew of her. "And you obviously think I fall into the category of women who don't make it. Is that a correct assumption?"

126

"If you'd asked me that question when I first saw you step from the train, I would've answered yes." His eyes narrowed. "But that's not my answer anymore."

Molly stared. He'd seen her step from the train. . . . Interesting.

His expression sobered, as though he just now realized what he'd revealed. "I didn't mean to make it sound like I was watching you. I simply noticed you step from the train. You looked a little . . . disappointed with your new surroundings. But that was only my impression. Maybe I misinterpreted your actions."

"My actions?" Molly couldn't even remember what she'd done.

James lifted his hand and touched his nose in a rather feminine and awkward-looking manner for him. "You did something like that."

She gave a laugh. "I did not!"

He nodded. "You did." A mischievous gleam lit his eyes, as when he kidded with the boys or with Rachel. Only, when the smile was aimed her way, Molly found it had quite a different effect on her.

She retreated behind the desk.

"I tend to watch people," he said. "Goes with the job, I guess. I didn't mean any offense."

"No offense was taken, Sheriff." She smiled as though what he'd said was of little consequence and gave the pedestaled globe on her desk a spin, thankful when he crossed the room to the window.

The world skimmed by beneath her fingertips, and with each revolution, she grew more determined to move into the boardinghouse by that evening. She liked James, Rachel, and the boys, and appreciated their offered friendship, but close friendships were the last thing she needed in her life. It would be best—for all involved—if she were on her own.

She stopped the globe and found North America facing upward. Locating the state of Georgia, she drew her finger over the hundreds of miles she'd traveled to get to the western territories. Colorado truly was another world away. And despite the second chance at life God had given her on that cliff, she couldn't forget what had prompted her move out west. She pressed a hand to her abdomen. As though forgetting were a possibility.

"Have you seen the view from this window yet?"

Knowing how proud James was of the surrounding mountains, and with reason, she indulged him and joined him at the window. The view was indeed spectacular—the snow-covered peaks, the sunlight playing across the lake. She sighed. "How will the children ever get any work done with all this to look at?"

He didn't answer.

She looked over at him, but he simply nodded again out the window.

"Take a better look," he said softly. "A little to your right."

She did as he asked. "I'm sorry, but I don't see anyth—" She pressed closer. Her breath fogged the pane.

There, nestled at the base of the Maroon Bells, not far from the lake and partially shielded by a stand of trees, was a cabin. She could only see the edge of it from where she stood. Something Rachel had said came back to her, and she looked up at him. "Is that yours? I mean, where you lived before you moved in with Rachel and the boys?"

"No, ma'am." He slipped his hat on and held out his arm as though to escort her somewhere. "The town got together and built it . . . for the new schoolteacher in Timber Ridge."

10

Idyllic was the first word that came to Molly's mind as the cabin came into view. She'd seen an Albert Bierstadt painting a handful of years ago, of a mountain scene with a cabin by a stream. The Rocky Mountains, she thought, but couldn't be sure. All she remembered was wishing then that she could walk straight into that painting and live there.

And now, in this moment, she felt as if she had.

She walked beside James, hand tucked in the crook of his arm, the field grass crunching beneath their feet. A breeze rippled across the surface of the lake, sending tiny waves lapping the muddy banks.

Rachel's and the boys' laughter carried from the play area across the meadow, and Molly couldn't recall ever hearing a more harmonious blend of sounds.

My first home . . . Of her own. Not her parents' home, but hers.

It didn't seem real. And she reminded herself that it might not be if Bolden and others on the town council disapproved of her. Staring ahead at the cabin, and thinking of the child inside her, she untwined her arm from James's and prayed that wouldn't be the case.

On either side of the cabin's front porch, flower boxes adorned the windows. Riots of color spilled over their sides. A woman's touch . . . Rachel's, perhaps. Trees bordered the cabin on all sides but the front, and the exaggerated scent of fresh-cut pine greeted her as she drew closer.

"Would you care to see inside?"

The way James asked the question told her he'd noticed her reticence, and she gathered her scattered thoughts. "Yes . . . I would. Thank you."

He took the pair of porch stairs as one and opened the front door.

She stepped inside. *Furniture.* The cabin already had furniture. A plum-colored sofa and matching wingback chair anchored a blue-and-yellow corded rug, and a table with a lace doily nested between them. A small kitchen table with two chairs huddled cozily beneath the window on the far wall, and looking through the open door into the next room, she spotted a bed and chifforobe. And in her mind's eye, she pictured a cradle in the corner.

"It's only got two rooms, but they're a nice size." He motioned. "The smaller room is your bedroom, and—as you can see—this larger one is your sitting room and kitchen. It's nearly done. They've got some final roof work to do along the sides and back, and then it'll be ready to move into."

She ran a hand along the back of the sofa. "I hardly know what to say."

"So this meets with your approval too?"

Her laughter came out breathy. "Do you even have to ask?" She looked out a back window to see a swiftly running stream behind the cabin, and a question rose inside her.

Why?

Why, after what she'd done, would God give her this? It didn't make any sense.

James came to stand beside her. "Are you all right, Molly?"

She nodded. "Yes, I'm fine." But she wasn't.

Little more than three weeks ago, she'd never heard of Timber Ridge. Then it quickly became a symbol of punishment and penance. And today she stood looking at all this, the red dirt of Georgia still clinging to her boots, and she couldn't understand what God was doing.

Part of her wanted to thank Him for His undeserved gift, while another part of her, a small but vocal part, was waiting for the other shoe to drop. God loved her, she knew, but people had to pay for their wrongs. That was the way of things.

"Sheriff McPherson! You in there?" someone yelled.

James peered out a front window and gave a sharp exhale. "You best stay inside and let me handle this."

Molly came alongside him to spot Bolden, Angelo's accuser, marching across the field with another gentleman. The second man wasn't as tall, but he carried his weight across his shoulders and chest, which gave him an imposing presence. And he moved at a blistering pace. Even at this distance, she could see the man's neck flushing crimson, and the color extended into his face.

He reminded her of someone, but she couldn't recall who. "Who's that with Mr. Bolden?"

"That's Mayor Davenport. Bolden's his brother-in-law. And my guess would be that the mayor's learned of your *arrival*."

The way he said it, Molly knew he was referring to her being "widowed."

"He looks angry." More in a mood to fire than a mood to hire.

James nodded. "He's got a temper—that's for sure."

"I didn't mean to cause such a problem."

He didn't answer right off, then finally turned to

her. "We may be out west, Molly, but along with furniture and keepsakes, people move their traditions with them too. Schoolteachers have always been unmarried." He looked at her as if to say, *"You know that as well as I do."*

"And even though you *are* unmarried again, there are some people who won't see it that way." He glanced back outside. "And here come two of them right now."

Speechless in the face of James's honesty, Molly watched the mayor through the window, noting the intensity in his eyes and the sharp confidence in his movements. And she realized who it was he reminded her of—President Northrop. And the heat of indignation simmered inside her.

"Molly?"

She turned to see James by the door.

"Promise me you'll stay inside until they're gone."

She shook her head. "I think it'd be best if I go ahead and get this meeting over with." If she wasn't going to be hired, it was best to find that out right away. Her heart was already putting down roots in this place, and with these people. If she was leaving—she whispered a prayer she doubted God heard—she needed to know.

"You need to meet Mayor Davenport, I agree, Molly. But now's not the time. It'll be better once he's cooled down, and when the town council is convened." James opened the door as if the issue were settled. "And one more thing . . . David Davenport doesn't favor the immigrants being in Timber Ridge. If he had his druthers, they'd be packed up and headed down the mountain by nightfall—every last one of them. So while I appreciate what you did earlier in town with Angelo, very much . . . I'm afraid that's already made you an adversary in Davenport's book."

James closed the door behind him, hoping Molly would do as he said and stay put. He was certain the men wouldn't do anything to threaten her physically—Davenport, anyway—but they were formidable men, and when paired, their intelligence and decency seemed to diminish at a rapid pace.

"The woman *lied*, Sheriff!" Purplish veins bulged in Mayor Davenport's neck. "She's married! And do I hear the news from you? No! I have to hear it from Brandon Tolliver!"

James held up a hand. "Tolliver told you wrong, sir. Mrs. Whitcomb is not married. She's widowed."

This news seemed to catch Davenport unaware, but he quickly recovered. "Widowed is still not *un*married, Sheriff McPherson. Have you allowed her to sign the contract yet?"

James shifted his weight, eying the man. He had Molly's contract in his desk drawer at his office. He was supposed to have had her sign it upon her arrival. And though that had been tempting after meeting her . . . "You know me better than that, Mayor. This is not one man's decision. It's for the town council to decide. So no, I haven't given her the contract yet." Though he knew that if he could win Davenport's favor, Bolden and the rest of the men in the mayor's pocket would follow like little ducklings.

Davenport exhaled through his teeth, jaw rigid. "If you remember correctly, Sheriff, you're the one who said she was most qualified for this job."

"She was and still is the most qualified candidate, Mayor." James kept his tone even. "That's why we chose her. Her husband passed away three months ago, *before* she applied for this position."

"But her correspondence stated that—"

"Her correspondence," James interrupted, mindful that Molly might be able to hear him, "simply referred to her as Dr. Whitcomb. So she did not lie to us. It was just a misunderstanding. Now, as I see things, with only two weeks to go before school starts—"

"Bolden here tells me she interfered with a situation in town this afternoon. That an immigrant boy stole something from Bolden's bakery. Sounds like he's a conniving little thief who needs to be tried accordingly."

James couldn't resist. "Which one, sir? Bolden or the boy?"

Davenport's starched collar seemed to shrink by two sizes. "Do you or do you not have plans to pursue that boy on charges of theft, Sheriff McPherson?"

Bolden stood wordless, his silence bleeding satisfaction.

"I have no intention of pursuing that boy on charges of any kind, Mayor. Bolden hired him, the boy worked for him, and then Bolden refused to pay the promised wages. Thanks to Mrs. Whitcomb, who interpreted, *and* to Lyda Mullins, who confirmed she saw the boy working for your brother-in-law here, I'm satisfied that I reached the truth in that situation."

"You're satisfied?" Mayor Davenport said, his voice low. "Let me tell you something, McPherson. Elections for sheriff of this town come up next spring, and we'll see how satisfied you are then." He pointed a finger, his voice lowering. "I've been telling the good people of Timber Ridge that we hired the finest possible teacher for their children. And I don't care how busy your office is, I'm placing you *personally* responsible for seeing that she does her job, and that she does it exactly to our specifications. Because if she doesn't—"

James heard the door of the cabin open behind him. Davenport and Bolden looked up in unison.

"Good afternoon, gentlemen." Molly's voice was gentle as the breeze, steady and confident. Though a mite thick on the accent.

She fairly floated down the stairs, and James

wanted to wring that pretty little neck of hers for not staying hidden. In their current state of froth, Bolden and Davenport could easily eat her alive. Not that he would let them.

"I couldn't help but overhear portions of your conversation, gentlemen, and I wanted to take this opportunity to introduce myself. I'm Dr. Molly Whitcomb from Franklin College in Georgia. And I appreciate the opportunity you've given me, Mayor Davenport, along with the town council, to serve as the teacher here in Timber Ridge."

Her gaze barely brushed Hank Bolden, and James felt the man bristle in response. When Molly looked at Mayor Davenport, however, the man reacted quite differently. David Davenport took Molly in from head to toe, assessing as he went, his thoughts plain as day to any other red-blooded male.

If James wasn't mistaken, Davenport sucked in his gut. It wasn't the first time he'd seen the town's mayor change tune when faced with a beautiful woman.

"Mrs. Whitcomb . . ." Davenport cleared his throat. "This is indeed a pleasure, ma'am. But I'm sorry, I didn't realize you were in our company." He shot James a look. "I trust your sojourn to Timber Ridge was a pleasant one."

She smiled. "As pleasant as a two-week journey by rail and coach can be." Her smile faded.

"Mayor Davenport, I wish to speak frankly with you, sir."

Davenport's brow rose. "Yes, ma'am. I . . . I welcome your frankness."

"If there are concerns over my employment, then I sincerely hope we can come to some—"

"There was some initial concern, Mrs. Whitcomb, only . . ." Davenport studied her—not in a tasteless fashion, but with more leisure than James would have preferred. "Understanding that the town council will have certain expectations of you, and that you'll be expected to make regular reports on the students' progress, I believe we can put that issue behind us. And that we can move forward together for the future of Timber Ridge and the betterment of its children."

James glanced at Molly beside him, fighting the urge to check his boots. Davenport was piling it on higher and deeper, as was his style.

Molly's smile was gracious beyond words. "I'm so relieved to hear that, Mr. Davenport."

"Ah . . . actually, ma'am, it's *Mayor* Davenport, Mrs. Whitcomb."

She smiled again. "I beg your pardon, Mayor. And not to be a stickler, but actually, it's *Dr.* Whitcomb, sir."

James felt the hidden thorn cloaked in the sweetness of her voice. A spark glinted in Davenport's eyes, and James half expected the man to challenge her.

"Dr. Whitcomb," Davenport repeated, his smile strained. "That'll take some getting used to, I'm afraid."

"Repetition is key to learning, Mayor. I'll happily remind you should you forget."

Davenport's patience and admiration of Molly's beauty visibly slipped a notch, and James got the impression from watching Molly that the discovery pleased her immensely. Then he saw it—

The tremor of her skirt.

He looked more closely. The woman was literally shaking in her boots. Yet you'd never know it from the confidence in her voice and how she conducted herself.

Dr. Whitcomb, he made note, had more depth to her than even her credentials led one to believe. And that was saying a lot for a woman who had graduated first in her class, with honors, who spoke at least four languages.

And the good mayor had just seen fit to put him in charge of seeing after her. An all-consuming job, for she was *one fiery lass*—James smiled, thinking of his grandfather—but somehow he'd find the time.

11

"Thank you, Mr. Daggett, for bringing these all the way out here." Molly motioned for him to place the first trunk in the front room of the cabin. "Right over there will be just fine. For all of them."

"Yes, ma'am, Miss Molly." Charlie Daggett set the trunk down with such gentleness he gave the impression it was filled with air. Only the sweat pouring down his face hinted at his exertion.

He left to retrieve another from the wagon, and Molly opened the trunk and began sorting the books and knickknacks she'd brought from home into stacks.

For the past two nights, she'd stayed at the boardinghouse, much to Rachel's dismay and James's efforts to talk her out of it. But it had worked out better that way. James's attempt to handle the situation with Mayor Davenport still sat uneasily within her, and she'd decided some distance would be a good thing.

As she'd stood inside the cabin overhearing him plead her case with the town's mayor, though she hadn't heard every word, she'd heard enough to realize that, yet again, a man was seeking to step in and control her future. Only this time, she could do something about it. And she had. Though she'd nearly gotten sick from the effort, she'd shaken so badly. She was relieved when none of the men seemed to notice.

But she was an intelligent, well-spoken woman, capable of representing herself, and she intended to do just that. She didn't need James acting as her champion, and didn't want to risk anyone thinking that he was. For both their sakes.

In the past two days, she'd spent time walking

the town, visiting the stores, and becoming acquainted with the shopkeepers, and something had become very clear. James McPherson wasn't simply well thought of by people in Timber Ridge—he was revered. And though he didn't realize it, their keeping a certain distance from each other was in his best interest too, especially considering the upcoming elections Davenport had mentioned—and the child growing inside her.

At James's request, she'd met him yesterday morning at his office to serve as translator for his meeting with Angelo. As he'd predicted, the boy showed up and the meeting went well. Already James had two job possibilities for the youth. Thirteen years old, Angelo lived with his mother and three sisters in a *che bella tenda*—a very nice tent—on the outskirts of town, along with other Italian families. But she got the distinct impression that most of the families had little food and few necessities.

She hadn't said anything to James—sensing he might try to dissuade her if he knew—but the boy had invited her to come and visit, and she'd accepted, eager to help in whatever way she could and to see the culture of a language she'd loved for so long.

After Angelo had left, James had presented her with the teaching contract. She'd experienced a moment of hesitation as she read it through. The document had clearly stated that, as the schoolteacher, she could not marry, and that if she chose to marry, she must resign her position immediately. She'd had no qualms about agreeing to that. Marriage was no longer on her horizon.

It was what *hadn't* been written in the contract—and yet what was there, between every word, every sentence, silently understood—that had given her pause. There was no mention of the schoolteacher having children. But of course there wouldn't be. What moral, decent person would ever think that such a clause would have to be included in an agreement with an unmarried woman?

Gripping the quill so tightly she'd feared it might break, she'd signed the document.

"Here you go, ma'am!"

Startled by Charlie's voice, she looked up.

"The last one!" He set the trunk down—along with her satchel from the stagecoach!

"Ah!" She couldn't believe it. "How did you get this!" She'd half expected to never see it again.

A grin split his face. "I climbed on down there yesterday and hauled everything up."

"Everything? You mean you hauled all that luggage up? By yourself?"

He shrugged. "It weren't that hard. I got a strong back, and Ben Mullins loaned me his wagon."

The satchel's cloth exterior was dirty, but the contents seemed much as she'd left them. She withdrew the soiled black day dress she'd worn to honor the anniversary of her father's passing and laid it aside to launder.

"Thank you, Mr. Daggett, so very much. That was going above and beyond the call of duty, as they say." She reached into her reticule for a bill and pressed it into his hand. The image of him walking into the saloon returned, and she wondered if that money would end up in those tainted coffers. She prayed it wouldn't, for Charlie's sake.

"Thank you kindly, Miss Molly. You got anything else you need done around here, you just say the word." He grinned. "The sheriff, he wants to make sure things go right for you."

She paused. "Sheriff McPherson said that?"

He wiped his brow with his sleeve, wriggling his bushy brows. "Yes, ma'am. He sure did."

She nodded slowly. "Wasn't that kind of him?" And it was. Still, she couldn't deny the spark of resentment over his close attention. "I can't think of anything else that I need right now, Mr. Daggett. But if I do, how may I reach you?"

"The sheriff knows how to get ahold of me, ma'am. Just let him know."

Molly forced a smile. Apparently all roads in Timber Ridge either led to—or through—James McPherson. Of all the towns she could have been sent to, she'd been sent to his.

Charlie turned to leave, and she worked to put aside her frustration, knowing he wasn't to blame.

"Mr. Daggett?"

He turned at the door.

"Thank you again for all you've done for me." She smiled up at him, letting only the slightest trace of humor show through. "It occurs to me that I've been nothing but trouble to you since the moment I arrived."

His expression took a sober turn. "Don't you worry about that, ma'am. That's just the way of womenfolk. You can't help it."

Realizing he was serious, Molly laughed, and was still grinning as Charlie cut a path across the field toward town. She closed the door and leaned back against it, admiring the tiny cabin that was her home.

At least for now.

Welcoming the task of unpacking, she opened another trunk to find her dresses covered in a layer of dust. They were wrinkled and bunched from the journey, and though she wouldn't be wearing the colorful frocks for months, she didn't want to leave them wadded up either. After digging for her fabric brush, she set to work, mentally counting the days until school started—August fourteenth.

Sixteen days to be exact, including weekends.

The list of items she was to complete before school started lay open on the table, and she already knew what was first on her agenda—visiting each student and their parents in their home.

Rachel had jotted down the names of as many children as she could think of. The total numbered twenty-nine, though Rachel had warned that not all parents in Timber Ridge were open to the idea of their children attending school. Especially if the children were girls.

"Not all folks here think it's important for girls to know how to read and write," she'd said. "Or to work their sums. They feel it's a waste of time. Some parents hold that teaching their girls how to cook and sew, keep a clean house, and be a good wife is enough."

While Molly appreciated the value of those lessons, she was determined to win those parents to her way of thinking.

She bent to retrieve another dress from the trunk and lifted the black silk gown she'd worn only twice—to her father's funeral a year ago, and her mother's four years previous. She ran a hand over a lace sleeve, still able to picture her parents' smiles, and still able to hear their voices. Her father had been in such pain at the end, it had almost been a relief when he'd breathed his last. Almost.

Before his passing, she'd tried to prepare herself for what it would be like when both her parents were gone. But nothing could have prepared her for the void inside. Or for those moments when she first returned home in the evenings to a house that was still and empty, and quiet as death.

That was the point when her relationship with Jeremy had taken a more intimate turn, and everything had changed for the better. Or so she'd thought.

Thinking of him brought a siege of emotions she didn't want to deal with. Wiping a tear, she suddenly decided she'd done enough unpacking for one day. Leaving everything as it was, she closed up the cabin and headed into town.

The fresh air felt good against her face, and she quickened her pace, welcoming the way her heart pumped strong in her chest and how her lungs burned. With each step, she told herself her life wasn't over. And tried her best to believe it.

"Are you accusing me of doing something illegal, Sheriff? Because if you are, I'd just as soon you state it outright rather than beating around the bush."

James followed Tolliver up the path to the construction site of the Colorado Hot Springs Resort. On his ride out, he'd anticipated this reaction from the man. "When have you ever known me to beat around the bush, Tolliver? I'm not accusing you of anything. I'm simply asking to see your drawings for the resort, along with the safety inspector's most recent report." James looked around, evaluating the stage of construction. "You must be what . . . fifty percent completed by now?"

"Sixty. And still on schedule for our grand opening in January. At least for the main building and two of the hot springs houses. The rest is slated to be finished by late spring—*if* we don't have any unexpected delays."

James caught his insinuation—and ignored it. "You've got a long way to go in a short space of time."

"We'll make it. There's no shortage of workers, and so far, supplies have been delivered on schedule."

James gestured at Tolliver's forehead. "How's the gash?"

Tolliver touched the wound at his hairline. "It's healing." He picked up a hammer and gripped it as though testing its weight, but James wasn't fooled. The man's clothes were perfectly pressed, and his hands were as smooth as an accountant's.

James stepped up to the next level of the expansive front porch of the main hotel, and a few of the boards shifted beneath his boots. He glanced over at Tolliver.

"That floor hasn't been fully nailed down yet, Sheriff. But the workers know to be careful. It's all part of working construction—keeping up with the project." Tolliver tossed a condescending smile worthy of Mayor Davenport himself.

"You speak Italian, Tolliver?"

The man's smile faded.

James shrugged. "I'm just wondering how you communicate with your workers."

"Vicenza, my foreman, speaks some English. He's in charge of relaying instructions."

James nodded. "So what happened to Sorrento the other day?"

"Who?" Tolliver's eyes narrowed.

"Your worker who fell through a second-story floor that"—he peered at the boards beneath his boots—"wasn't fully nailed down yet. Dr. Brookston treated him for a broken leg. Said the guy was lucky, that it could've been much worse."

"Accidents happen on construction sites, McPherson. It's the way of things."

"Too many are happening on yours, Tolliver. Eight in the past month. When a complaint is filed, I'm obligated to check out each one."

"Obligated to whom?"

James stilled. "To the workers, who are members of this community, just like you and I are." Not waiting for Tolliver's response, James stepped off the porch and started around the building, looking for anything that might be suspect. He was no expert on building a resort of this size, but he knew a few things about basic construction.

He stopped and looked up to the fourth story. This hotel was going to be impressive. It already was, even at only sixty percent completed.

Men poised on makeshift scaffolding high above the ground pounded lumber into place, speaking to each other in their native tongue. They kept working, looking down on occasion. James wished Molly Whitcomb were here with him so he could ask the workers some questions. Then again, he was hesitant to involve her. A construction site wasn't the proper setting for a woman, and translating for him certainly wasn't part of her job.

He'd asked her to lunch after they'd met with Angelo, but she'd declined, saying something about needing to get started on her teaching duties. But it was when she'd added that she'd probably be busy for some time that he'd begun to wonder if he'd said or done something to cause her to—

"Hey . . . Sheriff!"

Tolliver caught up with him, and James pulled his focus back.

"I run a safe operation here. I've been in construction for nearly twenty years. Just let me do my job. I guarantee you'll be pleased. Because when I'm done, this resort stands to bring a lot of revenue to Timber Ridge."

As well as to your own pockets—which James didn't begrudge. It was the exorbitant amount of money that he had qualms with. Especially knowing firsthand how little Tolliver was paying his workers.

"I know what you're thinking, Sheriff. And I've never denied that I'll make a handsome profit. I'm a businessman, after all. Not some kind of—" he chuckled—"man of the people."

The sarcasm in Tolliver's voice didn't kindle James's anger as much as the man's cavalier attitude. "I've wired Denver to send a building inspector."

Tolliver's smile faded. "You have no right to do that."

"I have every right, on behalf of these men here. Keeping the people in this town safe is my job. And if the inspector from Denver finds anything that doesn't meet regulations, you'll have a week to fix it. Either that or I'll halt construction until you meet your obligations." James strode back to his horse, hearing footsteps behind him.

"This could end up causing a delay, which means I could be forced to change the date for the opening. Which will cost me a lot of money, Sheriff."

James untethered his mount and turned back. "You know, as I understand it . . . that's all part of doing construction." He swung into the saddle.

Tolliver's expression hardened. "Do you have any idea how costly it is to build something like this way up here? To haul supplies up this mountain, I pay triple the shipping costs a builder pays in Denver."

"What goes on in Denver isn't my concern. What goes on in Timber Ridge is." James fingered the reins. "The inspector will be here in the next couple of weeks. He'll file his report, and you'll have until the end of August to comply with his findings. And that's being generous." He half expected Tolliver to explode. But he didn't.

Instead, a pensive look came over his face. "Say, Sheriff . . . I hear that come election time next spring, Mayor Davenport's thinking about backing another man for your job. You heard that rumor yet?"

James said nothing.

"Something else you may not know . . . Davenport has an interest in this hotel now. Just recently invested. Did you know that?"

He didn't.

Tolliver took a step closer. "My thinking, Sheriff, is that if we could work together on this, keeping costs low, keeping the project on schedule, then we all win. Me, the mayor, the town, even you."

"You didn't mention the workers, Tolliver. The ones risking their necks to build this place." James looked up at the men climbing in and out of the scaffolding, forty feet off the ground. "How do they win?"

"They have jobs, Sheriff. They're earning money."

"Their wage is less than half of what you'd pay a man from town to do the same job."

Tolliver's patience evaporated. "I pay these men well! Yes, they work more cheaply than men from Timber Ridge. But can I be faulted for hiring the cheapest labor? That's just good business sense."

"Their families barely have enough to eat. And have you seen where they live?"

"That's unfortunate, Sheriff, but it's not my doing. I didn't ask them to come here. And just so you remember, I'm hiring them. That's more than most folks around here are doing. These people made a choice."

These people . . . James looked back at the hotel, sick to his gut. Tolliver's argument was nauseating, but he was right—there was nothing illegal about his paying the men who worked for him less than what he'd pay men from town. And then there was Davenport—willing to benefit from the Italians' backbreaking labor while they were here, while doing his best to see that they didn't stay.

James doubted whether Tolliver had visited the shanties where these men and their families lived. He probably considered it beneath him. But James *had* visited, and the living conditions were inexcusable. Rachel had wanted to go out there on her own to see what help she might be, but he'd discouraged her. It wasn't safe for a woman to go unaccompanied. He'd promised to take her with him sometime.

Staring down from his horse, James worked to set aside his personal feelings and to view Tolliver and these circumstances through the strict eye of the law. "These people made a choice to come here, that's true. But you've got a choice to make too, Tolliver. Improve the working conditions for your men, take greater precautions for their welfare—or wire New York and tell them your resort won't be opening on time." James dug in his heels and the mare took off at a gallop.

He let her have her head, and they were halfway

back to town before he finally reined in. Even then, she whinnied and tossed her head as though she still had some run left in her. He reached down and gave her neck a good rub. "I needed that too, girl."

Tolliver's attitude toward the immigrants was frustrating, but Tolliver wasn't the only one in town who held that opinion. That was the problem. And James didn't know how to fix it.

He dismounted and led Winsome to a stream that ran alongside the road, to a shaded place where the water ran more tranquil and deep. The horse drank. He did too, and he knelt and washed the road dust from his face and neck. He'd been sheriff of Timber Ridge for nearly eight years, and he'd wager that most folks were pleased with the job he'd done. He'd made some enemies along the way . . . no way not to in his job. And last year things had gotten rough for a spell.

He thought of Josiah Birch and what had happened to him, and his throat tightened. Finding Josiah beaten like that, left naked by the stream for dead, had shaken him. In his head, he knew that no sheriff could be everywhere, every minute. But he'd felt so responsible, so powerless to protect.

After sneaking Josiah out of town, he'd received threats on his life and on his home. *Rachel's* home. It was the first time as sheriff of Timber Ridge that he'd actually feared for Rachel's and the boys' safety. He hadn't said anything to her, then or since, but his deputies had known, and for weeks following, Willis and Stanton had helped keep watch.

The threatening notes had been anonymous. Anger kindled inside him again, remembering. Cowardly, gutless men who hid behind paper, afraid to sign their names. Same as the ones back home in Tennessee who hid behind sheets, afraid to show their faces.

He stood and sighed, and stretched the muscles in his shoulders and back. He knew what prejudice was. A person didn't grow up in the South ignorant of that. His father had owned slaves, and that was something that, he admitted—in the quieter, more honest moments—he'd never thought much about as a young man. When a fellow grew up with something as normal, he tended not to question it. He accepted it as part of life.

But there came a time when he *did* begin to question, when he saw things more clearly. And he'd wondered how he hadn't seen it before. It had shamed him. He couldn't go back and change the past, however much he wished he could. But he could make a difference in Timber Ridge, in the lives of its townspeople. And he intended to do just that.

He stooped and picked up a couple of rocks and smoothed away the dirt.

He couldn't imagine doing anything else with his life other than being sheriff of Timber Ridge, and didn't know what he'd do if the door wasn't opened to him again. He didn't fear Mayor Davenport. David Davenport held influence in town, true. But in the end, when people cast their vote for the next sheriff, they'd vote for the man they trusted most. The man they thought would best protect them and their families.

And James pledged, again, to be that man.

But if he wasn't their choice, for whatever reason, he knew that nothing ever surprised the Creator of heaven and earth. As the circuit preacher had said a month or so ago, *"God never leans over the balcony of heaven and gasps."*

James lifted his head and settled his gaze on the Maroon Bells. He liked that thought—that nothing ever took God by surprise. There was comfort in it, and the possibility of so much good, even in the midst of bad.

He led Winsome from the shade of the trees, climbed into the saddle, and rode on toward town, his mind more at ease. He considered stopping off at Molly's cabin to check on her, see if she needed anything, yet somehow didn't feel quite right about it. Uncertain his company would be welcome.

But there was another woman in town whose arms were always open to him, and whose peach cobbler could soothe just about any woe a man might have. And both of those things sounded mighty good right then.

12

Molly peered into the mare's mouth, mindful of the horse's teeth. Which were rotten!

"I'll give you a good deal on her, ma'am. Just say the word." The livery owner nodded to her from where he stood by the forge.

Molly shook her head. No doubt he would. Of the horses Mr. Atwood had shown her, she doubted any of them would live to see next year. Two of them appeared to be going lame.

"Thank you, Mr. Atwood, but I think I'll keep looking."

He intercepted her at the open double doors. "Hang on just a minute, Mrs. Whitcomb. I can't remember if I told you about the gelding I got in the back. He's a real beauty. I was thinkin' of keepin' him for myself, but I might could let him go. Would cost you a bit more. Then again . . ." He stepped close enough for her to count the veins in his bulbous nose. "I'm thinkin' I could see fit to give a pretty little widow a break in price."

Already having questioned the man's motives, Molly was finished with his games. "I've changed my mind, Mr. Atwood. I'm no longer interested in buying a horse today." And when she was, she wouldn't be buying it from him.

At the general store, she purchased a few items—a tin of ground coffee, a package of crackers, and other staples. She started back in the direction of her cabin, feeling better for having gotten out for a while, when an aroma enticed her off course. It smelled of comfort and home.

She took a deeper whiff, almost certain it was fried chicken and . . . biscuits?

She walked to the corner, looked both ways, and spotted an outdoor cafe at the far end of the street. A banner with the name *Clara's Cafe* hung between two poles, and she headed straight for it.

Word about her arrival had indeed spread. As people passed her on the boardwalk, those who didn't call her by name—"Good day, Mrs. Whitcomb"—greeted her with silent nods accompanied with smiles. Adults' respect was evident in the way they dipped their heads. Children's showed in how wide their gazes grew.

In a way, she felt more esteemed here than she had as a professor at Franklin College.

Judging by the number of patrons, the cafe was well liked. Various-sized tables, most occupied, dotted the smooth dirt floor beneath a twisted-limbed tree whose trunk was as big around at the bottom as the cast-iron stove hulking off to one side. The leafed canopy overhead provided shelter from the late-day sun, and Molly lingered at the edge of its shade, a sack of groceries in one hand, her reticule in the other, uncertain of the custom. Should she wait to be seated? Or seat herself?

From the edge of her vision she saw someone

standing stock-still across the cafe. Curiosity guided her attention and she turned to look.

It was a Negro woman, tall and slender, stately looking with skin the color of cream-laced coffee. Recognition sharpened the woman's expression, and Molly glanced to see who might be standing behind her. No one was there.

When she turned back, the woman was approaching.

She carried herself with quiet dignity, a faint frown on her face. "Dr. Whitcomb?"

"Yes, that's right."

"You're the new schoolteacher, ma'am."

"I am." Molly smiled. "Is this your cafe?"

"Oh—no, ma'am." Her soft laugh was lyrical. "I'm afraid I don't cook well enough for the likes of Miss Clara."

Molly squinted, regretting her hasty speculation. "I'm sorry. I just assumed—"

"No harm done, ma'am." And still, that steady stare. "But I'll be sure to tell Miss Clara what you said. She'll have herself a good chuckle at that."

"What will I be havin' a good chuckle at, Belle Birch?" An older woman bustled up beside them, her eyes bright and attentive, her apron nearly dragging the ground. Balanced on the curve of one arm were three bowls of the most appetizing peach cobbler Molly had ever seen. If it tasted as good as it smelled . . .

Belle Birch edged closer to Miss Clara, a conspiratorial look in her eyes. "I was just telling our new schoolteacher here that you wouldn't dare let me into your kitchen."

"Why, lands no! I want my customers to keep comin' back, don't I?"

As Molly laughed along with them, she watched the two women and felt an old familiar longing. Since reaching college age, and in the years following, her friendships with women had been scarce. And those she'd had were more competitive in nature. Nothing like what she saw before her now.

She'd secretly dared to hope that such a close friendship might develop between her and Rachel Boyd, given time. But James's tie to Rachel complicated that possibility.

Miss Clara waved to a nearby table before scooting off to another task. "Take a seat right there, you two. I'll be over to serve you soon."

Pleased not to have to eat alone, Molly started toward the table but felt a touch on her arm.

Belle's expression held apology. "I wish I could join you, Dr. Whitcomb, but my husband, Josiah, is waiting for me at home. And I make it a point never to be late in meeting my husband. Time with him is precious to me."

Molly found herself the one staring this time. What a sweet way for a wife to state her affection for her husband. And the woman's voice—it was rich and deep, oak-tree strong. Hearing her give a recitation or deliver a lecture would be sheer pleasure. "I completely understand. It was nice to meet you, Mrs. Birch. And I hope we have occasion to speak again."

"I'm sure we will, ma'am. And before I go . . ." Her brown eyes softened. "May I say how sorry I am about your husband. I heard about his passing from Mrs. Mullins at the store."

Molly looked anywhere but at Belle. "Thank you," she whispered. Belle walked on, but Molly stood there for a moment, still and silent, searching her heart—and not liking what she saw.

With the exception of Mayor Davenport and his brute of a brother-in-law, the people she'd met here were so kind and accepting, and it made her wonder. . . . If she'd chosen differently in Sulfur Falls, if she hadn't purchased the ring—she twisted the band on her finger; it was already losing some of its luster—might she have found acceptance in this town anyway?

But in her heart, she knew the answer.

She took a seat as Miss Clara had indicated and looked around. She was the only person dining alone. Not that she'd never dined alone before. A woman didn't reach the age of thirty-one without eating by herself on occasion. But being new in town, and everyone knowing it, made her feel more conspicuous.

She made eye contact with an older couple sitting closest to her, then with another couple two tables away. She smiled, and they did likewise. Two women at a table by the stove glanced in her direction, smiles noticeably absent, and leaned close to speak to each other.

Molly's imagination kicked in and began filling in the blanks. Then she caught herself. It was probably nothing. Though chances *were* fairly good—given what Rachel had said about her arrival being such a buzz—that those women were talking about her. But that didn't necessarily mean their conversation was negative.

Perhaps they were simply acknowledging her arrival. Or were sharing their surprise in discovering she was widowed. Molly looked down. Did they recognize this black dress as belonging to Rachel Boyd? The gown was lovely, after all. And memorable. Perhaps they were wondering why she was wearing a borrowed dress. *"Maybe she doesn't have enough money to buy her own clothes,"* she imagined the dark-haired woman whispering. *"Or maybe she's not a widow at all and simply purchased a ring in Sulfur Falls to cover up her being with chi—"*

"Here we are!"

Molly nearly jumped out of her seat.

Miss Clara set a plate of food before her. "Now don't you fill up on this. Once you're done"—she patted Molly's shoulder the way a grandmother might—"I have some peach cobbler with your name on it, Mrs. Whitcomb."

"I wouldn't dream of it," Molly assured, her heart still pounding in her throat. "That cobbler looks too good."

Beaming, Miss Clara moved to other tables, addressing every customer by name. And from their responses, they all seemed to know her well too.

"Pardon me, ma'am."

She looked up to see a young boy holding a cup and pitcher.

"Would you like some water? Or maybe hot coffee? I'll get it for you."

"Water will be fine, thank you." The server was a handsome boy, or young man, judging by his size. Maybe thirteen, fourteen? Anyone looking on would have labeled him a Negro, but that description, while partly true, didn't take into account the lighter color of his skin, nor the striking green of his eyes. Molly guessed at his lineage, not something hard to do having been raised in the South.

Though her father had never owned slaves, many of their family friends had. It wasn't until Molly was thirteen that a sickening reality had been brought to light. She'd visited Carolyne Anderson's home for a birthday party, and one of the girls whispered an ugly rumor about Carolyne's father. Molly told her she was wrong. But over dinner, the girl indicated a Negro woman who was serving. The woman was striking, with warm brown eyes and an exotic beauty. After dinner, the same girl lured Molly on a "casual stroll," where they ended up by the kitchen housed in the building behind the main home.

The oppressive heat was the first thing Molly noticed. The second was a young Negro girl of lighter complexion who shared the same exquisite beauty as the woman who had served them at dinner—and whose eyes were the exact brilliant blue of Carolyn Anderson's father's.

Colonel Graham Anderson was an upstanding member of the church and community, someone Molly respected and revered. And she rejected her friend's conclusions, as well as the ones forming in her own mind—until she delicately posed the question to her father at home. He gave a gentle, honest explanation, as he always did.

And Molly never looked Colonel Anderson in the eye again, nor did she ever return to the Anderson home.

"If there's anything else you need, ma'am, you let me know."

Molly blinked and found herself staring at the young man. "Oh yes, I'm sorry. Thank you, I'll do that."

She unfolded her napkin and pressed it in her lap. Fried chicken, whipped potatoes, and creamed peas crowded the plate. Delicious! And a warm biscuit slathered with butter hugged the rim. From habit, she bowed her head. But her eyes didn't seem to want to close.

She grew conscious of others around her, and of how she appeared. New teacher in town, draped in widow's garb, bowing her head so piously to offer thanks. Nothing out of the ordinary. Except the woman people were seeing was not the woman she was.

Remembering the compassion in Belle's eyes, Molly felt a stinging behind her own. She'd memorized countless petitions from her father's favorite book of prayer, but each one deserted her now. A tenacious fear, one she'd managed to keep at bay in recent days, strong-armed its way past her defenses, and the lace on her sleeve cuffs began to tremble.

What would happen to her when her . . . condition became apparent?

For a while she could mask the swell in her belly with fuller dresses and aprons. And with a long coat, come winter. All of which she must commission to have sewn. But if Mayor Davenport had been furious when he heard she was widowed, how would he react when he discovered she was pregnant? How would James react? And what would happen when it came time for the baby to be born?

And this with the town still believing that she had been married?

Fear tightened its grip in her chest, and a solitary tear fell onto the napkin in her lap.

Pressing her lips together, she forced her eyes

closed, her mind a prayerless fog. She tried to form the words, but they wouldn't come. Her head was bowed but her heart seemed reluctant to follow.

After a moment, she finally gave up and began to eat.

The chicken, potatoes, biscuit . . . Each bite was mouth-watering. Did every woman in town cook with such savory skills? Enjoying the meal, with the breeze coming off the mountains, and even the cadence of conversation around her, Molly slowly began to relax.

She glanced up to see Miss Clara hustling toward her, two bowls of peach cobbler balanced in one hand and a full plate of food in the other.

"Here you go, Mrs. Whitcomb." Miss Clara set the cobbler in front of her and the other two dishes at the place setting across from hers. "You don't mind some delightful dinner company, do you, ma'am?"

Molly looked around, not knowing to whom she was referring—until he spoke from behind.

"Dr. Whitcomb, would you mind my joining you for dinner, ma'am?"

13

Despite what she'd said, James saw the real answer in Molly's eyes. He waited for Clara to leave before asking again. "You're sure you don't mind if I join you, Dr. Whitcomb?" He nodded to the couple watching them one table over. "If you do, I could easily—"

"Of course I don't mind. Please . . ." She motioned to the chair across from her, her smile tight. "You're welcome to sit, Sheriff."

He did, and noticed she kept eating. At a faster pace, if he wasn't mistaken. "How are you this evening?"

She nodded, swallowing before answering. "Fine, thank you." Then continued to eat.

He waited, thinking she might reciprocate with a question. When she didn't, he took a bite of chicken. Where had he gotten off on the wrong foot with this woman? Maybe *wrong* wasn't the right word, but there was a definite barrier between them that hadn't been there at first.

Wishing he had a token of friendship to toss over that wall of hers, he thought of something that might serve that purpose. "Have you had an opportunity to meet Dr. Rand Brookston yet? He's our town physician. I was speaking with him about you the other day, and—"

Her head came up. "Why would you be speaking to a doctor about me?"

He paused from chewing, taken aback by the defensiveness in her tone.

She dabbed at the corners of her mouth and a semblance of a smile returned, but it didn't ring true. "I'm simply wondering, Sheriff, why I was the topic of conversation between you and the town doctor."

James scooped peas onto his mashed potatoes and stirred. "I wouldn't say you were the topic of conversation, ma'am." He loaded his fork. "Dr. Brookston simply inquired about your arrival date and I told him you were already here. He wants to speak with you about a proposal he made to the town council regarding the schoolchildren. I think you'll be pleased."

Molly pushed aside her dinner plate and moved her bowl of cobbler closer.

Swallowing, he pointed with his fork. "That's the best-tasting stuff you've ever put in your mouth. Miss Clara has peaches brought over from the western slope. I guarantee it's the tastiest you've ever had."

"What exactly was the nature of the doctor's proposal, Sheriff?"

James eyed her. Apparently casual dinner conversation wasn't part of Molly Whitcomb's vast vocabulary.

"More coffee, Sheriff?"

James looked up to see a familiar face. "Yes, Elijah, thank you."

Elijah refilled his cup. "Ma'am, would you care for coffee now? It's right good with Miss Clara's cobbler."

"Yes, I believe I would, thank you."

The boy pulled a cup from his apron pocket and poured. James noticed him stealing glances at Molly, and couldn't blame Elijah in the least.

When he'd ridden up a moment ago and spotted her sitting alone, he'd experienced a lightness of spirit he hadn't felt in a long time. And all that from just looking at her.

He hadn't planned on being her dinner companion. But as he'd hugged Miss Clara, the last couple of open tables had filled, much to his favor. And when Miss Clara made the suggestion, he hadn't discouraged it.

James sipped his coffee. "How're your parents, Elijah? I haven't seen them in a while."

"They're fine, sir. My mama was just here a while ago, and my papa"—Elijah's face widened in a grin—"he's doin' real good. I'll tell him you asked after him, sir. That'll make him smile."

The image of Josiah Birch's smile quickly faded in James's mind and was replaced with that of him lying naked and beaten by a stream. And the same stirring that tightened his chest earlier returned. "I'd appreciate that, Elijah. And please pass along my compliments on the work he did for Dr. Whitcomb's cabin. It turned out mighty fine."

Molly looked up. "Your father helped build the cabin I'm living in?"

Pride lit Elijah's expression. "Yes, ma'am. He built the kitchen cupboard and the chifforobe in the bedroom. And your desk in the schoolhouse too. I helped him some."

"Well, you're both very talented. I appreciate your contribution."

"Elijah . . ." James motioned. "Have you met Timber Ridge's new schoolteacher yet? Dr. Molly Whitcomb of Franklin College in Athens, Georgia."

"No, sir, not where we've exchanged names." Elijah ducked his head and came up smiling again. "But I know who you are, Dr. Whitcomb. Nice to meet you, ma'am."

Each time James was in this boy's company, he was more impressed. Judging by Molly's expression, so was she.

"Dr. Whitcomb, may I present Elijah Birch, son of Josiah and Belle Birch, originally hailing from Franklin, Tennessee."

"It's nice to meet you, Elijah. How long have you been in Timber Ridge?"

"About a year, ma'am."

"Do you like living here?" she asked.

"Yes, ma'am. I like it a lot. I hope you will too."

She stared at Elijah for a few seconds, then laid her spoon aside. "Elijah," she said softly, her voice lowering. "Have you ever attended school?"

James paused midbite, fork halfway to his mouth.

Elijah gave a quick laugh. "No, ma'am. But my mama, she taught me growing up. She's real smart. So's my papa."

Molly leaned forward in her chair. "What would you think about attending a real school, Elijah?"

The boy stilled. His eyes went round. "Me? You mean . . . go to your school, ma'am?"

"Yes." There was nothing fake about her smile now. "Go to school right here in Timber Ridge, where I'll be teaching."

James didn't turn to look, but the two men conversing at the table behind him had fallen silent. And the man and woman one table over had stopped speaking as well.

Molly's voice was soft, but her enthusiasm was unmistakable. "One of my tasks this next week is to visit all the students and their parents. If you're interested, Elijah, I'll stop by your home and speak with your mother and father."

Elijah hesitated and looked at James, his silent question clear.

James already knew the answer, and it was one he didn't like. Change like this took time. It came slowly, and with a price. And in the middle of Clara's Cafe wasn't the place to discuss it either. Not with young Elijah at its center. And not when considering what had happened to the boy's father only last year.

James leaned forward and spoke loudly enough for those listening close by to hear. "Dr. Whitcomb, you'll be pleased to learn that Elijah here already knows how to read and cipher. He tallies receipts for Miss Clara and works part-time at the town's newspaper. The *Timber Ridge Reporter*."

Disappointment shadowed Elijah's eyes . . . and Molly's. Hers narrowed slightly, telling him she didn't appreciate his rerouting of the conversation either. James only hoped she wouldn't push the issue. She already had one strike against her with the town council for having arrived widowed. She didn't need a second. And he didn't need the disruption the rumors about this conversation would cause among townsfolk, not on top of everything else he was dealing with.

"Two jobs? Is that so, Elijah?" she finally said, her smile returning. "And the newspaper . . . That's impressive for a young man your age."

Elijah's smile lacked its previous fullness. "Thank you, Dr. Whitcomb." He briefly bowed his head and stole another look at James. "Well, I best get back to work now."

James watched the young man move from table to table, filling glasses and cups. Elijah spoke politely and was efficient in his tasks, but his spark was gone. And James felt responsible. He also knew Molly wasn't pleased with his interference, and he needed to try to set that aright.

He kept his voice to a whisper. "I apologize for interrupting you just now, and I'd be happy to discuss this after we're through with dinner."

"Contrary to what you might believe, Sheriff—" Her volume matched his as she spooned another dollop of cobbler, lifted it to her mouth, then stared at it and set the utensil back down. "It isn't my intention to be difficult, I assure you. And I'm not blind to what challenges there may be in these first steps. But"—she leaned closer, and James saw the man seated at the table right behind her do the same—"it's wrong to not allow a boy like Elijah Birch to study and learn, to improve himself. I'll teach him after hours, if that would work better."

"Dr. Whitcomb, if you're finished—"

She put her hand on his arm. "I saw you in town the other day with a Negro gentleman, shaking his hand, treating him like you would anyone else. That's just what I'm trying to do too. I *know* transitions like these aren't without their difficulties, but I'd gathered that, or rather hoped that—" Her hand tightened, sincerity glistening in those beautiful eyes. "I'd hoped that people might be more accepting out here."

Keenly aware of her touch, James would've bet good money she wasn't. Sure enough, she glanced down and quickly pulled her hand back. Pink tinged her cheeks.

Mindful of others looking in their direction, James tucked his napkin by his plate and stood. He chose a more formal tone in the hope of avoiding further discussion, and rumors. "If you're finished with dinner, Dr. Whitcomb, then perhaps I could give you a tour of the town. I'll show you where the church is located so you'll know how to get there in the morning. The community of Timber Ridge is eager to give you a proper welcome."

She looked at him and blinked, then managed an almost imperceptible nod. "Yes," she said, apparently catching on. "Of course, Sheriff. I'd like to offer my compliments to Miss Clara first, and then I'll be right with you."

James waited while she gathered her things, nodding to the couple seated nearby. "How are you, Mr. and Mrs. Foster?"

The parents of two school-age children, the Fosters smiled at him, then looked at Molly. And their smiles fell away.

James walked to where he'd tethered his horse. He wished now that he'd never sat down at Molly's table. If only for her sake. Mrs. Foster was a nice enough woman to your face, but she could talk a porcupine from his quills, and she tended to pass along everything she saw and heard with little attention to whether or not it was true.

Molly Whitcomb was obviously a woman impassioned about her beliefs, and he admired that quality. Very much. But if she wasn't careful, she was going to *impassion* herself right out of a job, even before she delivered her first lesson.

14

Molly thanked Miss Clara for dinner and settled the bill with Elijah. She gave the young man a handsome tip, which he declined, as she'd expected. But her persistence won out.

Grocery sack in hand, she slipped her reticule over her wrist and walked to meet James where he waited for her on the street. She felt as though the man had rescued her—again. She appreciated his alerting her to eavesdroppers, and though she'd thought she'd spoken softly enough, she shouldn't have extended the invitation to Elijah without speaking to the town council first. She'd allowed her personal desires to rule over her sensibilities. Something her parents had always warned her not to do.

Yet it hurt her to think that there was no room for Elijah and children like him in her school. They were castoffs, as it were. Children perceived as unworthy. But every child was worthy of receiving an education. Boys *and* girls. Whites *and* Negroes. Italian children too—although the language barrier would present a significant challenge if the children attended together. Already, her mind was spinning with possibilities.

James stood holding the reins to his horse. He wore that patient look of his again, one she was becoming accustomed to seeing from him. He started to speak, but she beat him to it, wanting to stay on his good side.

"Sheriff, please let me apologize for speaking out of turn. I feel strongly about certain issues, and sometimes I tend to get carried away in my effort to defend them."

"Carried away?" He frowned. "Really? I hadn't noticed."

A slow smile tipped one side of his mouth, and

he winked. She felt its effect in places she didn't know had nerves.

He gestured to his horse. "Would you care to walk or ride, ma'am?"

Still reeling inside from her involuntary response to him, she remembered their only other ride together, and how . . . stimulating that had been. "I'd prefer to walk, I think. It's such a lovely evening."

"All right, walk it is, Dr. Whitcomb. Here, let me take that for you." He pointed to her sack of groceries. She handed it to him, and he fit it into a saddlebag, then set a comfortable pace, leading the horse behind him.

She laughed softly. "Don't think I don't know what you're doing, Sheriff. I do."

Surprise lit his face. "I'm afraid I don't follow."

"With calling me *Dr.* Whitcomb. You're only doing that because of what I said to Mayor Davenport the other day."

He ran his tongue along the inside of his cheek. "Guilty as charged. What can I say? You scared the livin' daylights out of me, woman."

She laughed, trying to think of a way to gently steer the conversation back to school, and to Elijah Birch specifically. Dust swirled as she walked, and it clung to her skirt. Half of her time in Timber Ridge would be spent brushing the dirt from her clothes.

"Speaking of the other day . . ." He looked over at her. "Did I do something to upset you?"

She knew what James was alluding to, yet let a moment pass. "Why do you ask?"

"Because you've seemed . . . different since then. More distant."

She slowed to a stop. "May I be completely honest with you . . . James?"

"I'd like to assume you'd never be anything else with me, Molly."

His words were a sword, and they pierced far deeper than he could have imagined.

In that moment, the regret she carried for her ill-considered intimacy with Jeremy Fowler carved into a deeper hole inside her. What she wouldn't do to go back and make a different choice with him that night. She'd given herself to a man like Jeremy Fowler when a man like James McPherson had been in the world. And that thought made her want to weep. What might her life have been like if she'd waited for someone like him instead?

The man before her would never be anything more than a friend; she knew that. But having him for a friend was far better than having him as an enemy. And as much as she didn't require his protection or desire that he make decisions in her life, she didn't ever want to be an enemy to him, or to see herself as that in his eyes.

She resumed walking, if only so he would stop staring at her. He followed.

"When you defended me to Mayor Davenport

the other afternoon . . ." Tempted to soften what she was going to say, she decided not to temper her words. Though she wanted to keep James as her friend, she couldn't risk having him too close. And this, she was certain, would provide the distance she sought. "While I appreciated your willingness to plead my case that day, I much prefer standing up for myself in those situations. I mean no disrespect, to you or the office you hold, but I'm capable of representing myself, of making my own decisions. I don't need a ma—" She caught herself and had to think fast. "A myriad of excuses made on my behalf. I'm used to fighting my own battles and am quite comfortable in doing so." But if that were true, why did she feel so weak inside? So brittle and lacking?

He didn't answer, and she stole a glance beside her. He stared straight ahead, his expression inscrutable.

When they rounded the bend and the schoolhouse came into view, then the cabin, she half expected him to turn back. But he didn't.

When they reached the lake, he gestured. "Mind if we stop here for a few minutes?"

Wanting to say yes, that she did mind, that she was sorry but she had work to do—she shook her head. "No, I don't mind."

Already, the sun had dipped low behind the highest peaks, on its way to making another age-old journey. Shadows spilled down from the mountains like a vapor and hovered in an ebon hue across the lake. Back home in Georgia, they would have called this a night for haunting. When spirits grew restless and roamed the earth, seeking to arrest their loneliness. Of course, she didn't believe in such foolish—

"Dr. Whit—"

She jumped.

"I'm sorry, I didn't mean to startle you."

"You didn't," she lied, her heart racing.

He turned to face her. "I owe you an apology, ma'am. You're right. I stepped in where I shouldn't have—that day with Mayor Davenport. My intentions were honorable, I assure you. But intentions, however innocent or well meant, don't change the outcome of one's actions. My actions were wrong, and I apologize."

Molly could only stare. *Who is this man?* Not only was he not easily offended, but he admitted when he was wrong?

"And for the record . . ." He shrugged his shoulders and smiled, and she was certain her jaw would've landed on her chest if she'd let it. "What exactly does . . . *myriad* mean? That's a new one for me, ma'am."

She laughed. She couldn't help herself. "You mean . . . you're not angry with me?"

"No, ma'am. I appreciate your honesty. I just wish you would've come to me right after. Then there wouldn't have been the strife between us."

He gathered the horse's reins. "Best get you on inside. It's getting cool."

Molly hadn't noticed before, but she was chilly. James walked her the rest of the way to the cabin, stopping short of seeing her to the door. He handed her the bag of items she'd purchased from the store.

"Can we continue this talk tomorrow, ma'am? After church? Rachel's asked me to invite you for Sunday dinner." He held up a hand. "And before I forget, there's a town council meeting on Thursday night, six o'clock. You'll need to be there. We meet at the church building."

Molly held back from answering. Seeing Rachel and the boys again would be nice. And the prospect of having crackers and coffee for Sunday dinner was none too appealing. But neither was opening up the possibility of starting a tradition of going to the sheriff's house each Sunday for dinner following church.

"Ma'am?"

She looked back at him.

"I'm wagering it's the part about Sunday dinner that's giving you pause, and not the meeting." He searched her eyes. "Am I right?"

She gave a slight nod. "It's not that I don't appreciate what you've done for me. I do." She lifted a brow. "I wouldn't be standing here right now if you hadn't come upon that stagecoach when you did." How much to reveal to him was an issue, and she treaded carefully. "You were right the other day when you guessed that part of my coming to Timber Ridge was to start over. And part of that new beginning is making a life for myself here." *Alone*, she almost added, then heard the silence do it for her.

She tried to guess his thoughts, but the steadiness of his gaze skewed her judgment.

"If it makes your decision any easier, *Dr. Whitcomb,* I promise not to act as your protector. I won't speak on your behalf. I'll let you fight all your own battles." He laughed softly. "I won't even make you eat your vegetables if you don't want to."

She made a halfhearted attempt to hide her smile. "So you'll put aside that badge of yours for the entire afternoon. Is that what you're saying?"

Nudging a rock with the tip of his boot, he sighed. "I could lay aside this badge about as easily as you could forget how to speak all those languages you know." He took a step closer. "What I'm trying to say—and am not doing a very good job of it—is that I'd like for us to be friends, Molly. We're going to be working together in getting the school started, and we'll see each other in town from time to time. It'd be easier, and far more pleasant, if we were on sure footing with each other. I'm willing to relearn some things if I need to, in order for that to happen."

His honesty left her near speechless. As did her

desire that she'd made a different choice with Jeremy Fowler. "Then . . . yes, I—" Her voice caught. "I would enjoy having lunch with you and Rachel and the boys. As for the meeting, I'll be there. And as for being friends, I look forward to that."

"Me too, ma'am." He tipped his hat and turned.

She was inside and had almost closed the door when she remembered. She stepped back onto the porch. "A multitude or very large number," she called.

Not far down the path, James turned back. His head angled to one side.

"That's what myriad means! And I'll expect you to be able to use it in a sentence by tomorrow."

Smiling, she dashed back inside and closed the door before he could respond. And that feeling was still with her when she crawled into bed a while later. The windows were closed, but she could hear the faint trickle of the stream behind the cabin and the wind sweeping down from the mountains.

Her first night in her new home . . .

Reviewing the events of the day, she realized that James had never answered her question about the proposal the town doctor had made on behalf of the schoolchildren. She plumped her pillow and snuggled beneath the covers that smelled faintly of lilac and sunshine. Whatever the proposal was, she would be fine with it, she felt certain. As long as it didn't require her spending time with the town doctor.

She would need his services eventually, but that was one acquaintance she intended to put off forming for as long as possible.

James saw her when she walked into the church building. All heads turned as Molly took a seat near the back, only a minute or so before services started. Had she awakened late? Or had she purposefully timed her arrival to avoid being inundated with greetings on her first Sunday?

"Uncle James," Kurt said in a loud whisper. "Can I sit by you?"

" 'Course you can, buddy. I was saving this spot for you." James lifted the boy over Rachel and Mitch, who sat beside him on the pew.

"Can I hold your Bible too?"

Giving Kurt's head a rub, James placed the black leather-bound Bible in his lap and gave his younger nephew a sideways hug. His heart tugged tight when the boy sidled up closer. It was hard to imagine loving a child more than he loved his nephews.

"Let's all rise," the circuit preacher said from the front. "And turn in your hymnals to page twelve . . . 'A Mighty Fortress Is Our God.' And let's sing it like we believe it."

James smiled at that last part. Pastor Carlson had been visiting them twice a month now since the snows melted in late May, and James liked the way the man led the singing and delivered a sermon. He didn't preach with a lot of hoopla or ranting and raving. It felt more like you were sitting across the dinner table from him having a real good discussion. And he quoted Scripture with an ease and confidence he admired.

James could still picture his brother-in-law standing up there, leading singing. Sunday mornings always pulled memories of Thomas extra close. Thomas's clarion tenor used to rise over the swell of this chorus of voices in such a way that James had often sat out a verse just to appreciate the gift God had given the man.

How he wished Thomas were still here to watch his sons grow up, to love Rachel as she needed to be loved and cared for, and to continue building the ranch he'd dreamed of owning for so many years. James chanced a look at Rachel beside him. No one could tell from looking at her now—singing, voice and face lifted to God—that she was bone-tired, and worried.

The ranch was barely bringing in enough money to cover the mortgage, and little was left to cover day-to-day expenses. He was doing as much as he could to help out with chores but didn't have more time to spare. He had a little money tucked aside and helped here and there when he could, unbeknownst to Rachel, who would've refused.

He'd paid down the bill at the general store some, and planned on buying both boys a new pair of boots before school started. But his pockets only went so deep. Being sheriff didn't exactly command a high-paying salary.

The song ended, and Pastor Carlson invited the congregation to sit down, then announced the next song.

Paging through his hymnal, James spotted movement from the corner of his eye. He turned. Brandon Tolliver loitered by the back door. What on earth was Tolliver doing in church? Not that the man wasn't welcome. He was. James had invited him more than once. He'd just never shown up before.

Tolliver's gaze connected with his, held only a second, and then moved back over the crowd. After a minute, Tolliver headed toward a pew on the right and took a seat—right beside Molly.

James sat a little straighter in the pew. So much for questioning Brandon Tolliver's motivation.

"She's pretty, ain't she?" Kurt whispered, a mite too loudly.

Realizing his nephew had caught him staring, James nodded once and held a finger to his lips.

A second later, as the voices swelled in song again, Kurt tugged his sleeve. "She smells good too, Uncle James."

James had to smile. Rachel would've corrected the boy for saying such a thing, but he couldn't bring himself to. Not when it was God's honest truth.

Through the singing and on through the sermon,

James managed to sneak occasional glances behind him. Each time, Tolliver was looking his way. Molly only looked his way once, but her smile was instant and full and had a lasting quality about it. Something a man could take with him, like a picture stuck in his vest pocket for safe-keeping.

He tried to view her through the eyes of a member of the community, a parent whose child she would be teaching. Molly hadn't cracked open a hymnal this morning, yet she'd known the words to every song. She'd brought her Bible with her too, and flipped the pages whenever the preacher referenced a verse.

He was glad they'd gotten things settled between them last night, at least on a personal note. He still needed to address the subject of Elijah Birch and other school-related issues, but he was saving that for either before or after the town council meeting. As much as possible, he planned on keeping business issues separate from personal with Molly Whitcomb.

Especially since Mayor Davenport had assigned him as her official go-between to the town council—something else he needed to address with her. After their discussion last night—even with how things had turned out—he had a sense she wouldn't react favorably to that news.

After the final amen was said, members of the congregation flooded Molly with greetings. A sense of satisfaction came over James as he watched. One thing he could count on was these fine folks making her feel welcome. He kept an eye on her as he visited. Courteous and pleasant, she handled herself with perfect aplomb, and he was assured, yet again, that the town council had made the right choice.

Hiring Molly represented more than just hiring a schoolteacher, as Mayor Davenport had rightly pointed out. It was a significant step in a long succession of hard-won strides that would move Timber Ridge from being a rough mountain town to being a thriving community. A community that could stake a firm claim to the future and that would be around for Mitch's and Kurt's children. And their children's children.

As his grandfather had always said, *"Dream big, laddie. The Maker of heaven and earth is right beside you, so go ahead and take a leap or two. You might fall, get a little bruised. But if you end up flyin' . . . Ah . . . think of the thrill that would be! For both you and our Maker."* Ian McGuiggan always threw in a wink for good measure.

"Sheriff McPherson."

James turned at hearing his name. "Tolliver . . ." Maybe it was his imagination, but the man's smile seemed more smug than usual. "Surprising to see you here this morning."

Tolliver smoothed a hand over his pressed suit jacket. "I've been meaning to visit for a while now." He turned a bold glance in Molly's direction. "And today seemed like the perfect opportunity."

James found himself imagining how good it would feel to deck Tolliver. Not too hard, just enough to knock that boulder-sized chip off his shoulder. He managed a smile. "At least we know your motives are pure, don't we?"

Tolliver's smile only deepened. "You know me, Sheriff. I'm not the type of man who allows purity of motive to encumber him. When I want something, I go after it. I've never been one to mask my intentions." He raised a brow. "As some do."

James felt the insinuation. So Tolliver had caught him staring at Molly during church. More than once. He had no secret intentions when it came to her. On the contrary, he'd been open about his desire for her friendship in his conversation with her last night. So why did Tolliver's insinuation sting? "You're right, Tolliver. I do know you. Better than you think. And what I'm thinking is that you—"

"Gentlemen . . ."

James turned at the sound of Molly's voice.

She came alongside them, her expression attentive, and not a little curious. "How are you this morning, Sheriff?"

"I'm fine, ma'am," James answered first, still itching for that solid right hook to Tolliver's jaw. "I hope your first night in the cabin was a good one.

And that you had a *myriad* of pleasant dreams."

Her laughter was musical, and well worth the earning. "Well done, Sheriff. I'm impressed."

It was juvenile, he knew, but James enjoyed excluding Brandon Tolliver from the private joke.

"And my first night in the cabin was wonderful. I awakened to a herd of elk grazing right outside my bedroom window." She beamed. "They were magnificent!"

Tolliver stepped up. "If you think a herd of elk is magnificent, Dr. Whitcomb, just wait until you see my resort. I'd be honored to give you a private tour, and arrange for dinner to be served, of course."

James laughed. "Dinner? The hotel isn't even built yet."

Tolliver shook his head. "Have you never heard of catering a meal in, McPherson? I can't exactly take a woman like Dr. Whitcomb to an establishment like Clara's Cafe, now, can I?"

James snuck a look at Molly, whose expression was guarded.

"Now, Dr. Whitcomb." Tolliver's tone was gratingly cordial. "Shall we say . . . six o'clock Tuesday evening? I'll call on you at your cabin."

"Your offer is generous, Mr. Tolliver. But I must decline. As I told you a moment ago"—she tossed the man a look similar to one she might give an unruly student—"I have too much to do before school begins. Just ask the sheriff here. He'll vouch for that. The town council gave me a list of tasks a mile long."

"She's right, Tolliver. I gave her the list myself." James smiled in Tolliver's direction, enjoying seeing him put in his place. "She's got her work cut out for her."

"I'm sorry to hear that, Dr. Whitcomb." Tolliver's attention flashed briefly to James. "And speaking of work, I wish now that I'd pursued a chair on the town council. Perhaps then I could have thrown my hat into the ring to be your new boss, ma'am. Like the good sheriff here did. I would've enjoyed that distinction."

James felt his face heat, while Molly's expression clouded.

She frowned. "I . . . . don't understand."

Tolliver's smugness deepened. "Oh, I'm sorry, ma'am, if I've spoken out of turn. Mayor Davenport informed me that he'd assigned the sheriff to act as your . . . supervisor, of sorts. You'll be reporting to him in regard to your duties as the schoolteacher of Timber Ridge."

Confusion and—if James wasn't mistaken—suspicion, shadowed her eyes.

"Mrs. Whitcomb—" James turned to her. "Mr. Tolliver is making this out to be more than it is. I'm not your new boss or your supervisor, ma'am. Far from it. Mayor Davenport merely suggested that you and I work together to make sure the opening of the new school runs smoothly, and that the lines of communication stay open between you and the town council. That's all."

Molly clutched her Bible closer to her chest. "And just when, Sheriff McPherson"—her voice was soft; her eyes were not—"did he *assign* you this task?"

This woman was about as trusting as a wounded field mouse in a cage of buzzards. And James wondered, not for the first time, what kind of man her husband had been.

15

"On the day Mayor Davenport came to the cabin, he requested that I be your go-between for the town council," James said quietly, watching suspicion deepen in her eyes.

Molly nodded, obvious conclusions forming. "The day you asked me to wait inside."

"Dr. Whitcomb . . ." Tolliver bowed at the waist, his grin declaring victory. "I'll take my leave of you, madam. For now. But rest assured I'll issue a future invitation at, what I trust will be, a more opportune time. And I'll take pleasure in showing you the newest and most modern resort in the West."

"Thank you, Mr. Tolliver. I look forward to seeing your hotel." Molly gave him a gracious—if not tolerant—smile.

Tolliver. James watched the man leave, noticing

he didn't bother to speak to anyone on his way out. Not that most of these people were overly fond of the resort owner. Tolliver had arrived last fall promising to create jobs with the construction of his resort. But the hopes he'd raised among towns-folk were soon dashed when he offered lower-than-expected wages and hired immigrants to do the work instead.

As if having waited for Tolliver to leave, Rachel walked up behind Molly and gave her shoulders a squeeze. "I hope you're ready for some roasted chicken and potatoes, green beans with fatback, and apple crumb cake with fresh cream."

Molly was slow to answer. "Actually, Rachel, I'm . . . not feeling too well this morning. Perhaps I should stay closer to home today."

Rachel's expression fell, and James felt respon-sible. Rachel had been up before dawn working on dinner, wanting everything to be perfect for her new friend.

"I'm so sorry . . ." Rachel, ever the nurturer, touched the side of Molly's cheek. "You do feel a little warm."

Molly offered a noncommittal shrug. "Yes, but I think some extra rest will take care of it."

Rachel nodded and bowed her head.

Knowing he was to blame for Molly's change of heart, James grew determined to change it back. "Please reconsider, Mrs. Whitcomb. The boys stayed up late last night. They both made something special in your honor. And Rachel's apple crumb cake took the ribbon at this year's spring festival. If you don't get it now"—with work, he managed to get her attention—"you might have to wait 'a whole 'nother year,' as Kurt says."

Whether it was his persuasiveness or Rachel's obvious disappointment—he wagered it was the latter—he detected Molly wavering. And when Rachel hugged her again and Molly hugged her back, he knew their plans were on again.

Throughout the afternoon, James felt a deepening certainty that Molly's coming to Timber Ridge was by God's design. And was for their benefit as much as hers.

Rachel outdid herself at lunch, and as the boys presented their gifts to their new teacher—excitement flickering in their eyes as he hadn't seen in a long time—he found himself more and more curious about Molly Whitcomb.

"I hope you like it, teacher." Mitchell stood close by her side, rocking from heel to toe, as he did when he was excited. "I made it myself."

Molly removed the brown wrapping paper to reveal a box made from cut branches whittled free of bark and bound tight with string. She turned it in her hands. "Mitchell, this is—" She firmed her lips, her eyes bright with emotion. "This is beautiful, and so thoughtful of you."

Mitchell beamed. "I made it for your desk at school."

Molly's lips trembled. "And that's exactly where I'll put it. I'll use it every day and think of you."

"Now it's my turn!" Kurt edged closer, grinning and holding out his wrapped package. "Be careful. They can break."

Molly took the package from him, brushing his cheek with her forefinger, her mannerisms reflecting his excitement. She gingerly removed the paper—and gasped. She held the board out as though trying to put distance between it and her. "Oh, Kurt! This is—" She swallowed. "This is w-wonderful."

Kurt leaned closer, pointing to the largest and hairiest bug pinned to the board. "I found this one here in the barn. In one of the stalls. Feel his wings. They're real soft."

James had trouble containing his laughter, and saw Rachel having the same reaction. Apparently Molly Whitcomb did not like bugs, and that was putting it mildly. But recalling the hours Kurt had spent "catching" his present for her, he hoped she would appreciate the offering for what it was.

"Oh, I bet they are soft. But I—" Molly gave a visible shudder. "I'd hate to break them." She looked closer. "Are they . . . all dead?"

Kurt giggled. "These are. But I've got some live ones in my room if you want to—"

"No, no," she said quickly, smiling. "These are

. . . amazing specimens." She shot a look in James's direction, seeming to draw a measure of calm. "And I appreciate all the time and effort you took in . . . catching them for me."

Kurt's little chest puffed out.

As the afternoon stretched on, James sensed Molly relaxing, and he got a glimpse of the woman she must have been before her husband died. She was vibrant, quick-witted, and possessed a natural curiosity of life that was engaging. And she was pretty as all get out. Even dressed head to toe in black.

He hadn't felt this depth of an attraction to a woman in—well, forever. And while he felt better knowing that his attraction to her wasn't based solely on the physical, knowing that also bothered him. If she'd been the slightest bit uppity or unkind, or even uninterested in the goings-on of others' lives, he could've more easily dismissed his feelings.

That evening he drove her home in the wagon and she sat quietly beside him, wearing his jacket. She'd said she was chilly, but the cool evening air felt good to him. This was his favorite time of day. When the sky had a golden purple wash to it and the mountains seemed even bigger, all dark and craggy, set up against a waning sun.

He'd kept his promise to himself about not mixing business with personal. They had some things to talk out between them, but he hated to ruin such a nice day. He tugged on the reins and brought the wagon to a stop in front of her cabin.

He set the brake and went around to her side to help her down. When his hands fit about her waist and he lowered her to the ground, James recalled what Brandon Tolliver had said about hidden motives. Molly stood looking up at him, and for all the world, he wanted to kiss her. Slowly, and thoroughly. Thoughts of what kissing her would be like, of what it would feel like to hold her, of the softness of her lips, were vivid inside him.

Desire bolted through him, unexpected and unfettered. And he quickly let her go and stepped back, putting distance between them.

Her brow furrowed. She stared, and James felt as though she'd caught him with his hand in the cookie jar. She'd been a married woman. She was familiar with the desires of a man and had no doubt just glimpsed that desire in his eyes. He felt as though he needed to apologize, yet that didn't seem quite right either.

What if he'd misread her and she hadn't noticed anything? He'd only be drawing attention to something that would bring further discomfort. To them both.

She touched his arm. "James . . ."

Whether his reaction was only internal or if she'd noticed too, he couldn't tell. He only knew that it would be best for her not to touch him right now. Yet he did not want her to remove her hand.

Her smile was slow to bloom. "I appreciate your allowing this afternoon to be what it was . . . a wonderful time with friends. Rachel is so lovely and kind." She moved her hand away. "And your nephews are endearing."

"I'm glad you enjoyed yourself, and that you changed your mind about coming." He found it easier to speak when he wasn't looking at her. He motioned to the cabin. "I'll wait here until you're safe inside."

She didn't move. "I'm sorry for my reaction earlier today . . . after church. It was childish and silly, and I apologize."

The sincerity in her eyes made him swallow. He'd prayed often through the years that God would remove the desire for a woman's touch, since a wife didn't seem to be in his future. And He had—up until now, it seemed.

The life of any sheriff, much less a sheriff in a town like Timber Ridge, didn't leave room for a wife and a family. Having Rachel and the boys in his care was hard enough. Not that he'd shirked his duties in enforcing the law since coming to live with them, but there were times when he'd carried out his responsibilities as sheriff and had worried that the threats made against him would extend to them as well.

Coming after *him* was one thing. Coming after Rachel and the boys—or his family, if he had one—was another.

"You were right, early on." Molly gave a gentle shrug. "About my not expecting to find things in Timber Ridge to my liking. I wasn't at all excited about the prospects of living here. I imagined the town would be rougher, the aspects of my job less desirable, and the people far less kind." Her expression grew earnest. "But I was wrong. I'm grateful for the opportunity the town council has given me, Sheriff," she said with a nod. "I want you to know that."

There it was again. That vulnerability. That briefest glimpse past her confident façade, as though she considered herself unworthy of the teaching position. Her humility only made her more special in his eyes, and increased his determination to keep their relationship on a right footing.

"And you need to know again, *Dr. Whitcomb*, that we're very pleased you said yes. Now . . ." He motioned toward the cabin, then remembered something and turned to reach into the back of the wagon. "Let's not forget these."

He handed her Mitchell's gift and she gave it a closer look.

"Mitchell said he made this himself." Her tone held a twinge of doubt. "But I'm thinking he had help."

"I showed him what to do, but he insisted on doing all the work himself. He started over three times. You'll find he's a stickler for doing things right, and for wanting to do it that way the very first time. He gets frustrated on occasion and needs to learn to be more patient with himself."

She nodded. "I can relate, and appreciate knowing that about him." She was slower to accept Kurt's gift and used care to hold the board by the edges. "Thank you"—she frowned—"I think."

James grinned. "Kurt likes bugs."

"Yes, I gathered that."

"And I take it that you don't."

"I'm not overly fond of them, no. But at least it's not a snake." She eyed the board, which served as the final resting place for ten near-perfect beetles and other insects.

"Kurt's always been interested in anything that creeps or crawls. When he was two, he came to church with a lizard in his pocket." James laughed remembering Thomas's and Rachel's response. "He took it out during Communion and about scared Lyda Mullins half to death."

Molly shuddered, barely finding a smile.

"Would you like me to carry this to the door for you?"

She nodded. "Would you, please? I'm not altogether sure that one on the far corner is dead yet."

He took the board and walked her up to the front porch, feeling at ease again with the woman beside him. His desire to kiss her hadn't lessened, but, with effort, he held it in check. Other than Rachel, he'd never been close to a woman before. This could be good. This being friends with Molly Whitcomb.

He kept telling himself that on the way home, and then again as he lay in bed later that night. The same bed she'd slept in, which—when thinking of that, and imagining the softness of her mouth—only pushed sleep further from his mind.

It was Monday morning and Molly had two over-full weeks of work ahead before school started. And it wasn't getting done with her just standing here, drinking coffee, staring out at the stream behind her cabin. She rinsed out her cup and left it by the washbasin.

Wearing her own black dress, freshly brushed, she grabbed her reticule, along with her teaching satchel packed with lesson samples and books, and checked her image in the mirror hanging by the door one last time.

Propped on a side table, the board containing the still-much-too-alive-looking bugs drew her attention. They were dead—she felt certain. But the way the big black one on the end stared back at her did make her wonder.

But better a collection of bugs than a snake. Her spine crawled just thinking about it.

A neighborhood boy had slipped a snake into her lunch pail once, and she'd nearly fainted when she found it—and she'd been fourteen at the time! From then on, whenever a fellow classmate made fun of her, the others would laugh and make a hissing sound.

Cute little Kurt Boyd had spent no telling how many hours collecting these for her. Still, she didn't like the idea of keeping them in her home.

An idea came. Why hadn't she thought of it before?

She slipped on her gloves and carried the board, along with her reticule and satchel, the short distance to the schoolhouse. She gave the insect collection a prominent place on a shelf and planned to use it for a science lesson the very first week. Surely Kurt Boyd would approve of that. But the best thing was—the bugs were out of her house!

Sunlight filtered through the bank of windows on her left, falling across the rows of desks and illuminating specks of dust in the air that otherwise would have gone unseen. She walked up the aisle to her desk and slowly took a seat in her chair, facing the classroom, memorizing the moment, and imagining the room full of children, all chattering as they bustled to their desks, the noise level rising to a deafening crescendo.

For now, quiet reigned. Everything was pristine. Perfect. Orderly and in its place. But it wouldn't stay that way.

Just as her life wouldn't. Not that her life was perfect. It certainly wasn't. But the imperfections were hidden. Where no one could see. And she wished she could keep them there.

A wave of dread rose fierce from somewhere deep inside her. Her days were numbered in Timber Ridge—she felt it. An ache settled in her chest. Tomorrow marked the first of August—and the third full month of her pregnancy. What was Jeremy Fowler doing this very moment? Did he even give her—or the baby—a passing thought? Especially now, as his marriage to Maria Elena Patterson drew closer.

Fall semester would soon be under way at Franklin College. Professors would return to campus, report for faculty meetings, and share lunch in the college cafeteria. Was the new administration building completed yet? And what of the new Language Arts facility? Where her new office would have been.

She'd known Jeremy for three years. They'd been colleagues, serving on committees together. Then they'd moved to being friends. He'd invited her to lunch, and they gradually began attending faculty gatherings with each other, even going to church together on occasion. But when her father fell ill, their relationship had developed into something . . . more.

Jeremy had stayed by her side during those last difficult days, then the ones leading up to the funeral, and after, helping her with details and being there whenever she needed support or someone to talk to. They'd discussed marriage but never made a formal announcement.

Looking back, Molly wondered if she'd inferred more than she should have. Remembering the last time she'd been to his house, she closed her eyes, feeling as if it were three years ago instead of only three months.

"I want you to know how much I appreciate your doing this for me, Molly." Jeremy had led her through the spacious lobby of his home into a front parlor. "You're an expert on grant requests. It won't take long, and your knowledge will benefit the entire college."

She tried not to be obvious as she took in the elaborate surroundings of his home again. She'd been there before for faculty gatherings and evenings spent with him discussing their shared love of literature. Antiques filled the home, and the plush Persian rug underfoot served to remind her how different his background was from hers.

Jeremy tossed his jacket over a wingback chair. "I'll make us some coffee before we get started. Mrs. Fulton's already left for the day, so I'm afraid you'll have to suffer through my sorely unrefined culinary skills."

Molly hesitated. *Mrs. Fulton isn't here?* The housekeeper had always been present in the home when she'd visited before. The elderly woman never joined them but could always be heard in the kitchen or upstairs in one of the bedrooms. "Perhaps I should leave, Jeremy. I didn't realize that—"

"Don't be silly." He tossed her a look that said she was being foolish. "You and I have been alone before. In my office. In your office. In our classrooms. We're mature adults, Molly. Not schoolchildren who need constant supervision."

When he put it that way, she felt as if she'd overreacted. Her father's passing had left a gaping hole in her life, in her heart, and Jeremy's companionship had served to fill part of that void. She laid aside her wrap and headed toward the kitchen. "I'll make the coffee, then. Just show me where everything is."

He caught up with her in the hallway and grabbed her hand. "You're a jewel, Molly Whitcomb." He brushed a kiss to her knuckles. "And for what it's worth, I think you should have gotten that promotion rather than Alex Hollister."

Molly bowed her head. Appreciating his reassurance, she was sorry he'd brought up the topic again. She'd managed to set aside her disappointment for a few moments.

Jeremy brushed the hair back from her temple. "I doubt President Northrop sees his mistake right now. But he will, in time. You're a gifted teacher, Molly. You'll do well here at Franklin. Just give it time." He quirked a brow. "You'll shake up this old men's fraternity yet."

She laughed at that, and when he kissed her cheek—once, twice—she couldn't decide whether it was pleasure she felt, or discomfort. They'd kissed before, and she remembered each one vividly. But she was also aware of how alone they were.

He moved closer, but she laid a hand to his chest. "You mentioned coffee?"

He smiled, giving a quick nod. "That I did." Taking her hand, he led her into the kitchen.

The creak of the schoolhouse door opening brought Molly's head up and swept aside the thick cobweb of memories.

A black man stood in the entryway, toolbox in hand. "I's sorry, Dr. Whitcomb, ma'am. Didn't know you was here. I come back directly."

"No, please." Molly rose from her desk. "You're not bothering me. In fact, I was just leaving." She gathered her teaching satchel and reticule, thankful for the interruption. "I'm on my way to visit the students and their parents." She paused by the door, smiling up at him. "But I'm afraid you have the advantage, sir. You know my name, but I don't know yours."

He dipped his head. "The name's Josiah Birch, ma'am. I just come by to finish hookin' up that stovepipe over yonder. The air in these mountains gets bone chillin' come fall, and I don't want these young'uns to be comin' down sick."

Molly quickly put two and two together. "You're Elijah's father?" As soon as she said it, she recalled the mossy green of Elijah's eyes and wished she could take back the question.

But the smile stretching Josiah's deep mahogany features bespoke nothing less than a father's heartfelt pride. "Yes, ma'am. Elijah's my son. He told me he done met you. Belle said she did too. We're sure glad to have you here, ma'am. Havin' us a school like this with a real teacher means a lot to this town."

What a gracious statement for this man to make, considering his son wasn't allowed to be a student in this school. Molly chose her words carefully. "I was planning on stopping by to visit with you and your wife this week."

His brow rose. "You comin' to our house?" He let out a soft whoop. "I best give Belle some warnin'. She'll be wantin' to fix up things, for sure."

The way he said it led her to think he was only kidding, but still Molly shook her head. "There's no need to do that. I just wanted an opportunity to speak with you both about—" she offered up a hasty prayer—"Elijah . . . and his education."

The man's smile faded. "His education?" Deep creases furrowed his brow. "I don't rightly follow your meanin', ma'am."

"Your son is very bright, Mr. Birch, as I'm sure you well know. And as much as I wish I could extend an invitation to him to attend this school . . . I cannot. For reasons I believe we both understand." She waited, and continued after his gentle nod. "But I would be more than willing to teach him, if you're open to that. After school, or on weekends, if need be. I could instruct him in advanced mathematics, literature, and the sciences. It would open up doors to him that he might not otherwise experience."

Josiah stared. "You done talked to Sheriff McPherson about this, ma'am?"

Molly felt censure in his question and knew it was deserved. "I've made no secret to him about my views on this, Mr. Birch. But I consider time outside of this classroom as my own, and therefore believe I can spend it however I wish."

"Don't mean no disrespect, ma'am, but the way I see it, the good folks that brought you here aim for you to be teachin' the white children. I don't have their word on it, but I'm thinkin' that's about all the children they's wantin' you to teach."

"But if I'm willing to sacrifice my time and effort, and pay that price, Mr. Birch, that should be my decision. Do you not agree?"

He seemed hesitant. His eyes darted to hers, then away again. "That's just it, ma'am. You won't be the only one payin' the price." He eyed her. "You from Georgia, that right, Dr. Whitcomb?"

She nodded.

"You ever wake up durin' the night"—his eyes narrowed—"peer out your front window, and see a cross burnin' bright as daylight outside your house?"

Emotion tightened Molly's throat. She steadied her voice. "In fact . . . I have. More than once. My father abhorred slavery, Mr. Birch. He did everything he could to stand against it, and"—she lowered her gaze, recalling the image of looking up at her father and seeing the reflection of a burning cross in the mirror on the wall behind him—"he instilled within me those same principles, and the will to fight for them."

Mr. Birch seemed to take this in. "I'm thinkin' your father did a lot of good in his life, ma'am."

"Yes, he did," she whispered.

"I know some white folks who worked hard to change laws up in Washington. Who talked to anybody who'd listen, tryin' to change the way things were." His expression was gentle. "The way things are."

"That aptly describes my father, Mr. Birch. He was that type of man."

His smile held understanding, and compassion. "On those nights, ma'am, when them crosses were burnin' out in front of your house, did your father send you outside? Alone? To reckon with those men hidin' in the shadows?"

Molly could only stare, hearing what he was asking, and knowing he already knew her answer. "No," she whispered. "He did not."

"And with all the respect I have in me, ma'am, I'm askin' you . . ." Earnestness sharpened the concern in his face. "Please don't be askin' me to send my child out there either. I won't do it. Not when I know what's waitin' in the shadows for him."

16

As the week progressed, Molly carried her conversation with Josiah Birch and his love for his son—not even his own biological child—with her as she visited students and parents in their homes. She introduced herself and evaluated each student's level of progress, and by late Tuesday afternoon, she realized what a formidable challenge awaited her. Not only with parents—a few of whom seemed resistant to the very idea of school—but with her potential students.

While a handful of the children could read and write, to varying degrees, most held only a limited knowledge of language and mathematics. And by Wednesday evening, she'd discarded any hope of teaching these children Italian or French. Instructing them in proper English, along with how to read and write and work their sums, would be the primary order of business.

Thursday afternoon, when she retreated inside Mullins General Store, exhausted and covered in dust, her once-fresh curls hanging limp at her temples, she felt as though she could lie down and sleep for a week. The task before her seemed overwhelming. She'd thought teaching college was a challenge, but this . . .

She had nearly thirty students ranging from ages six to sixteen, and they fell everywhere on the scale in regard to ability and knowledge. She'd visited twenty of the pupils on the list Rachel had made and still had half again that number to meet, and the list didn't even cover all her potential students.

She'd taken a lunch and snack with her that day, along with her canteen, to keep up her strength, but she still felt depleted. And the only thing she could attribute it to was the baby inside her, which somehow brought her thoughts back full circle to Josiah Birch and his son.

Josiah Birch loved Elijah as if the boy were his own flesh and blood. But he wasn't.

She didn't know Josiah and Belle's story, but she knew Elijah's—at least in part. It was written in his face, quite literally. The child nestled in her womb was part of her. He, or she, was her *own* flesh and blood, yet her feelings toward it didn't begin to resemble those of Josiah Birch's for his son—a son fathered by another man.

"Mrs. Whitcomb?"

Molly looked up to see Lyda Mullins, the proprietress, arranging pairs of boots on a side table. Molly offered a smile, hoping it communicated more verve than she felt. "Good day, Mrs. Mullins."

Lyda's patient assessment was telling. "Has it been that long of a week already, Mrs. Whitcomb?"

Molly made a show of blowing a curl from her

forehead, and enjoyed the giggle it drew from the older woman. "I'm afraid it has been." She sighed. "And it's not over yet."

Lyda gestured. "Wait here." She returned a moment later with a full glass. "Here you go. This should liven you back up."

"Thank you." Molly took a ladylike sip at first. But when the cool, sweet wetness hit her throat, she tossed propriety aside and downed half the glass.

"There you go!" Lyda Mullins said, laughing. "You'll be one of us in no time."

Grinning, Molly dabbed the corners of her mouth, hoping the woman's words would prove true. She held up the glass of tea. "This is delicious. What's in it?"

"It's my mother's recipe. It has some spices mixed in and plenty of sugar. I make it with water from the stream out back, so it's nice and cold. I just mixed up a fresh batch. It's Ben's favorite."

"I can see why." Molly took another drink. "It's delicious, and just what I needed. Thank you again."

Nodding, Lyda returned to arranging boots. "So your first official meeting with the town council is this evening, I hear."

Molly raised a brow. "You know about that?"

"Everybody in town knows about that. Mayor Davenport sent someone from his office around town earlier today. She invited me and Ben and what customers were here to attend. I saw her head on down the street, asking more folks as she went. My thinking is that the mayor wants to make a good impression on your first meeting."

Recalling Mayor Davenport's initial reaction to her, Molly wondered if he had some other motivation. "If that's what he's trying to do, then he needn't bother." She raised her glass in a mock cheer. "Timber Ridge has already made a very favorable impression on me." She drank the rest of her tea.

"I'm glad to hear that, Mrs. Whitcomb. I hope you'll be very happy here. The children of this town deserve a teacher like you."

"Do you and your husband have children, Mrs. Mullins?"

Lyda stilled and stared at the child-sized boots in her hand. And the question grew louder in the silence. "No, Ben and I don't have any children," she whispered, smoothing a hand over the lace ties. "Not anymore."

Molly pressed her lips tight. "I'm sorry, Mrs. Mullins, I didn't mean to pry—"

"You're not prying, Mrs. Whitcomb." Lyda put the boots down and smoothed the front of her apron. "It's been several years ago now." Though telling by the pain in her expression, the wound was still fresh, in some ways, at least. "I'm usually fine talking about it, but today—" Lyda looked at her hands knotted at her waist. "Today would have

211

been their twelfth birthday. Twins," she said softly. "A boy and a girl." Loss and longing shadowed Lyda Mullins's expression. "I don't know why, but their birthday is always harder for me to get through than the day they—" She bit her lower lip, then reached out. "Here, let me take that for you."

Molly handed Lyda the glass and their hands touched.

Lyda looked at her, hesitating. "You and your husband . . . you never had any children."

It wasn't a question, and yet Molly saw the opportunity for what it was. And part of her wanted to take it. She wanted to tell the truth. She could say it aloud right now, right this minute, and—certain that nearby patrons shopping one aisle over would hear—the news would be all over town in no time. And just as certain, her time in this town would be all over too.

No more job. No more fresh start, or new friends. For however long they might last. Heart beating in her ears, Molly slowly shook her head.

Lyda took hold of her hand. "Well, don't you worry. You're young yet, Mrs. Whitcomb, there's still time. Once you're ready to open your heart again, I'm sure there'll be a good man to come along, ready to steal it."

Molly felt herself tearing up.

"Oh, there, there, dear . . ." Lyda touched her cheek. "Don't cry. It'll be all right. I'm living proof that God gives you strength for each new day. I know you miss your husband. And I'm not sure that'll ever stop, not completely. But there'll come a day when someone else will touch a part of you in a way that maybe he didn't. And you'll know, just like you did that first time."

Molly couldn't meet her gaze.

"Pretty as you are, you'll have your choice of men too." She laughed softly. "I'm surprised they haven't already started lining up outside your cabin."

Molly took a hiccupped breath, wishing she had the courage to tell Lyda Mullins the truth. But she didn't.

"Excuse me, ladies . . ."

Recognizing the voice behind her, Molly worked to dry her tears.

"Sheriff McPherson . . ." Lyda gently touched Molly's arm as she stepped past. "How are you today, sir?"

"I'm doing well, ma'am. And you?"

"Better now that you've stopped by. Is there something I can help you find?"

Molly knew Lyda Mullins was buying her more time, and she could have hugged her for it.

"I'm interested in getting both my nephews a pair of boots before school starts. You don't happen to know if Ben has measured their feet recently, do you?"

"No, but I can check with him," Lyda said. "I'll be right back."

Hearing Lyda's retreating footsteps and feeling James's stare, Molly turned to greet him, aware of others nearby. "Sheriff, how nice to see you." She forced a lightness to her voice, but the concern lining his features said he wasn't fooled.

That half smile tipped his mouth. "Pleasure's all mine, Dr. Whitcomb. I assure you." He glanced downward. "I take it you've been out visiting your students today?"

Molly took a meaningless swipe at the layer of dust coating her skirt. "Yes, and the meetings are going very well. I'm eager to make a report to the town council tonight." *Eager* was stretching the truth, but she wanted to appear competent and in charge.

"Actually, I was hoping to speak to you about something before the meeting this evening. If that's possible. It has to do with the proposal I started telling you about the other day, the one Dr. Brookston—"

"Sheriff McPherson!" Ben Mullins came up from behind and clapped him on the shoulder. "I hear you're looking for boots for Mitch and Kurt. I have their measurements right here." Mr. Mullins looked her way. "Mrs. Whitcomb, how are you, ma'am? Fill me in on how things are going for our new schoolteacher."

"I'm doing well, thank you." Matching his exuberance, she told Ben Mullins about preparing her lessons and about getting the room ready, but spared him the details on her meetings with parents and their children, not wanting to bring up any unwanted memories for him. "But I'll be ready come that first day."

"I'm sure you will," Ben said. "So what kind of boots would you like to see, Sheriff?"

James touched Molly's elbow. "Would you mind waiting for me, Dr. Whitcomb? I promise I won't be long."

As James looked at boots, Molly picked up the soap and coffee she'd come into the store for, paid for it, and met him on the boardwalk minutes later.

"That's very kind of you," she said, gesturing behind them to the store, thinking of what he'd just done for Mitchell and Kurt.

"They do far more for me than I do for them, I assure you." He cocked his head to one side. "Are you hungry?"

She smiled at his impulsive question. "Yes, in fact, I am. But—" She pulled her father's pocket watch from her skirt pocket—five o'clock—and glanced down at the dust layering her dress. "Doesn't the meeting begin at six?"

He nodded, apparently following her line of thought. "Tell you what . . . why don't you ride Winsome on to the cabin, I'll go to Clara's and bribe her into letting me have two plate dinners, with cobbler, and I'll meet you on your porch in about twenty minutes. We'll consider it a pre-town-council meeting. How does that sound?"

She stared up at him, thinking of the "friend truce" they'd made just days ago, and weighed that against her determination to keep some distance between them.

"It's just a meal, Molly. And everyone needs to eat. Even you."

She considered his overly patient look. If only he knew her hesitance was for his sake, not hers. From how he described it though, they'd be eating on her front porch. No one would even see them together. She laughed softly. "I gladly accept, James. Thank you."

She followed him over to the pretty chestnut mare tethered nearby, and James handed her the reins. "She's about as gentle as they come, but she'll fly if you give her the lead."

"Then I'll make sure not to give her the lead." Molly climbed into the saddle and arranged her skirt over her legs, halfway wishing she *could* see what his little mare could do. If such a thing would even be permitted in her condition.

She guided the mare down the street, drawing an occasional stare. It didn't hit her why until she was nearly through town—it was because she was riding the sheriff's horse. If she'd thought it through, she would have declined James's generous offer. As it was, she hurried the mare along.

Back at the cabin, she changed into Rachel's dress and was putting the finishing touches on her hair when she thought she heard something—an explosion. But it sounded far away. Pausing, comb in hand, she waited, didn't hear anything else, and went back to her task.

Then it sounded again. Her hand stilled.

She walked to the front door and stepped outside—and heard a chorus of gunfire erupt. She looked toward town. The blasts carried over the lake and echoed off the mountain before turning back again.

Alarm spread through her. Was there an emergency in town? A fire? Is this what they did to call for help? She grabbed her reticule and ran to where James's horse stood tethered. She yanked the reins free, swung into the saddle, and gave Winsome a good kick in the haunches.

James was right. His pretty little chestnut mare about sprouted wings and flew!

Molly held the reins, heart pounding, as Winsome's hooves ate up the path toward town. She had no idea what help she could offer once she got there, but faces of people she'd met came to mind. She couldn't even remember all their names but was determined to repay them something of what they'd already given her.

Leaning forward, close to the horse, she felt an exhilaration she hadn't experienced in a long time. She'd ridden since she was a little girl and was skilled at it. The mare's stride was sleek and smooth, and as they rounded the last corner toward town together, Molly didn't feel a pinch of fear. Not for herself, or her baby.

Her baby . . .

The thought caught her off guard. But when the main thoroughfare came into view, she found she couldn't give the thought the attention it needed. Throngs of people clogged the street, guns and rifles firing one after the other. She reined in, sending bits of gravel flying.

And that's when she saw him—James striding toward her through the crowd, two covered plates in one hand and his gun in the other.

17

James slipped his gun back into his holster and negotiated a path through the crowd, trying to get to Molly. From the confused look on her face, he realized she had no clue what was happening. People slapped him on the back as he went, hugging him, hugging each other. Someone bear-hugged him from behind, and he had to steady the plates in his hand to keep from dropping them.

He turned to see Charlie Daggett hanging on to him.

"We did it, Sheriff!" Charlie yelled, liquor heavy on his breath. "We did it!"

James laughed. "We sure did, Charlie!" He clapped him on the shoulder, then looked him in the eye. "You go easy on the celebrating tonight, okay?"

"I will, Sheriff. You want me to swear on it?"

James shook his head. "You've already given me your word. That's good enough in my book."

Charlie straightened a bit—as much as he probably could in his current state—and pointed. "She's waitin' for you over there."

James glanced in Molly's direction, then back at Charlie. He narrowed his eyes. Maybe Charlie wasn't as far gone as he'd thought.

Charlie grinned. "I'm a little drunk, Sheriff. But I'm not stupid."

James felt himself smiling despite knowing the reaction would reveal more than he wanted to. But he also knew that, come morning, tonight would likely be a blur for Charlie Daggett. As most of them unfortunately were. "One thing you're not, Charlie . . . is stupid. Don't ever buy into that lie, friend."

Charlie stared for a second. "Yes, sir, Sheriff." He gave him another bear hug before plunging back into the celebrating mob.

By the time James reached her, Molly had dismounted. She held the reins to Winsome and eyed the crowd behind him, a curious half smile on her face. He deposited their dinners on a nearby bench. Seeing the flush of her cheeks and the mussed look of her hair, he threw caution aside and gave her a spur-of-the-moment hug.

Eyes wide, she laughed. "What was that for?"

"Colorado's been granted statehood! We just got the telegram. President Grant signed the bill, so it's official."

Her eyes lit. She giggled. "I heard the commotion from my cabin and thought something was wrong. So we came to see what it was." She stroked Winsome's neck. "You're right. This little girl rides like the wind."

"And you don't ride too badly yourself either. I saw you rein in. That was impressive."

Her cheeks flushed a deeper shade of pink. "I've done some riding in my day."

"That would've been my guess." He gestured to the plates on the bench. "You still hungry?"

"Starving. But won't the meeting be starting soon?"

He raised a brow. "The mayor's off writing a new speech, so we have time, believe me."

She laughed again, and James thought of how easy it would be to get used to that sound.

They ate dinner on the bench, watching the celebration and laughing at the crowd's antics. Grown men hugging each other and dancing around like little girls. When they saw people heading toward the church building, they moved in that direction too.

They stepped through the doorway, and James directed her toward the front of the room, where Mayor Davenport was already situated behind the podium. "Mayor Davenport will speak first, then he'll want to introduce you."

"I think I've already met just about everyone in town."

He leaned close as they walked down the aisle. "Humor the man, Molly. You'll find that much of what he does is not for the reason you see on the surface."

Molly flashed him a smile. "I've already figured that one out," she whispered.

She sat on the front pew, and James settled in beside her, keeping an appropriate distance, especially remembering Charlie Daggett's observation.

The moment Davenport began speaking, James knew they were in for a long one, and that this wasn't going to be a normal town council meeting. It was more like a town hall gathering. He glanced behind them. The pews were packed. People stood in the back and crowded the open doorway. If only they could get such a crowd on Sunday mornings.

Nearly an hour later, after the mayor had recounted the entire history of Timber Ridge, as well as every accomplishment he could possibly give himself credit for, he turned to Molly.

"And so it is, on this auspicious occasion, as we celebrate the announcement of Colorado's statehood, we also celebrate another milestone in the history of our illustrious town. After receiving numerous applications from *many* highly qualified applicants—" Davenport shot James a look.

James immediately thought of Davenport's sister, who had applied for the job, and hoped Davenport wouldn't try to make reference to that tonight. He leaned forward in the pew, arms resting on his thighs, and tried to get that message across to Davenport as clearly as he could.

Davenport cleared his throat. "However, I am wholly persuaded that we have chosen the most qualified of them all. *Dr.* Whitcomb," he said with emphasis, "has already begun meeting with parents and students, many of whom are joining us this evening." He looked out over the crowd. "And we're so glad you're here. But for those of you who haven't had an opportunity to meet our new teacher, I'd like to introduce her to you now." He indicated for her to join him at the front.

It took her a moment to rise and walk to the front, and James got the impression she didn't welcome being the center of attention. Odd for a woman who made her living at the front of a classroom.

"Dr. Molly Whitcomb is a language professor from Franklin College in Athens, Georgia"— Davenport read from notes now—"and she speaks Italian, French, Spanish." Impressed gasps and whispers skittered through the crowd, and the mayor paused. From the pride on his face, one might have thought they were *ooh*ing and *ahh*ing over him. "She graduated first in her class and has held prestigious positions on faculty service committees in addition to her duties as a professor. . . ."

Davenport continued to list Molly's accomplishments, and James continued to enjoy the opportunity to watch her, already familiar with what she'd achieved. Molly Whitcomb was intelligent, cultured, refined. She was the essence of grace and comportment. Rachel had summed it up well when she said, "The woman simply has no flaws."

So taking all that into account, what was it about Molly Whitcomb that still gave him the slight nudge inside that something just wasn't quite right?

When he saw Dr. Brookston walking up to the front, James realized he'd let his mind wander. He also realized he'd failed to explain to Molly about the doctor's proposal. Though not for lack of trying. They'd simply been interrupted. But he wasn't worried. She would respond to Brookston's plan with customary graciousness, he was sure.

Davenport greeted Dr. Brookston as though they were the closest of friends. "Our good doctor here made a recommendation to the town council, which we heartily approved and for which I personally campaigned."

Rand Brookston glanced in James's direction, and James returned the silent commiseration, remembering how much discussion it took to even get Davenport on board with the idea.

Grinning, Davenport patted Rand Brookston on the back. "For every student entering school this fall, Dr. Brookston will administer a complete physical examination . . . free of charge!"

Spontaneous applause filled the room, and James joined in. He noticed little Emily Thompson, on the opposite aisle, lean up and whisper something to her mother. Mrs. Thompson whispered back and Emily's eyes grew wide. The applause subsided. "But I don't want to visit the doctor! He uses needles! Becky Turner said so!"

Mrs. Thompson shushed her daughter, but Emily began crying. Frantic high-pitched whispers dotted the gathering, and a chorus of comforting shushes rose to compensate.

"Now, now, children." Mayor Davenport raised his hands in a calming manner. "There's nothing to be afraid of. In fact, as your teacher and the one responsible for your education, Dr. Whitcomb here has volunteered to set the example—by having her examination first. Haven't you, Dr. Whitcomb?"

James wasn't sure which was most amusing, the pitiful whimpers coming from all corners of the room or the look of sheer terror on Molly's face. Apparently, their new schoolteacher did have some slight flaws—in addition to being terrified of bugs, she was scared spitless of doctors.

Molly knew she needed to say something but couldn't decide on what.

Mayor Davenport stood beside her, smiling wide. Dr. Brookston watched her with keen eyes so discerning she had to look away, and James stared from the front pew, apology lining his expression. Why hadn't he told her about this? Then again—she recalled that afternoon at Miss Clara's, and then just a while ago—her guess was that he'd tried.

"Come now, Dr. Whitcomb—" Davenport used a tone more suited for speaking to a child than to one's peer. "Don't tell us that you harbor a fear of physicians too."

Her laugh came out strangled. "No, not at all. I have the highest regard for physicians and the care they provide. In fact—" Her voice sounded overly loud in her head and she couldn't seem to gain a true sense of its volume. "Before leaving Georgia, I had an examination with my physician there and he pronounced me fit as a fiddle." Which was true—eight months prior. "So I promise you, students, there's nothing to fear."

"You see, children?" Davenport said, motioning in Molly's direction. "Your teacher isn't afraid of Dr. Brookston. Are you, Dr. Whitcomb?"

"Of course not." Smiling, she looked with confidence out over the crowd, connecting gazes with every child looking her way—and noticed that not one of them was Italian or Negro.

"And my guess is that you'd happily undergo an examination with Dr. Brookston if it will help your students to feel more comfortable. Am I right, *Dr. Whitcomb?*"

Molly looked back.

The challenge in Mayor Davenport's eyes was subtle but unmistakable, and she wondered if anyone else saw it. This was a form of payback. His way of putting her in her place. And there wasn't a thing in the world she could do about it. For the time being.

She tilted her head. "If it helps my students to feel more comfortable, I would be happy to undergo the same examination they'll receive."

One little girl on the front row—was her name Emily?—lifted her head and sniffed. Her eyes began to brighten. As did other children's around the room. The parents' expressions also reflected gratitude.

Dr. Brookston held up the black bag in his grip, and every boy and girl in the room seemed to hold their breath. "To all the children who will be students in Dr. Whitcomb's class this fall, I have something for you in my bag tonight. Is there a brave boy or girl among us who's willing to look inside and tell us what it is?"

The children stared, wide-eyed and unmoving, as though Dr. Brookston might not see them if they kept still enough.

On the left side, the fourth pew back, a little girl—dark-haired and dark-eyed, with a waifish look about her—peered out from behind someone. Molly didn't recognize her but couldn't help smiling. The girl responded by sliding off the pew and stepping into the aisle.

Dr. Brookston knelt where he stood, encouraging her without words.

The girl made it as far as the first pew, then froze. And looked at Molly.

Instinct kicked in and Molly walked toward her, hand extended. A hush fell over the crowd. Molly felt every eye on her and realized—too late—how risky a move she was making. What if the child rejected her offer of assistance? Or turned and ran back to her parents, crying?

The little girl stared up, dark eyes fathomless, then glanced behind her to a man Molly presumed was her father. Fearing the child was about to make a mad dash back to her father's arms, Molly prayed she wouldn't.

But then, as if on cue, the child faced her again and took hold of Molly's hand.

"Shall we go together?" Molly asked softly.

A single nod, and the girl's grip tightened.

They reached Dr. Brookston, who was still waiting on one knee, his smile patient, and Molly knelt to be at eye level with the little girl. "What's your name?" she whispered, not recognizing her as a member of any of the families she'd visited.

"Ansley," the girl whispered back. "Ansley Tucker."

Molly smiled again, hearing—and admiring—the brave determination in the girl's reed-thin voice. "Ansley, you have a beautiful name. Now, can you peek into Dr. Brookston's bag and tell the other boys and girls what he's brought for you all?"

Ansley slid a cautious gaze in Dr. Brookston's direction, then looked back at Molly.

"I'm right here with you," Molly encouraged. "I know you can do this."

Ansley inched closer to the medical bag and stood on tiptoe to see inside. Then beamed. "Stick candy!" she cried, and excitement rippled through the crowd.

Molly gave her a quick hug. "I'm very proud of you, Ansley."

"So am I," Dr. Brookston added, leaning forward. "And since you were so brave, you get to choose your piece of candy first."

Ansley reached forward, then stilled. "Can my brothers and sisters have one too?"

Dr. Brookston's expression softened. "Of course they can. We'll make sure of it."

By the time Ansley finished choosing, a line of children trailed behind her, and Molly introduced herself to each one—working to remember their names—as they chose a sugar stick from the doctor's bag. After the sixth child in line claimed the last name of Tucker, she began to question how many brothers and sisters Ansley had.

Molly mingled and chatted with parents, answering questions about lessons and about how a typical school day would progress, always aware of where James was in the crowd. Every time she looked his way, he was looking hers, which lit a spark inside her—much like his hugging her had done earlier. Except when he'd hugged her, it had felt like a thousand fireworks going off inside her at once. He'd taken her breath away. No. He *took* her breath away.

Gradually the crowd began to dwindle, and she was thankful. The week's events were catching up with her.

She felt someone's attention and turned to find Mayor Davenport and Brandon Tolliver staring at her from across the room. Davenport said something she couldn't hear, and both men laughed. But neither of their smiles fell within the definition of friendly. She read warning in Davenport's expression, and something else entirely different—and uninvited—in Tolliver's. And she determined, as much as possible, to steer clear of both men.

"Well done, Dr. Whitcomb." Dr. Brookston appeared on her left, holding out a piece of stick candy. "I believe you've earned this."

She took the sugary treat and offered a slight curtsey, cautious not of the man but of his profession. "Thank you, Dr. Brookston. That was nothing short of brilliant on your part."

He shrugged off the compliment. "One of the best pieces of advice I received in medical school was from a nurse. She told me to try my best to crawl inside the skin of my patients and see things from their perspective." He made a face. "A gruesome-sounding prospect, I realize. But that counsel, more than any other, has helped me to be more empathetic. To see the world through the eyes of those I'm treating. Because only then," he said, sounding now as though he were quoting, "will I ever be able to understand their apprehensions and fears." He held up a piece of candy. "And their proper motivations."

Molly liked him instantly and heard in his voice—as she did in James's—a trace of the South. Had all of the honorable Southern gentlemen fled west after the war? She was starting to believe it.

"I have some openings this week"—Dr. Brookston adopted a more professional tone—"for your examination, if your schedule permits."

"I believe that would work . . . ." Molly acted as though she were mentally checking her appointment book. She had given her word on having the examination and would follow through. But she planned on delaying it as long as possible. Then again—considering her thickening waistline—having the examination sooner rather than later might be the better option.

"I can vouch for his services, ma'am," James said, walking up with Kurt fast asleep on his shoulder. "But I must say, Dr. Brookston, that I'm a little disappointed you didn't offer *me* candy when I was in your office earlier this week."

Laughing, Brookston tossed a sugar stick at him. James caught it one-handed and popped it in his mouth.

Grateful for James's shifting the focus from her, Molly didn't have any trouble imagining both of these men in childhood years, tromping to their respective creeks, fishing poles in hand, and pockets stuffed with worms.

Dr. Brookston raised his candy in mock salute. "If you'll both excuse me, please, I need to catch some families before they leave. Dr. Whitcomb, it was a pleasure to finally meet you."

"You as well, Doctor." Watching him go, she worked to suppress a yawn.

James shifted Kurt's weight in his arms. "I need to see Rachel and the boys home directly. It's past the boys' bedtimes."

Molly patted Kurt's back. "Yes, I can see that. And it's past mine too!"

He smiled. "Rachel's still outside, visiting with a friend. Mitch is with her. But . . . I'd be honored to see you home first, if you're ready to go. Since it's dark out."

Molly glanced at the open window. Sure enough, the sun had long since set. "I'd appreciate your escort, Sheriff. Thank you."

As they walked, she swirled the stick candy between her lips. Grape. Her favorite. "Something I've been meaning to ask you . . . Where might I buy a horse other than from Mr. Atwood at the livery?"

"Didn't care for Mr. Atwood, did you?"

"It's not that. Well . . . not entirely. Let's just say I

wasn't impressed with a certain *offer* he made me."

"Fair enough. I'll have him arrested first thing in the morning."

She laughed, knowing he was kidding yet enjoying the seriousness in his tone. She could barely make out his dark outline beside her, and that of Kurt's sleeping form cuddled against his chest. It was a touching picture, and one she tucked away for later.

The cabin loomed ahead, lightless and uninviting. She appreciated the cabin's seclusion and the quiet it offered, but sometimes she wished it were closer to town.

"I'll check with a couple of ranchers in town. Rachel might be interested in selling a horse too. I could ask her, if you'd like."

"Yes, please." Though slightly embarrassed to broach the next subject, Molly needed to know. "I realize I haven't been here long, James, and that I haven't started teaching yet, but my funds are fairly limited, and I'm wondering whe—"

"When you're going to be paid." He sighed. "I'm sorry. Some kind of go-between I am. An account's been set up for you at the bank here in town. Your first month's salary, plus some extra for moving expenses, according to the agreement, should have been deposited into your account this week. If the money's not there, let me know and I'll track it down for you."

"I'll do that. Thank you."

They paused at the bottom of the porch stairs. "Why don't you go on inside, get a lamp lit. I'll wait here."

"You just read my mind, thank you."

Holding the stick candy between her front teeth, she fumbled to get her key into the lock, finally managed it, and lit the lamp she'd left on the kitchen table. Feeling braver knowing James was outside, she made a quick check of the cabin, unable to account for her reluctance but feeling better once she discovered everything was as she'd left it.

Candy in one hand and lamp in the other, she walked back to the porch.

"All okay?" he asked.

"Yes, everything's fine. Thank you for waiting, and for seeing me home."

The way he stood there, one boot poised on the bottom stair, his nephew snuggled dead-to-the-world against him, and with that silly sugar stick between his lips, she found herself more than a little attracted to the man.

He slipped the candy from his mouth. "You did good tonight, Molly. Up there in front of every-body. Especially when Davenport put you on the spot like that."

She balanced the oil lamp on the porch railing. "You noticed?"

He nodded. "But only because I know him so well. I doubt anyone else did."

"He was paying me back."

"Yes, he was." He smiled. "But that only proves you got him good and flustered the day he was out here."

"The day I scared the livin' daylights outta you?" She laughed.

"Yes, ma'am," he whispered. "That's the day I'm thinking of." Kurt sighed and his little head dipped forward. James eased it back to his shoulder. "I need to get this tired little bronco on home." He kissed the top of the boy's head.

Molly watched him, having no business imagining what she was imagining at that moment, which was what it would be like to kiss this man, and to have him kiss her, to be the object of his desire. And even more, to be worthy of it. But some things, once gone, couldn't be regained.

The secret nestled inside her—its tiny heart beating as surely as hers was now, though she couldn't feel it yet—would soon be making its presence known. *God help me in that moment. And in this one now. . . .*

James moved up a step, surprising her, his expression reminiscent of the little boy in his arms. "Rachel and I used to do something as kids." He held out his sugar stick.

Molly stared, not following.

"Hold yours out," he said softly.

She did and he touched the end of his to hers. Once, twice.

She giggled, feeling like a child. "What does this mean?"

"You might say it's a kind of *toast,* I guess. When Rachel and I were little, we crept downstairs one night to spy on a fancy party our parents were hosting. All the grown-ups were in their finery, raising their glasses in a toast, and Rachel wanted to do it too. But I knew my father would tan our backsides—mine especially—if he caught us out of bed. Much less if we got into the champagne at that age." He shook his head. "But Rachel had her heart set on taking part in the evening. So . . ." He sighed. "I snuck down real careful-like, crawled beneath the dining room table, and waited for just the right minute—then snatched something off the dessert tray and hightailed it back upstairs. We toasted with that instead."

Molly smiled. "What did you take from the tray?"

He looked down, scuffing the wooden plank with the toe of his boot. "Couple of ladyfingers."

She laughed, picturing the scene. *Oh, this man . . .*

He laughed along with her, and then the quiet of night slowly crept back around them. The singsong trickle of the stream behind the cabin filled the silence.

James touched his sugar stick to hers again and held it there. "I'd like to raise a toast to you, Molly Whitcomb. For your bravery in coming west when you could've stayed right where you were and had a fine, safe life."

Sincerity deepened his gaze, and Molly told herself not to cry.

"For all the pain you've endured in recent months—the loss of your father, and of . . . your husband. And for all the joy I pray that your future holds."

A tear slipped down her cheek. If only she'd known James McPherson had been waiting in her future, she would have chosen differently. Then again, would he have been in her future had she not made such a poor choice to begin with?

He held her gaze. "And for the difference you're already making in this town. In the lives of its children and their parents. And in the lives of so many others."

Wordlessly, he slipped the candy back into his mouth, tugged the brim of his hat, and turned to walk away.

Molly watched his shadowed form until she couldn't distinguish it from the darkness, then went inside, closed the door behind her and locked it, and walked into the bedroom. With a quick breath, she snuffed out the flickering flame of the oil lamp, and crawled beneath the chilled covers.

She searched the darkness, shivering. "Heavenly Father, why am I here?" *Why did you bring me here?* Her coming to Timber Ridge had been more of a punishment than a choice. But since the first day she arrived, she'd felt more blessed than cursed. And she hadn't been able to figure out what God was doing. . . .

Until a moment ago.

God was meting out justice, teaching her a lesson. Only, she hadn't expected Him to do it in such a cruel and teasing way. A sob wrenched up from somewhere deep inside her.

She turned onto her side and stared through the window at the thumbnail moon. A pain, sharp-edged and strong-willed, throbbed hot inside her chest, and she wrapped her arms around herself and her unborn child.

Not only was she bearing the consequence of having given herself to a man who wasn't her husband, but she was being made to witness what her life might have been like had she not chosen so poorly. The cruel irony of that thought caught like a rusty nail over silk and tore at something deep inside her.

It wasn't simply that the consequence of sin was causing such pain in her life, as costly as that was and would be. It was what sin robbed from her future—the possibility of who she might have become, and of what she might have done with her life—that made sin so heinous.

It was funny, in a brutal sort of way. . . . The characteristics that attracted her to James—his integrity, his honor, his unwavering sense of duty—were the very traits that would prevent him from ever really caring about her once he saw her for who she really was.

But apparently that was God's punishment for her sin. If so, He'd hit His mark.

18

Molly could hardly believe the morning had finally arrived—the first day of school.

She peered out the window of the cabin. The palest hint of pink tinged the dark eastern horizon. Apparently the sun was still contemplating whether or not to awaken. But Molly had hardly been able to sleep for her excitement. Already, she was up and dressed with her satchel packed and ready by the door.

And yet along with her excitement was woven a strand of uncertainty.

She stepped outside and drew in a breath of cool mountain air. Her lungs tingled with the chill of it, and she tasted a hint of approaching fall—that sweet, sometimes elusive promise of leaves turning crimson and gold, and of nature stripping branches bare to reveal the intricacies of God's handiwork beneath.

Hidden somewhere high above her in the trees, a bird warbled a tune as though he'd been saving up for days. Surely he'd have to stop for breath soon.

Despite her past experience with teaching children, she pledged again to do everything she could to make Timber Ridge's school a success. And not just a success—she would make it the best it could be. The rustle of leaves drew her gaze to the bottom porch step and she pictured James standing there, sugar stick in hand.

She'd only seen him in passing since that evening of the town council meeting.

Something had definitely changed between them, though she couldn't rightly put it into words. It was as if they shared a secret. A secret paid homage to only with glances and smiles.

If she'd had any question about her attraction to him, it had been answered that evening with his "toast." Simply thinking about how he'd looked at her made her heart do an odd stuttered skip, and made her more determined than ever to remain "only" friends.

She'd stopped by Dr. Brookston's clinic last week, and—to her partial relief—he hadn't been in. She'd left a note so he would know she'd made the effort. With her waist and middle thickening by the day, it felt like, it would be best to get the examination completed before letting too many more days pass.

The whistle of the teakettle called her back inside, and she divided the boiling water between a pot of oatmeal and a cup containing the last of her tea leaves. Her stomach growling, she dropped the last bit of butter into the oatmeal and watched it melt. She hadn't experienced morning sickness in several days. Perhaps she was beyond that now.

She'd awakened with the sniffles and a tickle in her throat, but a warm breakfast should see to that. She hoped each of her students was having a good breakfast, but recalling two or three of the houses—or shacks, as they were—that her students called home, she realized that was unlikely.

Angelo Giordano.

The boy's face appeared clearly in her memory. She'd thought of him numerous times in recent days, and intended on visiting him, as promised. The next time she saw James, she would inquire as to whether or not a job had panned out for the boy.

She sat down at the table, the aroma of oatmeal and cinnamon wafting together with the crisp scent of steeping peppermint tea. She bowed her head and stared through the steam rising from her bowl, thankful for so many things. And yet feeling so very far away from the One to whom she needed—and wanted—to offer her thanks. She slowly lifted her head and looked around the room, waiting, listening. For what, exactly, she wasn't sure.

Ever since the night of the town council meeting, after James walked her home, she'd felt as though she and God were at an impasse. As if both of them were waiting for the other to take the first step. Deep down, she knew what He wanted her to do. But what He wanted was asking too much.

How could she be expected to start over, to have any kind of future for her baby, and herself, if everyone in Timber Ridge knew the truth about her past?

She skimmed her spoon over the top of her oatmeal, then took a bite, and another. It warmed a path down her throat and into her belly. And with deliberate effort, she steered her thoughts toward the day ahead.

She had no doubt she could teach Timber Ridge's children. She'd been trained in studies far more rigorous than anything she would be called on to teach in a one-room schoolhouse. She'd taught college students, for heaven's sake, and had been challenged by them in class—intelligent young men and women only slightly younger than she, who were more advanced academically than any of the students who would fill the seats in that schoolhouse today.

So why was she so nervous?

After breakfast, she straightened the cabin, made her lunch, checked her lesson notes for the fourth time, and then began the brief walk to the schoolhouse. The sun had barely risen, and still an hour remained before she would ring the bell for the first time, officially signaling the start to the Timber Ridge school year.

Evergreens partially shielded the schoolhouse from view from the front of the cabin. So it wasn't until she was well on the path that she made out the structure, sitting quiet and still in the field. The tranquility of its walls would be laid waste in no time.

A light fog hovered over the lake and extended across the field. She cut a path through it, feeling the cool moisture on her face. Thirty-four students had enrolled. Not every child in Timber Ridge, but nearly. James relayed to her that the town council was pleased, which was enough to please her.

She pulled her shawl closer about her shoulders, wondering if she should have asked Josiah to build a fire in the stove. If she could figure out how to work the contraption, she'd build it herself.

As she drew nearer the schoolhouse, she detected the faint murmur of voices, but saw no one. The clomping of horses' hooves and distinctive rumble of wagon wheels drew her attention. A wagon rounded the bend, still some distance away, its passengers masked by the silver veil of first light. Who would be arriving so early?

Molly turned the corner of the schoolhouse and came to a standstill.

"Mornin', teacher," little Ansley Tucker said, bunched together with her brothers and sisters. "Pa got us here early."

"We ain't wantin' to be late, ma'am." A little towheaded boy tucked beside Ansley wore thin trousers with a holey jacket and wagged his head when he spoke. "We's supposed to help and be good, Mama says."

Their father, Mathias Tucker, who had accompanied his children, stepped forward, removing his hat. "Morning, Mrs. Whitcomb. My wife and our children had the pleasure of your company at home last week, but I missed out on account of being out in the field."

"Yes, Mr. Tucker." Molly smiled at his children. "Pleasure to see you again, sir."

"The children have been up and dressed since before dawn. They're nigh on to busting to start their learning with you, ma'am. It's a good thing you've done, coming all the way out here to teach our young ones."

"It's an honor and a privilege for me to do this, Mr. Tucker. I assure you."

"Dr. Whitcomb!"

She turned to see Mitchell and Kurt Boyd waving from the back of the wagon as Rachel guided the team into the school yard. Rachel smiled in greeting, with a woman Molly didn't recognize seated beside her.

Another wagon appeared at the end of the road, followed by two older children covering the distance afoot. Molly smiled to herself. Seems she wasn't too early after all.

She made her way toward Rachel's wagon.

"Dr. Whitcomb," Rachel said with a formality Molly knew was for the benefit of little ears. "I'd like to introduce Mrs. Elizabeth Ranslett. Mrs. Ranslett, this is our new schoolteacher, Dr. Molly Whitcomb."

Molly couldn't help herself. She'd been waiting for this moment. "Mrs. Ranslett, it's such an honor to make your acquaintance. Your article, the one in a recent issue of *Harper's Weekly,* was such an inspiration to me. I read it, and reread it, on my journey to Timber Ridge. Reading the story of how you came here, your adventures, your love for this land—I found it all very . . . compelling."

"Compelling," Elizabeth Ranslett repeated, smiling. "Now there's a word I like. And thank you for your compliments, Dr. Whitcomb. They mean a great deal. As does your coming to Timber Ridge. I've been excited to meet you as well."

Rachel set the brake on the wagon and climbed down. "Elizabeth's father is the generous party responsible for coordinating the donation of all the supplies and furniture for the school. And Elizabeth has a special surprise. . . ." She gave Mrs. Ranslett a knowing look.

"If you don't mind, Dr. Whitcomb, I'd like to take a photograph of you and your students some-time today. I'll make copies for you and each family represented in the school." A sheepish smile lit her face. "As well as for my father, who's been eagerly awaiting this day."

"The students and I would be honored, Mrs. Ranslett. Thank you." Molly gestured for them to follow. "Please, won't you join us inside for a minute? I'd love for you to see the schoolroom. . . ." She grinned, lowering her voice. "Before it gets 'lived in.' "

Molly was reaching for the bell to ring the first

day of the Timber Ridge School to order when the gentle thunder of horses' hooves stayed her hand.

A group of men on horseback made their way up the road, and she recognized the man at the forefront. James rode with authority and presence worthy of his office. Mayor Davenport and Hank Bolden rode behind him, along with other men she recognized from the town council. They hadn't said anything about coming, but she should've known Mayor Davenport would insist on being present.

The mayor reined in and dismounted. "Good morning, Dr. Whitcomb. I hope we're not too late."

"No, sir. You're not late at all. We were just about to begin the school day." Molly felt James's attention and gave him a subtle look.

Sidestepping students, Davenport worked his way up the stairs and moved to stand by the bell. "Shall I do the honors on behalf of the town council, which brought you here to Timber Ridge, Dr. Whitcomb? Or would you like to?"

It was silly, she knew, but she'd been looking forward to ringing that bell all week. But doing so would come at a cost. "By all means, sir, you do the honors."

Mayor Davenport pulled the rope, and the bell pealed a clear, clarion tone that carried across the field and that no doubt could be heard in town. A chorus of cheers broke out, and Molly felt a rush of readiness. She still wasn't at peace with why God had brought her to Timber Ridge, but she knew she was ready to teach its children.

Mayor Davenport stepped forward to open the door, but James blocked his path. "Dr. Whitcomb," James said softly. "After you, ma'am."

Not missing Davenport's glower, Molly took James's lead and reached for the door latch, knowing she would remember everything about this moment. The chilly morning air, the sunshine on her back, the eager looks on each child's face, and the sense of anticipation and fresh beginnings. If only the latter could be true for her. But in a way it was.

That day on the cliff, when the ravine opened wide beneath her, she'd been certain that she would die. But she hadn't. God had spared her life. But for what purpose?

She thought of the baby inside her, and of James standing beside her. Certain opportunities were closed to her now; that much was clear. But a voice inside whispered that other opportunities might be waiting. Perhaps ones she hadn't yet thought of. She opened the door, praying that would be true.

A warm wave of air greeted her, and she spotted Josiah Birch kneeling by the stove. As the crowd of students and parents filed in behind her, she went to greet him.

"Mr. Birch, you must have read my mind. I was thinking on my walk here that a fire would serve us well this morning."

His grin was at the ready. "I's thinkin' the very same thing when I got up this mornin' and felt the shiver in the air, Dr. Whitcomb, ma'am." He reached for his slouch hat on the floor where he'd been crouched. "I'll be back this afternoon to make sure she's out for the night."

"Oh, I'm sure I can—"

"Don't want you to worry none 'bout havin' to see to it. It be my pleasure, ma'am."

This man's kindness seemed without limit. Especially considering his own son wasn't counted among the students. "Would you be willing to do a favor for me, Mr. Birch?"

"I reckon. If it don't get me in trouble with our sheriff over there."

Molly turned to see James watching them and smiled. "No problems with the sheriff, I promise." She crossed to a bookshelf where she'd added her personal volumes and withdrew one. "Here . . ." She held it out to Josiah. "I'd appreciate it if you'd share this with Elijah. It's an intriguing read, and one I think he'll enjoy. Then"—she tried for a casual tone—"if he'd like to discuss it when he's done, I'd welcome that opportunity."

Josiah looked at the book, then at her, and slowly shook his head. "I's thinkin' it'd be best, ma'am, if you'd just—"

"But, Mr. Birch, I truly believe that Elijah would enjoy—"

"Dr. Whitcomb."

Molly felt a hand on her arm and heard the gentle warning in James's voice. She nodded. "Very well, Mr. Birch. It is your decision, after all. I'm sorry to have pushed you on the subject."

Josiah stepped closer and ran his thick, scarred fingers over the top of the book. "What I's gonna say a minute ago, ma'am, was that it'd be best if you was to take this book to Elijah yourself. He'd like it a heap more comin' from your own hand."

Later that morning, after parents and town council members had taken their leave, and after Elizabeth Ranslett captured a photograph of Molly and the students, Molly stood in front of the classroom, her lesson notes neatly arranged in front of her on her desk. She picked up her roll book. "Each morning, students, I'll begin by taking roll. When I call on you, I'd like for you to respond by saying—" Where was her pencil? She'd just had it.

Unable to find it, she opened her desk drawer to get another—and let out a squeal! She jumped back, heart thudding.

Laughter erupted in the classroom, and children rose from their seats to come forward.

"Please, stay in your seats, students." She made a conscious effort to lower her voice. "Don't be alarmed. There's simply a—" she swallowed, fighting a shudder—"a mouse . . . in my desk drawer." That wasn't moving.

"A mouse?" Zachary Tucker strained to see from

his first-row seat. "All that screamin' over a mouse, teacher?"

A fresh wave of giggles swept the class.

Molly squared her shoulders. "I was simply taken by surprise, that's all." She looked closer at the vermin, unable to decide whether it was deaf or deceased. With all the commotion and still no reaction, she guessed the latter. But how to get it out of her drawer? And even more worrisome, how did it get in there!

"Want me to fetch it out for you, teacher?"

She looked up to see sweet Mason Tucker raising his hand. "Yes, Mason, I would—" Right behind Mason sat Kurt Boyd, whose smile seemed to hold a trace more exuberance than the other children's. Or did it? She couldn't be sure. But since Kurt was Rachel's son, and *the sheriff's* nephew, and for a host of other reasons, she decided not to pursue it. "Yes, Mason. I would appreciate if you'd dispose of it for me. And please take time to wash your hands at the stream."

By the time Mason returned, Molly had regained her composure. She took roll and stood in front of her desk to address the class. "Before we begin our lessons this morning, students, I'd like to know a little bit about each of you." She usually asked her college students to take out a sheet of paper and write down their favorite book, era in world history, and what U.S. president—alive or deceased—they would most like to spend one hour with. She found it told her a great deal about them as a person, and also about where they were in their studies.

Her question for these students would be somewhat different.

"I'd like for each of you to tell the class what your best day this summer has been, and what made that day so special. I'd appreciate your standing by your desk when you address the class, and please remember to give your name." Some of the collegiate practices would translate well, even in Timber Ridge.

Wide-eyed with lips in firm lines, the children stared.

Mitchell's hand crept up. "Is this a test, Dr. Whitcomb?"

Molly curbed a grin. "No, Mitchell, it's not a test. This is an exercise to help me get to know each of you better." She approached his desk. "Why don't you start for us? Can you tell me what your best day this summer has been? And what made that day so special?"

Clarity lit Mitchell's face, yet he said nothing.

"And let me remind you, students," Molly added, sensing his apprehension to share, "that there is no wrong answer to this question. Each answer will be right and for each student who answers, I'll draw a star by their name in my grade book." She retrieved the book from her desk, along with a freshly sharpened pencil, and turning back, noticed the students sitting up a little straighter.

Mitch raised his hand and stood by his desk. "My name is Mitchell Boyd, and my favorite day this summer was when my uncle James took me hunting with him. Just me and him alone . . . over on Crawley's Ridge."

Kurt's hand shot up one row over.

Mitch looked at his brother. "He took my brother with him too, later. They went on their own trip."

Apparently satisfied, Kurt lowered his hand, and Molly could already guess what his favorite day was going to be.

"And why was this day so special to you, Mitchell?"

The boy started to answer, then stopped. He fingered the side seam of his pants, and his chest rose and fell with exaggeration. "It was special because . . . we went back to the spot where . . . where they found my pa—" The boy's voice broke. "At the place where the bear got him."

Molly's throat tightened. She looked around the room. Not a single child's expression revealed surprise. And then it slowly made sense. Timber Ridge was a small community. She'd already witnessed how quickly news traveled. Each child already knew what had happened to Mitchell and Kurt Boyd's father.

"My uncle James, he's the sheriff," Mitch continued, pride in his voice. "He and I camped up there for a night. We caught us a rabbit and roasted it like he and my uncle Daniel did when they were boys. Then Uncle James told me all the stories he could remember about my pa. He met my pa when he wasn't much older than me, so he knows lots of them. My pa was funny, especially when he was my age." Mitch managed a smile as he took his seat. "That was my best day, ma'am."

Molly looked down to draw a star by Mitch's name, and the names of the children blurred on the page. "Well done, Mitchell Boyd," she said softly, taking her time before speaking again. In the margin, she simply wrote *James, where pa died,* so she would remember what Mitchell shared—as though she could forget. She tried to push aside the image of what finding Thomas Boyd on that ridge must have been like. And of how it must have been for Rachel discovering how her husband had died. She cleared her throat. "Now, who would like to go next?"

Half of the children raised their hands. Molly made eye contact with one of the girls and nodded. The girl rose from her seat.

"My name is Emily Thompson, and my best day was when Mama and I made peach preserves. I got to stir and add the sugar just like she did with my grandma when Mama was my age. When we got done and the pot was cooled, we sat on the porch and licked the pot clean. We didn't use spoons or anything, just our fingers. My mama never lets us do that." The girl grinned. "That was my best day, teacher."

Molly wrote *peach preserves with mama* in the side margin, then drew a star, almost able to taste the syrupy sweet peaches, and remembering a similar day with her own mother, a memory that felt as if it were a lifetime ago.

Another student raised his hand, then stood. "My name is Billy Bolden, and my favorite day this summer was when I got shot out of a cannon and was sent to the moon." He smiled, his brown eyes sparkling.

Having met with Billy and his mother in their home last week, Molly still couldn't believe that he was the son of Hank Bolden, the shopkeeper who was so cruel to Angelo. She had been thankful Mr. Bolden wasn't home at the time of her visit. Billy was fair-haired and of thinner build than his father, and held not a hint of the same harshness.

Molly eyed him, already having an idea of what his "favorite day" referred to. "And tell us, Billy Bolden, why did you enjoy reading the book *From the Earth to the Moon*?"

His brow rose. "You know it, Dr. Whitcomb?"

She nodded. "I've read it twice. Have you read *Twenty Thousand Leagues Under the Sea* by the same author?" At the shake of his head, she smiled. "Then you indeed have a treat awaiting." She wrote *books, Jules Verne* by Billy's name. "See me after class and I'll share my personal copy with you."

"Yes, ma'am! Thank you, Dr. Whitcomb."

The exercise took longer than Molly had planned, but by the time each child shared their special memory, she felt as though she truly knew them better, and their families. In many ways, these children already knew more about life—real life—than had her college students.

"Thank you, children, for sharing. Now—" She checked her father's pocket watch that lay on her desk. "We have about a half hour before lunch recess, so I'd like to—"

Ansley Tucker raised her hand.

"Yes, Ansley?"

"You haven't told us about your favorite day, teacher."

As though they'd rehearsed it, the rest of the students nodded in unison, their attention focused on the front of the room.

Molly walked to the front of her desk, trying to decide what she would share—when her mind went to one specific moment. She phrased it with purpose. "My name is Dr. Whitcomb—" she waited until the giggles subsided—"and my best day this summer was . . . when the stagecoach I was riding in on the way up to Timber Ridge nearly went off the mountain."

Gasps filled the room and little jaws gaped, as she'd expected.

Kurt shot up by his desk. "It did too! She coulda died. Everybody coulda died. Uncle James said so."

"Thank you, Kurt." Molly motioned for him to be seated. "But please remember to raise your hand and wait for me to call on you before speaking."

He nodded and sat, his enthusiasm seemingly unfazed by the correction.

"It had been raining that day," Molly continued. "The roads were muddy and the carriage slipped going uphill." She decided to forego the terrifying details. "It turned over and nearly slid off the side of the mountain."

Kurt's hand shot up again, but Molly shook her head. With a pained expression, he lowered his arm.

"As I was in the coach, hanging there on the edge of that cliff, I stared down into the ravine and thought about what my life had been like up to that point." How to phrase it in a way these children would understand, and in a way that they might perhaps glean something from her mistakes. "And I decided that if I lived, I wanted to do better. I wanted to make better choices with my life."

Mostly blank looks stared back—except for a handful of the older children. She hoped the older ones were grasping some of what she was saying, at least. "I realize how much older I am than all of you, but I wish I could convey to you how quickly the years will pass." She shook her head, still able to feel what it had been like to be their age, having no idea what the world held—both for the good, and bad. "I decided that afternoon that I wanted to make more of a lasting difference in this world than I had in the past. So I—"

She felt an uncomfortable prick of tears and cleared her throat, aware of something deep inside her, curled tight in a ball, slowly beginning to unfurl. Nothing in the room changed. And yet something did. "And so I asked God to give me another chance." She took a breath. "And He did," she whispered, hoping He was listening, not only to her words but to what was inside her heart that words had failed to capture in recent weeks. "With all of you." And with the child hidden inside her womb.

In the freshly washed faces of her students, she saw a hunger for knowledge she longed to fill. Her position as professor at Franklin College had held considerably more prestige, but she had an inkling that being schoolteacher of Timber Ridge might prove even more rewarding.

19

Teaching children hadn't worked the first time; why on earth had she thought this experience would be any different? Molly checked her pocket watch again. Another hour until she could dismiss school. It felt like an eternity. Her head throbbed. Her lower back ached.

With each passing day that week, she'd felt progressively worse. Thank goodness it was Friday. For the third time that afternoon, she rapped the ruler on the side of her desk, barely able to hear it above the din of high-pitched voices.

She felt a tug on her skirt.

Tears rimmed little Ansley Tucker's eyes. "I don't understand this, teacher." She held up her slate.

"That's okay, honey. I'll explain it again in just a—" Molly looked up in time to see Kurt lift the globe from its stand on the back table and bend low, as though he were going to roll it down the aisle. "Kurt Boyd!" she said, louder than intended. Ansley shrank back. "No, no, sweetie, you're all right." Molly patted the girl's shoulder and headed to deal with Kurt.

The boy straightened as she came closer and tucked the globe under one arm. "I was just going to—"

"I know what you were 'just going to do,' young man." She rescued the globe from his clutches. As cute as Kurt was, he was proving to be a pistol in class. His brother, Mitch, was the complete opposite—studious, well behaved, finishing his work in a timely manner and asking for more. "Kurt, I want you to be seated, and I don't want you to get up again until I give you permission. Do you understand me?"

"Yes, ma'am, Dr. Whitcomb." He plopped down, but his tone smacked more of placation than penance.

"Teacher, I'm done with this." Zachary Tucker held out his slate. "This was easy. Can I have something else?"

Molly massaged her right temple. The past five days of teaching made the language classes she taught at Franklin College seem like a summer vacation. The constant chatter, the questions, the disruptions. She couldn't wait to get back to her cabin, to stillness and quiet. The popular saying "Silence is golden" had taken on a whole new meaning.

"Teacher, I need permission to use the privy, please. Time is of the essence!"

Molly turned to see thirteen-year-old Amanda Spivey looking as if she needed a fainting couch. She appreciated the girl's manners but not her flair for the dramatic. Amanda was a hard worker but was average in her marks, and had so far shown none of the propensity toward "extreme gifted-ness" that her mother, LuEllen Spivey, had insisted her daughter possessed.

Molly gestured. "Permission granted, Amanda."

"But I'm scared! I saw a snake out there last time. And I loathe snakes with a vengeance, teacher!"

Kurt jumped up from his desk. "I *like* snakes!"

Molly stared him down until he plunked back into his seat, then she rubbed her forehead, the area behind her eyes aching. Maybe she was just over-tired or had spent too much time writing in recent evenings. She'd been so touched by what the students had shared on Monday about their best days of summer that she'd written each of their parents a note, sharing the gist of what their child had said and telling them how much she appreciated being their child's teacher.

Her gaze traveled the room. Perhaps that had been a premature move on her part. She felt another sneeze coming on but fought the urge.

"Teacher, does your head hurt?" Amanda peered up, her face a stage mask of sympathy. "Because when my mama does that, it's because her head's hurtin' something awful. Right now my head is hurtin' too, teacher. Really bad. And I still desperately need to . . ."

Molly closed her eyes, not exactly certain when she'd lost control. But lost control she had. And she needed to get it back before a parent—or worse, a council member—stopped by to see how the week had progressed.

What if one of the children went home and told their parents how unruly recent days had been? Especially this one. If Hank Bolden found out, he would go straight to Mayor Davenport, and that would be the end for her.

She took a deep breath, her temper teetering on the edge. "Children, I need your attention, please."

Only a handful responded. She obviously hadn't spoken loudly enough.

"Children! Give me your *attention!"*

The room stilled. Children froze as if time had stopped and rendered them immobile.

Molly swallowed, willing calm. Her throat hurt more now than it had that morning. "Rebecca Taylor, would you please accompany Amanda Spivey to the privy?"

The older girl nodded and put down her book. "Yes, ma'am."

"Everyone else, I want you in your seats. Immediately!" She smiled at Ansley Tucker to soften the command. But the girl's tears flowed anyway.

Molly walked the short distance to her desk. She had her doctorate in language studies. She could speak three foreign languages fluently. She had chaired committees with senior members twice her age, earning her colleagues' respect. From most of them, anyway.

So why couldn't she handle a roomful of children?

This experience was turning out to be worse than her first. Her first class consisted of nine students. She'd been sixteen at the time and full of energy. Now she was thirty-one, unmarried and expecting a child, and could easily put her head on her desk and be asleep within seconds.

She sank down in her desk chair, breaking one of President Northrop's cardinal rules. He had strict guidelines against a professor sitting when they addressed a classroom. But this was her classroom, not Northrop's. And it wasn't as if she hadn't already broken about every one of his cardinal rules anyway.

"Students, thank you for giving me your attention. We're nearly through our first week of school"—*Thank you, Lord*—"and I appreciate those of you who have listened and worked hard these past few days." She looked at every child she considered part of that group—and rewarded them with a smile. "To those who have not listened and who have not given their best effort—" Starting with Kurt Boyd, she addressed the other children. "I will not tolerate disruptive behavior in my classroom. The town council brought me to Timber Ridge to teach. However, if some of you choose not to develop an attitude of learning, then I'll be forced to speak with your parents, and together we'll see if we can't arrive at some . . . motivation that will encourage you to come to school with a readiness to learn. Do I make myself clear?"

"Yes, Dr. Whitcomb," a few of the children muttered.

"Do I make myself clear?" Molly repeated with more boldness.

"Yes, Dr. Whitcomb," they all said in unison.

"Thank you. And now, students, you are—" She sneezed, and the throbbing in her head pounded harder. Pulling a handkerchief from her sleeve, she saw the book for Elijah still occupying the edge of

261

her desk—something else she'd intended to do this week and hadn't yet. *Just add it to the list.*

She sniffled. "You are dismissed."

Achy, fighting chills, and glad the week was nearly over, Molly opened the door to the newspaper office, peering through the front window as she went. A bell jingled overhead. She didn't want another day to go by without sharing this book with Elijah Birch, especially considering that Josiah might have mentioned it to his son and that Elijah might be anticipating her visit.

The office appeared to be empty, yet the door had been unlocked. "Hello?" Feeling another sneeze coming on, she held her breath until the sensation passed. "Is anyone here?"

It wasn't overly cool inside, but she pulled her shawl tighter about her shoulders, warding off a shiver. This had to be a cold she was getting—as if she had time for such a thing. She would stop by the store on her way home and get another tin of chamomile tea. A cup of hot tea and a quiet weekend buried beneath a mound of covers sounded like heaven about now.

She was turning to leave when the door at the back of the office opened.

Elijah walked in carrying a box. He glanced up. "Dr. Whitcomb! I'm sorry, I didn't hear you come in, ma'am." He set the box aside. "Is there something I can help you with?"

"Good afternoon, Elijah." She scanned the office. "Are you minding the shop by yourself today?"

"Yes, ma'am. Mrs. Ranslett—she's the editor— she and her husband live a ways from town, so she only comes in three days a week. If there's something I can do for you, I'd be pleased to."

"Actually, it's you I came to see." Molly pulled the book from the teaching satchel slung over one shoulder. "I have something for you." She turned the book toward him. "Have you ever had the opportunity to read this?"

His brow furrowed. "No, ma'am, Dr. Whitcomb. I never even heard of it before."

"It's by a Frenchman. He writes stories that stretch the imagination, and this is one of my favorites. If you like it, I have others I'd be willing to share."

She held it out, but he only stared, not taking it.

"You want to share your book with me, ma'am?"

"Yes, Elijah, I do. You can keep it for as long as you like—and once you're done, I'd like to discuss it with you. Hear your opinions on the author's ideas. See if you think what he's proposing is possible or not. But only if you'd like to, of course. I'll leave that up to you."

"Oh yes, ma'am, I'd like to read it *and* talk with you about it, but . . . maybe I should ask my father first."

Like father like son. Such integrity for a boy his

age. "I've already asked your father, and he said it was fine with him. He suggested I give you the book myself."

Slowly, Elijah took the bound volume and turned it over in his hands. "Thank you, Dr. Whitcomb. I'll take good care of it, ma'am. And about what you said at Miss Clara's. About me attending your school . . ." Understanding far beyond the boy's years moved into his expression. "I appreciate the thought behind that, just the same."

His acceptance tugged at her heartstrings, and as she continued on to the store, Molly wished again that circumstances were different.

She prayed that life would be kind to Elijah Birch, that the people of Timber Ridge would come to see him for who he really was, and that God would use her, in whatever way He saw fit, to help bring that about.

"Did you actually *see* the mountain lion?" James studied Arlin Spivey's expression, wanting to make sure the man had actually seen something and wasn't merely jumping to conclusions. Secretly, he hoped it *was* a mountain lion that had gotten Spivey's calf. Better that than what the evidence pointed to.

"It was dark and I didn't see it happen outright, Sheriff, but I've seen a cougar's damage before. I heard the calf bawlin', and by the time I made it out here to the corral, the calf was gone. Cougar must've drug it across the field and into the brush over there. Come daylight is when I saw the mess in the brush. I only mentioned it to your deputy here in passing yesterday afternoon." Spivey nodded to Willis, who stood nearby. "Didn't mean for him to bring you all the way out here on a Saturday morning. It was just a cougar." Spivey shook his head. "But that was my prize calf. Sure hurts to lose it."

James scanned the field. "If that calf was anything like last year's, you would've taken top prize again."

"He was every bit and more, Sheriff."

James motioned to Willis to join him. "Willis and I will have one last look around, if that's all right."

"Help yourself. LuEllen has an apple pie in the oven." Spivey arched a brow. "Poke around long enough and she'll bring you both a piece to take home." He walked back into the barn.

Rifle in hand, James started back across the field to survey the area again. "That makes two calves in two days. First Ray Ballister's and now Spivey's."

Willis matched his stride. "Yes, sir. Except Ballister's was snatched from the field."

James reached the edge of the brush and knelt. Drag marks in the dirt, traces of blood on the leaves and ground. Broken limbs, but split up high, by the tips. He sighed. "You seen any cougars around your place lately, Willis?"

"Not in a while. I heard one, though, a few nights back. A female, in heat. Eeriest-sounding thing you ever heard. It about scared Mary to death. She still won't go outside alone to bring in the wash from the line."

James glanced behind him to the corral, his mind working in two different directions at once. "How's Mary doing? Is she getting along okay?" The corral was a good two hundred feet from the edge of the woods. Not impossible for a cougar to drag a calf that far. Shoot, he'd seen a full-grown male drag a three-hundred-pound elk a thousand yards back to its cave. But the cougar had no place to hide around Spivey's barn. No place to pounce and take its prey by surprise.

Willis crouched beside him. "Mary's fine. She nudged me awake the other night, told me to put my hand on her belly and wait for a second. Then I felt something move. She says to me, "That's our baby kicking." He laughed. "I told her it was just Miss Clara's cobbler mixing up with all those pickles she'd eaten after dinner."

"Did she slap you?"

Willis nodded. "Good and hard."

James laughed along with him, but he also felt a bitter twinge way down deep. And he realized what it was. He was jealous of Willis. Not person-ally—of him and Mary—but of what Willis had. A wife, and a child on the way. A life outside of the sheriff's office.

As much as he enjoyed being sheriff and had dedicated himself to upholding justice and making Timber Ridge a safer place, he couldn't escape the sense that God had something else for his life. It was just a feeling, a hunch, and one he couldn't explain. Or shake.

Willis fingered a broken branch. "Beats all I've ever seen. Or felt," he whispered.

Without asking, James knew the deputy wasn't referring to the branch in his grip, or how Mary had slapped him. "Does the doctor think she'll carry this one all the way through?"

"Brookston says if she can make it another four weeks, to her seventh month, then she'll be past the time when she—" He looked away. "When we lost our son. I don't think she'll be able to take it if she loses this one too, Sheriff. Last time about killed her."

James stood, and Willis followed suit.

"All three of you are in my prayers, Willis. Now why don't you take on off and surprise Mary by getting home a little early? I'll scout around here a bit more, see if I can locate the kill."

"Thank you, Sheriff. I appreciate that." But Willis didn't make any move to leave. "I've been meaning to talk to you about something, Sheriff. But—" He bowed his head. "This is hard. And I . . . I don't know quite how to put it."

"I've found the best way to say something is usually just to say it."

With a deep breath, Willis raised his head. "I respect you, Sheriff. And I'd never do anything to undermine you or your authority. You know that."

James nodded. "Something tells me you're not to the hard part yet, Deputy." He smiled in hopes of easing his deputy's tension.

"The mayor's approached me about putting my name forward for sheriff next spring. His exact words were that—" Willis sighed. "That he wants to 'back me' for sheriff of Timber Ridge."

James slowly sifted the news, weighing Davenport's motivation behind it, and Willis's struggle. He thought of his grandfather and knew what Ian Fletcher McGuiggan would have said if he were standing there. "And what does God have to say about it all?"

The stress in Willis's features lessened. "I told Mary that'd be the first thing you'd say." He shook his head. "That's part of the problem, Sheriff. I haven't heard Him say anything yet. Either for it or against it. And Davenport's pressuring me for an answer."

Behind Willis rose the Maroon Bells, and James's gaze was drawn to a particular peak he'd climbed by himself last summer—not long after Josiah Birch had been beaten so badly. He'd spent the night alone, praying, asking God for guidance in that situation. And God had given it, tenfold.

A measure of that same peace returned to James again. "If you haven't heard God speak, Willis, then I wouldn't give my answer. I'd wait and get my direction first."

"But . . . what if I feel His direction is saying for me to put my name in the hat?"

"Then you put your name in that hat."

"But I can't go against you, Sheriff. I won't. When you took me on as deputy, I didn't know anything. I've learned everything I know from you."

"I appreciate that, Deputy, but . . ." James rubbed the back of his neck, wearier now than a few heartbeats before. "If God wants you to be the next sheriff of Timber Ridge, then I'll step aside. Because that'll mean He has something else in mind for me."

"But this job is your life, Sheriff. You've told me that a thousand times."

"So I have," James said quietly. *"This job is your life."* The statement stung. "What I want more than anything, Willis, is to be right where the Almighty wants me. I wasted way too much of my youth pushing to be something I wasn't. And I refuse to spend one more day going in that direction. So"— he put his hand on the deputy's shoulder—"you go on home, see to that pretty wife of yours, and we'll both wait and see what direction we get on this other question. And I appreciate you confiding in me, Willis. I won't say anything to Davenport."

Willis stared for a second. "Yes, sir, Sheriff. Thank you, sir."

For the next hour, James scoured the hills around Spivey's ranch, looking for signs of a recent kill, or even a set of paw prints. But the ground gave up nothing. It hadn't rained in days, and the paths were dry and dusty. The higher he climbed the chillier the air, and the more the leaves were beginning to turn. It wouldn't be long before the mountains were in full fall color, which spawned an idea for an outing with Molly.

As quickly as the thought came, he dismissed it. It wasn't a good course to pursue their "friendship," and he knew it. But it didn't mean it wasn't still appealing.

Standing on Molly's porch stairs nearly two weeks ago, toasting sugar sticks, he thought he'd detected a softening in her that resembled an invitation for more than friendship. When he'd looked closer at her—standing there smiling, with that candy between her lips—he was sure of it. Afterward, though, when he'd seen her again in town and things were "normal" between them, he realized he'd just imagined it.

Finding no leads on the mountain, he returned to the Spiveys' ranch and was climbing into the saddle when LuEllen Spivey hustled out the cabin door.

"I've got a little something for you, Sheriff. I gave Deputy Willis some pie for him and Mary. And I've wrapped up a couple of pieces for you too."

He took the pie, grateful, and hungry enough to eat both slices himself. He caught the spark in Mrs. Spivey's eyes and decided to play along, as he always did. "Now what am I going to do with two pieces of pie, Mrs. Spivey?"

"You're a resourceful man, Sheriff McPherson." She half sang the words, winking at him. "You'll think of a *friend* to share it with, I'm sure. Or I can always make some suggestions, if you need a little help."

James smiled as he tucked the pie into a saddlebag. The dear woman was forever trying to match him up with someone. Either the latest unmarried woman who moved to town—not that many unmarried women moved to Timber Ridge—or one of the widows at church, most of whom were ten years his senior, at least. Last summer *and* fall it was her niece visiting from Texas. A nice enough lady, but not the woman for him.

There *was* someone he would have liked to share the pie with, but his position as her liaison to the town council only went so far. And it didn't include delivering pie to schoolteachers on Saturday mornings.

"I appreciate your kindness, ma'am. And I'll find someone to share this with, I'm sure." He motioned to the barn. "By chance, do you know if Arlin's selling any of his horses? I might know of an interested party."

271

She nodded, hands on her hips. "He posted an advertisement on the board at the Mullinses' store for a couple of the mares."

James tipped his hat. "Good enough, then. I'll have the person contact you."

He rode back toward town, taking a path that led over the ridge behind the schoolhouse and by a series of caves that dotted the mountainside. He kept alert for any sign of a cougar, hoping to spot something.

Barrister and Spivey had both lost a calf. And in both instances, the cougar had dragged the animal a good distance to get him to the woods. Yet there was hardly any blood until he reached the brush. Didn't make any sense. Unless the cougar broke the calf's neck when it pounced. That would explain it.

Or maybe it wasn't a cougar taking the calves.

There'd been rustlers in the area months ago, but no other thefts had been reported since then. And those guys had simply taken the animals. They hadn't bothered trying to fabricate a cover-up.

Buzzards flying overhead got James's attention first. Followed by the smell.

He dismounted and drew his rifle from its sheath, and took only a handful of steps off the path when he came upon it. He grimaced at the ravaged carcass.

But even more at the claw marks on what little was left of the calf's hide.

20

James wasn't sure this was Spivey's calf, but this calf had been killed by a mountain lion. That was for certain. Behind him on the trail, Winsome whinnied and pawed the ground.

"Easy, girl," he whispered, rifle at the ready.

He scanned the woods around him and above him on the ridge, paying special attention to the trees. Cougars were formidable predators. He'd seen one shoot straight up a lodgepole pine, as if gravity meant nothing, and then perch there, waiting, only to leap straight down—some thirty feet at least—to take down a bull elk twice the animal's size.

His attention keen, he climbed back in the saddle and continued down the twisting path.

The newspaper office was closed over the weekend, but come Monday he'd ask Elizabeth Ranslett to put a line about the killings in the next issue. Just so people would be on the alert with their animals. Cougars were shy of people, so that typically wasn't a worry—although folks being more attentive wouldn't hurt.

When he reached the fork in the trail, he paused. The narrow path leading upward to the left followed the ridge, skirting around the lake, and would take him directly into town. He could stop by the office and get some work done. The path to the right sloped downward and emptied out by Maroon Lake—and the schoolhouse.

He smiled to himself. The choice wasn't a hard one.

Molly couldn't remember ever feeling worse.

Holding her robe closed, she gripped the porch railing and eased down the front stairs of the cabin. The twenty-odd steps to the outdoor privy might as well have been a mile.

Her aches and chills had turned into a fiery sore throat during the night, along with constant sneezing and a fever potent enough to give her the shakes. She hurt all over, even on the soles of her feet, and her nose was raw from sniffling all night.

She longed for something more than tepid water, maybe some tea, but lacked the strength to make anything. She'd been alone often enough since coming to Timber Ridge, but she'd never felt truly lonely—until now.

Maybe it was lying awake through the bleak hours of night, unable to sleep, listening to the clock on the mantel ticking off the seconds, her body alternating between hot and cold. Or being hungry and thirsty, worn out, thinking of the families in town who were together, who had one another if they needed anything, and meanwhile, she had no one.

But the realization was sobering. She'd made many acquaintances while in Timber Ridge. She would even call some of them friends. But when it came down to it, she was alone.

What would she do right now if the baby were already born? How would she care for a child when she was sick? She wouldn't be able to continue teaching once the baby was born, but she'd have to have a job. What would she do? Who would hire her?

Her head throbbed from the brief walk to the privy, and the squeak of hinges sounded overloud in the hush of morning. The air inside was chilly and her hands shook. The outhouse was an inconvenience, but it wasn't foreign. She'd grown up using an outhouse during warmer months and a chamber pot come winter. But that had been years ago, before her father had indoor water closets installed.

When she finished, she arranged her gown and robe and stepped from the privy, adding a chamber pot to her list of items to purchase. The door closed behind her with the same high-pitched complaint as before—and the world suddenly tilted, taking her with it.

Landing on all fours, she squeezed her eyes shut, breathing hard, trying to cease the spinning in her head. Weakness washed through her. The porch blurred—all four of them—in her vision. The ground was dry and the sun was shining, but she shuddered with cold.

She took in gulps of air through her mouth, punishing her throat with the effort. She had to get back inside. . . . A splashing noise sounded from somewhere in the stream behind her, then the pounding of a horse's hooves.

"Molly!"

She heard footsteps and looked up to see James running toward her. Her head felt as if it were about to split wide open.

He felt her cheeks and forehead. "You've got fever!"

"It's just a cold," she whispered. "I got dizzy . . . and—" It hurt to talk. "Would you mind helping—"

Before she could finish, he lifted her in his arms.

Touched by his lack of thought for himself, she turned her head away. "Don't get too close."

"I'll take my chances," he whispered, his voice holding concern as he started for the porch stairs.

She was only too aware of her gown and robe, and her hair hanging loose and limp around her shoulders. The door to her cabin stood open. She didn't remember leaving it that way, but neither did she remember closing it.

He carried her inside, then strode straight back to her bedroom. Perhaps she should've been more uncomfortable—with her past experience with Jeremy Fowler—but all she could think about was lying back down and getting warm again. Her bare feet were like ice. And besides, this was James McPherson—the man who did no wrong. The thought might have made her smile if she hadn't felt so sick.

"Here you go." He eased her down by the bed, never letting go, and pulled back the covers.

She crawled in, keeping on her robe for modesty, and warmth. The sheets had cooled in her absence and only served to deepen the chill inside her. James laid aside his hat and leaned down and tucked her in as though she were a little girl.

He felt her forehead again. "Have you seen Dr. Brookston yet?"

"No, but I'll be fine," she whispered, drinking in the warmth from his hand. She was so cold. Her chin trembled. "It got worse during the night." A thought occurred. "I hope none of my students are ill."

"I wouldn't worry much about that. Chances are, you got sick from them. I seem to catch everything Mitch and Kurt come down with." He glanced at the bedside table where her empty teacup sat, beside her Bible. "Have you had anything to eat or drink today?"

"I've had some water."

"I'll haul some in fresh from the stream. Are you hungry?"

She teared up, but the mere thought of crying made her throat hurt even worse. She didn't know why, but she was embarrassed to admit her need to him. Especially when her cupboards were so bare.

"Yes," she said, looking away. "I am. But I'm sorry to put you to such—"

His hand, gentle against her mouth, silenced her protest. He drew her face back to him. "Don't you dare say that to me, Molly Whitcomb." Smiling, he touched the side of her cheek. "This is what friends do. They take care of each other."

She looked up at him, her throat aching with emotion. "And that's what we are . . . aren't we, James?"

He cradled her face. "You bet we are." The blue of his eyes deepened. "Now, I'll be right back with some fresh water and something to eat. Don't you go fighting any battles while I'm gone."

Smiling, Molly curled onto her side. Covers pulled close beneath her chin, she imagined the cool water on her throat and thanked God James had stopped by.

When James returned, she stirred, not realizing she'd drifted off. He laid something bundled in a checkered cloth on the bed and let her drink her fill of cold water until her thirst was satisfied.

He set the glass on the table and grabbed the straight-back chair from the corner. He pulled it close. "Have I got a treat for you." He unwrapped the checkered cloth. "It might not be chicken soup, but I guarantee you're gonna love it."

She couldn't see what it was until he brought the fork to her mouth. She moved to slip her hand from beneath the covers to take the fork, but he shook his head.

"No, ma'am. That's against the rules." He winked.

Every inch of her body hurt, yet she felt better just being in his company.

She took the bite and chewed, her hunger winning out over the dread of swallowing. She couldn't taste anything at first, then she sniffed and swallowed again and caught the sweetness of apples and cinnamon and pastry. Oh, it was heaven. He doled the apple pie out in small bites, and when it was gone, her appetite was sated, though she still craved the taste.

"Where did you get that?" she whispered, raising her head for the glass he held to her lips.

"I got it this morning from LuEllen Spivey—Amanda's mother. LuEllen's famous for her apple pie. A deputy and I were out there and she insisted I take some. A piece for me, and a piece to share with 'a friend.'"

Such sincerity and kindness in his face. Molly couldn't help but think of the woman she was, versus the woman he thought he knew. "Thank you for sharing it with me, James."

"You're welcome . . . Molly." He rose. "I'll get you a cool cloth, and then I'll ride for Dr. Brookston."

She offered no protest about the doctor this time, hoping Dr. Brookston would be able to give her something for the achiness and chills. She told James where to find the linens, and he returned to lay a cool, damp towel on her forehead, which only made her shiver more.

Teeth chattering, she looked up. "Are you trying to make me worse?"

"I'm trying to keep your fever down."

She shuddered. "I think you missed your calling, *Dr.* McPherson."

He stilled. A look moved across his face that she couldn't decipher, but she felt as if she'd misspoken.

"I'm sorry, did I say—"

He shrugged. "It's nothing. My father was a physician, and . . . it's just been a long time since I've heard his—" He looked away. "Since I've heard someone say that."

Molly felt something from him she'd never felt before. An evasiveness. He wouldn't meet her eyes, and she quickly decided that the quality didn't suit him well.

He reached for his hat. "If you think you'll be all right for a few minutes, I'll head out."

She nodded. "Thank you."

"Is there anything you need before I go?"

She started to respond, then hesitated. She thought of two things—a chamber pot and a bed warmer. No manner of coercion could bring her to admit the first. She would ask the doctor for that. "Would you mind stopping by the store and seeing if Ben and Lyda Mullins have a bed warmer?" She frowned. "I just can't seem to get rid of these chills."

He smiled again. "I can do that." He felt her cheeks and forehead again. "But you sure feel warm enough. I'll be back with Brookston soon."

Hearing the pound of Winsome's hooves, Molly removed the cloth, laying it aside, and rose on one elbow to peer through the window at James riding toward town. Whoever ended up winning that man's heart would be a queen. She'd have to be, to deserve him. She sank back into the mattress.

What a difference between James McPherson and Jeremy Fowler. She hadn't felt a moment's unease with James McPherson in her bedroom, but he would never act unseemly. Much less coerce or pressure a woman to do something she had misgivings about. She closed her eyes and was back in Jeremy Fowler's kitchen that night nearly four months ago.

"Here's what you need for the coffee," Jeremy had said, reaching for the tin. His arm brushed against her breast and he paused. "Oh, I'm sorry. I didn't mean to—" He looked at her, leaned over, and gave her a chaste kiss on the mouth. Then went on about his task.

Cheeks burning, Molly set aside her discomfort. He hadn't meant to do it. It had been an accident. Yet she couldn't deny a flush of excitement.

After the coffee was made, they retired to a sitting room down the hallway and sat for a long while drinking coffee and talking university politics. She felt an ease with him and the camaraderie of common goals within academia.

She noticed how late it was getting. "Would you still like for me to review that grant proposal before I go?"

Jeremy took her china cup and set it aside. "You know, it's so late now, and it's nice to just sit here and talk. Why don't we wait on that until tomorrow?" He eased closer to her on the couch and put his arm around her shoulders. "Have you thought any more about what we discussed last week?"

He said it so matter-of-factly. But he'd never been one to show his emotions. "Yes, I've . . . thought about it." Only every other moment.

"And?" He trailed a finger down her arm.

"And, I think . . . it's a very promising idea."

He turned her to face him. "We will make the most wonderful couple at Franklin College, Molly Whitcomb." He kissed her cheek, then the corner of her mouth. "I'll make you happy, Molly. I give you my word. I'll work to be everything you desire in a husband."

He kissed her and the rest of the world had faded. For a while. Then she grew uncomfortable.

"Jeremy—" Her breath came heavy. She put a firm hand to his chest.

He did as she silently asked but didn't move

from where he lay beside her on the sofa. "Do you know that it's been three years since we first met? I still remember you walking into that curriculum committee meeting for the very first time. You look scared to death."

"I was scared to death." Despite her father being an esteemed professor emeritus at Franklin College—perhaps even more so because of it—she'd been so nervous. So eager to prove herself and gain acceptance among her father's peers. "Until you came over and asked me to sit with you."

"We managed to get every piece of new curriculum pushed through that semester." He brushed the tip of her nose. "We make a good team." He kissed her again. "Let me love you, Molly. Let me show you how I can love you as your husband."

His attention, his desire, his words—they all rushed in to fill a void inside her that had been empty for so long. Her closest friends had long ago married. They'd been busy having babies while she'd been busy gaining degrees. She felt elevated in Jeremy's eyes. He made her see what she could be, especially with him by her side.

Realizing how far they'd gone, Molly drew back. "No, Jeremy, we shouldn't. I—"

"We're going to be married, Molly. I love you, and you love me." He pressed closer, his kisses convincing.

And in the end, she'd relinquished, and had reluctantly given herself to a man, even while not fully wanting to.

Molly hiccupped a sob and turned over in the bed. She stared out the cabin window, shaking uncontrollably. She'd been so innocent, so trusting. So *foolish.*

The back of her throat was raw. She tried to sit up to reach the glass of water James had left, but the pain in her head prevented it. She eased back down and closed her eyes, and moved her hand over her belly, praying her baby was all right. It wasn't the child's fault . . . how it came into the world. *Oh, God, please . . . let him, or her, be all right. Please, let them be . . .*

She drifted on a wave, only to awaken sometime later, a voice calling to her from far, far away.

21

Dr. Whitcomb . . . with you now. Can you—"
Molly blinked. The voice, broken and fragmented, floated toward her in a fog. She tried to keep her eyes open and couldn't. Fire had replaced the ice in her veins and something mercifully cool touched her forehead.

"It's Dr. Brookston, and I need you to . . . if you can . . . to respond."

The thud of her heartbeat pulsed hot in the tips of her fingers and in the bottoms of her feet. "Yes," she finally managed. "I . . . hear you." But why did he sound so far away?

A cool rush of air swept over her body. She sat up, but not of her own volition. She felt herself being lifted, then carried. Her head bounced with each step, growing heavy. When she couldn't hold it up any longer, she let her chin slump forward on her chest. If only he would let her sleep. She was so tired. She just needed to sleep.

"Dr. Whitcomb, this is not going to be pleasant. But, I assure you, it's necessary."

He was carrying her. But to where?

Her answer came when icy cold water hit her body. She sucked in a breath. Her eyes flew open. Dr. Brookston still held her, but they were standing in the middle of the stream! What was the man think—

The water suddenly rose to chin level, and she tightened her hold around his neck as a million tiny pins pierced her all at once. She shivered, her teeth chattering.

"Your fever spiked, Dr. Whitcomb." He rose to his full height, taking her with him, and she felt the muscles in his arms tightening. "I checked your temperature one minute . . . it was fine. The next, you were burning up. Now, hold still."

He went down a second time, and again the pins stuck everywhere the water hit. She opened her mouth to say something and water splashed in. But she welcomed the cold against her throat.

She lost count of how many times Dr. Brookston repeated the dunking. She knew how to swim, but if he had let go of her, she would drown. Her arms and legs felt as if they were tethered to weights that would drag her under. She wasn't certain she could even stand.

Finally, he started toward the shore, and as the waters receded, Molly became conscious of her wet gown. As a physician, the man was no doubt accustomed to seeing . . . certain things. But doctor or no doctor, she still laid an arm across her chest and was glad when the cabin came into view.

"Thank you . . . I think, Dr. Brookston," she whispered, shivering again.

"You're welcome, Dr. Whitcomb." A smile warmed his voice. "The sheriff tracked me down, and I came right away. He had an emergency in town but said he'd be here as soon as possible." He opened the door and carried her inside. "You were sleeping when I arrived. You still had a fever, but it wasn't high. I went to get fresh water for compresses, and when I came back, you were having a seizure." He set her down by the side of the bed. "It was a febrile seizure, one relatively common with high fevers. But still . . . you gave me a good scare."

"Then I'd call us even." She returned his smile and glanced down at her gown.

"Where do you keep your nightclothes, ma'am?"

She gestured. "In the third drawer there."

He withdrew her a gown and laid it on the bed. "Can you manage this on your own?"

Molly nodded, uncertain whether she could or not but determined to die trying.

"I'll be outside. Call me when you're ready for me to come back in."

As soon as the door closed, she unbuttoned the first few buttons and pulled the wet gown over her head. It landed in a puddle on the floor. Her skin was like gooseflesh, all prickly and raised. She reached for a blanket crumpled at the foot of the bed and rubbed it over her arms and legs, then squeezed the excess moisture from her hair.

Looking down at her body, she paused.

The slight mound in her belly was noticeable, but only at this stage of undress. It fit perfectly beneath the palm of her hand, and if she didn't know better, she would have thought she'd simply gained a little weight. She would be able to conceal her condition for a few more weeks. But the dress she'd borrowed from Rachel was plenty snug, as was her own black gown. She would need to address that issue soon enough.

Along with others . . .

She slipped the fresh gown over her head and began buttoning the front. Dr. Brookston would be able to answer many, if not all, of her questions about the coming months—the progression of the baby's growth, the changes in her own body, what to expect as the time of birth drew near. But could she trust him to keep a confidence? She needed to tell the town council, and she would. In time. First, she had to prove her worth as a teacher. And heaven knew, the past week hadn't been testament to that.

No, now wasn't the time to tell anyone yet. If she started having problems, such as bleeding or discomfort, she would confide in the doctor. But not yet.

A knock sounded on the door. "Are you all right, Dr. Whitcomb?"

"Yes. I'm nearly done." Shivering, she slipped the final button through its paired hole and crawled back in bed, welcoming the chance to lie down again. "Come in."

Dr. Brookston entered with his black bag and claimed the same chair James had sat in earlier. The doctor had a decidedly different manner about him than James. It wasn't anything she could put into words, but if she'd seen photographs of each man sitting in that chair, even not having met them and even if they'd been identically dressed, she would've known which was the doctor and which was the sheriff.

Rand Brookston was about James's age, and hers, she guessed—and handsome. Dark-haired with chiseled, almost aristocratic features, he was considerably younger than any physician who had tended her. His youth wasn't a cause for discomfort, however. He exuded a confidence coupled with an approachability that made a person almost instantly at ease in his presence. His bedside manner resembled that of a dear family friend more than a studied medical professional.

Brookston felt her forehead, then her cheeks. "Considerably cooler." He nodded. "Very good. How are you feeling?" He reached for his bag and withdrew a stethoscope.

"Weak and tired, but better than before." Simply being in bed again encouraged her eyes to close, but her feet . . . Her feet were freezing again.

Dr. Brookston leaned close. "I'd like to ascertain the strength of your heart and lungs."

She nodded, and he unbuttoned the first few buttons on her gown.

Only then did Molly notice the scar on the lower left side of his neck. Long healed, the gash appeared to have been deep, telling from the pucker of gathered skin, which disappeared behind his collar.

"Have you ever taken laudanum, Dr. Whitcomb?"

"Yes, sir. When I was younger I took it for headaches."

"Headaches?"

"I read a great deal as a child. Our doctor said the headaches were due to"—she remembered the physician's explanation verbatim—"the overexertion of my eyes, and the strain to my delicate female acumen due to excessive inculcation."

Dr. Brookston laughed. "Sounds like one of my old medical school professors. He was forever referring to the female gender as the weaker sex. And unfortunately, he meant it in every way." He moved the stethoscope to various places on her chest, listening. "When, in my experience," he said, his eyes narrowing the slightest bit, "I've found quite the opposite to be true."

"Where did you attend school, Doctor?"

"The College of Physicians in Philadelphia."

She raised a brow. "Impressive." Anyone in her circle who attended school in the North was either from a wealthy family—wealthy before the war, anyway—or was a person of considerable intelligence. Or both. Looking at Rand Brookston, she guessed he was both.

His suit was tailor-made, expensive-looking, but his frayed collar and the worn seams of his dark trousers revealed another chapter in his story. If he *had* been born into a life of privilege, that wealth had parted ways with him some time ago.

"Impressive hardly describes me, ma'am. However, you, *Dr. Molly Whitcomb*"—he said it with a dash of Southern formality that made her smile—"are most impressive. Both on paper and in person. Or perhaps I should say 'in the paper.'" He pulled down the bottom lid of each of her eyes and peered close. "Mrs. Elizabeth Ranslett included a very nice article about you before you arrived."

"Yes, I've heard about that, but I have yet to see

it." Rachel said James had saved it for her. She would remember to ask him. A wave of fatigue hit her, and she looked forward to going back to sleep.

Dr. Brookston laid aside his stethoscope and gently probed her throat, then moved to the sides of her neck. "Have you experienced any vomiting?"

"No. It all started with a tickle in my throat earlier this week. I had a headache, then the sneezing started, and the sore throat and fever."

"And I assume you pushed on through, hoping it would go away?"

She heard the gentle reprimand in his voice and nodded.

"Have you been drinking plenty of fluids?"

"Hot tea earlier in the week, then mostly water."

"And your appetite?"

"I've been hungry but . . . I haven't felt well enough to get out of bed to fix anything. Sheriff McPherson brought me a piece of apple pie earlier, and I ate that."

"From Mrs. Spivey?"

She smiled. No matter this town's growth, Timber Ridge was still a small community. "Yes, and it was delicious."

"Best I've ever had." He gave a playful wince and glanced upward. "Let's just hope my dear mother's not listening, God rest her soul."

Molly laughed, liking the man more and more.

He finished his examination and eased back into the chair beside the bed. "So, Dr. Whitcomb . . . are there any medical conditions you need to tell me about, ma'am?"

Thinking she detected a certain tone in his voice, Molly searched his face but found nothing revealing in his expression. She smoothed a hand over the top of the blanket and vowed not to lie. "Let's see . . . I'm thirty-one years old. I broke my arm when I was twelve, climbing a tree, trying to keep up with the boys in my neighborhood. But other than that, I've been quite healthy all my life. And I haven't ever had this bad of a cold before."

Dr. Brookston's gaze remained steady, compassionate. He leaned forward. "This is more than simply a cold, Dr. Whitcomb. It's a strain of virus, similar to influenza but, thankfully, without the intestinal ravages on the body. Healing is usually much quicker." He looked down at his hands. "Unfortunately, there can be . . . consequences to a fever as high as yours was."

It felt as if the world began to spin a little slower.

Molly knew she wasn't imagining the tone in his voice this time. Nor the concern in his gaze. "W-what kind of consequences are we speaking about?"

He covered her hand on the blanket. She knew he intended it to be a comforting gesture, but it had the exact opposite effect on her. And a split second before he spoke, she read the truth in his eyes.

"What concerns me most, Dr. Whitcomb . . . is the child you're carrying. And how this fever may have affected him or her."

22

Molly stared up at Dr. Brookston, a hundred questions blurring her mind. How did he know? Would he keep her secret? Would he feel compelled to tell the town council? But only one question was of utmost concern at the moment. "How might this fever have affected my baby?"

He kept his hand atop hers on the blanket. "First of all, let me reiterate that I said *may* have affected your baby, Dr. Whitcomb. Remember, just because a fever *can* cause problems doesn't mean that it *will*." His sigh hinted at frustration. "Unfortunately, there's still much we don't know about the development of a child inside a mother's womb. What we do know is that there is a direct correlation between the mother's health and the child's."

"Meaning that my baby suffered the same high temperature that I did?"

He shook his head. "Not as direct as that, necessarily. God's design in a woman giving birth to a child is nothing short of a miracle." Subtle awe swept his face. "Studies have proven that there seem to be . . . safeguards in place. A mother will suffer the effects of say . . . a certain medicine or even poison, and yet the child within her remains unharmed. Then there are other instances when a mother carries her child for the full term with no complications whatsoever—no illnesses, no fevers—and yet the child is born with certain . . . challenges."

"What kind of challenges?"

"They're developmental in nature. The child still walks and talks and is able to perform many of the same tasks as a child born without these difficulties, but the progress is delayed. Learning those skills comes more slowly for those children."

A knock sounded at the front door. Dr. Brookston looked in that direction.

Molly rose up on one elbow and reached for his arm. "Please, Dr. Brookston," she whispered. "I know I should have told the town council about this child, but—"

"Dr. Whitcomb." His stare was direct, yet kind. "I am first and foremost a physician. *Your* physician, if you'll trust me to serve in that capacity on your behalf, and on that of your child."

When he didn't continue, she nodded.

"Everything you share with me, ma'am, will remain confidential. I will always offer my medical opinion when it concerns your health, or that of your unborn child, without reservation. But, unless requested, I will refrain from offering opinion of any other nature. Unless asked."

A second knock sounded. "Brookston? Molly?"

She recognized James's voice.

Dr. Brookston stood. "Unless, of course, you're planning on holding up the morning stage." He angled his head. "Then I might have to speak with the sheriff on that count."

Molly was too relieved and exhausted to laugh. "Thank you, Dr. Brookston. And I promise, I *will* tell the town council," she whispered. "When the time is right."

He nodded. "And I promise that, in time"— warning laced his smile—"they're going to know, whether you tell them or not."

"This should warm things up some." With care, James slid the bed warmer between the fresh sheets, tossing Molly a grin.

She sat in the chair beside the chifforobe, rubbing her arms and gazing at the bed as if she hadn't slept in a month of Sundays. He'd told Brookston he'd stay with her for the afternoon, in case the fever returned, until Brookston could make it back to check on her that evening. Brookston agreed. Both of them had already been exposed to whatever she had, so it made sense. James was just contented to have Molly all to himself, sick or not.

But he *was* glad that the schoolteacher's house wasn't located right smack in the middle of town. That would've made visiting her like this a little harder. Being mindful of appearances, especially as sheriff, he knew how quickly rumors could start and spread. And while he looked forward to time spent with this woman, he also meant to guard her reputation.

He carefully maneuvered the bed warmer around on the mattress, then slid it to the other side. Molly crawled back into bed, sighing as she snuggled deeper.

Her eyes fluttered closed. "This is heaven on earth, thank you."

He claimed the chair. "Hey, no going to sleep yet. You promised me another round of checkers. You can't expect to win an entire bagful of penny candy and then not give a fellow the chance to redeem himself."

She giggled. "You make it sound like we were gambling."

"No, we were just playing checkers with candy as the stakes. But it wasn't gambling." He smirked. "Not for you anyway, because you won it all." Having seen his nephews pout often enough, he tried mimicking their expressions, which earned him a grin.

"Now you look like Kurt." She peered at him over the covers, her smile softening. "Thank you, James."

He didn't have to ask what she was thanking him for—he knew. "If I were to tell you that this was all my pleasure, that wouldn't even begin to come close."

The warmth moving in behind her eyes made him intensely aware of how alone they were, and of how desirable she was, even with her feeling poorly. She was a beautiful woman, and not only on the outside.

Just today, four parents had stopped him in town to tell him they'd received a kind note from the new teacher, describing the "favorite day" their child had chosen to share with the class the first morning of school. His throat tightened when he thought of the *letter*—not note—Molly had written to Rachel, and how she'd gone into detail about what the boys had said. Rachel had shared it with him, and he'd been glad he'd read it in private.

Taking the boys on those overnight sojourns had been special for him, a way to honor Thomas's memory, and Rachel's abiding love for him. But it meant even more now, knowing how much it had meant to his nephews. And he had Molly to thank for that.

"What if"—she raised up slightly and tucked the corner of the pillow under her head—"I promise to buy you an entire bag of penny candy if we could just talk for a while?"

James stretched out his legs, more than satisfied. "Sounds good to me." He noticed her nearly empty glass. "You want more of Lyda's tea? Or soup? She made it special for you."

She shook her head, yawning. "I'm fine. I just

enjoy your being here." She shrugged softly. "Sitting with me."

He stared at her, more convinced than ever that being friends with this woman was going to prove near impossible. But still, he aimed to try. For both their sakes.

She'd surprised him earlier by calling him *Dr.* McPherson. It had been years since he'd heard that name spoken aloud. And it suited him just fine if that same amount of time passed without his hearing it again.

"Do you miss the South?" he asked, determined to turn his thoughts from their present course.

She weighed her answer before giving it. "No. And yes."

Silence had never bothered him, so he didn't seek to fill it. He liked how the tumble of the stream could be heard through her open bedroom window. That sound always aided his sleeping at night.

"I don't miss it the way I thought I would."

"But there *are* things you do miss."

She smoothed the hair back from her face. "I miss waking up to mornings wrapped in fog and mist. With everything cloaked in feathery white. The trees, the houses, the—"

"The barns, the rolling hills," he continued. "Everything's draped in it."

She nodded. "We have fog here, but it's not the same."

He liked how she used the word "we." "That's because it doesn't cling to things here the same way it does back home."

She laughed, her eyes widening briefly. "I hadn't thought of it that way, but that's exactly what it is."

He motioned to the picture on the wall beside her bed. "That turned out well."

She trailed his focus. "Yes, it did. Elizabeth Ranslett made copies for every family in the school. It was so generous of her."

"She's a very generous person. So is her husband, Daniel. Have you met him yet?"

She shook her head, fighting a yawn. "But Elizabeth told me—the day she was at school—that you and her husband have been friends since childhood."

"We sure have."

A sneaky sparkle lit her eyes. "So I would assume, then, that Daniel Ranslett would be the one to speak with if a person wanted to know anything about you. Besides Rachel, of course."

He leaned forward. "If there's anything you want to know about me, Molly Whitcomb, all you have to do is ask." He'd guessed the statement might catch her by surprise, maybe even encourage a giggle. But he'd guessed wrong.

Her eyes glistened with unshed tears.

He was tempted to offer an apology, but something within him held back the words. Watching her, he sensed a hurt he wished he could do something about. Heal, in some way. Or at least help shoulder. If she'd only trust him enough to tell him what it was.

She laughed softly and sniffed. "Always so direct."

"Not always," he whispered, wishing she would offer him the same invitation he'd given her—to ask her anything he wanted. He would ask about her husband, how he'd died, when they'd gotten married, what kind of life they'd had together, and if the pain he sensed from her now was from a past hurt, or a present one.

But the main question he would ask, and that he so wanted the answer to, was how—after being widowed only four months ago—she could look at him the way she was looking at him now.

Struck by an uncharacteristic measure of spontaneity, he struggled against the desire to go to her and take her in his arms. His mouth went dry at the thoughts filling his head. Thoughts that were certainly warm, but that weren't all that "friendly," not in the sense he and Molly had agreed to be friends.

A knock on the front door jerked his thoughts back, as did Brookston's greeting as he entered. James didn't know whether to be disappointed or relieved. Molly definitely looked relieved.

Brookston entered the bedroom, medical bag in hand. "How's my newest patient, Sheriff?"

James stood, still holding Molly's gaze. "I think she's on the mend, Doc."

"No more fever, then? That's good news." Brookston retrieved his stethoscope. "I've just left the Tucker family. There's no need to be alarmed, Dr. Whitcomb, but two of their children—Ansley and Zachary—are ill with something similar to what you have."

Molly frowned. "Are they going to be all right?"

"Without a doubt. Neither had the high fever you did, and children always seem to bounce back from these things faster than adults. I hope you won't take me to task for this, but I've exercised the liberty of recessing classes for next week, in order to give you time to gain your strength, for your body to fully heal, and to lessen the chance of this spreading to others. I told the Tuckers as much, while I was there, since they live the farthest from town."

James half expected Molly to protest, but she didn't.

Standing by the bedside, Brookston fingered the stethoscope in his hand, and James gathered he was waiting to examine his newest patient.

He reached for his hat, throwing Molly a discreet wink. "I'll stop by tomorrow after church with some more food. Several of the parents are planning on bringing meals throughout the week, too."

Molly's expression revealed gratitude—and question. "And I'm wondering, Sheriff, just how does everyone in town already know that I'm sick?"

James kept his smile as innocent as possible. "Beats me. I'm guessing the doc here just can't keep things to himself. So much for that oath he took." Seeing Brookston's grin, James slipped his hat on, having waited for this moment. He hadn't been reading a dictionary for the last few nights for nothing. "Perhaps later this week, ma'am, once you're better, you'll feel like . . . ambulating with me around town."

Seeing Molly's slow smile, James quickly took his leave before she could respond.

By Monday afternoon, Molly felt well enough to get out of bed. By Wednesday, Dr. Brookston told her she could be around others again without fear of being contagious. But her full strength still hadn't returned, and since she had more food than she knew what to do with, there was no reason for her to leave the cabin, which suited her fine. She wasn't in any frame of mind for company.

She spent the morning curled on the sofa by the fireplace reading past issues of the *Timber Ridge Reporter* that James had brought by, including the one with her article in it. Elizabeth Ranslett had certainly painted a glowing picture of her and her academic accomplishments. Molly cringed reading the newspaper headline—*Woman Professor Comes West To Teach Children*—just as Brandon Tolliver had quoted it to her that day on the stagecoach.

At one time in her life, she'd sought such public affirmation, such praise for her accomplishments. She'd *needed* it. Perhaps it was due to being a woman in what was still—despite the strides being made—a man's world. And having her work acknowledged in public arenas had served as confirmation of her abilities in the face of what had been, on many occasions, heated opposition.

A bittersweet realization moved through her, for which she knew the cause. She no longer required that public recognition. Nor did she desire it. Quite the contrary, and for good reason.

Not only were her efforts as a teacher presently failing, but her *accomplishments* in recent months didn't exactly merit accolades. Nor did she deserve the acceptance that the people of Timber Ridge had offered. Or her friendship with James.

James . . .

He'd been so kind, so thoughtful. Their friendship was one of the best parts of her life right now. Only it wasn't best for him. He simply didn't know it yet.

She'd wanted so badly to ask him about his father, *Dr.* McPherson, after his reaction to hearing the name. But curious as she was, she hadn't felt at liberty to, even with his invitation to ask him anything. How could she ask him personal questions like that when she wasn't willing to—when she couldn't—entertain them from him?

She laid aside the newspaper and picked up the

stack of envelopes—notes of thanks she'd penned to those who had brought meals and desserts during the week. Pencil drawings from students adorned her walls. James had tacked them up for her, and she appreciated each one.

She'd been asleep when he'd stopped by on Sunday, but seeing him ride up the path yesterday, she had been ready. "Are you here to . . . ambulate with me, James? Because if so, I'm not sure I'm quite up for a stroll around town yet."

His smile was telling. "So did you have to look it up, or did you know already?"

She formed a playful pout. "I grew up reading a dictionary for fun. So I fear . . ." She chose her most formal tone. "It is going to be difficult to find a word for which I do not already know the definition."

He shook his head, the gleam in his eyes never dimming. "That's all right. I like a good challenge, ma'am."

Molly smiled, remembering the conversation.

She moved to the window and stared up at the mountains soaring high above the cabin, feeling so small and insignificant in comparison, and so unworthy. *You've given me so much, Lord, and I've given so little in return.* "And just like this town, and James, you haven't treated me as I've deserved either." She pulled her shawl closer about her shoulders, not a trace of doubt within her that God was listening.

Even though she'd told herself her mistake with Jeremy was her own fault—deep down, in a dark hidden-away corner of her heart, one she preferred not to acknowledge—she'd assigned a portion of the blame to God for what she'd done. When she'd first discovered she was with child, she'd made excuses for her behavior, and they resurfaced again.

Except now, she saw them for what they were—lies.

God could have spared her father's life and therefore she wouldn't have been so lonely, and she wouldn't have sought Jeremy's comfort. So God was also to blame. How often had her friends confided in her about how long it had taken them to become with child? And her very first time, she'd conceived. God could have prevented that if He'd wanted to. So He was also to blame. God could have worked in Jeremy's heart to coerce him to stand by his promise to marry her. He could have prevented Jeremy from catching the attention of the daughter of the college's wealthiest donor. But He didn't.

And so today, in Athens, Georgia, Jeremy Fowler would wed Maria Elena Patterson, guaranteeing him not only a place among the social elite, but also a secure future with the college. And, one day, very likely, his own college presidency. None of which, Molly knew, he would have gained by marrying *her*.

Tears slipped down her cheeks. After all, she was only carrying his—

A pounding on the door sent her heart to her throat.

Hand to her chest, she worked to catch her breath and smoothed the front of her robe. Once composed, she opened the door. "Mrs. Spivey, how nice to see you." She glanced past Amanda Spivey's mother to see the horse and buggy in the yard. "How are you?"

"How are *you* is more the question, Mrs. Whitcomb." The woman absolutely beamed. "I saw the doctor in town yesterday, and he said you might be up for visitors now. So . . ." Scrunching her shoulders tight, LuEllen Spivey held out a covered dish. "I thought you could use one of my *famous* apple pies!" She removed the checkered cloth. "And it's still *warm*!"

She spoke in a high-pitched, singsong voice, and Molly's hunch as to where Amanda had inherited her dramatic flair was confirmed.

Molly managed what she hoped was a pleasant countenance. "That's so thoughtful of you, thank you. Dr. Brookston said I'm not contagious anymore, but I'd hate to take the chance of—"

"Oh . . ." LuEllen stepped closer. "I'm not worried about that! I trust Dr. Brookston's judgment implicitly."

Seeing no other alternative, Molly made a welcoming gesture. "Then, won't you come in, please?"

"I'd love to. Thank you!"

LuEllen Spivey breezed past her, and Molly was surprised she wasn't dragged along in the woman's wake. She closed the door, reaching deep for hospitality she didn't feel.

"Where do you keep your plates, dear?"

It took Molly a second to realize what Mrs. Spivey was suggesting. And another to shake off the odd feeling of the woman calling her "dear." She guessed they were right around the same age. "Ahh . . . the plates are right behind you, in the cabinet on the left." A piece of warm apple pie didn't sound half bad, actually. And it smelled delicious, which she already knew it would be from the piece James had shared.

Minutes later, seated at the table, Molly listened as Amanda's mother began with the latest news in her own household, then went into a dissertation of everyone else's business in town. Molly couldn't have gotten a word in even if she'd tried, which she didn't. But if ever she needed news spread quickly around Timber Ridge, she knew whom to tell.

"My daughter informs me that you've decided to put on a Christmas drama this year, Mrs. Whitcomb. A first for our new school."

"Yes, that's right." Molly had only mentioned it to the class once, December still being so far away. But, of course, Amanda Spivey would have keyed in on the word *drama*. She hoped to get several of the parents involved in the production, to foster relationships but also to help ease her own workload for such an event. "We'll host it at the church building, since the school isn't large enough to hold everyone." She pointed to her plate. "Your pie is delicious."

"Thank you so much. Will the whole town be invited, do you think?"

Molly nodded. "I've already spoken with Sheriff McPherson, and he said the town council thought it was a wonderful idea."

"Well, I completely agree!" LuEllen took a bite of her scarcely touched pie. "And I am hereby volunteering to organize the ladies' sewing circle at church. We'll make all the costumes." She reached over and patted Molly's hand. "So that's one less thing you have to worry about when the time comes."

Molly's smile came easily this time. "How kind of you, Mrs. Spivey. Thank you."

"Don't you mention it, dear. Mr. Spivey and I appreciate what you're doing for all the children in town." She laid her fork down. "Every afternoon last week, Amanda came home"—she made a talking gesture with her hand—"giving us all the details. She says that classes are going splendidly."

Molly thought she detected a false ring to the woman's tone but couldn't be sure. In case Amanda had told her mother the truth—and looking across the table at LuEllen's oversweet expression, Molly was certain now that the girl had—she decided to be more forthcoming. "I'm not sure I'd use the term 'splendidly' quite yet, Mrs. Spivey." She laughed softly. "But at the beginning of every school year, there's always a phase where the students and teacher are getting to know one another. I'm certain things will only get better from here on out."

"I'm certain of that too." She rose from the table. "Well, I'll let you get back to writing your notes."

Molly glanced behind her at the table by the couch and saw her box of stationery and the stack of envelopes. Then quickly looked around for anything she might not have wanted LuEllen Spivey to see, not that it mattered now.

LuEllen paused in the doorway. "Just bring the pie tin to school whenever you're done. Amanda will bring it home."

"I'll do that. And thank you again for stopping by, and for the pie." Molly started to close the door.

"Oh—" Mrs. Spivey raised her hand. "One last thing. . . . How do you envision the Christmas drama, Mrs. Whitcomb?"

"How do I envision it?"

"Yes, from the standpoint of each student's involvement."

And then it became clear—the reason for Mrs. Spivey's visit. Molly felt like she'd been blind-sided. She should have seen this coming. She hadn't given much thought to choosing parts, but she wasn't about to admit that to LuEllen Spivey, thereby inviting her to step in and plan every detail. "I'll give the students more information on the auditioning process when the time comes. I'm sure Amanda will let you know."

Mrs. Spivey grinned. "I'm sure she will! You're so organized and have everything planned. Now you be sure and enjoy the rest of that pie. I made it especially for you."

"I will." Molly attempted moderate enthusiasm. "As soon as I saw it, I was eager to taste your creation again. Sheriff McPherson shared a piece with me the other day, so I already knew how good your pies were."

LuEllen's smile stretched wider, if that were possible. "Sheriff McPherson? Shared a piece of my pie with you?"

"He did. And he said yours are the most delicious apple pies he's ever had." No harm in passing along a compliment. Molly grinned as Mrs. Spivey's face flushed red. Yet another woman, it would seem, who had fallen under the good sheriff's spell.

"Well, isn't that kind of him. . . . He's *such* a good man."

"Yes, he is." Molly took care to keep her tone neutral.

LuEllen leaned closer. "Don't you dare tell him this, but I'm working hard to find him a good woman. Someone who's as kind and gentle-hearted and deserving as he is. And who will make a good sheriff's wife for this town." She winked. "I know I haven't found her yet, but I will!"

Mrs. Spivey waved as she drove away in the wagon, and Molly returned the gesture, staring after her, quickly reaching the decision that it would be best to keep LuEllen Spivey at arm's length at all times, but definitely remain on the woman's good side.

23

Using the step stool, Molly situated herself on the end of the patient table, watching Dr. Brookston pull down the shades on the windows. "I've brought a list of questions with me." She slipped the paper from her reticule. "I hope you don't mind."

He smiled at her over his shoulder. "You don't know how refreshing that is, Dr. Whitcomb. Most patients tell me they had something they were going to ask me. Yet once they get here, they can't remember what it was."

"It's a rather long list, I'm afraid. I've had a lot of time to think in recent days." She reread the questions again, knowing they revealed not only her lack of knowledge in this area but her lack of friendship with women as well.

Considering how well she felt today, she could hardly imagine that only one week ago James had found her by the outhouse. She'd rested and recuperated, following Dr. Brookston's orders to a T, and was eager to face the challenge of teaching again.

Along with taking time to contemplate her coming months of pregnancy, she'd also spent time reviewing her lessons, as well as each student's strengths and weaknesses, which had become apparent during that first week. And she had an idea for restructuring class in a way that would, theoretically, allow her to maximize the use of her time, as well as that of her students. Now, to put her theory to the test come Monday morning.

Dr. Brookston silently read her list, nodding. "Excellent questions, Dr. Whitcomb. You *have* been doing some thinking. We'll address each of these before you leave today."

"Thank you, Doctor."

"One thing you didn't address, however"—his gaze held understanding—"and it's not imperative that you decide right now, but I'd like you to be considering . . . who might assist you during the birth. A woman you would be comfortable with and who could be a comfort to you. There are a couple of ladies in town who have assisted me in deliveries before. Belle Birch being one of them. And another lady from church, Jean Dickey. I'm sure either of them would be happy to help you, if you'd like."

Molly nodded, appreciating his forethought and

attention to detail. It boded well for his care as a physician. In answer to his suggestion, someone immediately came to mind, and she already felt certain of her response. Who better than Rachel to assist her, who had already been through this twice herself? She would ask her the next time they were together.

"If you'll go ahead and lie down now, Dr. Whitcomb." Dr. Brookston gently held her elbow as she leaned back, then took time to explain everything before he started his examination.

Molly had harbored more than a little apprehension as she'd anticipated this first appointment, but soon discovered that had been time wasted. Dr. Brookston's gentle bedside manner and the ease and humility with which he communicated not only his procedures but also his findings helped put her at ease.

After the examination, Molly smiled as he helped her sit up. "I'm curious, Doctor. That day you nearly drowned me in the stream, how did you know I was with child?" She didn't know quite how to phrase the rest of her question. "Was it the . . . swell in my . . . tummy?"

He laughed softly. "I wish I could say it was due to my acute powers of observation, but I'm afraid it wasn't anything like that. When I arrived, your fever was escalating. You were restless, talking to yourself. I couldn't understand what you were saying, at first. You kept holding your stomach, and I thought you were going to be sick. Then . . . I heard what you were saying." He leaned toward her. " 'Don't take my baby,' " he whispered. "You said it over and over, 'Please, don't take my baby.' "

Molly's eyes burned, and she looked down to see her hand sheltering the child in her womb. Her affection for the precious life inside her had been slow in coming, and still wasn't void of all regret, but she truly did love this baby—*her* baby. And then it occurred her. . . . "I imagine that must have sounded odd for you to hear me saying that."

"Not at all, Dr. Whitcomb . . . under the circumstances."

Seeing the compassion in his eyes, she realized what conclusion he'd drawn. God had allowed her "husband" to die recently, so she had been begging for the life of her child.

Dr. Brookston patiently answered all of her questions and assured her again that there was nothing she could have done to prevent the fever from spiking. "I'd like to see you once a month, which is more often than normal, granted. I'm not expecting any difficulties with your pregnancy, but I'd like to keep a closer watch, if you don't mind."

Encouraged, and not wanting to be late for her appointment with Belle Birch at the general store, she thanked him and opted to take the street instead of facing the throng of Saturday shoppers crowding the boardwalk.

"Mrs. Whitcomb," a man said, tipping his hat. "Glad to see you out again, ma'am."

She returned his greeting.

"Morning, Mrs. Whitcomb," a woman said seconds later.

Molly could hardly take five steps without people welcoming her back to town. By the time she reached the Mullinses' store, she wondered how she could have ever felt so lonely earlier in the week. She spotted Belle waiting for her in a curtained doorway toward the back. "Hello, Mrs. Birch. I hope I'm not late."

"Not at all. You're early." Belle grinned, and held her gaze a little longer than necessary. "I've got your dresses hanging right in here." She retrieved them from a hook. "Go ahead and slip on the first one, then I'll be in."

Curious over how Belle looked at her sometimes, Molly stepped into a side room, closed the door, and slipped on the first dress. She hadn't known Belle Birch was a seamstress until Belle brought a meal by earlier that week. It had come up during conversation, and Molly had commissioned her then and there to make two new dresses. Belle had borrowed one of her gowns to use as a pattern, and Molly had intentionally chosen one that was especially roomy through the bust and waist.

"I'm ready, Mrs. Birch." She admired Belle Birch's handiwork in the mirror on the wall.

"Gifted with a needle and thread" was the only way to describe the woman. The simple black day dress buttoned up the front, but the detail work—the tiny black beads sewn onto the collar and around the wrists and accenting the bodice—was exquisite.

Belle returned, pincushion in hand.

"You outdid yourself, Mrs. Birch. This is absolutely lovely!" And far nicer than anything she had expected.

"I'm glad you're pleased, ma'am." Belle's smile bloomed. "Now, hold still while I fit it to you." Her gaze lowered. "What did I do wrong here?" She gathered the extra fabric at Molly's waistline, frowning. "I cut this way too big for you, ma'am. I'm so sorry."

"Oh no, it's fine. I like it like this."

Belle huffed a soft laugh. "Like what? Big enough where you can 'bout walk right out of it?" She reached for a pin. "I'll just take the waist up about an inch or so on each side. That'll still give you plenty of—"

"No, please, it's fine." Molly stayed Belle's hand on her waist, softening her insistence with a smile. "I've lost weight in recent months—" Which was true, even after becoming pregnant. "But I'm already gaining that weight back. Especially with the way I've been eating this past week. Which reminds me—that stew of yours was delicious."

Belle's frown smoothed. "You liked it?"

"Liked it? Right after you left, Sheriff McPherson stopped by to see how I was. I told him about our visit and what you'd brought, and I just cried."

"You didn't," Belle whispered, her dark eyes sparkling.

"I'm afraid I did. I was an emotional mess." Molly laughed along with her. "I'd been feeling a bit lonely, and the first week of school hadn't gone as—" She caught herself, uncertain how much to reveal. But Belle seemed so genuine and kind. "To be candid with you, it hadn't gone as well as I'd thought it would. I was exhausted and disappointed, and you bringing your stew . . ." She sighed. "Well, it felt like a taste of home."

Belle's eyes went moist. "That's one of the nicest things anyone's ever said to me, Dr. Whitcomb. Thank you, ma'am."

Molly felt herself tearing up too and was surprised when Belle laughed.

"Aren't we a pair?" Belle shook her head. "Look at the two of us, standing here cryin' over stew."

Molly gave her hand a squeeze. "I nearly had to arm-wrestle Sheriff McPherson for the last slice of your corn bread."

"Is that so?" Belle raised a brow, a glint of mischief accompanying the gesture. "My guess is that he would've let you win, ma'am."

Too late, Molly realized that what she'd said could easily be misconstrued. "When he came by,

Sheriff McPherson hadn't eaten yet, so I asked him to join me. That's all."

Belle stared, a smile tracing her lips. "You don't have to offer explanation to me, Dr. Whitcomb."

But Molly felt as though she did. "Sheriff McPherson and I are friends, Mrs. Birch. He's a very kind man, but he doesn't treat me any differently than he treats anyone else."

Belle nodded and began adjusting the hem of the dress. "Yes, ma'am. Whatever you say."

Hearing the doubt in Belle's voice and knowing the woman meant no harm in her teasing, Molly decided that further protest would only make her appear defensive. Which didn't serve her purpose, or James's.

When Belle finished the fittings, they walked outside to the boardwalk together.

"I'll have the dresses ready for you by midweek, ma'am. I'll leave them here at the store."

"Would you like the other half of your payment today?" Molly reached into her reticule. "I can—"

"No, ma'am. When the dresses are done is when I get paid my other half. Thank you, though."

Molly sensed Belle looking at her again, as she had earlier. Feeling they'd formed enough of a friendship, she posed the question gently. "I hope you won't think me forward for asking this, but . . . I'm wondering. . . . On occasion, I get the feeling that . . . you're staring at me. Though maybe I'm imagining it."

Belle looked away, sighing. "No, ma'am. It's not you imagining it. It's me. I try not to stare, but it's hard not to. I'm sorry." Wistfulness softened her features. "You're the spittin' image of the woman whose husband owned me when I lived back in Tennessee."

Molly stared. No matter how hard she tried, the words wouldn't come, not seeing the depth of emotion in Belle's face.

"She was a real good woman, Dr. Whitcomb. She taught me how to read and how to write. But as good as she was—and as innocent—her husband was just as wicked."

Heaviness settled over Molly, and thinking of Elijah, she thought she understood what Belle meant but wasn't saying.

"So that's why I sometimes stare at you, ma'am. I'm sorry for doing it."

Molly took hold of her hand. "There's no need to apologize. I'm just sorry that I remind you of something so painful."

Belle tightened her grip. "What was done to me was wrong, and God's heart broke . . . each time. But I could never be sad over what came out of it. I love my son with all my heart. My husband does too." Unshed tears glistened in her dark eyes. "That man who owned me did me wrong." She shook her head. "But God, in His great mercy, He worked it for good. Like He does, in time, for those who are His and who love Him. So when I look at you, ma'am, it's not pain I'm feelin'. I'm thankin' the Lord for standin' beside me through those dark times, when I thought I was alone"— she smiled—"but never was."

Molly was halfway through town on her way home, her thoughts still with Belle, her tears barely dry, when she heard someone calling her name.

"*Signora* Whitcomb!"

She didn't have to look to know who it was. She waited until he drew closer. "Angelo Giordano!" she said with an Italian accent, and he beamed. She asked him how he was, but as he answered, she drew her own conclusions. She tried to convince herself that he'd gained some weight, but the thinness of his arms lent little evidence of that. And the sallow look of his skin didn't either.

"Did Sheriff McPherson find you a job?" she asked in his native tongue.

"*Si, signora.*" He spoke quickly, and twice she had to encourage him to please talk more slowly— *Parli lentamente.*

James had indeed helped find him a job, which was encouraging. Angelo worked at a ranch outside of town, mucking stalls and baling hay. It was hard enough to imagine the boy lifting a pitchfork, much less hefting bales of hay.

But it was his question to her that Molly found most interesting. And compelling.

She stared, a smile coming to her face. *"Dimmi, vuoi imparare l'inglese?"*

"Si, Signora Whitcomb. *"Sarò bravo, ve lo prometto."*

He wanted to learn to speak English, and she had no doubt he would be a good student, as he'd said he would be.

They arranged their first meeting for an afternoon the coming week, and his face lit when she invited him to meet her at the schoolhouse after classes were dismissed.

His next question came more slowly, and she sensed it held great importance to him.

She was touched by the sincerity of his invitation. *"Si,* Angelo." She would be honored to come to his home and meet his family soon.

He dipped his head repeatedly. *"Grazie, Signora Whitcomb. Grazie mille."*

They walked together to the edge of town, where he continued on down the road. Molly took the turnoff toward the cabin, eager to get home.

She was nearly past the schoolhouse when she looked over to see the door ajar. Strange. Maybe Josiah hadn't closed it firmly enough on his last visit. He'd volunteered to hang some maps for her. But it wasn't like him to leave the door unlatched. He was always so thorough in his work.

Molly climbed the stairs and pushed open the door. She spotted a boy seated at one of the desks toward the front. Hunched over, intent on whatever he was doing, he didn't look up. She took a closer look.

"Billy?" she asked quietly, not wishing to scare him.

Billy Bolden jumped up, nearly knocking over the desk. "Dr. Whitcomb!" His face reddened as a book hit the floor with a *thwak!* "I didn't know you would be in today, ma'am."

Molly approached, looking around the empty room. "What are you doing here, Billy? And on a beautiful Saturday afternoon, no less." As if she didn't already have a good idea.

His gaze darted to the book on the floor. "I'm sorry that I broke the rules by being in here outside of class time, ma'am."

She smiled in the hope of putting him at ease, more than a little curious as to what book he was reading. "You haven't broken any rules by being here, Billy."

"Oh yes, ma'am! Pa says I'm not supposed to come in here anytime outside of school hours. He said it's a rule."

Molly didn't know of any such rule existing, but she didn't wish to go against the boy's father either. She still wasn't in good standing with Hank Bolden, not since the incident with Angelo Giordano. Every time Mr. Bolden saw her, he gave her a withering glare. She couldn't understand how a man as hard-edged and hostile as Hank Bolden could have a son as kind and thoughtful as Billy.

Then again, perhaps she did know.

Billy's mother, Ida, was Billy in female form. Ida Bolden had brought by dinner one afternoon last week with instructions that she would pick up her dishes sometime later, and for Molly not to bother bringing them to church. Which made her wonder if Hank Bolden was aware of his wife's kindness, and if so, might he disapprove?

Question lit Billy's eyes. "How are you feeling, Dr. Whitcomb? Better, I hope?"

"Much better, thank you." She glanced at the book on the floor, unable to read the title. "May I ask"—she indicated the book with a nod—"what you're reading?"

Billy nodded and bent to retrieve it. Guilt clouding his features, he held out the volume, his shoulders slumping. "You said not to take any books off the special shelf without your permission, ma'am. I'm sorry, but I started reading this the last afternoon of class, and"—his voice grew more earnest—"I just couldn't wait any longer to find out what happened next."

Molly read the title and lifted a brow. *"The Life and Strange Surprising Adventures of Robinson Crusoe of York, Mariner."* It was her personal copy and an early edition. Not rare or particularly valuable, but special. Her father had read it to her when she was a child.

"If you need to tell my pa—" Billy's swallow was audible—"I-I'll understand, ma'am."

Molly urged his chin back up. "I would never encourage you to do something against your father's—or mother's—wishes, Billy. So, since your pa said you're not to be in here outside of school, you'll need to leave."

He nodded, turning to go.

"But—" She waited until he looked back. "You'll have to take this with you." His sudden grin drew one from her. "Under one condition! You'll have to tell me when you get to the part about the shipwreck."

"Which one, ma'am? There've already been two!"

She laughed. Billy Bolden was by far her most avid reader in class. "I don't want to spoil anything for you. Finish the book, and then we'll discuss it. Agreed?"

Grinning, Billy nodded, a hank of hair falling into his eyes. "Thank you, Dr. Whitcomb. I'll take good care of it too." He was almost to the door when it opened.

Elijah Birch stopped short in the entryway. "Excuse me," he said quietly to Billy, then turned in her direction. "I knocked on your cabin door, ma'am. You weren't there. I didn't mean to . . . I don't aim to be a bother."

"You're never a bother, Elijah." Molly joined the boys at the door, seeing the book she'd loaned Elijah in his hand.

"Have you read that?" Billy asked, excitement in his voice.

Elijah gave a shy nod, as though uncertain whether he should admit to such a thing.

"I loaned Elijah this book a week ago," Molly offered. "He's a very—"

"You read it in a week?" Billy's eyes widened. "It took me two!"

Normally Molly would have corrected Billy for interrupting, but hearing his enthusiasm and seeing Elijah's proud smile, she didn't have the heart to.

Elijah nodded again. "I liked it. A lot." He laughed softly. "I thought it was funny in parts."

"Me too!" Billy moved closer. "What part did you like best? Mine was when they started digging the hole for the cannon, and then Barbicane says to . . ."

Molly looked between the boys as they spoke, marveling at their love for the story, but even more at the unlikelihood of their pairing. She knew Hank Bolden wouldn't approve of the friendship. And while she doubted Josiah and Belle would disapprove, she couldn't help but think they would be cautious about it, knowing what kind of man Billy's father was.

"Have you read the next book yet? This one here?" Billy walked to the shelf and pulled off *Twenty Thousand Leagues Under the Sea*. He glanced at Molly, and she nodded her approval. "It's really good too."

Elijah took it, holding it like a prized gift, just as Molly had done with her books when she was their age.

"Thank you," Elijah said, directing the comment to them both. He turned to go, and Billy followed him out the door.

"When you're done with that one, I'll pass this one along to you. Dr. Whitcomb just loaned it to me today. It's got shipwrecks and . . . ."

Molly watched the boys as they headed away from town and toward the stream, wondering if their chosen direction was intentional. They were both old enough to know that being seen together in town wouldn't be viewed as right by some. Feeling somewhat responsible for their friendship, she prayed for them.

Several times later that night, she awakened, not feeling anxious or scared, but thinking about what Belle had told her. She viewed both Josiah and Elijah through that lens, and found her respect for their family deepening. Angelo Giordano came to mind. She could hear his strong Italian accent, see his dark eyes and too-thin arms, and was eager to teach him English but hoped to do much more.

Billy Bolden . . . so bright and studious, such an unquenchable imagination. She sighed and plumped her pillow. Billy would do well, if only she could be the teacher to him—and to the rest of her students God had brought into her life—that she'd once thought she could be.

And then there was James, who was never too far from her thoughts. She hadn't seen him since Tuesday, which was surprising in one way. And not, in another. He had a job to do after all. She scooted her feet closer to the bed warmer, relishing the warmth.

She was much fonder of him than was wise, and felt certain he had a fondness for her too. But not until today, when she'd heard Belle's reaction to his name being mentioned, had she realized that perhaps others had taken notice of that fondness as well, which she couldn't afford to have happen.

But even more, neither could James.

24

On Monday morning Molly walked the short distance to the schoolhouse, a little jittery inside. Though eager to face the challenge before her, she wished she felt more confident. Sunlight streamed through the windows to illuminate the still-shiny finish on the students' desks and cast a sheen on spines of books she knew like old friends. Halfway down the aisle, she slowed her steps.

Her desk wasn't as she'd left it.

She couldn't help her smile, wondering just who had gotten up so early to surprise her. Then again, she didn't have to wonder. She already knew.

She'd seen James briefly at church yesterday; they'd acknowledged each other across the room. More mindful now of being seen together in public, she'd made a point of visiting with others until he and Rachel and the boys had left.

She continued down the aisle, eyeing the bouquet centered on her desk. A beautiful spray of late-blooming wildflowers crowded an amber glass vase, blooms cascading over the sides, dew still on the petals. She deposited her reticule and satchel in her chair and spotted a red-ribboned box of sugar sticks propped up by the vase, along with a folded piece of stationery with her name on it.

He shouldn't have done this. Yet she couldn't deny that part of her was happy he had.

The sound of a rider approaching drew her attention to the window. Seeing who it was, she went to meet him on the front steps, his unread note in hand.

"Good morning, Sheriff."

James's smile came easily, as it always did. He was freshly shaved and his hair was still damp around the collar. "Morning, *Dr.* Whitcomb."

He tethered Winsome to the post and climbed the stairs, glancing at her dress. "You look real pretty this morning. How are you feeling?"

The black dress she wore he'd seen countless times before, but she still appreciated his compliment. "Thank you, and I'm feeling better. Actually, I'm feeling *much* better since I found a surprise on my desk."

An odd look came over his face; then he smiled. "Since you found a *surprise* on your desk?"

She nodded and walked back inside. He followed.

She gestured to the flowers and candy, then back at him, careful to word her response as a "friend" might. "I haven't read your note yet. . . ." She held it up. "But I appreciate your thoughtfulness, James. Since the day I moved here, you and your sister have treated me more like family than an outsider. And then with everyone bringing food this past week, making me feel so much a part of the community. I have you to thank for that too. You've come to my aid in so many ways. Even when you had no cause to, especially when I fairly much told you exactly that early on." She laughed softly. "What I'm trying to say is how grateful I am for your friendship."

He continued to look at her, his assessment patient, and somewhat of a mystery.

She ran a finger over the edge of the note, and held it up. "Shall I read it now?"

He shifted his weight. "You can if you want to. But one thing you should know before you do"— he removed his hat and set it aside—"is that I didn't write that. But you can believe that right about now—" he gave a humorless laugh and his expression turned decidedly more intimate—"I'm sure wishing I had."

Molly stared for a second, then laughed along with him, realizing he was kidding her again. The man's modesty was endless. Eager to reveal him, she opened the stationery with a flourish and began reading.

And nearly choked.

He stepped closer, and she pressed the note against her chest.

"I'm just guessing here, Molly, but I'm thinking the name you just read at the bottom there . . . it's not mine."

How could she have been so foolish? "James, I'm sorry, I . . . I feel so completely silly right now." That was an understatement, and the quiet stretching between them only accentuated her foolishness.

James withdrew something from his pocket. An apple, shiny and red. He held it out. "I *did* bring something to welcome you back." He glanced beyond her toward the front of the classroom. "But obviously I'm not your first caller of the morning, nor your most elaborate."

She wished the floor would open up and swallow her whole. She took the apple from him, or tried. He held on tight. Her fingers overlapped his, and neither of them let go.

"I didn't write you a note this morning, but I would like to say some things to you. If you have the time."

She could not let happen what she thought was about to happen. She motioned behind her. "I wi-wish I had time, James, but I—"

A smile tipped up one side of his mouth, and Molly felt her own go dry.

"I'd be less than honest with you, Molly, if I let

you keep thinking that all I feel toward you is friendship. I've tried not to feel more, understanding you being so recently widowed, and you being the new schoolteacher." His sigh was self-deprecating. "Not to mention that being 'more than friends' with a man in my profession isn't exactly what most women would aspire to."

Oh, if only you knew. How could a man be so astute about some things, and yet so blind about others?

"I didn't come here this morning with the intention of saying this, so it may come out all wrong." He looked down at the apple, then covered her hand completely with his other. "You're still in mourning. I respect that. I want to be sensitive to your loss, and the life you shared with your husband."

The embarrassment Molly felt quickly faded and gave way to the enormity of her greater predicament. If she had revealed her circumstance from the start, James McPherson would not be standing here now, looking as though he wanted to kiss her.

If she'd arrived in Timber Ridge an unmarried pregnant woman, he would still have treated her with sensitivity, even a certain measure of respect. That's the man he was. But he would not have allowed himself to look upon her as he was doing now, which only added to her regret, and to her dread of the moment when he would learn that she was with child—when she would *tell* him she was with child.

He would view her choice to withhold the information from him, and from the town council, as deceitful. And he would be right. Yet even then, he wouldn't know the full extent of the truth.

Reality curdled the pit of her stomach. In stepping off the train in Sulfur Falls and doing what she'd done, she'd started down a path that gave her no other choice but to continue. Either that, or tell the truth and lose everything.

He stepped closer. Reading his intention, she bowed her head. If only she were the woman he thought she was.

To her surprise—and panic—he tilted up her chin.

She shook her head, a weight pressing inside her chest so that she almost couldn't breathe. "I can't," she managed, her voice wavering.

She knew what it was like to care for someone only to discover they were not who you thought they were. She lived with the pain of that deception every day, and would for the rest of her life. She wouldn't do that to someone else. And certainly not someone she cared for so deeply.

"I know," he said quietly. "That's why I was only going to do this." He kissed her forehead, and lingered there, his breath warm on her skin, then pulled back. "But just to be clear, I'd still like to do the other."

Surprised she was still standing, Molly couldn't help but smile at his honesty. Seeing the truer blue of his eyes so close up, something inside her crumbled. It took her a moment to realize what it was—part of the wall she'd erected to keep herself safe, to keep anyone from hurting her again.

Her sensibilities told her sentiment to shore up the breach, but her heart paid no mind.

"I'll be your friend, Molly Whitcomb, the best friend I know how to be." He caressed the side of her face and traced her lower lip with his thumb. "Until you're ready for me to be something more."

He let go of the apple, and only then did Molly remember it. It would have fallen on the floor if not for his quick reflexes. His smile revealed his pleasure, and he held the apple out again. She took it this time and held on tight.

He slipped his hat back on and walked to the door. "As your friend, Dr. Whitcomb, I hope to see you around town real soon. Maybe we could even . . . ambulate together one evening around the lake."

Molly turned the apple in her hands and nodded, knowing that when that time came, she would have to fabricate some excuse—any excuse—why she couldn't.

Putting her roll book aside, Molly drew her focus from the apple on her desk and to the task at hand, and prayed her idea would work as well in practice as it seemed it would in theory. "We're going to do something a little different this morning, students. I'd like the following pupils to come to the front of the room when I call them, please. Billy Bolden, Amanda Spivey, Bradley Tucker, Benjamin Foster, and Rebecca Taylor."

She waited until the five older children had joined her before continuing, aware of the remaining students whispering amongst themselves.

"These five students are going to be the leaders of five different groups this morning." The students standing beside her exchanged expectant smiles. "I'm going to give each group an assignment, then will take turns working with each group as you apply yourselves to the lesson. We're going to meet in these groups but will also have time to interact together. Each person in the group will have a job, and I'll give that to them personally." She looked at Billy standing next to her. "Billy, I want you to take the following students and arrange your desks up here in the right corner."

She began reading the list of students belonging to Billy's group but heard someone talking. She looked up to discover it was Kurt Boyd. No surprise there. The boy quieted as soon as she looked at him, but the glint in his eyes again confirmed his lack of remorse.

She counted on this new plan to keep him more on task. Because if not, she would be forced to speak with Rachel about his discipline problems, and that was one conversation she didn't want to have.

Once the groups were assigned and the students

congregated their desks in various parts of the room, she gave them their first lesson. "Take out your *McGuffey's Readers,* please," she said, then went around to each group and gave them a specific page number.

As the morning progressed, the five older students clearly enjoyed their role, and the younger students in their groups—assigned based on level of study, as well as age and personality—seemed to as well. Her ability to interact with each child was also markedly improved.

She checked her pocket watch a while later and realized they were late in taking lunch recess—by twenty minutes! The morning had flown by and nearly every student seemed to have benefitted from the new methodology.

During recess Molly remained at her desk, making adjustments to the upcoming mathematics lesson for two of the groups based on their performance that morning. The sound of children laughing and playing drifted in through open windows.

"Dr. Whitcomb?"

She looked up to find Rebecca Taylor standing in the doorway. "Yes, Rebecca?"

The girl's lips moved but nothing came out at first. "I . . . I just wanted to thank you, teacher . . . for picking me to lead one of the groups. I liked it."

Molly leaned forward at her desk. "And what did you like most about it?"

A shy smile broke through. "What I learned."

The girl could not have said anything more perfect. "Thank you, Rebecca." Molly checked her pocket watch. "In five more minutes, would you ring the bell, please?"

Squaring her shoulders, Rebecca nodded. "Yes, ma'am." She left with an uncustomary spring in her step.

Molly let out a satisfied sigh. In all her years of training, in all the settings in which she'd received instruction, the most productive for her had been when she'd been forced to grapple with the lessons individually. When she'd had to explain what she'd learned—or thought she'd learned—to others. That sense of responsibility and ownership had been a powerful motivator for her, and it seemed to have struck a chord with these children too.

She leaned back in her chair—relieved, excited, hopeful—and reached for the apple on her desk. She cradled it in the palm of her hand, remembering the scene from earlier that morning—and finally allowed herself to think about James.

They'd spent considerable time getting to know each other in recent weeks, and yet, that he would have grown to care for her so much was something she could hardly fathom. She rubbed the smooth red skin of the fruit. Then again, he didn't really know who she was, now did he?

The question stung.

She stared at the apple, thinking of it in the context of another story, one ages old and well-known to her. Except in that story, the woman had given the man the apple. But one thing was the same. The woman had been the one to deceive.

She needed to tell him—and the town council—about the child. And she would. Soon, as though she had a choice. She just needed more time to prove her worth as a teacher. Maybe they would let her stay on then.

Even as the thought formed, she pictured Mayor Davenport and Hank Bolden and knew her chances of that happening were nil.

A breeze stirred the flowers on her desk. The box of candy remained unopened. She appreciated Brandon Tolliver's thoughtfulness, but his offerings paled in comparison to what she'd already been given, and she planned on declining his invitation, yet again, for dinner at the new resort.

The bell signaling the end of recess rang, and she realized she hadn't eaten anything. She took a bite of the apple and its juice rolled down her chin. She swiped at it with her finger. When she pulled her hand away, she looked at her wedding band. The ring had lost much of its shine and was darker in places now than it had been. The thin layer of gold was wearing off, as the salesman had guaranteed it would.

She took another bite of apple, just now seeing the resemblance between the ring she'd purchased and the life she'd chosen. And suddenly she wasn't hungry anymore.

25

"T his meeting of the Timber Ridge town council
will now come to order." Mayor Davenport
pounded the gavel three times, which was three
times more than needed seeing that everyone was
already quieted down and looking at the man.

James settled back into his chair and rubbed the
taut muscles in his neck. He wasn't of a mind to
listen to Davenport's ramblings this evening. Not
with what he'd dealt with in the past couple of
weeks. It had already been a long day, and being
Tuesday, the week wasn't even half gone yet.

Davenport had moved the town council meeting
to his office. Fifteen men gathered around a table
meant for ten. The space was tight, but at least
someone had opened a window, and the brisk fall
evening offered a welcome breeze. His thoughts
turned to Davenport going behind his back to push
Dean Willis to run for sheriff come spring.

He'd opposed Davenport on several issues, so
the man's dislike of him wasn't surprising. Neither
were his underhanded tactics. If there was one
thing James valued in a person above all else it was
honesty, straightforwardness. Tell a man to his
face, whatever it was. Even if it was something he
wouldn't like. Don't make him find out from
somebody else.

He peered through the open window to the street.

It wasn't like Molly to be late. She was scheduled to give an update on how the first few weeks of school had progressed.

Davenport cleared his throat the way he always did before he began. Ben Mullins had jokingly named the habit "the second gaveling." James caught Ben's attention down the table and found the man smiling his way.

James nodded, welcoming the subtle humor.

"The first order of business," Davenport began, "is to review the minutes from the last meeting." He turned to his brother-in-law. "Hank Bolden will read those for us."

As Bolden read, James watched the door.

He still didn't know what had gotten into him that morning when he'd stopped by the schoolhouse to welcome Molly back following her illness. He went there to give her an apple and wish her well. Next thing he knew, he was telling her the truth of his feelings. But when she'd mentioned his friendship again, it just hadn't sat right with him to let her go on thinking that was all he felt.

Of course, that wasn't the whole truth behind his motivation that morning, and he knew it.

Part of him was flat bothered to have discovered someone leaving her gifts, and he had a good idea who that someone had been. Brandon Tolliver. Turns out, the man had delivered the safety report as requested and on time. Everything *seemed* to be in order.

James couldn't prove anything, but he was suspicious: How much had Tolliver paid to secure the report? Beyond the safety inspector's regular fee and travel expenses.

James shifted in his chair again, restless.

Hank Bolden continued to read the notes from last month's meeting, and James let his thoughts wander.

Another calf had gone missing this week, and this time no trace of a carcass had been found. Accusations were already being made, with fingers pointing to out-of-work miners surly over the recent dry spell in silver ore deposits. The men were bored and needed work and weren't finding it, so they were finding trouble instead.

Three of them sat in his jail cells right now, awaiting transport to Denver, where they'd stand trial. Two had beaten an Italian worker nearly to death out near Little Italy—the area where Italian families had erected shacks and makeshift tents. The men said they were angry over "his kind" taking their jobs at the resort.

Then one miner shot another point-blank in a game of poker yesterday at one of the saloons. Over a twenty-seven-dollar kitty. James sighed and raked a hand through his hair. He'd wired the U.S. Marshal's office, and they were sending one of their men to transport the prisoners to Denver later next week.

He'd posted Willis at the jail, with another

deputy scheduled to relieve him during the night. Tension was escalating between the different groups in town, threats being made back and forth. More and more, his job felt like trying to keep a lid settled on a boiling pot.

He'd ridden out to Little Italy earlier this week to see the family of the man who was beaten. He'd taken a meal Rachel had prepared, and the family was grateful. But he was glad he'd discouraged her from going with him. The people in the settlement had so little, and it was painful to see how they lived. The church had helped some, but so much more still needed to be done. Come hard winter, he didn't know how they were going to make it through.

The door opened and he looked up.

"Dr. Brookston," Mayor Davenport said. "Glad you could join us, sir. We've already begun the meeting."

"I apologize for my lateness. I just came from seeing a patient."

Seeing Brookston coming his way, medical bag in hand, James pulled up another chair. Men shook the doctor's hand as he walked past, thanking him for tending their families during the recent illness.

"Gentlemen—" Davenport pounded the gavel again. "The town council has been called to order."

James suppressed a sigh, thinking of someone *he'd* like to pound.

Dr. Brookston took a seat beside him and slid an

envelope toward him on the table, then leaned close. "Dr. Whitcomb asked me to give this to you, Sheriff," he whispered. "It's her report for—"

"Dr. Brookston"—Mayor Davenport's expression showed clear interest, and mild disapproval— "we very much look forward to hearing your contribution at the appropriate time, sir."

Brookston hesitated, then cleared his throat. "Thank you, Mayor. I appreciate the invitation to be here."

Hank Bolden resumed reading the notes again, and Brookston raised a subtle brow as if to say, "We almost got ourselves in trouble." James made a feeble attempt to mask his smile.

"Now we'll move to new topics of business," Davenport said. "And we'll begin with . . ."

Halfway listening as Davenport spoke, James discreetly opened the envelope from Molly, wondering why she hadn't come herself. He pulled out a sheet of paper, and a smaller sheet came with it. He read the smaller first.

Dear Sheriff McPherson,

Enclosed is the report I intended to present to the town council this evening. If you would deliver the report in my stead, I would be most appreciative. It only seems fitting, since you're my appointed liaison.

With a myriad of thanks,
your friend, Dr. Whitcomb

With a myriad of thanks . . .

James felt a smile inside. She could be downright persnickety when she wanted to be, in an attractive sort of way. He'd been reading his dictionary lately and had come across plenty of words he hadn't known, but none yet that he was willing to bet were new to Molly. But he'd find one. . . .

He scanned the report she'd written and found himself wanting to read more slowly. Impressive . . . and not what he'd been expecting. Already, he could predict the mayor's initial reaction at hearing what she'd done, then the change in him when Davenport heard the results thus far.

But it was Molly's closing paragraph that struck a chord inside him.

"Dr. Brookston—"

Hearing Davenport address the doctor, James looked up.

Mayor Davenport arranged the papers before him. "We'd like to hear the outcome of your proposal now, Doctor. Would you say that offering physical examinations to the schoolchildren was met with success?"

Brookston stood, his chair scraping the floor. "Yes, Mr. Mayor, I would. I would even venture to say great success. But, before I broach that subject, I'd like to tell you that, on my recommendation, Dr. Whitcomb has stayed home this evening."

James sat up straighter.

"She's fine. She simply feels a bit under the weather," Brookston continued. "Several of her students have colds and sniffles, and since Dr. Whitcomb was so ill last month, I encouraged her to stay in and get her rest."

Frowning, Davenport opened his mouth, but the doctor pressed on.

"I encouraged this not only for her health, sirs, but in the interest of all students and of keeping the school year moving forward, as I'm sure you gentlemen will agree." Brookston gave the mayor a nod. "However, as you would expect from our dedicated professor"—his tone held admiration—"she prepared a report on the school's progress, which I've given to Sheriff McPherson, per her request."

James worked to pay attention as the doctor summarized his findings to the group, but all he wanted to do was head over to Molly's cabin to make sure she had everything she needed.

He'd seen her a handful of times in recent days. Rachel had invited her out to the house to eat and she'd accepted. And he'd taken her out to the Spiveys' one afternoon to buy a horse. James was just glad LuEllen hadn't been there. He didn't want the woman to get any ideas about him and Molly, not with her matchmaking ways.

He'd tried twice to collect on that walk around the lake, but each time Molly had been busy. After reading her report, he knew why.

"Sheriff—"

He was pulled back by Davenport's voice. "Yes, Mayor?"

"Would you provide us with an update of what's happening in the sheriff's office and of the current . . . climate in town regarding safety and well-being within the community? Then would you please follow with Dr. Whitcomb's report?"

Ignoring the formality in Davenport's manner—the man would have them all wearing robes if he could—James told them about the prisoners sitting in his jail, and the charges against each.

Davenport set down his glass of water. "Will Mrs. Ranslett be including an article about these crimes in the *Timber Ridge Reporter*?"

James stared, not sure where the mayor was going with his question. "Mrs. Ranslett customarily reports on events that happen in town, both the positive and negative. So, yes, I'd say she would be reporting on these two incidents."

Mayor Davenport frowned and leaned forward, hands steepled before him. "Is there any way she might be persuaded to delay publishing her stories until after the town's celebration at the end of the month? That's just over two weeks away. It seems fitting that the town be given an opportunity to celebrate Colorado's statehood without the occasion being overshadowed by these . . . recent occurrences. Let the people believe," he continued, his voice gaining emotion, "in the goodness of Timber Ridge, and be proud of what a fine place this is to live."

Silence filled the room.

James stared. "Mayor Davenport, a man was killed and another was nearly beaten to death. Without Dr. Brookston's skills, he would have died. I believe people have a right to know what's happening in their town—both the good and the bad. Mrs. Ranslett has used excellent judgment up until now, and I wouldn't presume to tell her what she can or cannot print in the town's newspaper. If I'm not mistaken, there's an amendment that protects that particular right."

Davenport's gaze turned steely, and in the silence, James heard Willis's ticket for sheriff being written in stone.

James picked up Mrs. Whitcomb's report. "If there's no further discussion, gentlemen, I'll read Dr. Whitcomb's report." When no further conversation ensued, he began. He got through the first paragraph and continued reading, surprised that Davenport hadn't—

"Groups?" Davenport asked, nearly coming out of his seat. "She has older students leading groups?"

"Yes, sir." James nodded. "Under her instruction and guidance. If you'll allow me to—"

"But we hired *her* to teach the students." The mayor grew red in the face. "Not for the students to teach themselves. Hank, your son's in her class. Did you know about this?"

"No, I didn't." Hank Bolden sat forward. "And furthermore, as a parent I think I should be informed before the teacher goes making any changes like this. After all, the town council's the governing body of this town, and—"

"Gentlemen." James held up a hand. "If you'll allow me to continue reading Dr. Whitcomb's report, I believe it will answer some of your questions. And objections." Out of respect for the mayor's position, he waited for Davenport's response.

"Very well, then. Proceed, Sheriff."

James started where he'd left off, imagining the lilt of Molly's voice in her words as she described her methods in more detail along with the students' increased enthusiasm and improvement.

But when he came to the final paragraph, he paused. This was the part he'd found so touching.

"As I understand it, gentlemen, you had many applicants for this position, yet you chose me. My state of arrival to Timber Ridge was somewhat unexpected, and you could have very well returned to those applications and chosen another person for this job, but you did not. You allowed me an opportunity to prove myself, to get to know your children, and your town, and I am most grateful. I will continue to work my hardest to prove my worth to the town council, to my students, and to the town of Timber Ridge.

Humbly submitted,
your teacher, Dr. Molly Whitcomb"

James stared at the page, hoping his softer tone there at the end hadn't given his feelings away. He looked up. Some of the men were staring at their laps, most were looking to Davenport to see how he would react.

Davenport clasped his hands on the table before him. "Thank you, Sheriff McPherson, for reading Dr. Whitcomb's report. It's most . . . informative. I, for one, would like more information on this 'method' of teaching she's developed, as she calls it. Sheriff, on behalf of the town council, would you request that she submit more information to us, and that she also provide future updates on the children's improvement? I think that information would be most beneficial to have on hand."

"I'll pass that request along to her, sir." James sat down, aware of Davenport watching him.

"It would seem, Sheriff, that your recommendation to the town council on the choice of schoolteacher paid off after all."

James felt the rub in Davenport's compliment. "I was judging strictly from accomplishments on paper, Mayor. I didn't know Dr. Whitcomb any more than any of you did, sir."

"But you said you had a gut feeling too, if I remember correctly." Davenport looked at his brother-in-law, Hank Bolden. Bolden nodded as if he remembered the exact moment in question.

James had learned long ago which battles were worth fighting and which weren't. "Yes, sir, I have those gut feelings about people from time to time." He leveled his gaze. "And I'm usually right on the mark."

Davenport slowly nodded. "Next on our agenda, gentlemen, is . . ."

James slipped the report back into the envelope, suspicious of what Davenport would do with the information from Molly once he received it. No telling what was going on in the man's mind. But whatever it was, his motivations were certain to be of benefit to himself first, Timber Ridge second, and maybe to Molly somewhere down the line.

As for Molly herself, he wanted to know how a woman so intelligent, so accomplished, so poised, and with so many reasons to feel worthy, could still possess the need to prove her worth.

26

Students, we only have ten minutes before class will be over, so—"

Groans and sighs, like music to Molly's ears, rose from the students. She tousled Ansley Tucker's hair, pleased when the girl beamed up at her. "So please record your solutions on your slates, and I'll come around to check everyone's work."

The week had flown by, and it had been a good one. But she was glad it was Friday afternoon. A chance to rest for the weekend.

She had missed the town council meeting on

Tuesday evening after telling Dr. Brookston she'd been experiencing some minor pelvic pain. He'd said it was routine with where she was in her pregnancy—like the swelling in her feet—and assured her it was nothing to be concerned about. But still, he had encouraged her to stay home and rest, and she'd happily agreed. She'd hoped to see James in town to ask him how the report she'd prepared had been received, but their paths hadn't crossed.

She looked down at the dress Belle Birch had sewn. She'd already worn it several times and loved the intricate beadwork—and roominess in the waistline. Her body was changing. The little pooch in her belly was growing more pronounced. At her last appointment, Dr. Brookston said she was progressing as she should be, which removed the fear of the effects of the fever one notch further from her—

She glanced across the room and caught Kurt Boyd making silly faces at little Libby Tucker. Libby chuckled, then looked back at her slate, chalk in hand. Libby made good marks but had to work hard to get them. Kurt made some of the highest marks in the class—when he tried, which wasn't often.

Kurt nudged Libby's desk with his foot, making an even sillier face this time. Libby giggled, which only encouraged him more.

Molly quietly made her way over to that side of the room. She'd assigned Kurt to Billy Bolden's group. Kurt was exceptionally bright, and he looked up to Billy. But Kurt had a tendency to not finish his work, something she'd been trying to work with him on.

"Kurt."

He looked up. "I already know the answer," he said matter-of-factly, and stated the answer outright.

Students in his group raised their heads. Billy Bolden looked at her and gave her an almost imperceptible shrug, as if to say, "I don't know what to do with him, ma'am."

Molly bent down. "I'm glad you know the answer, Kurt." She pointed to his clean slate. "But I want to see how you arrived at that answer."

"But I don't see how come—"

"And you're going to stay right here in your seat until you complete the task."

His expression was anything but silly now. "But Uncle James is meetin' me at the store to get me a—"

"Kurt." Molly gave him a studied look.

He frowned and gave her one right back. "Yes, ma'am." He hunched over his slate.

Tempted to make him stand in the corner, Molly reminded herself of what had already happened in his young life. The loss of a parent was a huge adjustment—even at an older age. She knew that firsthand, so she reached for extra patience.

She continued checking the other children's

answers while keeping an eye on him. To look at him—redheaded, freckles sprinkled across his nose and cheeks, eyes a dusty cornflower blue—you'd think he'd been kissed by angels on his way to earth. But his attitude in the classroom . . .

One of her most frustrating challenges as a teacher was the child who could and yet didn't. It was like finding a rare diamond in the rough. The qualities of a brilliant jewel were right there, beneath the dull and deceptive exterior. But it took hard work to reach the stone, and even more to unearth the diamond within.

Then there were children like Elijah Birch and Angelo Giordano, who would jump at the chance to learn. Yet who were denied.

"You've all done very good work this week, students. I'm proud of you. Now, all of you are dismissed . . . except for Kurt Boyd. Kurt, I'd like for you to stay after class, please."

Chatter filled the schoolhouse as children gathered jackets and slates and books and, with surprising quickness, emptied from the room into the beautiful fall day waiting outside.

Molly sat down at her desk. "Kurt, please join me, and bring your slate."

The boy did as she asked, his expression decidedly less rebellious.

She checked the work on his slate. Perfect. She looked at him, tempering her frustration with a smile. "Kurt, why does it take you so long to finish your work when you clearly understand the material?"

He shrugged. "I don't know." He looked back at her. "Why do you keep my present here at school?"

She frowned, not following. "I'm sorry?"

"What I made for you." He looked over at the shelf. "You always keep it here."

She trailed his gaze to the insect collection. "Well, I keep it here so I can use it for science projects. Like the one we did last week on insects." She'd made a special point of using his board and had praised him in front of his peers, hoping that might improve things. It hadn't.

"But I made it for you. Not for here."

Molly opened her mouth to respond, then closed it, seeing the situation from his perspective. "You know, I think I *will* take it home with me this weekend. So I can—" she swallowed—"see it when I get up first thing in the morning and when I go to bed at night."

His face brightened. "I can bring you more bugs for it too, if you want. Uncle James will help me cut another board."

"While that would be good, and very much appreciated, I would prefer that you concentrate more on your studies, Kurt. And spend less time trying to make other children laugh in class. It's disruptive and causes students to fall behind in their work."

His nod was anything but enthusiastic. "Yes, ma'am."

She stood on the steps of the schoolhouse and watched him walk toward town, his little shoulders slumped. She prayed for him, for Rachel and Mitchell too, and took a deep breath of cool air, welcoming fall's arrival. The aspen trees covering the mountainside caught the sun, their leaves glistening gold in the light. And the sky was as blue as she could remember, not a cloud in sight.

She glanced in the opposite direction down the road, hoping Angelo wouldn't be late for their lesson. She'd agreed to go with him to meet his family this afternoon and considered getting her horse from the livery, where she kept the mare boarded. But seeing what a lovely day it was, she decided to walk instead. Standing for long periods of time was becoming more of a chore, but Dr. Brookston had encouraged walking.

There she saw Angelo, cresting the hill. She looked back to see if Kurt had rounded the bend in the road. Seeing that he had, she relaxed. There was nothing wrong with her tutoring Angelo. She was teaching him after school hours, on *her* time. Still, she was sure some members of the town council wouldn't like it if they knew.

But Angelo's learning English would improve his life, and his family's. And how could she deny him that opportunity?

She waited for him by the door. "Good afternoon, Angelo."

He grinned coming up the stairs. "Good after-noon . . . Dr. Whitcomb."

"Very nice!" She patted his arm as he came through the door, noticing he wasn't wearing a jacket. It wasn't cold out, just brisk. But his skin felt chilled. "You have been studying." She was careful not to use contractions with him yet. Those were often confusing when someone was first learning the language.

"Yes, ma'am. I have . . . much study."

"I can tell. Your pronunciation is very good."

"*Graz—*" He stopped himself, a shy smile forming. "Thank you . . . ma'am."

This was their third week of studying together. The first week he'd come to the schoolhouse three afternoons. Last week four afternoons. And this week, he hadn't missed an afternoon yet.

"I made more cards for you." She held them up and loved how his eyes lit. She went through the cards, one by one. She'd written Italian words at the top and the corresponding English word at the bottom. She said the word aloud in English, and he repeated it. Then she used it in a sentence in Italian and waited for him to translate.

She wished he had a partner to work with him, but none of his family spoke English. Repetition was what had helped her learn languages more than anything else. That, and simply hearing the language spoken.

Once they'd circulated through the cards three

times, she put them aside. "Very good, now let's try a few more sentences. Ready?"

He nodded.

"Dov'e la Posta?"

He thought for a moment. "Where is . . . the . . . post office?"

"Excellent! And another—"

The door to the schoolhouse opened, and she turned.

Billy Bolden and Elijah Birch stopped inside the doorway. They looked at her, then at Angelo, and their expressions revealed surprise, as hers no doubt did.

She stood and Angelo did the same. "Billy, Elijah." Smiling, she met the boys at the back of the room, trying not to think about Mayor Davenport and Hank Bolden, Billy's uncle and father. "Can I help you two with something?"

Elijah peered past her in Angelo's direction, a half-eaten piece of jerky in his hand. "We just came by to get another book to read this weekend, Dr. Whitcomb."

"You said we could, ma'am," Billy chimed in, angling his head to look around her too. "Remember?"

"Of course I do. Here, let me choose one you haven't read yet." She walked to the bookshelf to make a quick selection.

"Good . . . afternoon."

Hearing Angelo's voice behind her, Molly

cringed. But not at his having introduced himself. She cringed at her own rudeness. She turned in time to see Angelo walk over and extend his hand, and for Billy Bolden to shake it. Emotion stung her eyes, and the significance of the simple exchange washed over her. Mere boys doing what their elders could not . . .

"My name's Billy Bolden."

"And mine's Elijah Birch." Elijah stuck out his hand too.

Angelo accepted it, then touched his chest. "Angelo Giordano," he said quickly.

Billy smiled, fingering the jerky in his hand. "That's sure a mouthful, isn't it?"

Angelo laughed, and Molly knew he was responding more to the kindness in Billy's tone, certain he hadn't understood what Billy had said.

Elijah gestured. "Is Dr. Whitcomb giving you English lessons?"

"Yes, I am." Molly pulled a book from the shelf and joined them. "Angelo is a quick learner and is doing very well."

"She . . . good . . . teacher."

Molly saw Angelo eyeing the jerky in the boys' hands, and so did Elijah.

Elijah tore his piece in half. "Here, want some? It's good, but I'm gettin' full." He patted his stomach and bloated his cheeks.

Angelo's shy smile returned. He shook his head, but the way he swallowed was revealing.

Elijah didn't draw back his hand. He just kept smiling, and Molly glimpsed both of his parents in the gesture. "How do you say *please* in Italian, Dr. Whitcomb?"

"Per favore," she whispered.

Offering the jerky a second time, Elijah repeated the words. But he said them without a hint of Italian inflection, and they all laughed.

Angelo accepted the jerky. *"Grazie,"* he whispered. *"Grazie mille."* He took a bite, then closed his eyes and chewed.

Molly nodded to Billy and Elijah, so proud of them. Of all three of them. "He says thank you. Thank you very much."

A while later, Molly stole a look at Angelo as she walked beside him toward his home. Billy had given Angelo another piece of jerky before they'd left, and Angelo had slipped it in his pocket, along with the rest of the piece Elijah had given him. She was certain Angelo could have eaten it all, but he was saving it. Presumably, for his family.

They'd spoken in English when they'd first left the schoolhouse, but when the conversation took a deeper turn, she'd switched to Italian, and Angelo followed her lead.

"So is your family expecting a visitor this afternoon?"

Angelo nodded. "I told them you were coming. I have told my mama about you." He grinned. "She is eager to meet the woman who rescued me from the mean shopkeeper."

Molly laughed softly. How would Angelo react if he knew that Billy was the son of that *mean shopkeeper*? "Thank you for carrying the basket. Is it too heavy?"

He looked at her as though she'd insulted him, but the sparkle in his eyes said otherwise. "I am a big strong Italian man. I can do anything!"

"Spoken like a true man. Regardless of heritage."

Gratitude deepened his smile. "Thank you, Dr. Whitcomb"—he indicated the basket in his arms—"for this."

"It is a custom where I am from." She'd already spoken to him about Georgia and where it was located in the country. "If you are from the South, then you must not go to someone's home the first time without taking something. So thank you for accepting my gift. You have allowed me to save face with my people."

He briefly bowed his head, and she glimpsed a gentlemanliness in the boy that would take him far—if he was given the opportunity to grow into a man.

Little Italy was not more than a half mile or so from town, but the stark contrast of how these families lived versus how families in town lived was numbing. Molly followed as they passed shack after shack, tent after dilapidated tent. The smell of human waste drifted toward her, then abated. Children were plentiful, most of them thin, like Angelo. None of them well nourished.

By the time they reached Angelo's *home*—which consisted of several tarpaulins tied together with rope, staked with what looked to be leftover pieces of lumber that had been nailed together—Molly wished she'd emptied her entire cupboard instead of bringing only a basketful of items.

Angelo lifted the flap of the tent as if living in such a place were normal. It took a moment for her eyes to adjust to the dim light. A woman sat in the corner on a pallet, and Molly guessed who she was.

The woman's head came up as they entered. "Angelo? Is that you?" Her voice was soft, her Italian accent even thicker than her son's.

"Yes, Mama. It is your Angelo." He put down the basket, went to her, and kissed her left cheek, then her right. "I have brought a guest as I said I would." He motioned Molly forward.

The woman held out her hands, and the milky white of her sightless eyes answered the question before it had fully formed in Molly's mind.

"Come close, Mrs. Whitcomb, I want to meet the woman who has shown such kindness to my son."

Molly knelt, and Angelo's mother ran her fingers over her face.

"It is a pleasure to meet you, Mrs. Giordano,"

Molly whispered. "Your Angelo is a fine son. You have every reason to be proud of him."

"Come and sit. Yes, my Angelo is a jewel. But you . . . you are teaching my only son this new language. He will be able to get a fine job and care for us."

Molly prayed that would be true.

"But you must speak to him about this . . . walking in the clouds he is doing. It is dangerous, no?"

Molly looked to Angelo, not following.

"I work at building Mr. Tolliver's hotel in my spare time. It is nothing." He hugged his mother again. "Mama, you worry for no reason. I will be fine."

For the next couple of hours, Molly mostly sat and listened as Angelo's mother spoke of their homeland and of how her husband had died shortly after they reached the Americas. She met Angelo's three younger sisters, all dark and lovely, and with the same shy smile as their brother. Neighbors came to visit while she was there. They all seemed to know each other and share a common concern for each other's welfare.

When it came time for her to leave, Angelo rose as well. Once to the edge of Little Italy, Molly turned to him. "I am fine to walk the rest of the way by myself, Angelo. It is not far, and I know the way." She pulled her shawl closer about her shoulders. "Besides, it is too cold for you to be out. You have no coat."

He waved off her concern. "I am not cold."

"Please, Angelo, go back home and help your mama and your sisters. I will see you next week for our lesson."

He did as she requested, though was slow to comply.

On her way home, Molly couldn't help but contrast her life with the lives of the people she'd just met. Not that she hadn't had challenges in the past and wouldn't have them in her future—she certainly would. But meeting someone whose life was so much harder than her own, and considering what it would be like to change places with them, made her own journey seem considerably less difficult.

The sun was half hidden behind the mountains to the west, and the brisk September breeze that had rustled fallen leaves earlier in the day now gusted through the stands of aspen, stripping leaves from their limbs.

Molly bowed her head against the wind and quickened her pace. She would make it home before dark—it was only a short walk—and was already looking forward to sitting in front of the fireplace with a cup of hot tea. As soon as she thought about it, she felt a touch of guilt, remembering the dwellings of the families she'd just left.

She raised her head to see two men walking in her direction on the opposite side of the road. Neither looked her way, and from habit, not recognizing them, she kept her head down as they passed. Farther down the road an inexplicable shiver scuttled up her spine. And an inaudible voice told her to *run*.

She chanced a look back and saw the men coming toward her.

27

Molly ran as hard as she could, cold air churning her lungs. But footfalls gained behind her. One of the men grabbed her shawl. She shrugged it off. The other man grabbed her.

She screamed and struggled, and nearly fell. But he held her arm tight.

"Where you runnin' to, ma'am?"

"She's in some big kind of hurry—I'll tell you that much."

Winded, Molly didn't respond. She searched the road both ways. No one. She wasn't five minutes from the schoolhouse. It was just over the rise and down in the valley.

The man holding her moved closer and brought a rank odor with him. "I've seen you in town. You're that new teacher." His breath was stale with smoke. "I hear tell you're real smart."

The men were younger than she'd thought at first glance. But their skin had an ashen tone to it, grayed and creased.

The second man, the larger of the two, fingered

the fabric of her sleeve. She pulled away, but the grip on her arm tightened. They both laughed. "We heard you can make that same talk as them foreigners who're taking all our jobs. Is that right, ma'am?"

Eyeing her slowly, he began unbuttoning his coat, and Molly felt sick inside.

"I tell you, ma'am. For knowing so many different ways to talk, you sure don't say much."

Oh, God, please help me. "I n-need—" She dug deep for courage. "I need to be on my way. Someone's expecting me right now." She jerked her arm away, but the man who held her only pulled her back against him.

His friend tossed his coat aside, nodding. "There you go. You *can* use that tongue of yours." He smiled. "Say something for me in that different talk. And make it sweet."

Molly shook her head.

He grabbed her jaw and forced her face back. "I said, say something in that—"

A thrashing noise sounded from deep within the woods.

The man holding her took a step back but didn't let go. He cursed softly. "What's that?"

His partner didn't answer. He just stared into the dense stand of evergreens.

Molly did the same, going from sickened and scared to petrified and unable to move. Of all the animals inhabiting these mountains, only one came to mind. As did the image of what Thomas Boyd's body must have looked like when they'd found him.

The thrashing grew louder. Sharp cracks and pops. It sounded as if trees were being trampled. Both men drew back. The one man let go of her arm.

Molly took steps away from them but couldn't take her eyes off the woods. The upper bough of an evergreen shook and she held her breath, praying—when Charlie Daggett crashed through the foliage, a bottle in his left hand.

He saw her and his eyes widened. He staggered a step as if trying to maintain his balance. "Miss Molly. What you doin' out here, ma'am?" He blinked and his gaze swung to the men beside her.

Confusion washed over his features, then quickly cleared.

Charlie looked back at Molly as if to confirm what he'd somehow deciphered.

She nodded, praying he was sober enough to understand.

What gentleness there was in the Charlie Daggett she knew disappeared. But he was drunk. She could smell it on him from where she stood, and the half-empty bottle in his hand confirmed it. Even as big as he was, he could barely stand. There was no way he could fight off—

Charlie started toward the men. The man without his coat drew a knife from a sheath on his belt.

Even watching, Molly wasn't sure how Charlie

got ahold of the man's wrist. But he did. And she heard a pop. The man screamed, dropped the knife, and cursed Charlie at the top of his lungs.

Charlie started toward the other man, who grabbed his partner by the shirt and hauled him down the road. Their trot became a run and neither looked back.

Charlie stood stalwart, watching their retreat. "You okay, Miss Molly?"

"Yes," she whispered, still hearing the sound of the man's wrist snap. "Thank you . . . Mr. Daggett." She took another breath. "For coming when you did."

He walked to where her shawl lay in the dirt, his steps slow and measured. He picked it up and walked back, stopping for the knife too. All while still cradling the bottle in his grip. "They touched you, Miss Molly. On your face."

She reached up and felt her jaw, and came away with black dust on her fingertips. "But that's all they did," she whispered. "Thanks to you."

Tenderness moved in behind his eyes, and he held out her shawl. "Miss Molly?"

"Yes, Mr. Daggett?"

"I heard about you losin' your man, before you come west. I don't know if I ever said how sorry I was about that." He slipped the knife into his coat pocket. "But in case I didn't, I want to now."

"Thank you, Mr. Daggett. That's most kind of you."

"I'll see you safely home, ma'am."

Dusk settled over the valley, and when the schoolhouse came into view, Molly touched his arm. "If there's ever anything I can do for you, Mr. Daggett—anything at all—please ask. This is the second time you've come to my rescue." She liked the way his eyes sparkled like a little boy's. "I'd consider it a privilege to return the favor, even in the smallest portion."

He stopped and stared at her for a second, then focused on the ground beneath his large work boots. "Do you know how to dance, Miss Molly?"

His voice was so tentative, and the question so unexpected, it took her a moment to respond. "I do, in fact, Mr. Daggett. Do you?" she chanced softly.

He shook his head.

Following the thread of his question, she peered up at him. "Would you care to learn?"

His bearded cheeks bunched in a grin that would've looked odd on the bear of a man he was had she not already known how kind and gentle a heart was within him.

"I would, Miss Molly. If it won't trouble you too much."

In her state of "widowhood," dancing was unacceptable, but she wanted to do something for this man and could see how important it was to him. Smiling, her mind jumped ahead. "Is there a special occasion coming up?"

He nodded. "The statehood celebration."

"In two weeks," she thought aloud.

"If you can't do it, Miss Molly, don't you fret over—"

"I would be honored to teach you how to dance, Mr. Daggett." She looped her arm through his, touched by how his chest puffed out. "But we'll need to get started as soon as possible."

Molly bolted the latch behind her, checked it a second time, and leaned against the cabin door, only then allowing to play out in her mind the possibility of what might have happened if Charlie Daggett hadn't come along. She hugged herself tight, so cold. It was a bone-numbing cold that went deeper than any chill.

A fire. She needed to build a fire. But first she filled the teakettle with water and lit the stove.

She closed every curtain on every window and thanked God again for sending Charlie Daggett along. She hadn't thought to ask him what he'd been doing out there in the woods. But then again, remembering the bottle, she thought she knew.

She knelt by the hearth and stacked the wood on top of old embers. She would need more wood before morning. It was just outside the door, on the side of the cabin, but she didn't want to go out in the dark. Not alone. She would make do with what she had.

Hands shaking, she struck a match. It failed to

light. She tried again. Not even a spark. She huffed in frustration. She'd just lit the stove, for heaven's sake. She would borrow the flame from there.

A gentle rap on the door brought her around.

"Molly? Are you in there?"

James . . .

She unbolted the latch and had no sooner turned the knob than he stepped through the doorway.

"Is it true?" he asked, breathing hard.

She took a step back, her hand trembling at her midsection. "Is . . . what true?"

"I just saw Charlie Daggett." A muscle flinched in his jaw. "Those men, on the road just now. Did they—" His eyes narrowed. "Did they . . . *hurt* you in any way?"

Tears rose, and she didn't try to stop them. "No," she whispered, relief pouring through her. Relief chased by guilt. "They didn't hurt me."

He exhaled, and a strangled sound rose from his throat. He briefly closed his eyes, and when he opened them again, Molly saw what she'd seen the morning he'd brought her the apple before school.

Except this time, the intensity in his eyes made that look tame.

He pushed the door closed and took her in his arms. He held her, his hands moving over her arms and her back, caressing her shoulders. She felt herself relaxing against him, knowing she shouldn't. But it felt so good to be held. Really held. His arms encircled her waist and pulled her against him.

He pressed his forehead to hers, his breath uneven. "I just had to make sure you were all right."

She nodded, mindful of how close they were. "I am." *Especially now*, she wanted to add but didn't, knowing that would only further encourage things in a direction they didn't need to go.

They stood that way for the longest time, her knowing she needed to stop whatever was happening between them and yet not knowing how to. And not fully wanting to.

"I don't guess you've changed your mind," he finally said, his deep voice soft.

She didn't have to ask what he was talking about. She wanted so badly to answer yes, that she'd changed her mind. She wanted to brush her lips against his and give him the answer he wanted—that *she* wanted to give—and that he was waiting for.

But instead, she shook her head, not trusting her voice.

A wry smile tipped one side of his mouth, telling her he didn't believe her. "I think I'm going to have to insist on a verbal answer, ma'am. That one wasn't very convincing."

Desire for him, swift and strong, swept through her. It left her light-headed and threatened to steal her resolve. Molly reached up and touched his face, and traced a path along his stubbled jawline. He caught her hand and kissed her open palm, again and again, and the tremble she felt in him resonated inside her.

She needed to tell him about the baby. Now was the time. She'd prayed for God to guide her steps, and she felt the gentle nudge inside her. Oh, but, Lord, this was harder than she'd imagined.

She looked up at him. "James . . ."

"Yes?"

His hand moved in slow circles on the small of her back, not making her decision any easier. But the precious child growing inside her, and between them—that he didn't know about yet—did.

She gently pulled her hand away. "I need to tell you something. Something you're not going to like." She glanced back at the sofa. "Maybe we should sit down."

But he didn't move. He brushed a finger against the side of her neck. "They touched you," he whispered. His jaw went rigid.

It wasn't a question. And she remembered Charlie commenting on the coal dust on her face. She thought she'd wiped it away.

"One of them touched my face. That was all."

A visible shudder passed through him. "If someone ever . . . touched you, or *hurt* you . . . in that way, I don't know what I'd do."

He pulled her close and she held him tight, hearing what he'd said, hearing the concern in his words. But also hearing a "difference" in what she might become in his eyes if those men *had* hurt her in that way.

The muted whistle of the teakettle sounded and quickly swelled to a loud shrill.

He drew back but seemed reluctant to let her go. "You didn't answer my question." He cradled her face. "Have you changed your mind, Molly?"

Thinking of herself brought the wrong answer to her lips. So she focused on him, and the man he was, and his reputation in Timber Ridge, and all the people who looked up to him. She thought of Rachel, Mitchell and Kurt, Josiah and Belle, all of them, and she shook her head. "No . . . James," she whispered, lying to him yet again, but this time for his own good. "I haven't changed my mind." She took a step back and out of his arms. "And I won't."

Needing to be away from him, she crossed to the stove and pulled the kettle from the flame, her hands shaking. The sudden silence seemed over-loud.

"I'll bring in more wood before I go."

The flatness of his voice cut her deep.

"You don't have to do that. I can—"

"I want to do it."

He returned with his arms full. With an amount that would have taken her three trips. A burst of cold air followed him inside, and she shut the door behind him.

Minutes later, a fire burned bright and hot in the fireplace. She walked him to the door, knowing again that the punishment for her sin wasn't the child inside of her. It was the life right before her that she would never have.

"Lock the door once I leave."

She nodded. "I will."

Standing in the doorway, he bowed his head. "Molly?"

"Yes?"

He turned back and reached out as though to touch her, then stopped. "I'll wait. And when the time comes, whenever you're ready—*if* you're ever ready—all you have to do is . . ." He didn't complete the sentence. He didn't have to.

His boot steps made a hollow thud on the porch stairs.

Molly closed the door and bolted the latch firmly in place, knowing that time would never come. Not unless she told him the entire truth. And if she did that, she would be risking it all with only the promise of rejection in return.

And friendship with James—though it was far from the relationship she wanted—was better than nothing at all.

28

But I don't want to do it now." Kurt drank the last of his milk, then slipped from his chair, eyeing his mother across the kitchen table. "I'll do it later."

Knowing it wasn't his place, James held back from saying anything. For Rachel's sake, as well as Molly's, who sat across the table, intent on smoothing the napkin in her lap.

Though the noon meal had been more tense than he'd expected, he was still glad she'd accepted their invitation for Sunday dinner, and he looked forward to time together, especially after what happened—or didn't—in her cabin two nights ago.

When Charlie Daggett had told him about finding her with two miners, a rage had overtaken him. He'd wanted to ride down that road and beat the men senseless, then haul them in and ask questions later. Charlie said he'd broken the wrist of one of the men. Knowing Charlie's grip, he could well imagine it, and hoped the two miners had moved on from Timber Ridge. If not, he would make sure they did.

Rachel looked tired, and he had a good idea as to why.

He'd heard her crying during the night. The ranch was a continuing source of worry for her, taking more time and energy than she had, and more than he could spare. She'd grown lax in following through with the boys in recent weeks, mainly with Kurt. Mitch had always been the more compliant of the two and rarely challenged her authority. Kurt, on the other hand, challenged her at every turn, especially these days.

Chances were good that Molly had witnessed this same behavior, or similar, from Kurt at school. But if she had, she hadn't said anything to Rachel. That he knew of, anyway.

"Kurt—" Rachel's voice grew more stern, but a weariness weighted her tone that weakened her attempt. "You'll go muck out those stalls right now with your brother, or I'm going to—"

Kurt turned as if to walk back to his bedroom.

Rachel stood, her chair nearly toppling over. "Young man, ge—" She steadied herself by placing a hand on the tabletop. "Get back here right now."

A tenuous thread of emotion undermined her threat. James heard it. And apparently, Kurt heard it too.

The boy paused and looked back at her, challenge in his eyes.

Rachel pointed. "You'll head out to that barn right now or—" She paused, her breathing audible. "Or you'll go to bed without supper tonight."

Kurt's brow furrowed slightly, revealing either doubt or lack of concern. James couldn't tell which. Earlier that morning in church, he'd watched Kurt intentionally drop a songbook in an attempt to draw a giggle from a cute little girl sitting in front of them. Rachel had scolded him afterward, but if appearances counted for anything, it hadn't made much of an impression. And the boy wore much the same expression now.

Kurt turned to leave, but James caught his eye and met his stare straight on.

Kurt stopped cold.

James didn't move. He didn't blink. And he sure didn't say anything, not with Rachel looking on, her authority teetering in the balance.

Kurt tried to keep up his courage, but James saw it slipping away. Just as his own had done when set against the unyielding steel of his grandfather's firm stare. Thank God his grandfather had been in his life—when his own father hadn't. For nearly twenty-one years, he and his father had lived beneath the same roof, yet James had never felt like he really knew the man. And the night his father died, he'd discovered why—because he was a constant reminder of something his father had spent a lifetime trying to forget.

Kurt's stare wavered, and he gradually lowered his gaze. "Yes, *ma'am*," he muttered, and trudged from the kitchen.

The front door closed louder than necessary, and Rachel looked across the table.

James read failure in her eyes—and irritation at him—and shook his head. "He's just testing you, Rachel."

"Do you not think I know that?" Her voice was soft, but her tone was brittle. "I am his mother, after all."

James didn't want to go where this conversation was headed. Not with their present company included. It was unlike Rachel to address something like this with guests, but he knew she felt comfortable around Molly and considered her a good friend. "Give it time, Rach—"

"I've given it time, James." She sank down in her chair and rested her head in her hands. "I've lost my hand with the boy."

"No, you haven't." James leaned forward. "He's simply trying to figure out where he fits in now that . . . Thomas is gone. And since he realizes his papa's not coming back."

The frustration drained from Rachel's face and raw uncertainty took its place.

James started to get up and go to her, but Molly reached out a hand. Rachel grabbed on and held tight, as if Molly were a lifeline in a stormy sea.

"I still miss him so much," Rachel whispered, closing her eyes. "It's not proper to speak of the deceased, I know. But—" She raised her head and looked at Molly, her eyes swimming with tears. "Do you ever still . . . *feel* your husband with you? Beside you?"

James watched, waiting. How many times had he wanted to ask Molly much that same question? Ask about her former life. Yet he hadn't felt at liberty to. And she'd volunteered so little.

He saw Molly's grip tighten on Rachel's hand. A single tear trailed her cheek. She opened her mouth as though to speak, then closed it again and said nothing.

"Sometimes . . ." A fragile smile curved Rachel's mouth. "Sometimes when I'm in the barn early in the morning, or when I ride up in the mountains like we used to do together, I'll sense him with me. I'll stop for a second, and—" she sighed a soft, humorless laugh—"I'll be so sure that when I turn, he'll be there." Her breath caught. "But he's not. I know he's gone, and that he's waiting for me in the hereafter, but . . . it feels like he took part of me with him when he went. A part I still need to get along in my life."

Tears slid down Rachel's cheeks, and James struggled to control his own emotions. Molly sat, quiet and pale. After a moment, she leaned over and put her arms around Rachel. Rachel hugged her back, and James sensed this moment might be best left to the women alone.

He rose. "I think I'll go check on the boys. See if they need any help."

He didn't wait for a response and noticed they didn't give one. He was nearly to the door when he remembered his coat. He quietly backtracked to his bedroom and was on his way out again when he heard Molly's voice.

"You and your husband, Thomas—" she took a stuttered breath—"shared something that I've—" A deep exhale, followed by a sob. "That I've never known," she whispered, her voice breaking. "I'm so sorry Thomas was taken from you, Rachel. I'm just so sorry."

James closed the front door noiselessly behind him and stood on the porch, looking out across the mountains that had become his home and where— for all he knew—he would breathe his last on this earth. Wiping his cheeks, he peered upward into the brilliant blue of a September sky and thanked God for bringing Molly Whitcomb when He had.

He wasn't about to guess what all God had planned, but he knew what he was going to do, and already felt God's hand in it. He was going to give Molly Whitcomb as much time as she needed to heal from her loss, while also moving ahead with loving her in a way she'd never been loved before.

Regardless of what she'd said to him the other night—that she wouldn't be changing her mind about him—he saw the way she looked at him. She just needed time. He remembered what it been like to hold her, to feel her against him, and a tender passion threaded through him again. He sensed a loneliness in her. One he understood. And that he wanted to fill, if she would only let him. But that would mean telling her the truth about his past, about who he was.

He couldn't change how he'd come into the world, but still—in moments like this, when he reflected on his heritage—he felt a layer of shame. Shame passed from father to son.

He shoved his hands in his pockets and strode toward the barn. He peered inside to find the boys working, and walked on down the path that led to the stream.

His eyes burned as he thought of his mother—not the woman who had given him life, but the woman who had loved him despite how he'd been given it—and he thanked God again for her generous heart.

His mother had been a kind and gentle woman, poised and gracious, and had supported her husband without question—even when he'd come home one night with a newborn baby boy wrapped in his arms. "The mother died this afternoon during birth, Savannah," his father had told her. "She had no family. No one to take the boy in." His mother had recently delivered her first child, a stillborn son. So at her husband's encouragement, she had taken the "orphaned" boy as her own, seeing him as a gift from God.

Only, he wasn't quite a *gift*, not in the truest, most innocent sense. Not when Dr. Andrew McPherson had kept a mistress on the side. One pregnant with his own child when she'd died during labor.

James paused by the streambed as a woman's faceless image rose in his mind. He didn't know anything about the woman who had given him birth, only that she'd died during it. But what kind of woman gave herself to a man like that? A man who wasn't her husband? And to a married man . . .

Having seen his father for the man he was when he confessed the night he died, and contrasting that with the man the city of Franklin, Tennessee, *thought* they'd known, he'd determined to live his life rooted and grounded in truth. His word would be binding. If he said he would be somewhere, he would. If he said he would do something, he would do it. And the man that people thought they knew would be the man he would try his best to be.

Not perfectly. Certainly not without fault. But without willful deceit.

And if he was expecting Molly to care for him in a deeper way, then it was only fair that she know the truth about his heritage, however much lesser it was than her own.

James kept Winsome at a slow pace, glad for the time alone with Molly. "Thanks for letting me see you home."

"And thank you for offering to accompany me." Molly rode beside him, handling her mare with ease on the winding mountain trail.

Shortly after he'd returned from the stream to check on the boys, Molly and Rachel had joined them in the barn. Once the boys had finished— with him helping to speed things along—they'd all hiked to the waterfall farther up the mountain. It was a place Thomas and Rachel used to take their sons, and Kurt had been especially quiet. James had hiked downhill with Kurt on his shoulders and had even managed to get the boy to smile a time or two.

Molly had also been subdued, but he could tell she'd enjoyed herself, and thought she could grow to love this place as much as he did. When they reached the ridge overlooking town, she reined in, and they sat in silence.

"I bet you never get tired of this view."

"No, ma'am," he answered softly. "And I don't think I ever will."

She turned, slowly, and raised a brow. "I was speaking of the mountains, James McPherson."

"Yes, ma'am. I know that." He fingered the reins, liking that she didn't look away from him but held his gaze steady. "But I hope you don't mind me looking . . . on occasion."

She gave him a smile he'd carry with him into the coming week.

"I don't mind," she whispered. "I'm touched that you would." Mellowness softened her voice, almost as if she was thinking of something else as she spoke. She urged her mare down the trail and he followed.

After a while, she glanced back. "You're certain the town council approved of my report?"

"More than approved. Davenport was chompin' at the bit for more information. I don't know what he plans to do with it, but he was eager to understand what it is you're doing in the classroom."

"I'll get started on it as soon as I get home."

The trail narrowed as it sloped downward into town, and he waved her on ahead of him. "So exactly what *is* it you're doing?"

Laughing, she described a typical day in the classroom, enthusiasm filling her voice. That she loved teaching was obvious. And that she loved teaching the children in Timber Ridge was too.

After a brief stop by the livery to board her mare, James leaned forward in the saddle as Molly snugged her boot into the stirrup, and he pulled her up behind him. They continued through town toward her cabin and met the stagecoach rounding the corner at the end of the street.

Lewis rode up top and waved when he saw them. "Evening, Sheriff." He pulled back on the reins, a wide grin on his face. "Evening, Dr. Whitcomb. Nice to see you again."

"You keeping busy, Lewis?"

"Yes, sir, Sheriff. This new stage is a beauty. And business is good." His focus shifted to Molly. "I hope you haven't forgotten, ma'am. My offer to you still stands. Anytime you need to go to Sulfur Falls, you just say the word and you've got free passage on my stage. Comin' and goin'."

"I haven't forgotten, Mr. Lewis. And thank you. That's very generous of you, sir."

From her tone, James could tell that a trip in that stagecoach—or any other—wasn't going to be happening anytime soon. Not that he could blame her.

James tipped his hat and nudged Winsome on. Down the road a piece, he glanced to the side. "A nice coach ride doesn't hold much appeal?" He grinned at the sharp jab in his back.

"I don't think I'll ever be able to ride in a coach again. And surely not on that road."

"How about this offer . . . Anytime you need to travel down the mountain, let me know. I'll accompany you. I'd even trust you to ride lead."

Her laughter was soft. "A sheriff who lets a woman ride lead—that's a first."

"I didn't say just any woman, Molly. I said I'd let—"

"Dr. Whitcomb!"

James saw Brandon Tolliver approaching and slowed up. Of all the luck. "Evening, Tolliver."

The man nodded, that smug look on his face. "Sheriff."

"Good evening, Mr. Tolliver."

The man reached for Molly's hand and kissed it. And it was all James could do not to goad Winsome into flying down the street, leaving Tolliver and his finely pressed suit in a cloud of dust.

"Dr. Whitcomb, I received your card in the mail, ma'am. To say the least, I was pleasantly surprised and appreciate your personal correspondence."

"I'm glad you received it, Mr. Tolliver. And I'm pleased you enjoyed my . . . *brief* note of thanks."

"I'm curious. Which did you enjoy more, ma'am? The candy? Or the flowers?"

James bristled inside but worked to hide it. He'd figured the flowers and candy had been from Tolliver but hadn't known for sure.

"The flowers were beautiful, Mr. Tolliver. But actually, I'm sorry to say I never tried the candy. I'd already been treated to a delicious apple that day—"

She paused, and James couldn't help but think she did it for his benefit.

"—but the students enjoyed the candy immensely. It served as a wonderful reward for those who completed their mathematics lessons on time that afternoon. Which, if memory serves, was everyone that day."

Tolliver looked like he'd just sucked on a persimmon. "Well, I can't tell you how much it pleases me, Dr. Whitcomb, that my gift was put to such . . . productive use, ma'am."

James smiled. "Consider it a donation to the education of children in Timber Ridge, Tolliver."

Tolliver's expression was barely cordial. "I'll do that, Sheriff. Now, Dr. Whitcomb, about that dinner at my resort. You declined my invitation once but indicated you would entertain another. I've been remiss in following up on that offer but would like to do so in the near future. If you're still open to that."

"Yes, I am, Mr. Tolliver. I'd like to see what the town of Timber Ridge is talking about."

Tolliver's smugness returned. "Very well, then. I'm leaving town in a few days, but when I return,

I'll be in touch." He tipped his fancy top hat. "Sheriff McPherson, my best wishes for a most pleasant evening."

"Tolliver," James said with a nod, and gave Winsome a soft kick in the flanks.

They reached the turnoff to Molly's cabin, and she leaned close. "The only reason I accepted Tolliver's invitation, James, is to see the resort. Angelo is working out there now, and when I visited his mother, she expressed concern for him."

James felt some missing pieces falling into place for him. Not in a pleasant way. "You . . . visited Little Italy? That's where you'd been on Friday afternoon?" Hearing the hint of accusation in his tone, he knew she probably did too.

"I walked there with Angelo. He was going to walk me back, but I told him it wasn't necessary. Everything was fine until—"

She didn't finish her sentence.

James stopped by the porch and dismounted, then helped her down.

He chose his words carefully, remembering the warning she'd given him, about not fighting her battles. "As someone who cares about you, Molly, a great deal, I'm asking you, please, not to go there again."

She stared up. "I would never consider going there, or coming home, unescorted again. But the families, they need help, James. They have so little. And the places where they live—"

"I know. I've been there. Many times."

"I told Mrs. Giordano I'd visit again and would bring food this next week. I'd like to keep my promise to her and the other families." She bowed her head briefly.

And when she peered up at him, James knew that whatever she was about to ask, it would have to be sinful in order for him to say no. And even then, it would be hard to deny her.

"Would you consider going with me? And helping me take the provisions?"

A compromise. He should've known she'd work toward that. He still didn't like the idea of her going, but at least he'd be with her and would keep her safe. "Yes, I'll take you. And thank you for asking me. Just"—he winced, smiling—"don't tell Rachel."

She frowned. "Why not?"

"Because she wanted to go and I discouraged her. I know this is hard to believe, but—" He kept his expression serious. "Some women actually listen to advice when it's given." She popped him on the arm, smiling, and he caught hold of her hand. "Thank you for being such a good friend to my sister. She enjoys your company."

"And I enjoy hers. I'm just so sorry about Thomas. She misses him so."

"And it's going on two years already since he's been gone."

"What she said today . . . about their marriage. They loved each other very much."

He nodded. "They did. You couldn't be in the same room with them and not feel it."

The change in her was subtle. Sadness moved into her eyes, and—based on what she'd told Rachel today—it didn't take much to know she was thinking about her late husband, and about how different their relationship had apparently been from Thomas and Rachel's.

Guessing what was on her mind, he decided it was only fair she knew what had happened. "It wasn't my intention to eavesdrop today, Molly, but I overheard some of what you said to Rachel . . . about your husband." He reached up and touched the side of her face. "There are all different kinds of marriages, and what Rachel and Thomas had was special. But just because your first marriage may not have been what you wanted it to be, it doesn't mean there's not the hope of that some-where in your future."

She looked at him for the longest time, and he sensed she wanted to tell him something, so he kept quiet, giving her ample opportunity. She finally stood on tiptoe and kissed him, high on the cheek, about as far away from his mouth as she could get. But that was okay. She'd kissed him.

It was a start. And he'd take it.

29

Molly glanced out a side window of the school-house as she pulled on her coat. The morning had been sunny and clear, but by midafternoon the weather had taken a surprising wintry turn. She watched Angelo from the corner of her eye, knowing he must be disappointed they couldn't work together longer, though he was doing a good job of hiding it.

What he needed now more than anything else was to practice what he knew. In conversation. But that took time she didn't have.

"Angelo, I am sorry to be in such a rush today." She made herself speak slowly. "I have an appointment"—she pointed to her pocket watch, thinking of Charlie Daggett and the trip to town she needed to make before meeting him—"and I cannot be late. I will do my best to give you more time on Thursday. Two days from now."

He nodded. "You . . . busy woman, Dr. Whitcomb." He looked toward the door. "I have . . . more friend meet me."

More friend? Molly glanced at the door, wondering if he was getting his words confused. Then it dawned on her who he must be referring to, and she didn't know whether to be happy—or deeply concerned. "You have someone else you are practicing your English with?"

He grinned and nodded. "Billy and . . . Elijah." He stuffed the new cards she'd made for him into his pocket.

She retrieved her reticule and satchel, debating whether or not to say anything to him. It was one thing for her to be tutoring him. And even a friendship with Elijah Birch was fine. She doubted Josiah and Belle would take issue with it. But Billy Bolden—Hank Bolden's son? That was another story.

She knew what Hank Bolden's opinion would be, and who he would blame if he found out. But it wasn't Angelo she needed to speak with about it. It was Billy Bolden. And she needed to broach the subject with care. *If* she decided to broach it at all.

Angelo opened the door and wind gusted inside. "You have . . . good evening, Dr. Whitcomb."

"Thank you, Angelo. And please tell your mother I will be out tomorrow afternoon with food. Sheriff McPherson will be coming with me."

Angelo grinned and nodded, then turned his body into the chilling wind. He was wearing a coat. One she'd seen Elijah wear before, if she wasn't mistaken.

The woolen coat she'd ordered had arrived, and she slipped the buttons through the slits. Lyda Mullins had seen her trying it on in the store and assumed Ben had ordered the wrong size. But Molly had assured her it was perfect. And it would be, soon enough.

She hustled from the schoolhouse, bracing herself against the cold. So much for fall. Almost overnight the wind had stripped the trees of autumn's color. She walked quickly, not only because she was cold, but because she didn't want to be late for her first dance lesson with Charlie Daggett. She smiled just thinking about it.

She reached the general store and had to use two hands to open the door, the wind was so stiff.

"Mrs. Whitcomb!" Lyda Mullins waved her on inside. "I'll get the door. You get on in here!"

"Thank you, Mrs. Mullins." Molly shivered.

Lyda stood at the door, looking out. "I smell snow."

"Snow?" Molly peered up into the gray clouds. "What happened to fall?"

Lyda laughed. "You're in Colorado now, Mrs. Whitcomb. Weather changes here on a whim. We normally get our first snow about now. But don't worry. We shouldn't get more than two or three inches this early in the year."

"Two or three inches? This soon?" Molly looked down at her heeled boots, imagining how she would manage snow in them. She looked up to find Lyda looking down.

"Are those your best winter boots, Mrs. Whitcomb?"

Molly smiled and turned a heel. "We don't get much call for winter boots in Georgia."

"I'll see what we have in stock that's around your

size. If none of those work, we'll order some in."

Lyda disappeared through the curtained doorway to the back room, and Molly waited in line behind a gentleman to post a letter. To James.

It had occupied most of her previous evening—after she'd finished the report the mayor had requested. It hadn't taken that long to write, but deciding what to write had. She eyed the envelope bearing his name, hoping what she'd said would be well received.

She needed to tell him about the baby, but whenever they were together, the words just wouldn't come. She'd been wrestling with how to say it the other night, summoning the courage to, when he'd confessed to overhearing part of her conversation with Rachel about "her late husband." And the emotion in his eyes when he'd told her . . .

She sighed. There'd been no way to tell him after that.

"Hello, Mrs. Whitcomb," Ben Mullins said, reaching for his hand stamp. "Just this one letter?"

"Yes, please. Thank you."

If he thought anything about her sending a letter to James McPherson, to his credit, he didn't show it.

Lyda returned with three boxes of boots. Only one pair ended up fitting and they weren't the most stylish. But considering her need, Molly decided stylish wasn't nearly as important out here as it had been back home. She pulled some bills from her reticule. "And would you add a loaf of bread too, please?"

"Oh, I'm sorry." Lyda glanced at the empty shelf. "We've already sold out for the day. But Hank Bolden's sure to have some. He always makes extra when the weather takes a bad turn."

Molly paid her bill and braved the cold wind again. She needed bread but didn't know if she needed it that badly. Remembering what Lyda said about coming snow, she decided hunger would quickly outweigh the discomfort of seeing Hank Bolden, if it came to that. Carrying her new boots, she covered the short distance to his store, mindful of the time.

The line inside the Boldens' store reached almost to the door. But true to what Lyda Mullins said, his shelves were full of bread, freshly baked and warm. Molly closed the door behind her, wishing she could live with this aroma. Delicious. How could something that smelled so delectable be baked by so rude a man?

She waited in line, sorry to see that Mr. Bolden was the one behind the counter.

The door opened and a rush of wind came with it. Chilled, Molly turned and glanced at the young woman now in line behind her, whose head stayed bowed.

"Do you think it's going to snow?" Molly asked.

The woman looked up. Then glanced behind her and back again. "I . . . I couldn't say for sure."

Molly watched a man rush by on the boardwalk outside, holding his hat on his head. "I've never been around much snow." She shrugged. "I'm from Georgia."

The woman nodded, a polite smile touching her mouth. She had a frail look about her, and kindness around her eyes that said she would do whatever she could to help someone, if only asked. "I would've guessed that. From your accent."

"Ah . . . true."

"Next!"

Hearing Bolden's voice, Molly cringed and turned to face him. "Good afternoon, Mr. Bolden. How are you, sir?"

His smile was anything but friendly. "Just dandy, ma'am." He gestured. "What do you want?"

Besides manners, or at least customary pleasantries? Molly eyed the shelves behind him. "Two loaves of bread, please. And . . . two sweet rolls." She'd had such a craving for sweets recently. She couldn't get enough of them.

Bolden wrapped each of her items. She paid and stepped to the side to slip the coins back into her change purse, the line of customers having deepened.

"I'd like the same thing . . . please, sir."

The meekness in the woman's voice drew Molly's attention.

Bolden reached for a loaf of bread and slapped it,

unwrapped, on the counter. "You can have one loaf, but that's it. I got other customers in line behind you."

Molly stared, disbelieving. The *rudeness* of that man! She half expected the woman to say something—but she didn't.

She merely laid her coins on the counter and took the bread, her gaze averted as she walked to the door.

It was all Molly could do not to confront Hank Bolden. But considering their history, she held back. Her gaze swept the other patrons, who, to the very last one, seemed nonplussed. None of them had even looked in the woman's direction as she'd left the store.

Molly hurried outside, searching to see which way she'd gone. There, at the end of the boardwalk. She ran to catch up with her. "Ma'am!"

The woman kept walking, head tucked against the wind.

"Ma'am!" Molly called louder and touched her arm.

The woman turned. Though not really knowing what she'd expected, Molly hadn't anticipated the calm composure on the woman's face.

"Yes?" Silent question lit her dark brown eyes.

Molly motioned behind them. "I'm so sorry about what happened back there. That man—Mr. Bolden—he can be rather . . . rude at times. And unseemingly terse."

The woman smiled. But this time, her face lit with humor. "Hank Bolden can be more than simply 'rather rude.' He's an insufferable bigot who looks only for what will bring him gain while taking every opportunity to diminish those around him. Especially those he considers less than himself. Which . . . is about everyone in town."

Molly stared, realizing too late that her mouth hung slightly open.

The woman's laugh held apology. "I'm sorry. I shouldn't have spoken my mind so completely. We don't even know each other."

Molly stared. "Which I would quickly like to remedy, seeing as we have such congruent opinions of the man." She smiled. "My name is—"

"I know who you are, Dr. Whitcomb. Everybody in town knows who you are, ma'am. I'm Miss Matthews, and it's indeed a pleasure."

The woman spoke with such eloquent confidence, yet Molly would never have guessed as much from her behavior back at the store. Molly turned her coat collar up against the wind. She liked this woman. Her candor. Her quick wit. Her honesty. "It's a pleasure to meet you, Miss Matthews." She reached into her sack and proffered one of the sweet rolls. "And I will not entertain refusal."

Miss Matthews held her stare, then slowly accepted the offering. "Thank you."

Aware of the time, Molly knew she needed to be on her way. "I'm sorry, but I've got an appointment to keep. Perhaps . . . we could have coffee sometime."

Miss Matthews nodded. "Perhaps," she whispered, her tone kind but noncommittal.

Molly hurried back to the schoolhouse, wondering how she'd not seen the woman in town before. And wishing she'd asked where she lived. She found Charlie Daggett sitting on the front stairs.

"Mr. Daggett! I'm sorry I'm late. Why didn't you go on in?" She opened the door.

"You're not late, Miss Molly. I'm early." He stepped inside and looked around. "I didn't want to bother nothing."

Molly deposited her items. "You wouldn't have bothered anything. I've been looking forward to this. It's been ages since I've danced!"

The mere mention of the word seemed to cause him unease.

"Here—" She motioned. "Let's scoot these desks back. It'll give us more room."

Together, they moved the desks. Then he stood in the middle of the room, staring. Looking shy and awkward. And huge.

Molly realized again just how large a man he was, and how massive his boots. "The most important thing for you to remember, Mr. Daggett, is not to step on your partner's feet."

He looked down, murmuring, "Don't step on her feet."

She touched his arm. "I'm only kidding, Mr. Daggett. That's not the most important thing. Although"—she looked up at him, brow scrunched—"it might be in your case."

That drew a smile from him.

"May I ask you a question, Mr. Daggett?"

He nodded again.

"Have you asked this lady you're wanting to dance with to the town celebration yet?"

His eyes widened. "Oh no, ma'am. I wouldn't think of doin' that. I'm just hopin' to dance with her once. If she'll have me."

Such humility and sweetness. "May I ask her name?"

The ruddiness of his face deepened. "Lori Beth."

"Lori Beth," she repeated. "That's a beautiful name."

"She's a beautiful lady."

Molly smelled the bourbon on him, though not as strong as before. What made a man as kind and good as Charlie Daggett drink the way he did? "I think you should consider asking her to the dance right and proper. I can't imagine Lori Beth saying no to you, Mr. Daggett." She squinted. "May I call you Charlie?"

He ducked his head. "I think that's fittin' enough. Recollectin' all we been through, and that I already call you Miss Molly."

"Well, all right, then . . . Charlie. Let's get to dancing."

James knelt to inspect the area again. Blood was all over the bushes, heavy in places. Twigs were broken and bent. Blood spotted the trail. But not a lot, and there were no drag marks. The dirt was smooth. Too smooth. It was as if the mountain lion had just leapt up into the trees with its kill. Which was impossible.

He turned his collar up against the cold and wind and studied the terrain. Overcast skies settled over the valley, and clouds shrouded the mountain heights. But the heavens had yet to unleash those storerooms, which had worked out well, since he'd escorted Molly to Little Italy yesterday. They'd delivered food to families, and the people all greeted her warmly, obviously having met her before. Angelo hadn't been there, but his mother and sisters had.

He'd invited Molly to have dinner with him tonight, but she'd said she had a "previous engagement." He determined again not to think about who she might be with.

Careful where he stepped, he moved over a couple of feet and peered closer. No blood on the boulders beside the bush. And none on the evergreens that lined the—

That's when he saw it.

He edged the foliage back to get a better look, and to make sure the afternoon sun wasn't playing tricks with the shadows. But there it was, outlined clearly in the dirt. A boot print, underneath, near the base of the bush, beyond where someone would walk. But not if someone had knelt there, hiding.

He sighed and nudged his hat back, experiencing that same feeling he'd gotten out at Spiveys' weeks before. He'd found a carcass that day, but he would bet his badge he wouldn't find one today. Not from this. Because this wasn't a cougar killing. It was cattle rustling. Yet someone had gone to a fair amount of trouble to try to make it look like a mountain lion's kill.

Walking back to the barn to speak with Glen Paulsen again, James decided not to reveal his hunch to the rancher just yet. Because that was all it was—a hunch. A boot print in the dirt didn't prove anything on its own. The new governor in Denver was pushing hard to put an end to cattle theft. Town council had received a recent report from the governor's office stating that the punishment for cattle rustling had been raised from one year in prison to three. And James knew that if Davenport got wind of cattle rustling in Timber Ridge, the man would try to use the opportunity to impress the new governor. All the more reason to keep things quiet until evidence was in hand.

Paulsen met him by the corral. "I told you. Cougar, right?" He gestured toward the barn. "One of my hands scouted the hills this morning. Didn't find a thing. The cat must've drug it off the path somewhere."

James nodded toward the mountains. "I want to take another ride up through there, see what I can find. If I come across something, I'll stop back by." He shook the man's hand.

"I appreciate that, Sheriff."

"Other than this—" James untethered Winsome from the post. "How are things going for you?"

"Going fairly well. Had a good summer." Paulsen laughed. "And fall, what little there was of it. I just hope the winter's mild. I don't know if I'll make it through another one like we had four years ago."

James remembered that particular winter. Snow fell in mid-September and didn't melt until April. Thomas and Rachel lost twenty head of cattle. Yet heavy snow in the mountains meant life-giving water to lowlands when the spring melt flowed into creeks and streams. It was a balance, and one of the . . . *dichotomies* of living in the mountains of Colorado. James couldn't help but smile to himself, looking forward to using that big word on Molly. He'd found it in the dictionary late last night. He was determined to stump the woman.

He slipped a boot through the stirrup and swung into the saddle. "I'm praying it's a mild one too. For all of us."

Angelo Giordano walked out of the barn, carrying a crate.

James nodded. "How's the boy working out for you?"

Paulsen looked in that direction. "Real well. I wasn't sure at first, like I told you. But he's a hard worker. And now that he can speak some English, that helps a lot."

James paused. "He's speaking English?"

"Yep, he says that new teacher's giving him lessons."

"Really?" Molly had failed to mention that to him. "I appreciate you giving him a chance, Paulsen. Means a lot to him and his family, I know."

As Paulsen walked back around the corral, James headed toward the road, trying not to dwell on what certain members of the town council would think of Molly's teaching Angelo English. There was nothing wrong with her doing that—in his book. But it would be in others'. He waved to Angelo as he passed, and the boy stopped to put down the crate he was carrying and waved big in return.

James smiled, glad the situation was working out. For everyone involved.

He scoured the mountainside for over an hour, looking for any sign of a carcass. But came up with nothing. He did find the remnants of a still, however, which he'd known was hidden away somewhere up in this area. Charlie Daggett had mentioned its vague whereabouts late one night after tying on a good one.

The wind died down, which helped with the chill, but the pewter blue-gray sky kept the promise of moisture close at hand.

On his way into town, James passed a trail leading to the creek that ran behind the school-house, and he caught a flash of something through the trees. He slowed up. Just a couple of kids, looked like. Sitting on a boulder. Reminded him of when he and Daniel Ranslett used to sneak off as boys to try their father's tobacco or drink the last nips of whiskey from a pilfered bottle. He shook his head. That felt like a lifetime ago.

He started to ride on past when one of the boys turned and looked back. James tugged on the reins. *Elijah Birch and . . .*

Elijah nudged Billy Bolden in the arm, and Billy turned. James would've waved and ridden on by if not for the guilt lining both their faces.

He dismounted, feeling an obligation to make sure the boys weren't doing something they ought not, and walked down the trail. "Afternoon, Elijah, Billy. How are you?"

"Fine, Sheriff, sir." Elijah's eyes were wide.

Billy scooted to the edge of the boulder and climbed down, holding something behind his back. "We're not doing anything wrong, Sheriff McPherson."

One of the last things James expected from either of these boys was trouble. Another was seeing them together. "I'm not accusing either of you of doing anything wrong, Billy. I was just passing by and saw you. You know . . ." He allowed a faint smile. "When I was a boy and got caught with something I ought not have, I always kind of . . . hid it behind me. Like you're doing now, son."

Billy hesitated, then pulled his arm from behind his back. He held a book. "It's Dr. Whitcomb's, but she said we could borrow it."

"Yes, sir, Sheriff, that's right," Elijah said, perched on the rock. "She says we can get whatever we want from her shelf."

James angled his head to read the title, and before he could catch himself, he smiled.

"See!" Elijah slid off the boulder. "I told you it was a girl's book!"

Billy's face reddened. "I didn't know. Dr. Whitcomb said it was her favorite. And she liked those other books we read."

James remembered seeing this book on Molly's desk. *"Little Women,"* he read aloud, and watched the boys cringe. If he wasn't mistaken, Rachel had a copy of the book at home. And if it was Molly's favorite, it might be good for him to give it a try.

Looking at Elijah and Billy, he found himself grateful for their friendship. Not just for the benefit to them both, but for what the friendship represented. Then he thought about how angry Hank Bolden could get—the man reacted first and asked questions later—and about what Bolden would say, and likely do, to Billy if he found his son

404

befriending a Negro boy. Josiah Birch would be cautious, with reason, after what happened to him in town last summer. But he wouldn't have the same objections as Bolden.

But bottom line, the boys weren't doing anything wrong, and James had no reason to interfere. It was his job to keep townspeople safe, not mandate whom they spent time with.

"So you boys read a lot of books, do you?"

"Yes, sir," they said in unison.

"Dr. Whitcomb has shelves of them," Billy added.

"Well, I think that's a real good thing. And I'm glad we've got a teacher who encourages that. For you both."

Back in town, James stopped by the office. It was nearly five o'clock, and Willis was already gone. Deputy Stanton was out making regular rounds in the saloons and gaming halls, serving as a visible reminder. A U.S. marshal by the name of Wyatt Caradon had picked up the three prisoners first thing that morning, so the place was quiet.

James tossed his hat on the desk and started to sit, intending to get some work done, then turned to watch folks pass by on the street outside.

Little Italy . . .

Molly had such hopes of making a difference there, which he was all for. But the changes she talked about yesterday—wanting better houses, more food—all that took money. Money his lean sheriff's budget didn't have, and the town's budget didn't either. Not that Mayor Davenport would have approved of it if it did.

Brandon Tolliver had the money, but he wasn't about to let go of it. Tolliver should be building those people houses for free. They were building his resort for practically that.

Needing to think things through, James grabbed his hat, closed up the office, and started walking. He always thought better when he walked.

He took the long way around town, checked on some of the buildings going up, and spoke with a couple of shopkeepers. Seemed everyone was getting excited about the statehood celebration coming up next Saturday night. He hoped the snow would hold off. A chill in the air was good, made the spiced cider taste all the better, but moisture wouldn't be welcome with the festivities being outdoors.

He chose the path leading around Maroon Lake and debated for about five seconds on whether or not to knock on Molly's door and see if she'd changed her mind about dinner.

He knocked.

But no answer. Apparently she was busy being "previously engaged."

It was getting dark and he continued on around the lake. While he'd been honest with her about his feelings, and she'd seemed touched by his admission, even pleased, she hadn't reciprocated.

Not in words anyway. Still, he sensed it. Or thought he did.

Passing the schoolhouse, he saw pale lamplight illuminating a side window and a curl of smoke rising from the chimney. Then he heard soft laughter—and voices—coming through a partially opened window.

"I'm sorry, ma'am!"

"No, no, that's all right." A soft mumble. "Let's try it again. Ready? One, two, three. One, two— *Ouch!*"

Concerned, but mostly curious, James scanned the field and then the road to make sure no one was watching. He then crept toward the schoolhouse, feeling most un-sheriff-like as he did. He stayed close to the building, finding both safety and discomfort in the shadows.

He edged his way to the corner of a window and peered inside, and what he saw drew a laugh he barely held back. *Oh, that woman . . .* Was there no end to the kindness in her heart?

30

Listening for the knock on her door, Molly turned sideways for a last look in her bedroom mirror. She smoothed her hands over her abdomen and pulled the fabric of the black dress taut. She'd definitely grown in recent weeks. Or, more rightly, her baby had grown.

The slight pooch in her belly was now a definite bulge, and it was firm. She pushed lightly against it, both in awe of the miracle growing inside her body and in complete dread of telling others about it. James first, then the town council, and finally everyone else. Then to pick up the pieces, whatever that would mean.

Classes had gone well over the past month, and parents routinely stopped her in town and after church on Sundays, thanking her for the difference they saw in their children. She hoped the men on the town council—Mayor Davenport, specifically—would take that into account when it came time to decide what to do with her future, which would be soon.

"Thou hast covered me in my mother's womb," she whispered, recalling a psalm she'd read recently. God already knew this child, intimately. But did He love this child, conceived in sin, as much as He would have had it not been? And was it any coincidence in recent days that her fingers had swollen to the point where her wedding ring no longer fit?

Her ankles were swollen too, especially after the dance lessons with Charlie Daggett. Charlie had to be excited about tonight. She was excited for him. And she couldn't wait to meet Lori Beth. She only hoped the woman was worthy of his admiration.

The expected knock came, and she opened the

door. "Good evening, Dr. Brookston. Please come in."

He stepped inside, medical bag in hand, his usual dapper self. Most doctors she'd known back east were married. Especially ones as handsome as Rand Brookston. How had he managed to avoid that union for so long?

"You look lovely tonight, Dr. Whitcomb. Are you ready to witness Timber Ridge in all its finery?"

She laughed. "I believe so. Lyda Mullins told me the whole town would be in attendance." She nodded toward his bag. "Expecting some mishaps this evening?"

He gave it a glance. "No, it's become a habit. The few times I haven't brought it with me places, something's happened, and I'd wished I had."

With his assistance, she slipped into her coat. "Thank you for that, kind sir. *And* for the offer of a ride this evening." She'd half thought that James might ask to accompany her. But even if he had, she would've refused. Being seen at an official town gathering was not part of keeping a distance, nor was it proper with her still being in "mourning." But at least she would see him there. Surely he had received her letter by now.

She reached for the entrée she'd prepared earlier that day. "Shall we go?"

"After you tell me what's in that pot. It smells delicious."

"It's chicken and dumplings. One of the few things I know how to cook."

He sniffed. "I'll be sure and have a bowl."

"If you do, you'll probably be glad you brought that bag along."

Laughing, he closed the door behind them and helped her into his buckboard.

Twilight lingered over the valley. The days were growing shorter, and this being the last of September, they would only grow more so. The air was crisp and cold, and the smell reminded her of rain, yet not the slightest quiver of a breeze stirred. Conversation came easily as they rode into town, an outcome of having spent quite a bit of time together.

She stopped by his office periodically to weigh herself on his scales and to ask whatever questions had come to mind since the time before. His knowing about the baby had brought an unexpected comfort. She didn't feel quite so alone in that respect anymore. And not once had he hinted at her needing to tell the town council about the child. Though he had to be thinking about it, as was she.

She waited for the right moment to broach the subject with him.

"So, I told the gentleman"—Dr. Brookston laughed, guiding the buckboard through town to church, passing droves of people already on their way—"that I'd never operated on a pig before, but that if he wanted me to, I would. And he did. That pig was like a pet to him. Old Cornwell used to lead it around on a leash." He shook his head. "I did my best to repair that pig's back leg."

"And was the surgery successful?"

"Let's just say that when I left Tennessee, that pig could outrun any fox."

Molly laughed, enjoying his humor—and sensing her opportunity. "Dr. Brookston . . ." She smiled and waved at a student on the boardwalk who called her name. "I wanted to let you know that I've decided to tell the town council about my . . . condition at their next scheduled meeting, two weeks from now."

He looked over at her. "Would you like for me to come with you?"

What a kind man. "No . . . thank you. This is something I need to do on my own."

"Do you have any sense of how they'll react?"

"I have every reason to believe it will not go well. Especially with Mayor Davenport."

He nodded. "David Davenport's not the most compassionate or understanding of men."

"Neither are terms I would use to describe him, no."

"Do you believe they'll let you keep your position as schoolteacher?"

She sighed. "I've done everything I know to do to make this school the best it can be, and I hope they'll allow me to continue teaching until the baby's born. But, as we both know, I've intention-ally misled them." *In more ways than even you know.* "So it's certainly within their right to grant me a swift and immediate dismissal." And if that was their decision, she didn't know what she would do.

Dr. Brookston brought the buckboard to a stop beside a row of wagons parked beside the church. "For what it's worth, Dr. Whitcomb—and I realize I'm in the minority on this—I believe a woman is capable of making a decision like that—whether or not to work—for herself. Especially a woman as bright and articulate as you."

He set the brake and came around to help her down.

"Thank you, Dr. Brookston, for your encourage-ment and your confidence."

He bowed low and formal, like a true Southern gentleman. "What else are friends for, Dr. Whitcomb, if not to believe in one another? And to operate on pet pigs?"

"Here, here," she said, laughing, acting as though she were raising a toast, which made her think of James again, and those silly sugar sticks.

Carrying her chicken and dumplings and thankful for the warmth from the pot, she fell into step beside the doctor and followed the crowd. When they rounded the corner of the church, her breath caught at the unexpected beauty of the set-ting.

Lanterns strung high on wooden poles dotted the field and were draped around a makeshift dance floor, illuminating the space with a warm shimmer of golden light. Streamers of red, white, and blue were wound around and hung from everything imaginable—naked tree limbs and boughs of ever-greens, tables laden with food and drink, even the picket fence that ran along the side of the church-yard. And the people! Lyda Mullins had been right. Everyone was in town for the celebration and dressed in their finest, from what little Molly could see past their coats and scarves.

Over the thrum of conversation, music rose and swelled, reminding her of home. Guitars and banjos and a fiddle! Not a violin, but a fiddle.

"Welcome, Dr. Brookston." LuEllen Spivey approached them, all smiles. "Mrs. Whitcomb, how nice to see you again too. Here, let me take that for you." She took the pot of chicken and dumplings. "I'll put this with the other dishes." She looked Molly up and down. "Don't you look nice this evening? Hardly any trace of having been so sick. But I can tell by those dark circles beneath your eyes that you're not completely back to health yet."

Molly touched her cheek, not having been aware, and somewhat at a loss for how to respond. "I . . . I actually feel quite well this evening, Mrs.—"

"As Dr. Whitcomb's physician, Mrs. Spivey, I can assure you she's fully healed. And"—he touched Molly's elbow—"I think she looks radiant."

"Thank you, Doctor," Molly said softly, not missing the pointed look Mrs. Spivey gave him—and her—as Dr. Brookston steered her on through the crowd. She searched her memory for how she might have offended the woman. But could think of nothing. She'd even made a point of assigning Amanda extra responsibilities in class, fully aware that the girl reported everything to her mother.

"Pay no mind to her comment, Dr. Whitcomb," Dr. Brookston whispered. "'O, beware of jealousy! It is the green-eyed monster which doth mock the meat it feeds on.'"

Molly recognized the quote from Shakespeare but wasn't certain about Dr. Brookston's meaning. Mrs. Spivey? Jealous of *her*?

He smiled. "Let's leave it at this: You are a lovely woman who has accomplished much in her life. And you exude a confidence that I dare say *some* could find a little threatening."

"Would you care for some cider, Miss Molly?"

Mulling over Dr. Brookston's comment, she turned, already knowing who it was. "Why, thank you, Mr. Dagg—" She stared, tongue-tied, startled at the transformation. Gone were Charlie's unkempt beard and hair and crumpled clothes. The man before her was clean-shaven and shorn and wore a suit. Granted, a suit that looked a size too small. But he wore it with distinction. Yet the most startling difference . . . was his eyes. They were clearer and brighter than she could remember.

"Charlie," she whispered, accepting the cup of cider. "You look positively handsome."

Brookston shook Charlie's hand. "I'll give that opinion a hearty *amen*, Mr. Daggett."

Charlie smiled big. "That's awful kind of you both." He looked around, rubbing his palms on his coat jacket. "Doc, do you know Miss Lori Beth?"

Dr. Brookston hesitated. "Ah . . . yes, I do."

"Have you seen her here yet?"

"No, no. I haven't. I'm sorry."

Charlie didn't seem to notice the subtle change in Brookston's tone, but Molly did. And her thoughts went in several different directions at once. But all collided at the same juncture—she hoped Lori Beth wasn't the type of woman who would hurt Charlie Daggett. Either unknowingly or on purpose. "When you find her, Charlie, please bring her over and make an introduction." Molly winked and sipped the hot cider, relishing its warmth. "I want to meet this special woman."

Charlie winked back and melded into the crowd.

She was turning to ask the doctor if there was reason to be concerned with this Lori Beth when she spotted Rachel and the boys arriving. Alone.

An older gentleman she'd seen in town before struck up a conversation with her and Dr. Brookston, but when he began describing his physical ailments in greater detail than she wanted—or needed—to hear, Molly politely excused herself and milled through the gathering, talking with students and their parents, and keeping an eye out for James.

Several loud whistles drew the crowd's attention, and she spotted Mayor Davenport making his way up onto the back of a wagon. A round of applause rose.

"Kind citizens of Timber Ridge," he began as the welcome died down. "We're gathered here tonight, on this memorable occasion, to celebrate the proud day that our territory became the state of Colorado! We all—"

Thunderous applause drowned out his next words, but Davenport didn't appear to mind. He raised his fist in victory, then shook it in the air like some prizefighter back east. Politely clapping along with everyone else, Molly continued to search the crowd—and spied James. Across the field. He was scanning the crowd too, and looking especially handsome tonight.

His gaze snagged on hers and she smiled. He did too, briefly, and nodded. Then turned back to watch Mayor Davenport.

Molly felt a portion of the air leave her lungs, but she pasted back on her smile and redirected her attention to the mayor, who was speaking again.

A half hour later, Mayor Davenport was still going strong, and Molly's feet—which had already been sore—now throbbed. She sought respite at one of the tables on the side, and found the only empty chair beside Mrs. Spivey and Mrs. Tucker. "May I please join you, ladies?" she whispered.

"Oh yes, please do." Oleta Tucker pulled out a chair for her and leaned close. "LuEllen and I were just talking about how we're going to start in on Frances's and Jean's desserts if our long-winded mayor doesn't finish soon!"

Molly grinned along with them.

"Mrs. Whitcomb," LuEllen Spivey said softly, leaning closer. "My niece is visiting from Dallas for a few days, and I've told her all about you. She's eager to make your acquaintance. She's a schoolteacher as well, or wants to be. She's quite talented, *and* single."

Molly nodded, wondering if she'd imagined that added emphasis. "Wonderful! I look forward to meeting her."

"Actually," LuEllen continued, "she submitted an application for the position here in Timber Ridge. When she wasn't chosen, we were disappointed at first, of course. But once we heard about you, and then met you—" She squeezed Molly's arm, a little too hard. "Well, we couldn't be more pleased. Her name is Judith Stafford and she's standing right over there." She pointed none too discreetly. "Right next to the sheriff."

Already knowing where to look, Molly saw a striking young brunette standing close to James, and she couldn't account for the bitter twist of emotion inside her. "She's lovely, Mrs. Spivey."

"Oh, isn't she? She's my brother's eldest daughter. Not married yet." She nudged Molly. "But I'm working on that."

Molly managed a smile, hearing exactly what LuEllen Spivey was saying. And *wasn't* saying. Apparently Belle Birch wasn't the only one who had noticed her "friendship" with James.

Applause rose again, louder now than before, and she looked to see Mayor Davenport step off the wagon. The guitarists began plucking while the fiddlers fired up their bows, and couples didn't waste any time taking the dance floor.

Molly searched for James again and saw him, walking with Judith straight toward their table. She'd thought he'd looked handsome from across the field, but seeing him close up—in a suit jacket, pressed trousers, a freshly starched white shirt and tie—she found herself attracted to him in a way she hadn't been before. But she knew her response was aided by the beautiful woman—no, the beautiful *unmarried* woman—beside him.

James looked at her and smiled, but something was different about it.

LuEllen Spivey stood. "Judith, I'd like to present Mrs. Molly Whitcomb. Mrs. Whitcomb, this is my niece, Miss Judith Stafford."

Molly rose and gave a slight curtsey. "It's an honor to meet you, Miss Stafford. Welcome to Timber Ridge."

Judith flashed a smile that only heightened her beauty. "Thank you, Mrs. Whitcomb. It's an honor to meet you too, ma'am. And, actually, I've been to Timber Ridge before. Many times." She gave James a shy glance. "I always enjoy my visits here."

Molly looked at James, who was looking at Miss Stafford.

The song ended and the couples on the makeshift dance floor clapped. Another tune began, slower this time, with the soulful blend of a harmonica joining in. "Beautiful Dreamer," if Molly wasn't mistaken. How apropos.

"Sheriff McPherson . . ." Mrs. Spivey's voice took on a matchmaking quality. "Why don't you and Judith run along and enjoy yourselves? Mrs. Whitcomb and Mrs. Tucker and I will do what older women do and get ourselves some dinner."

James gave a shy smile. "I'm not very light on my feet, ma'am. I'm not sure Miss Stafford wants to chance—"

"I'd love to, Sheriff," Judith said softly.

Molly met James's gaze and reminded herself to smile. And to breathe.

"Well," he said. "All right, then." He offered his arm to Judith, and she slipped her hand through. He led her to the dance floor, and Molly couldn't help but watch them. They made the perfect couple, and James didn't look her way again.

Mrs. Spivey looped her arm through Molly's. "Are you ready for dinner, Mrs. Whitcomb?"

Molly felt the knife in her back sink a notch deeper. She wasn't the least hungry, but wasn't about to admit that. "Yes, dinner sounds good."

Oleta Tucker rose from the table. "And let's not forget Frances's and Jean's desserts. Mrs. Whitcomb, if you haven't tried Frances's cherry pie and Jean's gingerbread cake, you're in for a real treat."

Molly followed them, doing her best to pay attention as they waited in line to get their food, agreeing to whatever they said, and telling herself how foolish she'd been. About so many, many things.

As though standing outside herself, she glimpsed what others saw when they looked at her. Only, her image wouldn't hold its shape. It wavered and shifted and faded, until she saw herself without the window treatment of lies and deceit, without the forgiveness she'd begged God to grant her.

She saw herself for who she was, and went stone-cold inside.

She looked around at the townspeople—many of them her friends now, who had accepted her among them, who had invited her into their homes and made her feel a part of the community. These people were good and kind and decent. And she had lied to them, intentionally misled them, and deceived them. And herself.

She turned and looked behind her at James, dancing with Judith, and a part of her broke away inside, down deep. She had brought this upon herself. She was here, now, because of her own choices. Emotions lodged like a painful fist at the base of her throat. *Oh, God, what have I done. . . .*

And was there anything He could do to lead her through this mess she'd made?

His answer came swift—and soft as a whisper, ageless and timeless, resounding as thunder. Molly gripped the edge of the table beside her, heart pounding, certain that at any moment the ground beneath her feet would give way. Her throat all but closed as her heart recognized His voice. And responded. And went to its knees.

Just as she would have done, if she could have.

31

M rs. Whitcomb, are you all right?"
Molly blinked, hearing Oleta Tucker's voice.

"You look pale, dear. Do you need to sit down?"

She nodded, still trembling inside. "Yes . . . please."

Once seated, Molly drew herself up. She dabbed at unshed tears and turned so Mrs. Spivey couldn't see her face. "I-I'm fine. I think I just went too long without eating, Mrs. Tucker, that's all."

"You're certain, dear?"

Molly nodded again.

"Well—" Oleta patted her shoulder. "You rest

right here. LuEllen and I will get your plate for you."

The women returned with food, and at their encouragement, Molly took a few bites. But it wasn't appetizing and sat uneasy on her stomach.

LuEllen Spivey leaned closer. "You're sure you're all right, dear? You're looking unwell again."

How could the woman manage so kind a tone when her manner clearly said she felt the opposite? Molly composed herself. "Please, you ladies go on and see to your families. I'm just going to sit here and enjoy the food and music for a while."

Looking only partially convinced, Oleta Tucker finally nodded. Mrs. Spivey just smiled.

Once they left, Molly tried eating again, vegetables this time, and managed a few bites, knowing the baby needed the nourishment, even if she wasn't hungry.

"Miss Molly?"

She looked up to see Charlie walking toward her, and had to look twice at the woman with him. It was Miss Matthews! The woman she'd met at Hank Bolden's store.

"Miss Molly—" Charlie gestured beside him. "This is Lori Beth. Miss Lori Beth Matthews," he added quickly. "I just asked her to dance with me." His eyes widened for a humorous instant. "But first, I wanted you two to meet. Lori Beth, this here's Dr. Molly Whitcomb."

Miss Matthews extended her hand. "Charlie, Dr. Whitcomb and I have already had the pleasure of meeting."

Molly grasped hold. "Miss Matthews, it's so nice to see you again. And please call me Molly." She couldn't help but look between Charlie and the woman, and she could tell by Miss Matthews's smile that she was aware of her surprise.

"Nice to see you again too, Molly. And it would please me if you'd call me Lori Beth." Her smile wavered. "So few people do these days."

Molly glimpsed the frailty she'd perceived in the woman the first time they'd met. "You need to know that Charlie speaks very highly of you, Lori Beth."

"As he does to me about you. Thank you"—she squeezed Molly's hand—"for welcoming me so warmly tonight. Town gatherings aren't easy for me to attend."

Molly caught her own frown a fraction before it formed, having the feeling she was missing something. Yet she didn't know what. Discovering that *Miss Matthews* was the object of Charlie's affection helped allay her earlier concern on his behalf. But she still had trouble pairing them, and a flicker of shame burned her when she realized why.

Because Lori Beth was much more polished than Charlie. More refined and well spoken.

The silence drew out—too long, Molly realized. Lori Beth's expression revealed awareness, and

Molly knew she'd failed to mask her thoughts.

Feeling at odds within herself, she borrowed a page from Mrs. Spivey's book, and felt years older in the taking. "Please, don't let me keep you two from enjoying yourselves. There's music playing!"

Charlie eyed the couples dancing. "I guess we *could* go dance now, Lori Beth. If you want."

"I'd very much like that, Charlie. Thank you." She turned to Molly. "I hope we can visit again, before the evening's through."

"Of course, I'll be sitting right here."

Molly took her seat again. Charlie glanced back when Lori Beth wasn't looking and gave her a big grin. Molly waved and watched as he took Lori Beth's hand and led her onto the dance floor. He bowed slightly—as she'd taught him—then took Lori Beth into his arms to dance.

If Molly wasn't mistaken, she saw Charlie's lips moving, counting in time to the music, which made her smile.

"Molly?"

Hearing her name, and the apology wrapped around it, she briefly closed her eyes. As much as she'd looked forward to this evening, and to seeing him, she now couldn't wait for it to end. She felt like such an imposter.

James claimed an empty chair beside her.

"Before you say anything, James—" She looked around to see if anyone was listening, but the blur of conversation and music provided ample cover.

Still, she kept her voice low, as he had done. "You owe me no apology."

"I feel as if I do. Can we go somewhere and talk? Quick, before Mrs. Spivey or Miss Stafford sees me again?"

She softened at the desperation in his voice. "I'm fine, James, really. And there'll be time to talk later."

"Something tells me you're not fine, Molly. And that maybe you haven't been fine in a long time."

His deep voice had a rasp to it that stirred something inside her.

Hearing the music reminded her she was supposed to be watching, and she turned to see Charlie dancing slow with Lori Beth, holding her gently, not once stepping on the woman's feet—that Molly could see. Charlie looked her way. She saw the pride and love on his face, and couldn't have been happier for him.

She felt James watching her.

"Thank you for your note."

She turned. "Did you read it?" What a silly question. Of course he'd read it. . . .

"Only about twenty times so far." He patted the pocket on his suit jacket. "But I carry it with me, just in case I need to read it again."

Molly told herself to look away from those blue eyes, but she couldn't. And without permission, another portion of her heart gave itself to him.

"What you wrote, though, it had a certain . . . dichotomy to it, don't you think?"

"Dichotomy?" She smiled despite the turmoil inside her.

He nodded. "That means a division or contrast between two things that are—"

"I know what the word means." She gave a soft laugh. "I just didn't know you did."

He feigned a wounded look. "And this after you said such sweet things in your note."

The tempo of the string music changed. A little faster tune, but the couples dancing still held each other close.

"I wish I could ask you to dance with me, Molly." His voice had softened. "Or maybe you'd agree to give me private lessons sometime."

He knew about Charlie. "Have you been spying on me, Sheriff McPherson?"

His face reddened. "I might have come by your cabin one evening to see if you'd have dinner with me. And then just happened to pass real close by the schoolhouse and sort of . . . happened to see through a window. For a few minutes."

"You just *happened* to pass real close by?" She made a *tsk*ing noise, able to see that he truly did feel bad about having done it. But not completely. "Are sheriffs allowed to spy on people through windows like that?"

"Actually, it's one of the advantages of being a sheriff. You can do it and it's considered part of your job."

"Really?"

He nodded. "It's in the Law Book. Section forty-two, code nineteen. A sheriff can skulk around a schoolhouse and spy on dance lessons for the safety of the town's teacher."

"May I see that book, please?"

"It's back in the office." One corner of his mouth tipped upward. "If you'll take that walk with me, I'll show it to you."

If it were up to her, she would get up from this table right now and go with him. But it wasn't. That timeless, ageless whisper reverberated inside her, reminding her of what she had to do. But this wasn't the right setting. She shook her head. "No, James. I can't." *I won't.*

Molly saw Charlie and Lori Beth making their way toward the refreshment tables, and felt James following her gaze. "That's the woman Charlie was taking the dance lessons for. Her name is—"

"Lori Beth Matthews," James said quietly, his tone going flat.

She tried to read his expression and couldn't. "What's wrong?" She glanced at Lori Beth, that same sense of having missed something returning. Her concern for Charlie renewed. "Do you know her?"

"Yes," James whispered, watching the couple. "I know Miss Matthews. I just didn't know that she and Charlie were—" He looked back at her. "That they were seeing each other."

Protectiveness rose within her, swift and strong.

"Is there something about Miss Matthews that Charlie should know? I'm not asking you to reveal a confidence, James, I just—" She sighed. "Charlie likes her very much, and I'd simply like an assurance that he won't get hurt."

"Charlie knows. At least I'm pretty sure he does. He's lived here for years."

Molly's curiosity and concern jumped about ten levels. It wasn't like James to talk about others, and she waited, sensing he might say more if she didn't.

A moment passed before he spoke again. "This is common knowledge to anyone who's lived here very long. And I tell you now only because I know you care about Charlie. And I do too." The fine lines around the edges of his eyes grew more pronounced, as they did when he was troubled. "Miss Matthews moved here about five years ago. From somewhere back east. She worked in the dress shop for a while, and did real well for herself, is my understanding. Then—" He looked as if whatever he was about to say pained him. "Then Miss Matthews came to be with child," he whispered, his voice thick with disapproval.

Molly heard the words, saw the objection on his face, and felt a severing deep inside her.

"We didn't know whose baby it was, and to my knowledge, we still don't. She's never said."

Glad she was seated, Molly swallowed. "And yet

she chose to stay here," she whispered, hardly aware she'd spoken the words.

"Yes . . . she did. But I'm not sure how wise a choice that was, given how she's been treated by folks."

Numb, Molly watched Lori Beth as she and Charlie went through the food line. The expressions of the women serving behind the tables didn't change—until Lori Beth passed. Then a handful of them turned and whispered to each other. And those who didn't also didn't speak to her.

"You're shaking. Are you cold?" James reached for her hands beneath the tablecloth.

Molly gently pulled away. "So she—" Her voice caught. She cleared her throat. "She has a child?"

James glanced around them, his expression unsettled. "The baby died at birth," he said, his voice barely above a whisper. "A boy, from what I was told. It was before Brookston came. There was something wrong with the baby, and the midwife didn't know what to do. Some folks said it was for the best, but I can't hold to that. A baby dying never seems right . . . no matter how it was brought into the world." His sigh came heavy. "Miss Matthews mostly keeps to herself now. She comes into town every so often, but I don't know how much contact she has with other folks." He looked up and came to his feet.

Molly turned to see Charlie and Lori Beth

coming their way. Her hands still shaking, she sat up straighter and tried to put on a pleasant countenance. But all she could think about was Lori Beth's baby lying somewhere in the cold dark ground. She covered her midsection, as though she could shield her own baby from a similar fate.

Charlie and Lori Beth joined them at the table, laughing, plates piled high.

"This all looks mighty good," Charlie said, holding Lori Beth's chair out.

"Yes, it does." Lori Beth beamed up at him. "I've never seen so much delicious-looking food."

James took his seat. "Charlie, it's good to see you. Miss Matthews . . . good evening to you, ma'am."

"Good evening, Sheriff McPherson." Lori Beth unfolded her napkin, pausing in the act. "If I could, Sheriff . . . I'd like to take this opportunity to thank you for your kindness and that of your friend, Mr. Ranslett, earlier this summer. The elk meat you left at my door was delicious."

Surprise sharpened James's features.

Molly stared, waiting for him to respond. But he didn't, which wasn't like him. If she read him right, he'd thought the meat had been left anonymously. But apparently that hadn't been the case. And for some reason, that caught him off guard.

As if eager to cover the sudden silence, Lori Beth motioned to Molly's plate. "You haven't eaten much, Molly. Are you feeling all right?"

Struggling to hold herself together, Molly nodded. "Yes, yes, I'm fine." But her voice came out stilted and unconvincing.

Lori Beth held her gaze, then looked at James, then back at Molly—and slowly lowered her eyes.

James rose. "If you'll excuse me, I should probably go help with whatever's coming next. Either that, or risk Mayor Davenport trying to speak again." That drew laughter, but only from Charlie. James touched Molly's shoulder. "I'll see you before you leave tonight, Mrs. Whitcomb."

Feeling his abrupt departure, and judging from Lori Beth's expression that she did too, Molly watched him work his way through the crowd. As always, he couldn't take four steps without someone shaking his hand or speaking to him. Mrs. Spivey approached him again, her lovely niece beside her, and Molly forced herself to turn back around, only too aware of Lori Beth's silent attention—and of her own feelings toward the woman now that she knew the truth.

She told herself she would have treated Lori Beth the very same—both outside Hank Bolden's store and again here tonight—even if she'd known. But glancing around them now, catching the subtle disapproving stares their table drew, she wasn't so sure. So this is what it would be like if people knew. No . . .

What it *will* be like, when they do.

A sudden streak of color screamed across the

dark night sky, followed by thunderous cracks and pops. Sparkling trails of red, white, yellow, blue, and green rained down over the field, and everyone clapped, *ooh*ing and *ahh*ing, as more fireworks launched and exploded in marvels of rainbow color.

But all Molly wanted to do was leave.

When the festivities were over, she spotted Dr. Brookston a few tables away. He saw her and pointed toward the wagons, raising a brow. She nodded and indicated she would walk on. Turning, she glimpsed James too, across the field, with Miss Stafford glued to his side.

Head down, she blended in with others walking in the direction of the church and kept to herself, mindful of the animals having been there. A light wind kicked up and she pulled her coat collar closer about her neck.

Then she felt it, something on her cheek. She paused and looked up.

Snow.

Tiny flakes drifted down, swirling and twirling on the wind. One landed on her lip and she licked it off. Her first snowfall in Timber Ridge. And the first in the new state of Colorado.

"I'm sorry, Dr. Whitcomb." Dr. Brookston ran up behind her, out of breath. "I got stopped by Mrs. Calhoun. God love that woman, but you ask her what time it is and she tells you how the clock was made."

Molly forced a smile as he helped her into the wagon.

He glanced up. "Looks like winter's here. We get a good deal more snow than Georgia does, so I hope you're ready."

Molly managed polite conversation on the way home.

Later, lying in bed, she finally fell into a fitful sleep only to awaken, thinking of Lori Beth and realizing how brave a woman she was. Far braver than she herself. Molly turned onto her side, unable to get warm. She hadn't taken the time to fill the bed warmer with hot coals and regretted it now.

Somewhere there was a man—perhaps still living in Timber Ridge—who had fathered Lori Beth's baby. He had let her carry the child, give birth to the child, and live with the public disgrace of it all. Just as Jeremy had done with her.

And as if that hadn't been enough, Lori Beth had stood by a tiny grave and buried a part of herself. And that man had allowed her to go through all of it—alone.

She tried to go back to sleep, and couldn't. She checked the clock. It was just after midnight but seemed much later. She needed to use the chamber pot but debated, weighing her need against the chill out from under the covers. Finally discomfort won out.

She crawled from bed and slipped into her robe,

the cold wooden planks prickling the soles of her feet. She made use of the chamber pot, then stoked the dying embers in the hearth and added two more logs. Stretching out her arms, she soaked up the warmth from the flames. Then cocked her head to one side, thinking she heard something.

She crossed to the window overlooking the stream behind the cabin and edged back the curtain. Her soft gasp fogged the icy pane. The world was draped in a blanket of white! She hunched closer to the window, careful not to touch the freezing glass. She couldn't believe how bright it was outside, and with a light snow still falling.

There. A jingle. She heard it again.

A knock on the door nearly sent her out of her skin.

Scared motionless at first, she grabbed the fire poker and wielded it where she stood. "Who is it?"

"It's James."

Still shaking, she clutched her makeshift weapon, having half a mind to brain the man with it for scaring her like that. What was he doing out at this time of night anyway? She returned the poker to its place and secured her robe, recalling what she'd promised herself, and more importantly, what she'd promised God, earlier that evening.

Bracing herself for more than just the cold, she pulled the door open and stepped back as snow drifted in. James was covered in it and held a bundle beneath his arm.

"Are you going to invite me in, or would you rather talk out here?"

Smiling, she motioned him inside and shut the door. "Do you have any idea what time it is?"

He lowered the scarf from his face, his slightest movement scattering snow everywhere. "It took me a while to get everything together." He pointed to the table. "May I?"

Uncertain, she nodded.

He unwrapped the bundle that turned out to be a blanket stuffed with clothes. Mostly men's clothes from what she could tell, along with a scarf, gloves, thick woolen socks, and boots.

"These are for you. And you've got ten minutes to get dressed."

She stared. "To get dressed? For what?"

Tugging off his glove, he led her by the hand to the front window and pushed back the curtain. She couldn't see anything at first—frost covered the pane—but he wiped it away. She took a closer look . . . and couldn't believe her eyes.

32

James tucked the blanket around Molly until only her eyes showed beneath the bundle of clothing and scarves and blankets. He wanted her to be warm, and he wanted to be next to her. Especially tonight.

He climbed into the sleigh and she tugged the

blanket up over him, then tucked it between them, her eyes smiling. He gave the reins a whip and the horses responded.

Snow drifted down without a hint of wind. The night was absolutely still, perfect, the only sound the muted tamp of horses' hooves and the soft jingle of bells. Two oil lamps adorned the front of the sleigh, but he hadn't bothered lighting them. With the moonlight reflecting off the world of white, the lamps weren't needed.

They reached the end of the path and he turned right, away from town.

She didn't ask where they were going. She just leaned back and stared up into the dark night sky. He would have been hard-pressed to explain it to anyone, but he'd never felt so much like a man as he did when he was with her. He wanted to protect her, provide for her, make her laugh, love her in every way he could. And he liked that she didn't have to fill every moment with words too.

Though she obviously knew quite a few more than he did.

It struck him as funny that a Tennessee boy and a Georgia girl had to come all the way west to Colorado to meet each other. But God's plans weren't necessarily his, he knew. And he'd walked with the Lord long enough to know that he wanted God's plans over anything else. No matter how much he might want what he wanted for himself.

He slowed as they came to a curve. The horses

pranced, their steps high and sprite, as though they enjoyed this middle-of-the-night jaunt as much as he did. He'd put extra blankets on both of them and had wrapped their legs to protect from the cold.

He guided the sleigh off the trail and down a gently sloped embankment, having been this way many times before. The fire he'd built earlier still burned low and bright. He pulled the sleigh up as close as he could get without hitting the drifts, then got out and came around to her side.

He tugged the scarf down from over his nose and mouth, and she did likewise. She started to climb out but he stopped her.

"The drifts are pretty deep through here. If you'll allow me?"

She slipped her arms around his neck, and he carried her the short distance to the fire, but he didn't set her down right off, and she noticed. The sideways look she gave him made him wish he'd known her as a young girl. No telling what trouble she'd gotten into. She'd looked beautiful earlier tonight, but now, with her hair all loose around her shoulders, mussed and hand-combed, she took his breath away.

"Thank you," he whispered.

Her expression turned quizzical. "For what?"

"For following God's lead in coming to Timber Ridge."

Arms around his neck, she searched his face, unhurried, and he welcomed it.

"I do believe God led me here, James. That's one thing I'll never doubt again."

He sensed something more might follow that thought, but when she didn't offer, he set her down and dusted off the log. "Make yourself at home, madam. I'll be right back."

Her soft chuckle behind him told him his grandfather had been right. There was something magical about kidnapping your sweetheart—or in this case, his "would-be" sweetheart—and taking her out during the first snowfall of winter. James only hoped it would turn out as well for him as it had for Ian Fletcher McGuiggan.

He retrieved the satchel from the sleigh, remembering Rachel's enthusiasm as he'd packed it earlier. She'd insisted on helping and had shared with him about the last time Thomas had done this for her. Aware of Molly watching him as he walked back, he set the satchel down and added more wood to the fire, then settled on the log beside her.

She laid a gloved hand on his arm. "I don't know what else you have planned for tonight, but it could be nothing else at all, and this would still be the best surprise I've ever had."

"Well, then . . ." He acted as if he was going to stand. "I might as well take this satchel on back to the—"

She grabbed his arm. "Don't you dare!"

Enjoying their ease with each other, especially considering their tension from earlier this evening, he thanked God again for bringing this woman into his life. He'd often wondered if the Almighty intended for him to go through this life alone, and that prospect, while lonely feeling at times, had never been a strong source of contention for him—until now. How could the mere thought of someone's absence from your life stir up such longing?

He tugged off his gloves and untied the satchel's leather straps. "This," he said, producing a canteen and two cups, "is my grandmother's cocoa." He poured and started to take a sip, but she touched his wrist.

"Aren't you forgetting something?" She raised her cup.

"Oh, you're right. It's not sugar sticks, but it'll have to do." He raised his cup to hers. "To friendships that grow, and deepen"—dare he add this last line—"and that last a lifetime."

She held his gaze, her eyes glistening in the firelight. "And for courage to follow God's lead," she whispered. "No matter where it takes us."

She drank, and James followed, somewhat reluctant. Not sure about the meaning behind her toast and the melancholy in her voice when she'd made it.

He pulled a covered plate from the satchel. "I also brought some of Frances Hines's cherry pie and Mattie Moorehead's gingerbread cake, if you're interested."

She waved it off. "No, thank you. This cocoa is delicious, and plenty."

Despite her being so quiet when they'd first left her cabin, conversation came easily. They talked about their respective homes and the differences between the South and Colorado, about school and Angelo learning English, about Billy and Elijah's unlikely friendship, and about the sheriff's office. Everything but his most pressing concern.

As the fire died down, he added more kindling. "I want to apologize to you, Molly, for what happened this evening at the celebration."

She shook her head as though knowing what was coming. "I've already told you, James. You have nothing for which to apologize."

"With all due respect . . ." He took her gloved hand in his, grateful he'd earned that privilege. "I believe I do. And I'd appreciate it if you'd hear me out before saying otherwise."

She stared at him for a second, then nodded.

"I want to apologize if, by my actions this evening, I gave you any reason to make you doubt my feelings for you. Two things figured in to my behavior tonight. First, LuEllen Spivey has a long history of playing matchmaker in this town." He shook his head. "And, unfortunately, I'm her current project."

"James, I know—"

"I'm not done yet. And it's rude to interrupt. As a teacher, you should know that."

She responded with an arched brow and a look worthy of any venerated professor.

He smiled. "I bet Kurt's seen that look before."

"Kurt has seen that look and far worse, I promise you. And more than once."

He nodded, well able to imagine. "The second thing, and this was intentional on my part, goes to something I've never had to deal with before as sheriff of Timber Ridge." He slipped off her left glove and wove his fingers through hers, surprised to find her fourth finger absent of her wedding band. "And that's wanting to spend more time—a lot more time—with just one woman."

She stared at their hands. "Is it safe for me to assume that you're not speaking of Miss Stafford?"

He laughed at the subtle mockery in her tone. "That's something you may very safely assume, Molly." He lifted her hand to his mouth and kissed the soft underside of her wrist, enjoying how her breath quickened.

The crackle of the fire filled the silence between them, and somewhere in the distance a wolf's howl rose lonely in the night.

"Watching you with Miss Stafford this evening wasn't what I would describe as pleasant, James, but I know with certainty that you, of all men, would never say one thing and do another. It's not within you."

While he appreciated her trust, he didn't welcome her elevated praise. "Don't paint me as being more worthy than I am. I've made my fair share of mistakes. But I've always tried to keep any hint of misconduct away from the sheriff's office. I don't want to give anyone reason to question my motives, and I don't want your reputation to be in question either, because of me."

She sighed, looking up at him. "You could never harm my reputation, James. You're too good a man. Too kind and honorable," she whispered, her brow knitting tight. "Which only makes—" She bowed her head. "Which only makes this so much harder."

He looked closer at her. "Which only makes *what* harder?"

"Being here . . . now, with you," she whispered.

"Being here with me is hard?" He laughed softly. "That's not exactly what I'd hoped to hear tonight."

She laughed, but it came out part sob, and tears rose to her eyes.

She turned her head, but he slipped his hands inside the collar of her coat and raised her face to meet his. And for the first time since they'd met, he sensed her resolve slipping. He heard it in her quick breaths and saw it in her face, and in the way she covered his hands framing her face. But her resolve wasn't just slipping . . . she *wanted* to let him through that impenetrable wall she'd built around herself. He could feel it, he was certain. He also felt her reluctance. Her fear was nearly tangible.

But given this opening, he wasn't about to let Molly slip back behind that barrier without a fight.

Molly couldn't think with James so close to her. She needed to move away. "I can't do this if you're touching me."

He drew her closer. "You can't do what?"

"Tell you," she whispered, hearing the tremor in her voice.

"Tell me what?"

She caught the scent of cocoa on his breath and imagined the taste of his kiss, which didn't help her concentration. She shook her head. *"This . . .* can't happen between us, James."

His hands were warm on her face. "You feel for me the way I feel for you, Molly. I can tell."

"No," she said softly.

"No?" His smile said he didn't believe her. "You're saying you don't care for me?"

"I'm saying—" Her breath came hard, the cost of her promise becoming clearer. "I'm saying . . . I c-can't."

She turned away, but he gently turned her back. She saw the desire in his eyes, and closed hers.

"Look at me, Molly."

She couldn't. Not and get through this.

He cradled the back of her neck. "Look at me," he whispered.

At the insistence in his voice, she obeyed, reluctant. He traced a feather-soft path over her lips, and her gaze went to his mouth. With a trembling hand, she touched his face. If she'd only known how it could be . . .

He kissed her cheek, then with utmost patience worked his way to the corner of her mouth, his breath warm against her skin. He drew back slightly, his question clear. And slowly, deliberately, knowing this would be their first kiss—and last—Molly closed her eyes.

His tenderness awakened an ache inside her, not only to be closer to him, but to be *more* to him. He tasted faintly of chocolate, smooth and sweet. He wove his hands through her hair, deepening their kiss, and Molly slipped her arms around his neck. She moved closer and heard his soft sigh, and sensed an urgency building—

She broke the kiss and pulled back, her breath coming hard. "We shouldn't ha—" She touched her mouth, still warm from his. "We shouldn't have done that."

His own breath uneven, he fingered a curl at her temple. "If it's any consolation, I don't regret it in the least."

He reached for her, but she rose and moved away, clutching the blanket tight about her shoulders. He stood, but she held up her hand.

"No, James, please . . ." She briefly closed her eyes, summoning the courage. "I made a promise tonight that I would—" She bit her lower lip. Her chin trembled. "I didn't plan on you," she whispered, remembering the first time she'd seen him in Sulfur Falls. Then again that same day, on the cliff. She took a stuttered breath, barely able to speak past the pain tightening her chest. "I never expected to meet you. You need to remember that . . . after I tell you this. Please promise me you'll remember that."

He moved closer. "Molly, I don't know what you're afraid of, but there's no reason to—"

"Say you'll remember."

"I'll remember." He took another step. "But whatever you're about to tell me isn't going to change the way I—"

"You don't know what you're saying, James."

"Trust me, Molly, I do." Firmness layered his tone. "I know exactly what I'm saying because there's something I've been wanting to—"

"James, I'm with child."

He stopped dead cold. He didn't blink. He didn't move. He just stared, as though seeing her from a distance, uncertain whether or not it was her.

Silence crowded the space between them, roaring in her ears and competing with the pounding of her pulse. A gentle thunder echoed deep inside her, and Molly closed her eyes, feeling the tears slip down her cheeks, knowing her promise to God was only half fulfilled.

"I don't . . ." James exhaled. "I don't understand. How can you be . . ."

"I was with child when I arrived in Timber Ridge."

He blinked and took a half step back. An unconscious move on his part, she felt sure. But it revealed so much.

His expression clouded. "And you didn't tell me," he whispered. "You never said anything."

"I tried . . . many times, I just couldn't—"

"When you first applied for the position here . . ." His eyes narrowed. He shook his head. "You couldn't have known then. . . . Right?"

He was so eager to believe the best. "Even then, James. I knew."

He frowned, and his gaze dropped to her midsection. "So . . . you lied," he said, disbelief thinning his voice. "All this time. You've been lying. To me. To everyone." Disappointment darkened his eyes as an invisible weight settled across his broad shoulders.

"I'm so sorry, James. Please, *please* forgive me. I've wanted to tell you. You don't know how much this has been—"

"Who else knows?"

The flat edge to his voice siphoned the air from her lungs. She swallowed. "Dr. Brookston."

His jaw hardened. "When did you tell *him*?"

"I didn't tell him . . . exactly. He found out when I was sick."

His stare grew heavy and daunting. She wanted to look away but couldn't. How was it that some moments seemed to pass in a blink, while others crept by with aching slowness?

"It's time I get you home," he said, his voice a monotone. Yet he didn't move.

And neither did she. She could feel him thinking, trying to sort things through.

"When is the baby due?"

She swallowed. "The first of February." Four months away.

She sensed the questions roiling inside him and waited, knowing she needed to tell him the rest—to keep the remainder of her promise—but she couldn't get the words to come, not when he was staring at her like that.

He reached for her glove lying on the ground where they'd been sitting and handed it to her. She slipped it on, careful not to meet his eyes.

The ride back to her cabin was tense and quiet. James stopped the sleigh and came around to help her out. He held her arm as she climbed the icy porch stairs, then quickly released her when she reached the door. She fumbled with her key, unable to fit it into the lock. She wiped her eyes, trying to see past her tears.

He took the key from her hand. "The town council will have to be told." He unlocked the door and pushed it open. "There's a meeting Tuesday night."

"I'll be there."

She stepped inside the darkened room and to her surprise, he followed her in. He lit the oil lamp on the table, then strode to the fireplace. Knowing it was useless to protest, she waited as he built a fire. When he finished, he walked past her to the door.

"Is there anything else I should do?" she asked. "To be ready for Tuesday?"

Hollowness filled his eyes. "No, I'll let everyone know you're coming. And that . . . that you have something to tell them." He turned to go.

"James?"

He paused at the door, his back to her.

"I'm so sorry," she whispered.

He slowly turned back, his eyes wet with emotion. "So am I . . . Molly. So am I."

33

Did she say when she expects the baby to be born?"

James glanced at Daniel riding beside him on the trail, grateful that Elizabeth Ranslett had come into the newspaper office that morning, and that she'd brought her husband with her. James needed the advice of his trusted friend, especially before the town council meeting that evening. And before seeing Molly again. "In February. Which means she's about five months along."

Wind gusted down the trail, frigid and biting, and

James tugged the brim of his Stetson lower. As they'd ridden up the mountain that morning, he'd confided in Daniel about Molly and the sleigh ride, and about the past several weeks. Daniel had listened patiently, never interrupting, with the same quiet attentiveness James had appreciated since their youth.

They reined in a good ways back from the cliff's edge and sat in silence. This vantage point was breathtaking, the mountains draped in their winter coats, standing stark and bold against the cloudless blue. James knew Daniel came up to this spot every now and then to think, and to be reminded of what God had done in his life here. But Elizabeth, Daniel's wife, vowed never to step foot on this particular mountain again.

Daniel looked over at him, his breath puffing white in the chilled morning air. "Are you planning on seeing Mrs. Whitcomb before the meeting tonight?"

James fingered a worn place on his leather gloves. "After the way I reacted to her news, I'm not sure she'd welcome me." He stared across the snow-covered peaks. "And, frankly, I'm still sorting things through—doing my best to take my personal feelings out of the equation. If you were to ask me how I feel about the situation as the sheriff, I'd answer one way—that she intentionally lied to the people in this town. And that I was the one who urged the town council to hire her in the first place, and then stood up for her when she arrived in town as a widow, putting my own reputation on the line. I don't welcome what some people are going to say about her, and quite frankly, about me, especially with the election coming up in the spring. But—" He sighed, shaking his head. "When you ask me my opinion as a man without the weight of this badge and the concern of the sheriff's office . . . I still believe what she did was wrong, Daniel, but my answer's not nearly so cut and dried anymore."

"That's actually reassuring to hear." Daniel laughed softly.

James frowned. "How's that?"

"As far back as I can remember"—Daniel shifted in the saddle—"you've had a fire in you for being a man of your word and for telling the truth. And that's a good thing—don't get me wrong. And lest you forget, I know where the seed of that came from."

James nodded, having told Daniel the truth about his father's infidelities years ago, though he'd never worked up the courage to tell him how closely one of his father's *wanderings* defined his own story. He was a few months older than Daniel, and Daniel had always held him in such respect. James knew deep down that it wouldn't have changed Daniel's opinion of him, if Daniel had known the truth. But as time went on, the less important it had seemed, and the more James had convinced himself it wasn't necessary for him to know.

"For years, James, you've placed what you thought would be best for the sheriff's office above what might be best for you. Again, that's admirable." A smile more reminiscent of a boy than a man turned Daniel's mouth. "But I can attest that sharing life with a woman is a mite better than what we used to imagine."

James smiled, remembering those youthful conversations.

Daniel rested his hand on the pommel. "And now you've met a woman who seems to mean a great deal to you. And as I recall, that's not happened before." He went quiet for a minute, which wasn't uncommon for him. "I realize you have responsibilities as sheriff, and that you need to be mindful of those, but I'd encourage you not to value those responsibilities over what might be best for you. You deserve the chance to have a life, a wife and children, just like everybody else. And I wouldn't put too much stock in what people *might* say over all this. There's always going to be 'talk.' That's the nature of some folks. Mrs. Whitcomb is a widow who's with child. And, yes, she lied about it. But it's not like she's some criminal." He prodded his horse. "As you've told me time and again, do as God leads you and don't worry about the rest."

They continued on up the trail, speaking on

occasion, but mostly not. James appreciated the time and space to sort out his thoughts in safe company.

From the very beginning, he'd sensed Molly had been hiding something, but never would he have guessed a baby. She hadn't been at church on Sunday morning, which he hadn't found very surprising, not after he'd gotten her home so late, and understanding how their evening had ended. He'd ridden by school on Monday morning to make sure she was all right. He'd only seen her from a distance and was fairly certain she hadn't seen him.

When the trail ended at the top of the mountain, he and Daniel nudged their mounts around and started back down.

"How's Elizabeth feeling these days?" James knew Daniel would know what he meant.

"She's doing well. But getting a little impatient for it to happen. As I am . . . I'll admit."

James knew they'd been trying for a baby, and had hoped Daniel might have good news for him this time. "We missed you both at the town celebration. Miss Matthews offered us her thanks for the elk meat that evening." He anticipated Daniel's glance.

"How did she know it was us who left it?"

James shrugged. "I'm guessing she saw us." He'd been caught completely off guard when Miss Matthews had thanked him that night. But even more, he'd felt like a hypocrite. Because it had been Daniel's idea to leave the meat for the woman. Not his.

He and Daniel rode on in silence.

"And for courage to follow God's lead, no matter where it takes us." That had been Molly's toast by the fire that night, and with hindsight, it made more sense. She'd been praying for courage to tell him about the baby, and he hadn't taken the news well. That was putting it mildly.

Thinking of the town council meeting that evening, and of what Molly must be going through as she anticipated standing before that group of men and telling them what she'd told him, James offered up that toast as a prayer for them both.

God, give us the courage to follow your lead, no matter where it takes us.

Sitting at her desk, Molly checked her pocket watch, her insides a sick tangle of nerves. Another fifteen minutes until lunch break was over—and another seven hours until the town council meeting when she would find out whether her life in Timber Ridge was over too. No matter what she did, she couldn't erase the memory of how James had last looked at her, and of the hollow disappointment in his eyes.

Though she'd told him the truth—part of it, at least—she felt no relief for having done so. No sense of finally having set things to right. Maybe that was because she'd only told him half the truth, or maybe it was because there would be no sense of "rightness" for her here in Timber Ridge, as she'd grown to hope. The uncertainty of her future corded the knot of emotions tighter in her chest, and she finally rose.

Maybe a brisk walk would help refocus her thoughts. Anything was better than sitting at her desk entertaining dark thoughts. She slipped on her coat and headed outside. Dr. Brookston had encouraged exercise, saying it would help ease the swelling in her hands and feet. Maybe it would also help her nerves.

Being careful of the ice and snow, she took the path that led around where the children were playing. The cool air and movement helped lessen her anxiety, but seeing the smiling faces of the students, hearing their laughter and giggles, and contemplating no longer being their teacher—even Kurt Boyd's, wherever he was—only deepened her regret.

Holding on with one hand, Ansley Tucker waved from the high end of the seesaw. "Teacher, is playtime over?"

"Not yet," Molly answered. "You have another ten minutes." She warmed at the surprised smile on Ansley's face when her cute little brother Davy brought her down a little sooner than expected.

Shoving her hands in her pockets, Molly continued on around the path, the memory of James's kiss pressing closer than she welcomed. She briefly closed her eyes, recalling his tenderness. At the time, he'd said he hadn't regretted that kiss. But that was before he'd known about the baby. And judging by his silence on the way home, then his response as he'd left her cabin, she guessed his opinion about that kiss—like his opinion about her—had changed dramatically.

And this without his knowing the full story, which she intended to tell him. As soon as she saw him next. Withholding the rest of the truth from him now—only to tell him somewhere down the road—would only make things worse between them. And not telling him wasn't an option anymore. He'd used the word *dichotomy* Saturday evening, and that's exactly what this was. The more she grew to care about James, the more determined she became not to continue to lie to him, and to everyone else. Even understanding the cost.

Claiming to be a widow who had hidden that she was with child was deceitful. But never having been married and saying she had been to cover for her carrying an illegitimate child—that was unforgivable. She'd been a fool to think the charade would work. She would have to leave Timber Ridge, and there was only one place for her to go—back to Athens and to her family home, at least until the baby was born. Then she would have to figure out her life from there.

She'd made so many mistakes in recent months,

and keeping her promise to God was one thing she could do, and *would* do. No matter what.

Emily Thompson rang the bell indicating classes were to resume, and Molly climbed the stairs to the schoolhouse. She did her best to focus on her afternoon lessons, but after bumbling through a summary lesson of the War of 1812, she sighed and closed her book.

"I'm going to write some addition and multiplication equations on the board"—she heard murmurs behind her—"and I want each of you to record your answers on your slates." She turned to write on the blackboard. "The first problem is—"

Her piece of chalk broke, which drew giggles. Normally she would've laughed along with them, but not today. She pulled open the top drawer of her desk. No chalk. She reached for the drawer below.

"Dr. Whitcomb?"

She looked up, pulling the next drawer open. "Yes, Amanda?"

"Are you going to give us marks on this?"

Watching other students nod at the question, Molly felt for the chalk. "I very well could, so please, be sure and do your—" Her hand brushed something odd. Something . . . *leathery*. She looked down—and screamed.

A snake! In her drawer. Belly side up. And she'd put her hand right on it! A chill slithered through her.

"What is it, teacher?"

"What's wrong, Dr. Whitcomb?"

Students rose from their seats, but she waved them back, shuddering inside and out. "I'm . . . f-fine, children. Stay seated, please."

She chanced a look back at the drawer, that old fear swelling inside her. *The snake is dead. This isn't the lunch pail. This snake is dead.* Her legs went weak and she reached behind her for her chair. *Breathe, just breathe.* She sat down and took big gulps of air, her flesh still crawling. She tried to unbutton the high collar of her dress, then realized the dress didn't have a high collar.

Hearing sobs, she saw some of the younger children crying. Older students wore concern, wide-eyed and watchful—all except for Kurt Boyd, who sat in the back, a ghost of a grin on his impish little face.

Her anger flared. Furious and embarrassed, she knew she needed to get ahold of herself. She was the teacher, after all, and—

The snake rolled over and raised its head.

Molly scrambled back so fast her chair toppled and took her with it. She fell hard on her hip and shoulder. The air left her lungs in a rush.

"Teacher!" a tiny voice screamed.

Lying curled on her side, Molly blinked, seeing stars, pain shooting down her back. She slowly pushed up to a sitting position, the clamor of footsteps growing close. She held her head and slowly regained her focus—in time to see the snake slither up and over her desk.

Later that afternoon, after tutoring Angelo, and with the children's marks recorded in her teacher's book, Molly sat up straighter in her chair and rubbed her lower back, trying to relieve the dull throb. The cushion in her chair helped, but her tailbone ached from the earlier fall.

Embarrassment flooded her again, recalling how she'd reacted to seeing that snake, and with every student watching. Including Amanda Spivey, who, no doubt, was reliving every dramatic detail to her mother at this very moment. Bless Billy Bolden's heart—the boy had removed the snake, then checked the rest of the drawers for anything else that might have been lurking.

What made her reaction to the snake even worse was that it wasn't poisonous. Billy had explained to her that it was a hognose snake, and that they "played dead" when they got scared. Thinking of it now, she should have told the class that was what she'd been doing too.

Massaging her left shoulder, Molly angled her neck from side to side. *That little Kurt Boyd . . .*

In front of the entire class, she'd challenged him about putting the snake in her drawer. And three times, he had denied it. She had no proof, but she *knew* he'd done it.

She checked the time—as she'd done repeatedly

all day—and felt the minutes ticking past, bringing her closer to her meeting with the town council. She looked down and placed a hand over the gentle rise hidden beneath the folds of her dress. As much as she'd hoped early on that this child couldn't detect her lack of love, she prayed now that the tiny life inside her would know how very much she *did* love him, or her.

The door opened with a creak, and she looked up.

Rachel stood in the entryway, somber and wordless. Kurt walked in behind her, head bowed. Together, they approached her desk.

Kurt took hesitant steps, his little chest rising and falling in quick, stuttered breaths. He looked up at his mother, then back at her, then tucked his trembling chin again, his eyes red-rimmed and puffy. This was a side of Kurt Boyd she'd not seen.

"Dr. Whitcomb—" Rachel's tone was understandably formal. "I've learned what happened in class today." She glanced sideways at her son. "Kurt and I have discussed it at length, and he has something he wants to say to you."

Kurt lifted his head, his little-boy cheeks smudged with dirt and damp with tears. "I put the snake in your drawer, Dr. Whitcomb. And I'm sorry."

He delivered the apology with surprisingly little effort, and Molly wasn't fully convinced of its sincerity, yet didn't feel at liberty to question it. "I accept your apology, Kurt, and I appreciate your coming back this afternoon to offer it."

"Mitchell told me what happened, when they got home." Rachel's voice wavered. She had a tired, defeated look about her. "I went and checked, and sure enough, the cage was empty. That's when I knew."

The cage? Molly cringed. Rachel allowed the boys to keep snakes as pets?

"Be assured, Dr. Whitcomb, that I've applied the appropriate discipline for what Kurt has done. And that I'm deeply sorry this happened. It *will* not happen again," she said, looking closer to tears than a tirade.

"Thank you, Rachel. I appreciate that." But looking at Kurt peering up at her beneath hooded eyes, Molly couldn't help but question the assurance of that guarantee. Something told her there was another motivation behind the boy's apology other than regretting the scare he'd given her, or even the threat of future discipline from his mother.

"Kurt, I've graded your slate from this afternoon." Molly motioned to the stack beside her desk, remembering how well he'd done. "Why don't you find yours and show your mother?"

As Kurt looked for his slate, Molly rose from her chair and retrieved her coat. She walked to the window and peered out. The sunshine from earlier in the day had given way to clouds, and the wind had picked up. She massaged her lower back, a dull ache throbbing low.

"Mama, do you think Uncle James will be proud of me again?"

Her coat halfway on, Molly paused, hearing the truth behind Kurt's apology—he wanted his Uncle James to be proud of him. Something she couldn't fault him for in the least, and something she would have liked as well.

"Molly?"

At the somberness in Rachel's tone, Molly turned and saw Rachel staring at her desk. Molly's first thought went to another snake, but Kurt wouldn't dare. Not with his mother here. She walked closer and realized what Rachel was staring at. Only, it wasn't her desk.

It was her chair, and the dark brown stain marring the cushion.

34

Molly shivered, both from the chill in the air and from fear of what Dr. Brookston was going to tell her. She tried to lie still on the patient table as he completed his examination, but thoughts of Lori Beth Matthews, and what James had said about some people having considered it a blessing when Lori Beth's baby had died, brought a shudder.

She cradled her abdomen. *Please, God, please . . .*

don't take my baby. Over and over she begged Him. Surely He wouldn't demand the life of her child in payment of a debt that was hers alone to settle. She didn't think He would, but she'd been wrong before when trying to anticipate His thoughts and ways.

"Please lie as still as you can, Dr. Whitcomb. I know this is uncomfortable, but it won't take much longer."

Detecting concern in his voice, Molly complied as best she could. She closed her eyes, willing a nonexistent calm. What must Rachel think of her? Rachel had driven her to the clinic in the wagon, and—knowing she had no choice—Molly had told her about the baby, careful not to let Kurt overhear. Shock best described Rachel's initial reaction, then disappointment, which Molly expected, but then Rachel's nurturing temperament had kicked in.

"Did you hit your stomach when you fell, Dr. Whitcomb?"

Tears slid from the corners of Molly's eyes. "No, I landed on my side."

"When exactly did the pain start?"

"There wasn't any pain, really. My back was hurting a little. But that's common these days; I didn't think anything of it."

When he was done with his examination, Dr. Brookston covered her with a blanket and pulled a stool up beside her. "The bleeding has stopped completely, and the examination revealed nothing alarming or abnormal. I do need to ask you some questions, but I don't want you reading anything into them, all right?"

Molly nodded, feeling her chin tremble.

"Have you felt the baby move yet?"

Her heart sank. "No, should I have?"

With a reassuring smile, he touched her arm. "I told you, don't be alarmed. As far as I can tell, you're well into your fourth month of pregnancy. And it's customary for a mother to feel the baby move for the first time somewhere in her fourth or fifth month. Have you had any spotting before this incident?"

She shook her head, knowing exactly how far along she was—entering her fifth month—because she knew the exact day she'd conceived. But telling him that would only raise suspicion, and since his assessment was correct, she decided to keep that knowledge to herself.

"Spotting during pregnancy isn't uncommon, Dr. Whitcomb, and most women who do, end up carrying their children to full term and delivering healthy, well-developed babies. So don't start borrowing trouble and thinking this portends an unhappy outcome. Because it doesn't."

"So there's nothing wrong with my baby?"

"I see nothing abnormal about your pregnancy. I *do* have a sense, however, that you've been under great stress recently, and that, along with the tumble today, may have contributed to the bleeding. I'd like for you to stay here at the clinic tonight. You can have my bed in the back room and I'll stay out here, so I'll be close in case you need anything."

She nodded. "Thank you, Doctor."

"I see no reason why you can't continue to teach, as long as you're careful. I would like for you to begin sitting more often during the day, instead of standing for such long stretches. And I'd like to see you in my office once a week, at least for a while, just to check the baby's heartbeat." He smiled. "Make sure it stays good and strong."

A short while later, Dr. Brookston left to pick up supplies from the general store and Molly rested in bed in the back room, finding herself more tired than she'd thought. And far more conflicted than earlier.

If she did as she'd planned, and confessed to James and to the town council that she'd never been married, that would mean leaving Dr. Brookston's care. And who would oversee the remainder of her pregnancy and the birth of her child then? Especially if there were complications as there had been in Lori Beth's situation. And though she tried not to dwell on it, she couldn't forget the high fever she'd suffered and Dr. Brookston's carefully worded warning about some babies being born with "challenges."

She turned onto her side and smoothed a hand over her belly. How could she tell them now, and jeopardize her baby's health? Feeling traitorous inside, she knew her decision was already made. And that God knew it too.

A soft knock sounded on the clinic door in the next room, followed by the telling creak of rusty hinges. Dr. Brookston wouldn't knock, so she knew it wasn't him.

"Molly?"

James. Her stomach did a somersault. "I'm back here." She sat up in the bed, dreading having to see him again, yet dreading the thought of not. He rounded the corner. She saw the concern lining his expression, and a portion of her apprehension fell away.

He removed his hat and stopped just inside the doorway. "Rachel came and found me. Are you all right, Molly? Is your . . . baby all right?"

"Yes, Dr. Brookston said we're both fine." Seeing a hint of his smile helped hers along. "He asked me to stay here for the night, though, just to be sure, so I won't be able to attend the town council meeting. But I don't expect you to tell them," she said in a rush, feeling a twinge of betrayal knowing she was still hiding something from him. "I'll do that. I could write a letter, if you want, but I think telling them in person would be best—if it can wait a day or two."

"I agree. And it can wait, until you're up to it." He stared. "I'm just so thankful you're all right." He turned his hat in his hands, worrying the rim.

"I wish I could do Saturday night over again, Molly. I would change how I behaved when you told me."

"You were right to behave as you did. I never should have kept this from you, James." *And I wish I wasn't keeping something from you still.* "Please forgive me."

That smile she loved tipped up one side of his mouth. "I already have. And I realize now how hard this must have been for you, all this time."

She bowed her head, finding the compassion in his gaze uncomfortable to sustain.

"Are you hungry?" he asked, surprising her.

She smiled. "Actually, I am."

"I'll go get you something to eat and bring it back." He turned to leave.

"James?" She waited. "You're a very good friend," she said softly, regretting the tremor in her voice. "And"—*wherever these next weeks and months take us, before they take me home again and away from you*—"I'm so grateful God brought you into my life."

James closed the front door noiselessly behind him and headed for the darkened kitchen, tired from the long town council meeting and from getting raked over the coals by Davenport and his pocketful of men in the group. He sat down at the kitchen table and rested his head in his hands, almost too tired to eat.

"James, you're home. Finally." Rachel swept through the doorway, oil lamp in hand. "I've kept dinner for you."

He rubbed his face. "Thank you, Rachel."

She withdrew his plate from the oven and set it before him, then filled two glasses with tea. "How was she when you left?"

Following her train of thought, James took her hand and offered a quick prayer of thanks, then lifted his fork. "She's doing fine. She said you stopped by while I was gone to get her dinner."

She nodded. "She said Dr. Brookston told her everything seemed fine. That he didn't see anything alarming, which is good news."

"Very good news." James took a bite of mashed potatoes, followed by meat loaf. "He wants to see her every week, looks like, just to be sure she's okay."

Rachel said nothing for a moment, but he could feel her wheels turning.

"Have you told her yet, James?"

He kept eating.

"You should, you know," she said quietly.

He took a long swig of tea, knowing how she must feel when he gently pushed her to make things right with Daniel. "It's not that simple, Rachel."

"It also doesn't have to be that hard, James."

He ate his dinner, grateful for it but wishing he could eat it in peace.

"May I ask you another question?" she said after a minute.

He finished chewing. "If I say no, will it make any difference?"

She laughed. "No."

"Then why are you asking me?" He cut his eyes in her direction, still a mite frustrated, but knowing she meant well.

She laid a hand on his arm. "I know you, James. And I know how you think. You're thinking that it wouldn't be right for the sheriff of Timber Ridge to have feelings for a woman who has lied about something like this. I was just as surprised as you were when I learned about the baby today too, but—"

"She told me about the baby Saturday night, on the sleigh ride."

Rachel said nothing for a moment. "So that's what's been wrong these past few days. I thought it was something related to the sheriff's office."

"It's that too." He sighed, staring at his plate. "But mostly, it's her . . ."

"Did the town council meeting go well?"

He kept his smile to himself, knowing she wasn't done pressing him about Molly. She was just biding her time. "It's not a cougar that's been taking the cattle. It's rustlers, which I've suspected for a while now. They hit Paulsens' ranch last night. I informed Davenport and the men tonight at the meeting, and they're wanting to form a posse before we even have suspects."

Davenport had also made a point of making sure that everyone knew it was Kurt who put the snake in Molly's drawer. But James kept that to himself, not wanting to add to Rachel's load. He sighed. "Another worker got hurt out at the resort too. A man fell through some loose flooring and hurt his back." He leaned forward, rolling his shoulders, working to loosen the knots. "Tolliver's building the finest resort in Colorado, while the families who are doing the work, and bearing the risks, don't even have enough to eat."

"It's coming at you from all directions, isn't it?" Rachel whispered. "Do the men know about Molly yet?"

He shook his head. "She and I agreed it'd be best coming from her. I'll call a special meeting later this week, once she feels well enough. I didn't tell her this, but the chances of her keeping her job after Davenport learns she's with child are slim."

"I think Molly knows that." Rachel refilled his glass. "She didn't say anything outright, but I could tell she's worried about that happening."

"And there's nothing I can do to stop it. It's the council's decision."

"But you have influence with those men."

He laughed softly. "Less every day, it feels like."

"No matter what happens, James . . . don't you let her get back on that train." Tender determination filled her tone. "Do you realize how rare this is, what the two of you have? When I watch the two of you together, I see—" Her eyes glistened and her smile went all wobbly. "I see Thomas and me. And I've never seen you look at another woman the way you look at her."

He couldn't argue with anything she'd said. He'd never cared for a woman like he did Molly. And as highly as he esteemed truth and integrity, as much as he'd based his entire adult life on upholding and building on those principles, maybe what Daniel said was right. Maybe he *was* letting his dedication to the sheriff's office dictate his view of things more than he should.

Despite the years having passed, James knew his father's infidelities—especially with that one woman—had greatly influenced the man he'd become. And seeing his mother shoulder the burden of his father's choices was a lesson he'd carry inside him forever.

But he was not his father. And Molly was not *that woman.*

"Mama, why are you cryin' too?"

James turned to see Mitch standing in the doorway, his hair rumpled and crushed to one side.

Rachel wiped her face and gave her eldest a smile. "These are just woman tears, Mitch." She held out her arms. "They come every now and then, whether I want them to or not."

James watched her hug her son, knowing that

statement to be true. But he also knew Rachel to be one of the strongest people he'd ever known.

Mitch rubbed his eyes. "Kurt's cryin' still. He woke me up again."

Rachel patted the boy's shoulder. "I'll come see to him."

"Why don't you let me go?" James tucked his napkin by his plate. "I'd like to, if you don't mind."

Rachel hesitated, then nodded.

James made his way down the hall, thinking back to what Rachel had said to him that afternoon when she'd first told him about the incident at school. *"I know it was just a prank, James. But I told Kurt you'd be ashamed of what he'd done. So please support me in this."* James pushed the bedroom door open, recalling how hard Kurt had been crying at the time. And it struck him again how much his and Kurt's relationship mirrored what he'd had with his grandfather.

He recalled the numerous times his father had meted out discipline. But it was four words from his grandfather's lips that had influenced his behavior more than anything. *I'm disappointed in you.* Those words had wounded him far deeper than any trip to the woodshed.

He knelt by Kurt's bed, feeling the weight of that responsibility, the wooden planks cold and hard against his knees. "Hey, buddy," he whispered. "You still awake?"

Sniffles and trembling covers gave him his answer, and told him more than words could have.

He gave Kurt's shoulder a gentle squeeze. "What you did today was wrong, but you already know that. What you also need to know, Kurt, is that no matter what you did, I still love you." His throat tightened, recalling the scent of sweet cherry tobacco on his grandfather's breath. "And that love's never going away. Nothing you can do will ever change it."

The boy sat up and grabbed him around the neck. "I'm sorry, Uncle James. Don't be disappointed in me no more."

James held him close, and heard a creak behind him. He turned to see Rachel and Mitch standing in the doorway.

He stayed with Kurt until the boy fell asleep; then he rose, knees stiff, and went to his bedroom. He lit the lamp and sank down on the edge of his bed, pulling the tattered envelope from his vest pocket. He slid the single sheet of paper from within, already knowing each word but liking the fancy way Molly made her letters.

Dear James,

Thank you for seeing me home last night. You've made me feel so welcome since I came to Timber Ridge, and I appreciate the support and encouragement you've given me. I count your friendship among the biggest blessings in my life and look forward to working with you in the future.

Yours most amiably,
Molly Whitcomb
P.S. Whenever I see a sugar stick, I think of you.

Yours most amiably. He ran a finger over that phrase, recalling the kiss they'd shared. There'd been nothing *amiable* about that. She'd seemed a touch hesitant at first, which he'd understood, with her having been married. Kissing someone other than her husband had to feel awkward, but she'd warmed up to the notion right quick. He smiled, remembering how she'd leaned into him, her arms coming around his neck.

His gaze fell to the postscript. That's where the *dichotomy* had come in for him. Her note had such formality to it, such reserve and properness. All except that mention of the sugar sticks, and that's what had given him hope.

After disrobing, he snuffed out the lamp and fell into bed, welcoming the cool of the sheets. He tugged the blanket up waist-high, his mind rabbit-trailing in a hundred different directions. But no matter how many paths his thoughts took, they kept returning to one central point. He had no doubt Molly was sorry for having deceived everyone, and that she regretted what she'd done, which made the question in his mind all the more frustrating and perplexing.

If he was convinced of her sincerity—and he was—then why did he still get the feeling something wasn't quite right?

A possibility gradually surfaced that made more sense than he cared to admit—perhaps his own history and the burden of carrying around, for so long, the silent stigma of his illegitimate birth drove him to question his feelings for her. And maybe that same history, somewhere way down deep, in places he didn't go very often, still drove him to question himself.

35

Y ou have placed the town council in a most difficult and *embarrassing* position, Dr. Whitcomb."

Molly stood by her chair at the table, head bowed, her face burning. Davenport's patronizing tone deepened her shame, as did the solemn stares of all the men around the table. All the men but James.

Across the table from her, James shifted in his chair, looking as if it were all he could do to stay silent. She'd made him promise not to intervene— no matter what was said, no matter the council's decision—and she threw a brief but pleading look in his direction as a reminder of that vow.

She'd contacted Mayor Davenport herself about scheduling a special Saturday session, not wanting to further compromise James's reputation by using him as a go-between. For the past hour, she'd waited in the hallway outside the room while these men deliberated her fate, and from the stoniness in James's gaze, she gathered the outcome was not good.

She forced her head up. "I fully realize that, Mayor Davenport. And, please, to all of you, I want you to know how very much I regret my actions."

The mayor leaned forward, hands clasped and expression stern. "You've heard the phrase 'Actions speak louder than words,' Dr. Whitcomb. I believe that's written on a plaque in your classroom. Is it not?"

"Yes, Mayor, it is. And my desire is that my actions always be consistent with my words. But . . ." A bitter taste tinged her mouth. "I'm afraid they're not."

Davenport's glare darkened. "Which leads me to wonder, ma'am—as it does others around this table—how we can believe anything you tell us in the future?"

Molly flinched at his well-aimed accusation. Sensing her sealed fate, she shivered where she stood. More snow had fallen during the week and bitter cold hung over the valley. She'd learned from James that another seven head of cattle had been taken from ranches. The pressure for him to find those responsible had escalated. She could see the tension in his expression even now and had felt it in his reticence with her that week.

"Dr. Whitcomb, the council has reached our decision." Mayor Davenport's tone held mildly reined enthusiasm. "Due to your deliberate deceitfulness to this board, and to the parents and students of Timber Ridge, and due in part to your choice of *questionable pursuits* outside the classroom, we are mandating your immediate dismissal."

Hearing the words stated so boldly caused her to shudder, yet something he'd said didn't make any sense. "Questionable pursuits?" she asked softly.

"Yes, Dr. Whitcomb. We've learned of the 'tutoring' you've been undertaking with certain children in this town who are not numbered among those whom we hired you to teach. But surely you were aware of what our opinion would be on that matter."

Wondering how they'd found out, she wished she could deny it, but she couldn't. She'd known Davenport and others wouldn't approve of her decision to teach Angelo or to share books with Elijah, but she'd done it anyway. And be it right or wrong in their eyes, she would do it again if given the chance, which only further sealed the inevitability of her fate in Timber Ridge.

Davenport fingered his large wooden gavel.

"You have two days to vacate the premises of the teacher's cabin and to remove all personal effects from the schoolhouse. Furthermore, it is our recommendation that you consider—"

A door opened behind her, and Molly turned to see a gentleman poke his head inside. He handed an envelope to Hank Bolden, who read the front and quickly passed it across the table. "It's a telegram. For you, Mayor."

Mayor Davenport ripped it open, obviously bothered at the interruption.

Molly's mind raced. Two days to vacate the cabin. Where would she live? And she had a sneaking suspicion Davenport had been about to recommend that she leave Timber Ridge, but how could she? When she still needed Dr. Brookston to care for her baby.

Davenport's frustrated sigh drew her back. He glared at her across the table, his complexion reddening by the second. "Dr. Whitcomb, your reckless behavior has yet again placed this council—and the entire town—in a most regrettable and compromising situation."

From the corner of her eye, Molly saw James lean forward in his chair.

Davenport glanced at the telegram clenched in his grip. "It would seem that a team of educators has taken great interest in the reports you've submitted on the school's recent progress."

Molly knew her surprise showed. She hadn't

heard anything about her reports being shared outside of the town council, much less with a team of educators. "But I don't understand. . . . How did they get my—"

"That is a moot point at this juncture, Dr. Whitcomb!" Davenport pounded the table with his fist. "The fact is, they have scheduled a trip to Timber Ridge and are coming to look at our school! And when they arrive, they're going to discover that there's not only no one to demonstrate this new teaching method of yours, but now there's no teacher!" His features twisted in anger. "Your selfish lack of concern for this town and its advancement, not to mention your lack of integrity in the application process for this job has caused—"

"Mayor Davenport!"

Molly startled at the uncommon harshness in Ben Mullins's voice.

Ben wore a look of surprise, as though he too was caught off guard by his own outburst. He cleared his throat, his quiet manner returning. "I believe, sir, that you've made it clear to Dr. Whitcomb, and to all of us around this table, how difficult a situation this is. Seems to me that instead of focusing on how we got here, we'd do better to focus on how to move ahead in a way that's best for everyone involved—including the children of Timber Ridge, who should be our utmost concern."

Gentle reprimand framed Ben's soft voice, and Molly thought again of his and Lyda's children, and wondered what had happened to them. She waited for someone to say something, feeling as though her fate were tied to the tail end of a kite.

As soon as the thought came, she took it back. She knew who held her fate. She had purposefully entrusted it to Him. And did so again in that moment.

Davenport held up the telegram. He took a deep breath and exhaled slowly. "The committee members arrive a week from Monday and are expressing an interest in learning more about these new teaching methods of yours and about the students' improved marks. They want to observe your classroom and interview you personally!" He tugged on his starched white collar, as though something were lodged in his throat. "If they like what they find, there's every chance they'll use our school as a pattern for others in this state."

The look in his eyes was as close to loathing as Molly could remember seeing.

She struggled to maintain her composure. It had galled him to tell her that, but she felt not a single ounce of pride or gloating. On the contrary—she would have thanked him, if she could have spoken, but she couldn't with the glut of emotion rising inside. Though he'd obviously shared her report with the intent of furthering the town's standing, and therefore his own, God had used Davenport's efforts to answer a prayer she'd had for as long as she could remember.

She wanted to make a difference in this life.

And she'd wanted to do that by teaching, in some way, somewhere. She'd imagined it in the halls of prestigious Franklin College, but no, God had answered her prayer in a tiny, dot-of-a-town-on-a-map in the hidden heart of the Rocky Mountains. And this after all she'd done wrong. Regardless of how Davenport had treated her, she wanted to do anything to help James save face, knowing that the mayor would lay the blame for any and all of her failure at James's feet.

She swallowed, hoping her voice would hold. "If it benefits Timber Ridge, Mayor Davenport, and if you and the rest of the town council deem it appropriate, I would be honored to continue teaching until after the committee from Denver has completed its visits or . . . until my baby is born."

After which time she would return home to Georgia to rebuild her life—this time without pretense, without deceit. But also without half her heart.

The next morning, Molly purposely left her cabin later than normal in order to arrive at church right when the service began, perhaps even a few minutes after. She'd debated whether to go at all, knowing how quickly news spread in Timber

Ridge, and feeling relatively certain that the men on the town council wouldn't keep her news to themselves.

But if she chose to stay home today, she would simply have to face people tomorrow. There was no hiding.

When she rounded the corner and the church building came into view, she spotted a line of people filing slowly up the stairs. And drawing closer, she realized why. A circuit preacher stood in the entryway greeting members of the congregation as they walked inside.

This particular preacher—a Pastor Carlson, if she remembered correctly—had been there several times before, and it lifted her spirits to see him again. She remembered him not only because of his manner of delivering sermons—as if he were having a conversation with you in your front parlor—but also because of his resemblance to the late President Lincoln.

She joined the line behind the Taylor family, wishing now that she'd walked more slowly. Mrs. Taylor glanced back in her direction and Molly smiled.

"Good morning, Mrs. Taylor. How are you today? Rebecca." She nodded to her student, including her in the greeting.

Rebecca smiled her usual shy smile, but Linda Taylor's response was delayed, as though the woman was deciding how to react.

"Morning, Mrs. Whitcomb," she finally managed, then did an immediate about-face.

What little doubt Molly had disappeared. People knew.

A thought occurred that probably should have before—she hoped none of the parents would withdraw their children from her class because of her confession. She told herself the chances of that happening were slim, that she was overreacting, and hoped she was right.

When it came time to greet the preacher, Molly worked to find a smile. "Good morning, Pastor."

"Good morning, Dr. Whitcomb."

She raised a brow, surprised he remembered her name.

He grinned. "My wife, Hannah, and I"—he motioned to a woman standing a few steps ahead, speaking with a group of ladies—"we stay with Ben and Lyda Mullins when we're in town. They've told us all about you, and the good you've done here in Timber Ridge."

"Mr. and Mrs. Mullins are very kind, but I'm sure they've exaggerated."

"I don't think so. Ben told me last night that a group is traveling all the way from Denver just to observe what you've done. I wish our daughter could meet you. Lilly fills in, on occasion, for the teacher in Willow Springs, where we live. But she has such hopes of having her own school one day."

It pleased Molly to know Ben would share that

news with the pastor and his wife. But had he also shared that she wouldn't be teaching for much longer, and why? Knowing she needed to move on in line, she didn't want to leave the pastor with the wrong impression. "I'm not sure if the Mullinses informed you, Pastor Carlson, but the position of teacher here will be opening soon. I'm stepping down," she said quietly, and watched shades of understanding move across his face, answering her earlier question as to whether the Mullinses had told him or not. "So perhaps your daughter should consider making an inquiry about this school."

He nodded. "Thank you, Dr. Whitcomb. But I think we'd be hard-pressed to get Lilly to leave Willow Springs. You see . . ." He leaned closer. "There's a young man named Peter who's fairly well wrapped up her heart." The knowing look in his eyes said that was an understatement, while it also hinted at his pleasure in the arrangement.

After greeting the pastor's wife, Molly spotted LuEllen Spivey and Mrs. Foster standing off to one side, speaking in hushed tones, staring in her direction. Molly quickly looked away before the daggers LuEllen Spivey was sending her way could sink any deeper.

She chose to sit in the back, on the opposite side from James, Rachel, and the boys, and didn't steal but half a dozen glimpses in James's direction during the service, selfishly appreciating the opportunity to watch him from the side. Ruggedly handsome, he looked as if he'd been born in the wilds of these mountains rather than on a plantation in Franklin, Tennessee.

The *amen* was scarcely uttered on the closing prayer before she skirted down a side aisle and out the double doors, not looking back. She didn't want James to feel forced to speak to her, and she wanted to spare others—and herself—the discomfort of overlong stares, stiff smiles, and cool responses, despite knowing she deserved them.

She spent the afternoon and evening reviewing her lessons for that week and preparing for the committee scheduled to arrive from Denver the following week.

Monday morning came and every student returned, to her relief. Some of the children looked at her a little differently, but Molly tried her best to act as if nothing had changed. Kurt Boyd was quieter than he'd ever been, but unfortunately, that didn't translate to his customary good marks, despite the extra encouragement she gave him.

Midweek brought more snow, and after leaving Dr. Brookston's office on Friday afternoon having received a good report, she decided to treat herself to dinner at Miss Clara's Cafe. The cafe had moved inside for the winter, and the building was only a fourth the size of Miss Clara's outdoor setting. But as the woman had told her, "My business slacks off something fierce come winter, so it's just as well."

Molly passed the sheriff's office, wishing she felt at liberty to ask James to join her, but that was out of the question. And the windows were dark anyway. She'd seen him twice that week and they'd spoken. Somewhat. Things were more than civil, but there was a distance between them that hadn't been there before. The determined set of his jaw and the invisible weight on his shoulders revealed the burdens he was carrying, and she regretted having contributed to them.

It would be better for him—for them both—once she'd left Timber Ridge. But if she missed him this much now, living in the same town and seeing him on occasion, how much more would she miss him when he was out of her life for good?

Somehow she knew that "out of sight, out of mind" wouldn't hold true in this instance.

She stayed to the road instead of chancing the icy boardwalk, appreciating the warmth of her snow boots. The snow had ceased falling, but an obstinate wind worked its chill inside her coat. Before she even opened the door to the cafe, she caught the mouth-watering aroma of fried chicken and buttermilk biscuits. She hurried inside, shutting the wind and chill outside behind her.

The cafe was busier than she'd anticipated, and the hum of conversation dropped a level as she stood by the door, lightly stamping the snow from her boots. Though she knew nearly everyone in the room either by face or by name, she felt as conspicuous as she had the first evening she'd eaten at Miss Clara's earlier that summer.

Except this time she had good reason.

"Good evening, Mrs. Whitcomb!" Miss Clara waved to her from back by the kitchen. "Wonderful to see you bravin' the Colorado cold, just like a true pioneer! Come on in and grab a seat somewhere. I'll bring you a plate."

Molly pasted on a smile, finding others doing much the same when they looked her way.

She glanced around the room and saw two open seats. One was at a table occupied by two gentlemen on the town council who agreed with everything Mayor Davenport did or said. The other was in the far corner, right by the kitchen door, where Lori Beth Matthews sat alone, her attention fixed on her plate. Yet somehow Molly knew Lori Beth was aware of her presence.

Just as Molly knew that everyone in that restaurant was waiting to see where she would sit. Or if under the weight of their stares, and her only two choices, she would decide to leave.

With the same certainty that told her she would teach Angelo English all over again if given the opportunity, and that she would share her books with Elijah, Molly knew that sitting with Lori Beth Matthews somehow played into the reason she was standing there right then.

She made her way through the maze of tables, feeling the stares as conversation dropped another notch. She wished her decision were more altruistic. But in reality, she had little left to lose.

"Good evening, Miss Matthews. Is this seat taken?"

When Lori Beth looked up, the emotion in her eyes betrayed her foreknowledge. "No, Dr. Whitcomb . . . it's not," she whispered.

Molly's back was to the rest of the patrons, but she sensed their close attention. She and Lori Beth ate dinner together enjoying pleasant, "safe" conversation, aware of eavesdropping ears. The more she and Lori Beth chatted, the more Molly grew to like her. Lori Beth was real. She knew who she was, and who she wasn't—something Molly was only now beginning to grasp about herself.

When they finished dinner, they left the restaurant together and headed in the direction of Molly's cabin, the frozen snow on the street crunching beneath their boots.

"May I ask you a question, Molly?" Lori Beth's voice held a candor it hadn't before.

Molly looked over at her. "Of course."

"Would you have treated me any differently the first time we'd met, then again when you saw me with Charlie, if you'd known who I was and what I'd done?"

Ashamed, Molly thought back to the night of the town celebration and to that awkward moment of silence at the table when Lori Beth had stared from James, back to her, seeming to have known they'd been speaking about her. "It shames me to say it," Molly whispered, not allowing herself to look away. "But, yes, I probably would have."

A faint smile touched Lori Beth's mouth. "Thank you . . . for being honest."

For being honest . . . Molly shook her head, laughing softly. "You wouldn't say that if you'd heard the latest news in town this week."

"That you're with child?" Lori Beth's brow arched. "Charlie told me. He heard from someone at the livery." She glanced down, her smile inching wider. "How far along are you?"

"I'm in my fifth month, and I just received a good report from Dr. Brookston this afternoon. He thinks everything should go well for the—"

Wistfulness moved into Lori Beth's expression, and Molly wished she could take back what she'd just said. She paused in the street. "I'm so sorry, Lori Beth, I shouldn't have—"

Lori Beth shook her head. "No, please. There's no reason to apologize. I'm happy things are going well for you."

Molly winced inwardly, the sincerity in Lori Beth's voice deepening her regret. "I'm so sorry about what happened to your baby, Lori Beth. I've thought of you often since finding out, yet didn't feel at liberty to say anything."

"That's all right. And thank you," Lori Beth whispered, motioning for them to continue walking.

"May I ask *you* a question now?"

Lori Beth smiled. "It only seems fair."

Molly could think of many things to ask, but only one question held significance for her at the moment. "Why, after all that happened to you, did you choose to stay in Timber Ridge?"

Lori Beth gave a soft sigh. "That's a question that took me a long time to answer." A moment passed in silence. "I know this is going to sound strange, but . . . it's because of my son." Her voice was feather soft. "I can't bear to think of leaving him here. It would be like abandoning him. And I . . . I can't bring myself to do that. . . . Not when I know so well how it feels."

Tears filled Lori Beth's eyes, and Molly felt her own eyes burning. A familiar fear crept in as she imagined a too-small box being lowered into the earth. Not knowing what to say, Molly did something that didn't come naturally for her but that felt right for the moment. She looped her arm through Lori Beth's, much as Belle Birch had done with Miss Clara that time, and Lori Beth smiled.

As they passed the general store, Molly glimpsed Ben and Lyda Mullins inside. The couple had treated her kindly when she'd stopped in to thank Ben for taking up for her during the town council meeting. They'd been quieter than usual, as was expected, but kind.

"What will you do, Molly . . ." Lori Beth asked after a moment, "after your baby is born?"

Molly started to shrug off the question and give an evasive answer, but then stopped herself. She was sick to death of pretense. Of lying. If there was one woman she could be honest with about what she'd done, it was Lori Beth Matthews. "I'll be leaving Timber Ridge, Lori Beth. I can't stay here because—" She exhaled, feeling a tiny sliver of relief. "Because . . . I'm not as strong as you are," she whispered, watching. Waiting.

Lori Beth's attention never wavered. She showed not a trace of surprise.

"You know," Molly whispered.

Lori Beth shook her head. "I only suspected . . . at the town celebration, after Sheriff McPherson told you about me." She smiled briefly, with a look that said she knew she'd been the topic of conversation. "But afterward, you kept looking at *him.* Not me. And it seemed you weren't so shocked to find out about me that night, as you were to find out about how James McPherson felt about someone like me."

Remembering his reaction, tears rose to Molly's eyes. She nodded.

Lori Beth grasped her hands. "Pain has a way of cutting through to what lies beneath. It lets you see into people in a way you couldn't before, I guess. But don't worry, I haven't said anything to anyone, Molly. And I won't. Your secret is safe with me, I promise."

Molly didn't doubt Lori Beth's promise for one

minute. But as she continued home by herself, she wondered if what Lori Beth had said about pain was right. And if it was, what had James endured in his life that gave him such insight into people?

36

Monday morning came, and she was prepared. Mayor Davenport arrived at nine o'clock with the group from Denver. Four of them. All men. And all stern looking.

She greeted them at the back of the room, then introduced them to the students. "These four gentlemen will be with us through Wednesday afternoon. They're here to observe how we learn, and they might even ask you some questions. All you need to do is answer their questions and then do exactly what you've been doing before they arrived—which is your very best." She smiled, and held Kurt Boyd's gaze a few seconds longer than that of the other children, praying he didn't have any snakes or mice in his pockets. Or worse.

Over the course of the next three days, the guests first observed from the back, then closer to the groups of children, then spoke with the students one on one. By Wednesday afternoon, they were evaluating the children's skill levels and making lengthy notations. Molly wasn't sure if she heard her future in the scribbling of their quills, or the death knell of her teaching career.

But whichever it turned out to be, she trusted that God had brought her this far and that He surely wouldn't leave her now.

On Friday afternoon when the last students left bundled against the cold and wind, she set the room aright so that it would be ready on Monday morning. She still hadn't heard from the town council as to whether or not she would be teaching the following week. But she assumed they would let her know when she was through. Until that time, or until her baby was born, she would show up each morning prepared.

She slipped her coat on and buttoned the buttons over her expanding middle. No movement from the baby yet, but she was definitely growing— according to Dr. Brookston's scales yesterday—so that had to be a good thing. And Dr. Brookston had assured her there was no cause to worry. So she determined not to, again.

Dark gray clouds hung close over the mountain peaks, and a smell similar to that of rain but with a sharper edge to it scented the afternoon air. More snow was coming. If not tonight, then by tomorrow morning for sure. She'd "gotten good at readin' the signs," as Charlie had told her the other day. And a trip into town would be easier this afternoon than tomorrow, so she bent into the wind and set out.

Typical of an afternoon before a storm, patrons crowded Hank Bolden's place, and business at the general store was bustling. Ignoring Hank Bolden's glare, Molly was thankful when he didn't slam her bread and sweet rolls unwrapped on the counter the way he had Lori Beth's. The possibility of that day loomed in her future, but she planned on leaving Timber Ridge before it came to pass.

At the Mullinses' store, she gathered what she needed and deposited the items on the counter, hoping Charlie Daggett was around to deliver them for her, as usual. Preferably this afternoon, before the storm hit.

Ben Mullins tallied her order, the satisfied look on his face becoming more so by the minute. He slid the bill toward her on the counter.

Her reticule open, Molly read the receipt and looked up. "But I don't understand. Why did you—"

"The other day, after you'd been in, Lyda told me where you asked for the food to be delivered, Dr. Whitcomb. It wasn't any of my business, ma'am, so I'd never asked you what you were doing with it all." He looked down at the counter. "But this is a good thing you're undertaking, and I'd like to help, if you don't mind, by discounting the price."

Molly's admiration for this quiet, somewhat timid, giant of a man grew tenfold. "I'd be honored to have your help, Mr. Mullins. As will Angelo Giordano's family, and the others. But, please, I'd like to spend the amount I'd budgeted. Let's just add more food to the pile." She had a second thought. "Or perhaps some blankets, if you have them."

He laughed. "We'll add both. I've got some miner's blankets in the back. They're none too soft, but they're warm and they keep away the moisture." He leaned close. "For what it's worth, ma'am . . . Being on the town council, I know your salary, and I don't think we're paying you enough as it is. Which makes this all the more kindhearted of you."

"Not at all, Mr. Mullins. I've been very blessed by my time here in Timber Ridge, and I appreciate the opportunity to give a portion of that back."

A shadow crept over his face. "You make it sound like your time here might be drawing to a close."

Wishing she hadn't spoken so freely, she also knew it was true. People had to be wondering if she would leave. "None of us knows what the future holds, do we, Mr. Mullins?"

He held her gaze, his features more reflective now than amused. "No, ma'am, we don't. So we best make the most of every day we're given. I'll see that Charlie gets this delivered to Little Italy this afternoon."

Thanking him, Molly turned.

"One more thing, Dr. Whitcomb." Ben gestured for her to wait and returned a minute later with an envelope in his hand. "For you," he said, his tone more businesslike than usual.

Molly eyed the envelope with her name penned neatly on the front, then fingered the bulge at the bottom. She looked at Ben, but he merely shrugged as if he knew nothing. But his expression hinted at just the opposite.

She moved off to the side, slid open the edge of the envelope, and pulled out a single sheet of stationery. Seeing the sender's name, her stomach did funny little somersaults.

Dear Molly,

We haven't seen each other much in recent days, but you've never been far from my thoughts. If you're still open to receiving my company, I'd like to come to your cabin on Saturday evening and fix us dinner. I don't want you to do a thing. I hope you'll be there.

With affection most friendly,
James
P.S. Here's a little something until then.

Molly peeked inside the envelope, and giggled. And smiled as she walked from the store, sucking on a sugar stick.

"Good day, Mrs. *Doctor* Molly Whitcomb!"

Without looking behind her on the boardwalk, she knew who it was. She slipped the candy from her mouth as she turned. "Good day, Mr. Tolliver." She hadn't seen him in a while, nor had she heard from him, which suited her fine. She'd been curious to see his resort, but since Angelo had told her he wasn't working there anymore, that desire had slipped in importance.

Tolliver's telling glance at her midsection said he'd heard *her* latest news. An almost comical grin edged up the corners of his mouth. "I hear you're in rather . . . full health these days, madam."

She gave him a sideways look. "I'm feeling quite well. Thank you for your genuine feeling of concern."

"Oh, my feelings are genuine." He quirked a brow. "They simply lean more toward surprise in this instance. You have considerably more mystery to you than I first judged, which I find to be a most compelling character trait."

That observation sat ill within her. "I'll choose *not* to take that as a compliment."

He frowned. "Well, that's indeed a pity. Because it was meant as one, I assure you." A sardonic grin lit his face.

Eager to be rid of his company, Molly thought of a way to hurry that along. Perhaps it would even put this man in his place. "I hope you're still on schedule to make your grand opening in January, Mr. Tolliver. I know how hard you've worked and how eager you are to show off your resort."

All mirth fled his expression, as expected. "With the recent snows, that's not looking favorable . . . as you're no doubt aware, Dr. Whitcomb."

Already having heard as much, Molly mimicked

his frown from before. "Well, that's indeed a pity, Mr. Tolliver." With a smile, she turned and continued down the boardwalk, sugar stick in her mouth.

James slammed the cell door and locked it, ignoring the string of expletive-loaded threats the two miners inside hurled at him. One of the men grabbed at him through the bars, and James caught his forearm and wrenched it back. "Try that again and I'll break it next time."

The miner glared but held his tongue.

James walked back into the office, dabbing at the corner of his mouth and still tasting blood. The miner who'd just tried getting at him again had put up a good fight. The fellow was younger and outweighed him and had gotten in a solid blow to his mouth before James had subdued him. The guy was accustomed to fighting; that was clear. It had been quite a while since James had been in a scuffle like that. It reminded him of days long gone, when he was faster—and younger.

Deputy Willis slumped on a bench, his head down.

James eased himself into his desk chair, his shoulder sore, but not as sore as it would be tomorrow. "You okay, Willis?"

The deputy didn't look up. "They said they'd come in peaceable."

"They lied." James sighed. "Folks have a tendency to do that when they're in a tight spot."

Slowly Willis raised his head, and James saw the shiner already forming around his right eye.

"Oh . . ." James tried not to smile—too much. "Why don't you go on home and let Mary see to that? Stanton's taking the night shift. I won't be here much longer."

Willis stood, looking steady enough on his feet but lacking his normal swagger. "The mayor will be happy, at least."

James pulled a kerchief from his pocket and held it to his mouth. Stubborn cut wouldn't stop bleeding. Davenport wanted the rustlers caught, and they'd caught them. Two of them, at least. "He'll be happy for a while, Willis. A short while. Then something else will come up, and your tail—and mine—will be on the line again. That's all part of it. When things are going well in a town, when things are quiet, the sheriff's office is doing a fine job. But when things go bad, whether we could have prevented what happened or not, the sheriff's office gets blamed. Better get used to it."

"So tell me again, Sheriff . . . Why is it you do this job?"

James rolled his neck from side to side. "Because I care about the people of this town, and about right winning over wrong. I do it because I think I can make a difference for the better. Same as you can. And same as you will, if you're elected sheriff next spring."

Willis stared at him, then gave a gentle shake of his head. "I'm not sure I want it."

"Some days . . ." James smiled. "I'm not sure I do either. Now go on and see to your wife. How much longer does she have?"

Willis got that look he always did when talking about his soon-to-be-born son or daughter. "About a month, give or take, the doc says."

"Well, you tell Mary for me that Rachel said she can hardly wait to hold and love on that baby."

Willis briefly closed his eyes. "Her and me both, Sheriff. Her and me both."

A while later, relieved by Deputy Stanton, James saddled Winsome and made a scheduled stop by the store to pick up items he'd ordered. Ben had them at the ready, along with an encouraging grin that James all but ignored. Mullins hadn't said a thing when he'd left his note for Molly a couple of days ago. But he didn't have to.

Ben could be merciless in his kidding when he wanted to be. And he didn't even have to say anything half the time. He managed it with just a look, which James enjoyed but didn't let on that he did. It was all part of the back and forth between them.

He rode on to Molly's, hoping she'd be there.

If she wasn't, and he returned home early, Rachel might not let him in the house. When he'd told his sister he might not be back until later, then shared the reason, she'd beamed. He'd missed being with Molly, more than he probably should have, given

499

the circumstances. But the extra time he'd spent with Kurt in recent days seemed to be helping—at least Rachel thought it was. He loved that little guy, ornery as he could be at times.

And he had some good news to give Molly from the town council too. At least he hoped she'd see it as good news. He did, when compared to what Davenport had wanted to do. The only thing keeping Davenport from dismissing her immediately was the benefit he hoped to receive from the attention of educators in Denver.

The scantly warm sun flirted with the western peaks, and a fresh fall of snow blanketed the mountains, turning the world to white. For as long as he lived, he didn't think he'd ever get enough of this country. It was inside him now, and he doubted he'd ever leave. November was still a good week and a half away, but winter had made its arrival, bold and unyielding, which boded for hard months ahead.

He had taken a supply of firewood and food staples out to Little Italy earlier in the week. When loading it up, nearly a wagonful, it had seemed like a lot. But when divided among the number of families, it had seemed far too little an offering. He thought about the story he'd read to Kurt and Mitch last night from the Bible, the one about the boy with the scant loaves and fishes and how— with that littlest portion—God had fed thousands. He prayed God would somehow see fit to multiply his efforts and would provide the families what they needed. Before it was too late.

Nearing Molly's, he passed the school building and glimpsed a shadow in the window. He slowed Winsome's pace, wondering if the fading light was playing tricks on his eyes. But no—there it was again. He glanced at the cabin across the field to find a curl of smoke rising from the chimney. Molly was home. So . . . who was inside the school?

The door to the schoolhouse opened and a person walked out, followed by two others. Boys. James nudged Winsome in that direction, just wanting to make sure everything was all right.

When he got closer and saw who it was, his gut told him the boys weren't up to any mischief. But seeing them together concerned him, with knowing how the town council had reprimanded Molly for teaching Angelo, and with being able to guess Hank Bolden's reaction should he see his son, Billy, befriending these two particular boys. Not to mention what Billy's uncle, the illustrious mayor, would say.

Billy Bolden was the first to look up. "Sheriff!"

The other two boys turned.

"Evening, boys. How are you?"

"Fine, Sheriff," they said in unison, Angelo's greeting bearing a thick accent.

James saw them each carrying a book, so guessed what they'd been up to. "Dr. Whitcomb hasn't run out of books for you to read yet, has she?"

Elijah laughed, his smile bright. "No, sir, but she will soon. Mrs. Ranslett's already written her father in Washington about sendin' us more."

James rested his arms on his saddle horn. "That's a fine thing for her to do. And my guess from her father's past response is that he'll be sending boxes of them before the year's out."

The boys smiled at each other.

Elijah nudged Billy in the side. "Maybe Mrs. Ranslett's father will send more of those women books. Billy read that one and liked it."

"Women books?" Angelo's brief question made James smile.

Billy shoved Elijah back, grinning. "You read that one too! You said you even got choked up."

"Did not!" Elijah said, but the way he ducked his head said otherwise.

James laughed along with them, remembering what it was like to be a boy, and telling himself again that he needed to read that "women book," especially it being a favorite of Molly's.

Angelo stepped forward. "Thank you, Sheriff McPherson"—he spoke slowly but clearly—"for what you bring my family . . . this week."

"You're welcome, Angelo. It was my pleasure." James reined Winsome toward Molly's cabin. "You boys be careful, and stay out of trouble." He said it with a grin, while part of him was very serious. Not that they would seek trouble. His fear was that trouble might seek them.

He guided Winsome up the path and smiled when he saw the curtain push back from the window and Molly's head appear. Frost covered the glass pane, so he couldn't see her expression. But that she'd been watching for him was a good sign.

He dismounted and tethered Winsome on the side of the cabin where the horse would be sheltered from the wind. Then he shouldered the saddlebags full of ingredients. That Molly had lied to him still stung, but after taking inventory of his own life in recent days, he'd noticed a fair number of discrepancies. He was far from perfect, and to continue down the path his feelings for her were leading him and *not* tell her about his past would be false.

A Southern woman like Molly, of fine breeding from an honorable heritage, with an honorable family name, deserved to know the truth. Even if it might change her view of him, which made the mere thought of the beef stew he planned to make sit ill.

But tonight was a time for mending. A time to put things back in place for them both. His feelings for her hadn't changed. If anything, they'd deepened in past weeks. He didn't know where her feelings were for him now, but he hoped to know more, after tonight.

He climbed the porch stairs, unable to imagine Molly Whitcomb not being in his life. And when she opened the door, one thing became clear. As long as he had breath in his body and she had that spark in her eyes when she saw him, no way was he letting her get back on that train.

37

James pointed to her empty bowl. "You're sure you liked it?"

Molly smiled, hearing a rare touch of uncertainty in his voice. "Liked it? I had two bowlfuls, James. And I would've eaten a third, but I wanted to maintain *some* semblance of decorum."

He sighed, sitting across from her at her tiny kitchen table. "That won't ever be a problem for you, Molly."

She sipped her tea, grateful things were more comfortable between them again. Conversation came with little prompting, similar to the ease they'd shared before she had confessed to being with child, though the topics hadn't strayed into anything overtly personal just yet.

She'd looked forward to this time with him since receiving his note yesterday, but wasn't about to fool herself into believing that this dinner was about anything other than mending a friendship. A cherished and treasured friendship, but that was all it would be. James McPherson would never allow his heart to lead him in a direction where his honor and integrity could not follow, which made her unacceptable for him. And, unfortunately, made him more attractive to her.

"That looks like it would hurt." She indicated the cut on his lip.

He shrugged, his gaze thoughtful. "It doesn't . . . much."

He'd told her about what had happened with the miners that afternoon, and it brought closer to home what he must face day to day as the sheriff of Timber Ridge. Rachel had said she sometimes worried about him, and no wonder. Molly was grateful he hadn't been hurt any worse, and that the rustlers had been caught. Now the incidents should stop, which would lessen the pressure he was under.

She summoned her most formal tone. "I'll make some coffee and we can retire to the parlor." Smiling, she gestured to the sofa three feet away and started to stand.

"Not just yet." He gestured for her to wait. "First, I've got something to tell you. And I think it's good news, everything considered."

"From the town council?" she asked quietly.

He nodded. "Davenport received a telegram this morning, from the men who came to observe your classroom. They were very impressed, Molly. Both with you and your students. They'd like to send another group to observe your work. This time, a group of teachers."

She wasn't sure which pleased her more. The news, or the tender pride in his voice.

"Along with that, the town council is asking you to continue teaching until the Christmas program you've got planned. Then they'll close the school until they can find another teacher, which hopefully, for the children's sake, won't be long. Though you're leaving awfully big shoes to fill, Dr. Whitcomb."

Molly smiled, appreciating him while contemplating the news. She sorted through the weeks ahead, thinking about the progression of her pregnancy along with all she wanted to accomplish before her final day of teaching. The Christmas program was mid-December. Her baby wasn't due until the first of February, so she would have to find some other place to live during the interim. That was doable. Under the circumstances, she considered the council's decision most generous. "I'm grateful to you, James, for all you've done to work this out for me. I know your hand was in it."

He shook his head. "This is due almost entirely to your own merit, Molly. And the fact that Ben Mullins is one feisty cuss when you get him riled."

She laughed along with him.

"And now . . ." A gleam lit his eyes. "How about some dessert?"

"You're making dessert too?" She'd been craving sweets, but since she hadn't seen any ingredients for dessert, she'd assumed it wasn't part of the night's menu.

"I didn't forget your sweet tooth." A sheepish look came over his face. "As I remember, Rachel started wanting more sweets about now when she was carrying the boys."

Molly's cheeks warmed at his mention of her baby, and at the attention he was showing her. "The same thing is happening to me," she said softly.

"Well, I aim to remedy that. For a while anyway." A wry grin tipped his mouth. "It's time for some homemade Colorado ice cream."

Her mouth watered. "Ice cream? Really?"

He laughed. "Do you have a bowl?"

She grabbed one from the cupboard and followed him outside to the porch.

"Stay here," he said, and strode out a few feet from the cabin and scooped several handfuls of snow into the bowl. He stamped his feet before returning inside. "I've got some milk and honey in my saddlebags there."

She found them and met him at the table.

He picked up a spoon. "I'll stir while you add just a touch of milk and a little honey. But we'll have to hurry because it melts fast."

Molly added enough milk to make it smooth, then added some honey. And more honey. And a little more honey. "I like mine sweet," she whispered, feeling him staring at her from the side.

"I gathered that." Once he stirred it together, he dipped the spoon and held it out. "You take the first bite."

She did and closed her eyes at the cold, smooth sweetness of it. "Oh . . . why have you not told me about this before?" She did her best to hide her smile. "But where's your bowl?"

He laughed and grabbed another spoon. "We can make more."

They sat on the sofa and ate that bowlful and another as the fire crackled in the hearth. Molly couldn't remember a more enjoyable evening, or a more desirable man.

Telling herself not to, she couldn't help imagining what it would be like if he were able to somehow forgive her of everything, once the baby was safely born. Once she'd told him. Would there ever come a time when, after he knew all her secrets, he could look at her as the woman he cared for, or possibly even loved, instead of a woman who had borne a child out of wedlock?

Later that night, she lay in bed on her back in the dark, thinking about the evening they'd spent together. The heat from the bed warmer radiated from the opposite side of the mattress, and she soaked it up, praying the families in Little Italy were sheltered and warm, and that they had enough to eat. She stretched and curled onto her side and drew up her legs, and felt an unmistakable twinge.

She paused. Maybe she'd moved in the wrong way or—

There, she felt it again. Something similar to butterflies. Only more so. Like there was one very large butterfly. And an overzealous one, at that.

Holding her breath, she waited, completely still in the darkness, palms pressed flat against her rounded belly, the *ticktock* of the mantel clock in the main room counting off the seconds. And she felt it again. She laughed softly. "My baby . . ." *Oh, God, thank you. . . .*

This was what Dr. Brookston had tried to describe to her, her baby growing and moving inside of her, a miracle of life she didn't deserve but would spend the rest of her life trying to be worthy of.

"Students, please take out your slates and work the problems on the board. And no discussion this time." Molly threw a glance at Amanda Spivey, who had been "all a twitter" this week, as the girl put it, excited over the announcement of auditions for the Christmas program. "This is a chance to work on your own and to show me—and the other teachers with us this week—what you've each learned."

Molly moved to the stool and sat down, still following Dr. Brookston's orders to a T. The events of the past month, coupled with the changes in her body and the baby growing inside her, had left her exhausted inside and out. But she was also greatly encouraged by the progress.

Three more teachers were visiting from Denver, all women younger than she, with an insatiable desire to improve their skills. They'd asked excellent questions, which spoke well of their abilities. As soon as school was dismissed, the teachers would meet Mr. Lewis and take the stagecoach to Sulfur Falls, then would catch an early-morning train with plans to be home in Denver for Thanksgiving the following day.

With the teachers shadowing her, Molly checked the students' slates and could sense each child's eagerness to begin their brief Thanksgiving holiday. Though she doubted they looked forward to it as much as she did. She had something very important planned and couldn't wait to get started on it.

She saw the teachers off to catch the stage, then walked back to her cabin, unlaced her boots, and fully clothed, lay down on her bed and pulled up the covers, smiling into her pillow. She was asleep within seconds.

She awakened sometime later to darkness and to the wind howling through the aspen trees outside the window. She nestled deeper beneath the covers, drifting on a cocoon of warmth, until she awakened again. This time with the irrepressible need to visit the chamber pot. While up, she ate a hunk of bread and cheese, drank a tall glass of milk, then returned to bed.

And slept through to the following afternoon when she awakened famished but rested, feeling better than she had in weeks.

"I insist on helping with the dishes, Rachel." Molly retrieved a clean cloth from the kitchen cupboard. "Since you made practically the entire meal!"

Rachel grabbed the cloth from her hand, feigning an affront. "You'll do no such thing. It's snowing harder and James is already harnessing the horses. So unless you want to be stuck here for the night"—she gave a playful smirk—"I suggest you bundle up and let my brother take you home."

Molly had noticed Rachel eyeing her and James during the Thanksgiving meal. She didn't have a brother or sister, but she'd gotten the definite impression—was certain, in fact—that Rachel was encouraging James to pursue a relationship with her. She'd even caught a wink Rachel had thrown him, but then had acted as if she hadn't seen.

And just now, in Rachel's playful banter, Molly sensed that "encouragement" again. While she appreciated Rachel's "approval" of her for James, she knew that approval wasn't valid. Not when it was rooted in a falsehood.

"Rachel—" She and Rachel were alone in the kitchen—the Birches and Mullinses had already left—but still Molly lowered her voice. "I appreciate what you're trying to do . . . between me and James, but . . ." How to say this in a way that would accomplish the desired outcome without offending Rachel or slighting James? "But I'm simply not interested in . . . pursuing a relationship with a man right now. Even as fine a man as your brother." Witnessing a spark in Rachel's expression, Molly rushed to bolster her explanation. "I'm about to have a child, Rachel. And I'm about to lose my job." Her sigh came without force. "I'm in no position to make a commitment to anyone."

"Actually . . ." Rachel tied an apron around her slender waist. "I'd say that your current circumstances would suggest quite the opposite. Remember what I told you when you first arrived? Things are different out here. We don't hold to tradition like back home. You don't have to wait, Molly. Especially being with child."

Molly briefly looked away. This wasn't going as planned. Perhaps coming at it from a different angle would be better. "Your brother means a great deal to me. I'm especially thankful for his friendship, but I simply don't think—"

"His *friendship*?" Rachel's eyes sparkled. "Come now, Molly," she whispered, her tone sweetly conspiratorial. "We both know that he hardly looks upon you as a friend. But since you're asking, in a roundabout way"—she smiled—"for me to mind my own business, I'll do my best to not try and help things along. Now, come on." She looped her arm through Molly's. "Let's not keep him waiting."

After saying good-bye to Mitch and Kurt, Molly slipped into her coat and followed Rachel to the front door. They hugged, and Molly glanced down at her protruding belly coming between them. She rolled her eyes. "Do you still think I need to gain more weight?"

Rachel patted her rounded tummy. "I think you're beautiful, and that you're carrying a healthy baby who'll be ready to join us in another couple of months." She frowned. "And you're not nearly as big as I was at this stage—either time. So I don't want to hear any complaining!"

Grinning, Molly pulled on her gloves. "Thank you again for agreeing to be with me during the birth. I can't tell you how much better that makes me feel, to know you'll be there."

"I wouldn't miss it!"

Rachel followed her outside to the front porch, where the snow was flurrying heavier than before. The stairs the boys had swept clean three hours ago were piled high again.

Molly pulled her scarf higher around her neck. "I wish Dr. Brookston could've joined us today. I know he would've enjoyed it."

"Yes, well . . ." Rachel stared at some distant point. "When James mentioned having invited him, I knew the chances of the doctor showing up were slim. Doctors aren't exactly the most dependable people in the world."

Hearing a *tone* in Rachel's voice, Molly silently questioned it. James had explained at dinner that Dr. Brookston's services were required today at Deputy Willis's home. Mary, the deputy's wife, was in labor. So it hardly seemed fair to label Rand Brookston as undependable due to that. "I'm not sure I'd—"

"Take care, you fair lassies!" In full Scottish brogue, James pulled the sleigh up beside the porch stairs. "A wicked storm's a brewin'!"

Molly's train of thought derailed as he climbed the icy stairs and slipped an arm around her none-too-tiny waist. She felt about as big as a barn these days.

"You best hang on to me for all you're worth, Molly girl!" He winked. "With both hands, if you'd like."

Giggling, Rachel raised a discreet brow as if to say, *"Friendship?"* "You be careful taking her home, James."

Molly did hold on tight to him, unable to see her feet these days without peering over her belly. Glad when they reached the safety of the sleigh, she settled in, pulling the blankets up, and James gave the reins a flick. The horses responded and with seeming ease cut a path through the freshly fallen snow.

Boughs of evergreens, laden with white, lined

the trail as James guided the sleigh down the mountain. The air was pure and sweet, and Molly knew without question that she would remember this day—and this man beside her—for as long as she had breath.

The town of Timber Ridge was ghostlike, its stores and businesses closed up for the day, half hidden beneath a thick blanket of winter white.

They arrived at her cabin, and James assisted her up the stairs and slid the key into the lock. When he opened the door, a drift of snow built up by the wind gave way and avalanched inside.

"I'll get you a fire started before I head back."

She grabbed the broom and swept the snow back outside. "You don't have to do that, James. I don't want you to get caught in the storm. And I'm capable of building my own fire." She motioned to the half cord stacked against the wall. "You brought in enough wood two days ago to last me for a week."

He did a poor job of curbing his grin. "You can never have enough wood come winter."

"I'm not so sure about that." She eyed the stack taking up half of her parlor.

"Okay, I'll go—right after I build the fire."

He set to work and had her fire blazing in a matter of minutes. Only then did she remove her coat and gloves. She sat down on the sofa.

He claimed the place beside her and brushed her cheek with his fingers, his hand lingering. "You get prettier every time I see you, Molly Whitcomb."

She laughed. "All right, now I'm sure of it. You *did* have too much of Ben's homemade wine."

He smiled and moved closer, the blue of his eyes deepening, and Molly realized his intent. Part of her welcomed his advances and wanted nothing more than to kiss him again, but she knew she shouldn't. Not knowing what was coming.

She rose quickly—too quickly—and a sharp jab poked her abdomen. She fell back on the couch, gasping for breath and laughing, holding her mid-section.

James reached for her. "Are you all right?"

"Yes—" She laughed at the shock on his face. "I'm fine—" She took a breath. "I just—" The baby moved again, and a spasm rolled across her belly. Dr. Brookston had told her about this. "I just tried to get up too fast and am being . . . scolded for it." She put a hand on his arm. "The baby's moving, that's all."

"Moving?" He looked down, his eyes widening. "Is that a good thing?"

"It's a *very* good thing." She grinned. "I thought your father was a doctor."

"Well, he was. But . . . this wasn't exactly a topic of discussion around our dinner table."

The baby turned inside her, and Molly took deep, steady breaths. "It's . . . very normal . . . for the baby to move. It just . . . takes me by surprise . . . at times."

"Yeah . . ." He shook his head. "I can see that."

On a whim, she reached for him. "Here . . . give me your hand."

He pulled away, his expression uncertain.

"It's all right," she whispered, seeing his eyes narrow. "Trust me, James." She took his hand, so strong and warm, and pressed it against her belly. "Shhhh," she whispered. "Just wait." She loved the anticipation on his face. "There! Did you feel it?"

His look of wonder already told her he had. He moved his hand, following the movement of her child, and slowly exhaled. "Thomas told me about this," he said softly. "About how it felt before the boys were born." He looked at her, his eyes misting. "This is . . ."

She smiled when he didn't finish his sentence. "A miracle. Yes . . . it is."

They stayed that way for a few moments, sharing the feeling of life inside her, the fire crackling and warming away the chill, casting a burnt-orange glow on the room.

Finally, the baby quieted, but James didn't move his hand away. He slowly slid it on around her waist and pulled her closer.

Molly felt herself responding to him. "James—" She needed to think of a distraction. For them both. "Would you . . . like a cup of coffee?"

He nuzzled her cheek, laughing softly. "No . . . I don't want any coffee." He moved closer to her, but with such gentleness, mindful of the baby. He brushed his lips against hers. "Thank you for sharing that with me."

Oh, the way he did that. Kissing her while not fully completing the kiss. "You're welcome," she whispered, finally turning her mouth to meet his.

He kissed her long and slow, his hands massaging her back, her shoulders. He edged the hair from her shoulder and kissed the curve of her neck. Molly closed her eyes. And she thought she'd had trouble breathing before! He kissed her mouth again, deeply and without a trace of reservation, as though she belonged to him. Which she wanted to, in every way.

Just when she determined she should discourage things from going any further—he drew back.

His breath heavy, he sat back on the sofa and brought her alongside him. "I love you, Molly," he whispered, combing his fingers through her hair.

Her head against his chest, she closed her eyes, able to hear the solid beat of his heart. "I love you too." What should have been a completely happy moment wasn't. Not the way it should have been. "And I always will," she whispered.

He leaned back and searched her eyes. "I want you to be my wife. And I want to be your husband. There's nothing stopping us, Molly. I know you're afraid. I see it in your eyes. But I'll take care of you. And your baby. I'll love you both. I already do."

She tried to look away, but he held her fast.

"Tell me what happened." He cradled her face, his own a mask of concern. "What did he do to you, Molly? Did your husband hurt you? Was he cruel?"

Tears coming, she shook her head, not ready for this conversation. Not until after the baby was born. She couldn't bear the thought of James being estranged from her. Not now. She needed him beside her. "It's not what you're imagining, James."

"Then tell me. Help me understand."

"I will," she said, trembling, feeling as though she were standing on the edge of a cliff, about to jump off. Or be pushed. "I'll tell you, I promise. In time." But she couldn't do it yet. "Just give me a little more time."

She held him, and his strong arms came around her. She would tell him everything. Soon. Very soon. After the baby was born.

38

And remember, children—" Molly whispered, overaccentuating every near-silent syllable, aware of the crowd of eagerly awaiting parents and friends packing the garland-strung church pews behind her. It was standing-room only for the school's first Christmas Celebration, and less than two weeks until Christmas itself. "Turtle doves don't screech or crow," she mouthed, looking pointedly at Kurt Boyd. "They *coo. Softly.*"

Kurt smiled back at her, that ever-mischievous gleam having returned to his eyes. She'd managed to reach somewhat of an unspoken truce with him, and he'd finished strong the final days of class. Still, she raised a brow of warning in his direction, praying as she did. She needed this evening to go off without a hitch. No mice and no snakes. It was her last official duty as teacher, and she wanted this event to be a gift, of sorts, to the town of Timber Ridge for entrusting their children to her.

Excitement shone in the students' smiles and in the expectant looks on parents' faces. Molly shared it. But along with the excitement, she felt a melancholy. This evening also marked an end. An end to the most rewarding teaching experience she'd ever had, and the beginning of the end of her life in Timber Ridge.

She'd received a letter from Mayor Davenport earlier in the week, on behalf of the town council. More of an eviction notice, really, without one mention of the teachers who had visited from Denver. While the teachers themselves had expressed appreciation before leaving town, Molly hadn't received any feedback as to whether the administrators were pleased. But apparently that wasn't high on David Davenport's list anymore.

Either that or his eagerness to see her gone had taken precedence.

The mayor had instructed her to vacate the cabin by the eighteenth. That meant she had the weekend ahead to finish packing and be moved by Monday. Miss Ruby at the boardinghouse had said she should have an opening soon. Until then, Molly planned on staying at the hotel.

She checked her pocket watch. Five minutes until they were scheduled to start. She glanced behind her to see people still arriving. Wreaths decorated the doors, and red-ribboned garland, its scent pungent and sweet, was strung from the pews and around the windows, giving the room a warm, festive feel.

James was seated on the right side, three rows back. He gave her a quick wink and then tactfully pointed to her, then back to himself, as if to remind her of their sleigh ride planned for later that evening. He'd said he had something important to tell her, but after what he'd said to her on Thanksgiving Day in her cabin, she feared it was a question he wanted to ask instead. She'd told him she would likely be too tired after the program tonight. But that had been an excuse and he'd known it, and apparently wasn't accepting it.

Sweet, stubborn man . . .

Despite his private smile, she detected lines of worry around his eyes. Another cow had been stolen two days ago. The first such incident in weeks. Just one this time, according to Lyda Mullins, but Lyda had told her—having heard from Ben—that Mayor Davenport had been furious at the news and was attempting to use the situation to discredit James in the sheriff's election come spring, which was preposterous. James couldn't prevent every crime. And she had every confidence he would find those responsible, as he'd done before.

He'd offered her use of his bedroom at Rachel's house, volunteering to bunk at his office until she found a "permanent residence," but that was out of the question. Rachel needed his help at the ranch, but more than that, Molly refused to be indebted to him any more than she already was.

Because in six weeks, when her baby was born, he would come to regret everything he'd done to help her stay.

Seeing it was time to start, she whispered final encouragements to the children, especially the youngest ones standing on the bottom steps of the risers before her, who looked a tad more nervous than excited. Taking a breath, she turned to face the audience. "Ladies and gentlemen, on behalf of the students of the Timber Ridge School, I welcome you to the first annual Christmas Celebration."

As if on cue, everyone applauded, and she motioned for Billy Bolden and Amanda Spivey to join her. She'd awarded them the lead speaking and dramatic roles. As Billy and Amanda delivered their scripted messages, Molly scanned the audience.

Sitting beside James now, Rachel scrunched her shoulders and flashed a smile. Ben and Lyda

Mullins were in attendance, as was Dr. Brookston. Charlie Daggett and Lori Beth stood in the back, all smiles. But what pleased her most was seeing Josiah and Belle Birch, along with Elijah. Molly smiled in their direction, but her smile faded as her gaze moved back toward the front.

Mayor Davenport and his wife, Eliza, sat on the first row, neither of them looking pleased. Same for LuEllen Spivey and her husband. Hank Bolden occupied the pew behind them with his wife, Ida. Ida wore a pleasant countenance, no doubt anticipating her son's role in the drama of the birth of Christ tonight. And she wouldn't be disappointed.

Molly had discovered that Billy's love for story came alive on the stage, even more so than for Amanda Spivey, who had asked if—in portraying Mary, the mother of Jesus—she could sing a special solo and wear her hair in ringlets as she'd seen in a recent issue of *Harper's Weekly.* "No solo and no ringlets," Molly had told her in no uncertain terms.

And yet . . . Amanda's mother had been in charge of the costumes, and lovely as they were, Molly had never seen so ornate a shawl as Amanda wore this evening, gathered in decorative tucks around her face—with rosettes on each temple. If she'd seen it before today, Molly would have asked for an alteration. But once Amanda had arrived, minutes before the program, it was too late. Amanda's and LuEllen's intention, Molly felt certain.

More applause as Billy and Amanda took their places on the risers again.

Molly addressed the audience. "The students and I appreciate your attendance this evening. Teaching the children of Timber Ridge—*your* children—has been a joy and a privilege I won't soon forget, and one for which I'm most grateful. I daresay I've enjoyed it far more than I ever did instructing on the college level." Proud smiles dotted the faces in the audience. "And now, without further adieu, we hope you enjoy tonight's festivities."

Turning back to meet the children's eager smiles, she hummed the starting note, and on her mark, the class began in practiced unison. " 'The first Noel, the angels did say, was to certain poor shepherds in fields where they lay. . . . ' "

As the innocent voices filled the corners of the church, she looked from child to child, thanking God for each one. Even incorrigible little Kurt Boyd. The pomp and prestige she had pursued and garnered at Franklin College paled in comparison to seeing the sparkle in Ansley Tucker's eyes as the little girl had learned how to read and write. Or Benjamin Foster's satisfied smile as he'd grasped the ordered world of mathematics. Or Billy and Elijah's shared enthusiasm over stories.

The way the two boys had continued to teach Angelo was also a wonder. Angelo was teaching them some Italian too, Elijah had told her. Earlier in the week, Billy had shared after school one day that he wanted to be a teacher when he grew up, just like she was. He could not have paid her a higher compliment. She was so grateful for the friendship those boys shared. And that God had used her, even in the smallest way, to bring them together encouraged a smile.

Now, if only some of the people in this room would learn from their example.

The next hour passed far too quickly, and Molly tucked away the nuances of the evening—the sprinkled *ooh*s and *ahh*s from parents, and the cute unscripted responses from students when they forgot their lines. The event could not have gone better, mistakes and all.

Cloth-covered tables laden with cookies, cakes, pies, and punch lined the back of the room, and following the program, families stayed and visited, as Molly had hoped.

Mathias and Oleta Tucker gently pulled her aside. "Thank you, Dr. Whitcomb," Mathias said, "for all you've done for our children."

Oleta took hold of her hand. "You've been such a gift to our children and to this town. We're so thankful God brought you here."

Molly appreciated their gratitude but squirmed beneath the praise. The more she mingled and the more people thanked her, the more uncomfortable she grew, knowing she wasn't deserving.

"Molly?"

She spotted Lori Beth standing off to the side. Their paths had crossed in town in past weeks, but only a handful of times and all too briefly.

Molly joined her. "It was so kind of you and Charlie to come tonight, Lori Beth. Thank you."

"We wouldn't have missed it for anything. It's been all the talk around town, you know."

Molly sighed, shaking her head. "Better that than other things, I guess."

"So true. Here . . . this is for you." Lori Beth held out a cloth bag. It was tied at the neck with a bright red ribbon. "Open it later, when you get home. And please know that I've been thinking about you, praying for you . . . and your baby," she whispered. "I so appreciate our friendship."

Molly took the bag. "I feel the very same way. And thank you for this—though you shouldn't have." She grinned. "I'll open it as soon as I get home."

Lori Beth turned to go.

"Lori Beth, if you have time this week . . ." Molly fingered the bow on the bag. "Would you like to have tea together? I'm moving out of my cabin this weekend and will likely be staying in the hotel, but I'd appreciate another opportunity to visit."

Lori Beth held her gaze. "I'd love that. But why don't you come to my house? Charlie's still working at the Mullinses' store. Just stop by there and he can show you the way."

Molly nodded. Watching Lori Beth and Charlie leave, she felt the same sense of rightness inside her as she had that night in Miss Clara's dining room.

"Mrs. Whitcomb!"

Recognizing the high-pitched singsong voice, Molly pasted on a smile and turned. "Mrs. Spivey, how are you this evening?"

"I'm doing very well!" Mrs. Spivey's hand fluttered over her heart. "I'm just so proud of my precious Amanda. Have you ever seen a better or more beautiful Mary?"

Molly had learned to read LuEllen Spivey fairly well, and no manner of theatrics could disguise the keenness in the woman's gaze. "I can honestly say that I've never seen a Mary quite like your daughter portrayed this evening."

LuEllen smiled, but it wasn't genuine. "Have you decided yet, Mrs. Whitcomb, whether you'll be staying in Timber Ridge? *After* your child is born?"

"As I mentioned to you last week, when you asked me then," Molly said softly, knowing she was walking a fine line and that she was far more errant than LuEllen Spivey knew. "My future plans are still uncertain."

"I see. . . . Well, my niece, Judith Stafford . . . Do you remember her? She's the woman Sheriff McPherson so enjoyed dancing with that evening at the town—"

"I remember Miss Stafford." Which LuEllen already knew, of course. "She's quite lovely."

"Isn't she, though? And so kind and good—and forthcoming." LuEllen's eyes narrowed in a manner incongruent with her pleasant tone. "She's applied for the teaching position here again, and as the mayor just told me, she's his first choice of the current candidates. As she was for many . . . of the town council members before you came."

Molly felt the barb and didn't do a good job of hiding it. Imagining what Mrs. Spivey's reaction would be once she knew the truth, Molly shuddered inwardly. *Merciless* was the first term that came to mind. "If your niece is awarded the position, I have no doubt she'll do a wonderful job, Mrs. Spivey. Now, if you'll excuse me, I need to—"

"Not only will she do a fine job as teacher, but my niece is the type of woman people in this town could respect, that they could look up to. Like they do Sheriff McPherson. You know, Mrs. Whitcomb"—LuEllen stepped closer and slipped her arm through Molly's, as though they were the dearest of friends—"having the right woman beside a man can make all the difference in his success. Wouldn't you agree?" She didn't wait for a response. "Men are often blind to things, no matter how intelligent they may be. They don't see what's best for them. They only see what they want. But we women"—she smiled—"we have discernment, do we not? We see things—and people—as they are. And sometimes it's up to us to make the right choice, not just for ourselves . . . but for others."

Molly swallowed. The room suddenly had less air than it had seconds before.

LuEllen patted her arm. "The election for sheriff will be coming up in the spring. James McPherson is a fine man, and he's done so much for Timber Ridge. It would be a shame if he were to make a . . . personal decision that could cost him his job."

Personal decision? Not believing what she was hearing, yet hearing it clearly, Molly felt a light sweat break out on her forehead. Did Mrs. Spivey *know* about her? No, that wasn't possible. Because if she did, then everyone else in this church building—in this town—would know. But the woman did suspect something. Somehow.

Feeling like an insect caught in a spider's web, Molly disengaged herself from the woman. "Please excuse me, Mrs. Spivey, I . . . I need to say good-bye to the Tucker family before they leave."

Setting etiquette aside, Molly didn't wait for a response but made her way toward the double doors at the back of the church, speaking to people who greeted her, trying to be the gracious school-teacher, but unable to ignore the tremor deep inside, like a gentle thunder.

She'd known there would be a cost to her rela-tionship with James. She'd known that from the beginning and had tried to put distance between them. But, selfishly, she hadn't tried hard enough. And not until now had she realized what an extravagant price he would pay once the people of this town—*his* town, all the people who knew he cared for her—discovered she'd never been married.

A sickly weakness fanned out inside her.

If only she could go back to that moment when she'd first stepped foot onto that train station in Sulfur Falls and make her choice again. She would choose differently this time. Sin's cost to her was one thing. But the cost of her sin to someone she loved was another. Hindsight was a thorough, if not oftentimes cruel, teacher.

"Well, Dr. Whitcomb, I'd say this evening was a great success."

Hearing James behind her, Molly briefly closed her eyes before facing him. "Why thank you, Sheriff McPherson. I appreciate that."

His brow furrowed. "Are you all right? You look a little pale."

She tugged at the high collar of her black dress. "It's just a little warm in here, that's all."

He glanced around them, then leaned closer, but not too close. "Are you ready for that sleigh ride? I just need to see Rachel and the boys to the wagon, then—"

A commotion sounded outside the church building. Among shouting voices, a woman screamed.

James made for the door and Molly followed, the

last of the families trailing behind her. But they were stopped by a crowd of people bottlenecked on the front steps. Murmurs drifted back, some gasps. Molly stood on tiptoe but couldn't see anything. James pushed his way through and she followed.

A handful of torches provided scant light in the churchyard. She made it to the front of the group, and it took a few seconds for her eyes to adjust to the shadows. When they did, she had trouble making sense of what she saw.

Four men formed a half circle, their rifles pointed down at someone who lay bloodied and crumpled on the ground. She stepped forward, peering over someone's shoulder, trying to see who it was—when Angelo Giordano raised his beaten and swollen face.

Her breath left in a rush. "Angelo!"

The boy struggled to rise, his thin arms pushing upward. One of the four men standing over him delivered a swift boot to his stomach, and Angelo went down hard.

Molly screamed, running for him.

39

James reached the boy seconds after Molly did and felt for a pulse on his thin arm. *Nothing.* Molly cradled Angelo's head in her lap and smoothed his blood-matted hair. Tears lined her cheeks, but anger lit her eyes.

Brookston knelt beside them, his bag already open. He gently probed the side of Angelo's throat with one hand while listening to the boy's chest through his stethoscope. James felt his own throat tightening, images of Josiah Birch crowding close. He could hardly breathe. *Oh, God, please . . . not again.*

Hearing murmurs behind him in the crowd, James rose, a bitter taste on his tongue. His attention went to one of the four men standing over Angelo. "Are you responsible for this, Rudger?"

Leonard Rudger eyed him, rifle in his grip. "This boy stole my cattle, Sheriff. I'm just protecting my land and my stock. I still have a right to do that in this town, don't I?"

James wanted to take the man's Winchester and gut punch him with it. "Do you have proof?"

"My men and I searched Little Italy. We found meat hidden in this boy's tent, and a burned carcass with my brand on it not too far away. That's enough evidence in my book."

"But you didn't catch the boy in the act?"

"Didn't need to." An unpleasant smile turned Rudger's mouth. "He confessed to doing it."

James gritted his teeth. "Was that before—or after—you beat him senseless?"

Rudger gave a shrug. "We just applied a little pressure, Sheriff. Something a man in your position knows a little about, I'm sure."

Brookston peered up. "Sheriff, I've got a pulse,

but it's faint. I need help getting him to the clinic."

Josiah Birch and Ben Mullins stepped from the crowd. With Molly close beside them, they lifted Angelo's frail body and carried him to a wagon. James saw Molly glare back at the four men, accusation fierce in her expression. He caught her gaze and indicated with a nod for her to go on, hoping she would. For her to say anything would only complicate matters.

She climbed into the wagon beside Angelo and Dr. Brookston.

James turned back to Rudger as the wagon pulled away. The rancher and his men could have killed Angelo and dumped his body on the side of a road somewhere, or could've dragged him onto Rudger's property to make a stronger case. But they hadn't. They'd brought the boy to town, tonight, to a public gathering, and a school gathering at that—to make a point. And he didn't have to look far to know who was behind it all.

Davenport stood watching the scene, an all-too-smug look on his face. James strode toward him, and the man's confidence wavered.

"Hold on, McPherson!" Davenport shielded his face with his hand. "You've got no—"

James stopped inches from his face, aware of the families gathered, watching. Especially Mitchell and Kurt, who stood with Rachel just feet away. "I want to speak with you and your *men* inside the church."

A nervous but affable grin lit the mayor's face. "Now, Sheriff . . ." He glanced around them. "I think Leonard Rudger is well within his rights to protect his property. The boy confessed to the crime and needs to be dealt with, according to the law. And it's up to you to see that the law's enforced, and that he's sent to Denver to stand trial for his—"

"Now, Mayor!" James included Rudger and the other three men in his stare. "You either get inside that church building and we talk, or I'll take you to jail and we'll do it there. Your choice."

Slowly, the men filed through the crowd and up the stairs, Davenport trailing them.

"Everyone else, head on home." James caught Rachel's worried look and crossed to where she stood. "Would you and the boys stop by Willis's place and ask him to join me here? As soon as he can."

She nodded. "Be careful, James."

As he made his way to the church, Billy Bolden caught his eye. Billy stood by his father and his mother, his face wet with tears. Billy looked at him, then bowed his head.

Hank Bolden shoved his son through the crowd. Ida Bolden followed at her husband's urging. But James couldn't shake the look on Billy's face, or the feeling that the boy knew something. And knowing about Billy's friendship with Angelo made him even more suspicious.

"Bolden!" he called out.

Billy was the first to turn. Then his father.

Hank puffed out his barrel chest. "You want something with us, Sheriff?"

James closed the distance between them. Thankful the crowd was dispersing, he kept his voice low. "I'd like to speak with you and your son, please. Over at my office, if you will."

Hank bristled. "If there's something you're wanting, I'd prefer you put it to me straight. I'm a busy man. If not, then I suggest you get on with the job of keepin' this town safe."

Ida slipped a protective arm around her son's shoulders, and sure as anything, James read guilt in Billy's eyes. He couldn't fathom that Billy Bolden could be mixed up in this—just as he couldn't imagine Angelo doing it either—but Billy *was* involved somehow, he was certain. "I'd rather not speak about this here, Hank. So, please . . ." He gestured. "Meet me at my office. I'll be there shortly, after I speak with Rudger."

Molly held Angelo's hand as Dr. Brookston sutured the gash on his forehead, the coppery tang of blood heavy in the air. "The doctor's almost done," she said, wondering if the boy could hear her. He hadn't awakened yet.

"Keep speaking to him, Dr. Whitcomb." Brookston pulled the needle taut, his manner calming and methodical. "I believe people can still

535

hear in situations like these, and a familiar voice can make all the difference."

Molly leaned closer. "Angelo, I'm here with you. You're going to be all right. I'm so sorry this happened. So sorry. *Mi dispiace.*" Without thought, she slipped into Italian. "I don't know if what those men are saying you've done is true or not, but even if it is, I want you to know that I'll stand beside you, Angelo. I won't leave you. Nothing you could do could make me turn my back on you. Because I know what it feels like to be alone. . . ."

Brookston looked up from suturing. "I don't know what you're saying to him, Dr. Whitcomb. But it sure sounds comforting."

Molly sighed and continued to whisper in Angelo's ear.

A knock sounded on the door, and Josiah Birch poked his head inside. "Is it all right if we come in?"

Brookston nodded. "As long as you're not squeamish."

Josiah ushered Belle and Elijah inside, then closed the door behind them. "How's the boy farin', sir?"

Brookston tied off the last suture. "His right arm is fractured. He's got multiple cuts and contusions. I'm watching for signs of internal injuries too." He grimaced. "His body couldn't have taken much more of a beating, and I'd feel worlds better if he would wake up. Even for a minute." He glanced at

Josiah and his expression softened. "Seems I remember someone else bein' on my table much in this same shape, and he pulled through. That gives me hope."

Josiah's smile was brief but telling, and a near tangible anxiety crept into the room. Belle slipped an arm around her husband's waist, her eyes filling with tears. But Belle's emotion didn't seem due so much to Brookston's comment as it did with the look of fear on her son's face.

"Doc . . ." Josiah dipped his head. "Dr. Whitcomb, ma'am . . . we was thinkin' that maybe the sheriff would be here."

Molly shook her head. "He hasn't stopped by yet, but I'm sure he will. When he's through meeting with . . . those men."

Elijah slowly approached the table and touched Angelo's arm. "Is there anything I can do for him?"

Something in Elijah's tone made Molly give him a closer look. His lower lip was trembling. Josiah came behind his son and laid a hand on his shoulder, and Elijah's countenance slipped. His slender shoulders began to shake.

Molly looked from Elijah to Angelo and back, and found Elijah's green eyes swimming with tears.

"I'm sorry, Dr. Whitcomb," he said, hiccupping a breath. "This is my fault, ma'am."

She frowned, not understanding. *"Your* fault? No, Elijah. How could this be your fault?"

Belle cleared her throat and it sounded overloud in the silence. "Elijah helped Angelo butcher the cow."

Elijah bowed his head, his breath coming harder.

Molly stared, fighting the conclusion forming in her mind. But deep inside, she knew. If Elijah was involved, then Billy Bolden had been involved too. The three boys were so close. And she was to blame for that. *Oh, God, help me. . . .* If she hadn't introduced them, then maybe—

"It was wrong. I know it," Elijah said beneath his breath. "But he and his family were so hungry."

Josiah laid a hand on his son's shoulder. "We aim to tell the sheriff everything. And my son and I will work to pay for that cow. Longer still for the wrong that was done to Mr. Rudger."

But Molly wasn't sure it would be that simple a fix. James had told her that the miners responsible for stealing the cattle before would stand trial in Denver, then would be sentenced to jail. But these were only boys! Surely there would be a distinction made, since they were so young.

Elijah sucked in a breath, and Molly looked back to see Angelo blink. Once. Twice.

James stared at Billy across his desk in his office, awaiting the boy's answer, and already knowing what it would be. The clock on the opposite wall indicated shortly after midnight.

He'd met separately with Davenport, Rudger,

and Rudger's three ranch hands. And they'd each given him the same information, almost verbatim—as if they'd rehearsed it. He hadn't met with Angelo yet. He wasn't even sure the boy was going to pull through, based on what he'd seen. But if he did survive the beating—and if the men's accusations were on the mark—Angelo would face charges for cattle rustling and would stand trial in Denver. And being an immigrant, things wouldn't go well for him.

But James's hunch told him something else was at play. He reached for patience beyond his own and prayed for the boy sitting before him. "I'll ask you again, Billy. Do you know anything about what happened with Angelo tonight? Or about the cattle being stolen from Mr. Rudger's ranch?"

Hank Bolden heaved a sigh and stood. "I've already told you, Sheriff, my son doesn't even know the kid, much less hang around with such—"

James raised a hand. "Consider this your last warning, Bolden. Next time, you're gone."

Red in the face, Hank Bolden sat back down. Ida reached out to touch her husband's arm, but Bolden shoved her hand away. She bowed her head, knotting her hands in her lap.

Billy sniffed and slowly raised his head. His eyes were bloodshot. His lips moved, but nothing came out at first. With force, he cleared his throat and began. "I-it was o-only one cow, Sheriff.

We—" His voice broke. "We didn't think th-they'd miss it."

Ida began to cry. Hank leaned forward, elbows on his knees, and cursed his only son. The words were like bullets, and Billy shuddered, wincing.

James fought the urge to round his desk and take the boy and hug him tight like his grandfather used to do with him. Either that or thrash Hank Bolden. The man didn't deserve a son like Billy. "I appreciate you telling me the truth, Billy. That took courage, son. A lot of courage."

Billy shook his head. "It was me who should've gotten that beating tonight, Sheriff. I stole that cow. Not Angelo. I got so scared when I saw what they'd done to him." He wiped his eyes. "But when I saw how hungry those people are out—"

"That's enough, Billy!" Hank Bolden came to his feet again. "Don't say anything more 'til I talk to your uncle."

James didn't want to make things worse for Billy, or to scare the boy. But he also didn't want Davenport getting to him and confusing the truth, and that's just what would happen if Hank Bolden got his brother-in-law involved. "Hank, Ida . . . I need to take Billy into custody, until we get this worked out."

Ida gasped and glanced at the hallway leading to the jail cells. "You can't put him in there, Sheriff. Please! He's only a boy!"

"He's the same age as his friend, Angelo

Giordano," James said quietly, watching Hank.

Hank grimaced. "That's different, McPherson. Those immigrants are—"

"It's not different, Pa."

Billy's voice came out small but had a strength to it that James felt deep inside him. And, if he wasn't mistaken, Hank had sensed that strength too.

"Angelo's my friend, Pa. And he's not anything like you said he was. None of his people are. They work hard for what they—"

"I said, that's enough, boy!" The muscles in Hank's jaw corded tight. He stared at his son, then at James. "What if . . ." He briefly looked away. "What if I say you can't put him in there?" he asked more softly.

James rose, hearing the real question behind Hank Bolden's threat. "He'll be all right, Bolden." He motioned for Billy to stand and rested a hand on the boy's shoulder. "I'll put him in a cell by himself, and Willis or I will be with him the entire time. You're both welcome to stay and sit with him until morning, if you'd like."

Hank and Ida both nodded, which also served to answer another of his questions—whether Hank was involved with his brother-in-law and Leonard Rudger. His guess was no. Otherwise, Hank would've left as quickly as possible to tell Davenport what had happened.

After Willis arrived, James made his way across the darkened town to the doc's clinic, praying the news on Angelo Giordano would be good. He couldn't help but admire Billy Bolden for standing up to his father. But what Billy and Angelo had done was wrong, and—if his earlier hunch was right—this night was far from over.

Because he still had one more confession he needed to hear.

40

James checked his pocket watch. Nearly eight o'clock. Leonard Rudger and Mayor Davenport were scheduled to arrive any minute, if they kept their word.

Feeling the effects of a sleepless night, he peered through his office window to the mountains reigning lofty above the town. The sun had risen over Timber Ridge this morning with a brilliance he couldn't recall, reflecting off the snowy peaks with a sheen so bright it almost hurt his eyes.

Boot steps sounded on the boardwalk, and he straightened. The door that led to the jail cells down the hallway stood open, as he'd left it.

The front door opened with a creak, and Rudger and Davenport walked inside.

"Morning, gentlemen." James met them and shook hands.

Davenport seemed well rested and almost chipper. Rudger wore his customary confidence like a cloak, more subdued by nature. James settled into his desk chair and motioned for them to sit.

Davenport eased his weight down. "Sheriff, I hope you won't waste our time this morning by trying to convince Rudger here not to press charges against that immigrant boy. Personally, I appreciate the work he and his men did in tracking down the culprit who stole the cattle." He smiled. "Since you seem to be preoccupied with other pursuits these days."

James eyed the men. "In case you're interested, gentlemen, it looks like *that immigrant boy*, as you phrased it, Mayor, is going to pull through, thanks to Dr. Brookston."

Rudger shifted in his chair but said nothing. Davenport's silent stare was answer enough.

James leaned forward. "So I take it, Rudger, that you still want to press charges against Angelo Giordano for cattle theft?"

"Absolutely, I do, Sheriff. The boy's a thief. He confessed to the crime, and I found evidence in his—"

James motioned, nodding. "I confirmed the evidence, so there's no question about that. I also saw evidence of 'the search' you and your men conducted."

Rudger's jaw hardened. "Those folks wouldn't cooperate, Sheriff."

"So you had to ransack their homes and have your men destroy what little shelter they had?"

Seething, Rudger looked away.

James pulled a piece of paper from a file on his desk, deciding to let Rudger stew on that for a minute. "I've prepared this document based on the testimony you gave last night. I just need for you to sign here, and here"—James indicated the locations on the page—"and the sheriff's office will proceed with the arrests."

Davenport looked up. "Arrests?"

James dipped the quill and handed it to Rudger. "Angelo Giordano didn't act on his own. He had two accomplices."

Rudger eyed him. "And they are?"

"Elijah Birch," James said quietly.

Davenport huffed an offensive word beneath his breath. "Not hard to see that one coming, now, was it? Who's the other?"

James looked beyond the men to where Billy Bolden stood behind them in the doorway.

"It was me, Uncle David."

Davenport's face went slack before draining of color. He turned and looked behind him.

Billy now stood with his parents, along with the Birch family, and Molly and Willis.

"I stole the cow," Billy whispered, his red-rimmed eyes filling again. "Not Angelo . . . not Elijah." He twisted the hem of his untucked shirt. "It was my idea. They only helped once I got the cow clear of the gate. Those families out there . . ." He sniffed and wiped his nose with his sleeve. "They're so hungry, and I just couldn't—" His voice caught. He winced. "What I did was wrong, Mr. Rudger. I know that. I just didn't think you'd miss one cow."

The silence lengthened, and James leaned forward in his chair. "I've spoken with each of the boys, and their parents, during the night. Including Mrs. Giordano, with the help of Dr. Whitcomb, who translated. The boys realize that what they did was wrong. They're sorry, and they want to make restitution. Either that, or . . ." He waited until Rudger and Davenport looked back. "You can proceed with your plan to prosecute. But you need to know that if you do, Billy Bolden will carry the bulk of the blame. He'll be charged with cattle theft, and he'll be transferred to the jail in Denver to stand trial."

Ida Bolden clamped her hand to her mouth but couldn't silence the whimper.

"Angelo and Elijah," James continued, "will face lesser charges, which I'll deal with here."

Rudger stared at the quill in his hand.

Davenport's reaction was more revealing. If the man could have thought of a way around this—to charge Angelo and Elijah, but not Billy—he would have. But there *was* no way around it.

"Sheriff, if that Italian boy didn't steal my cow"—Rudger's voice held considerably less confidence—"then why did he let me and my men believe that he did?"

"Because Angelo was protecting his friend,

Rudger." James pulled another sheet of paper from the file. "Which leads us to another matter." Rudger's gaze sharpened as James slid the page toward him. "That of you and your ranch hands beating an innocent boy . . . nearly to death."

Rudger pointed a finger. "He should have said something if he wasn't guilty!"

"Would you have listened to him if he had?" James shook his head. "We have laws, Rudger, not only to punish the guilty, but to protect the innocent. And you had no right to take that law into your own hands." He included Davenport in his stare.

"See here now, Sheriff . . ." Davenport tugged at the collar of his starched white shirt. "I'll not sit here and allow you to place all the blame on Leonard Rudger for—"

"I'm not placing all the blame with Rudger. I'm placing it square on your shoulders too, Mayor. I believe you had a part in this, and that you attempted to use this as an opportunity to advance your own ideas and plans for this town."

Davenport's glare darkened. "You have no proof of that."

"Not yet. But I will . . . after speaking with Rudger's ranch hand." James said nothing. He just stared, hoping his poker face was convincing. Watching the mayor turn three shades of crimson told him it was.

Rudger ran a hand through his thinning hair. "I

don't know what you're getting at, Sheriff McPherson, but—" His laugh held no humor. "I'm not the guilty party here. And I'm not spending time in jail for something I didn't do."

"And my aim isn't to put you there, Rudger." James sighed. "My aim is to find a way through this that, first, upholds the law. And, second, that will bring the most good from the bad that's happened." He gestured to the quill still in Rudger's hand. "You can sign that piece of paper and I'll arrest these boys—and you. Or . . ." He prayed again for God's guidance, as he had the better part of the night. "We can work out some alternative, for both sides."

Rudger slowly returned the quill to its holder. "What do you mean by alternative?"

"The boys have offered to work for you, Rudger, on your ranch, to pay for the cow, and even beyond that, for the wrong they did."

Rudger considered that. "You said *both sides*. What's my part?"

"Seems to me your restitution needs to be directed to Angelo Giordano and his family. You've been out there to Little Italy. You've seen how those families live. No houses to speak of, no warm shelter. Especially not now."

Rudger laughed. "Are you suggesting I go in and build them homes? All by myself?"

"No," James said quietly, knowing Rudger had enough money to do that ten times over, without feeling the loss. "Not all by yourself. If I were you, I'd look around and see if any of my . . . *associates* might have a vested interest in this opportunity, someone who might've encouraged you to do this. Someone who needs to share that burden with you."

Rudger looked pointedly at Davenport, who looked away, and James saw Molly smile.

Rudger stood, his expression resigned. His chair legs scraped against the wooden floor. "I'll have one of my men contact you about getting that started. And I'll be expecting those three boys at my ranch, Sheriff. They'll work off the cost of that cow, and then they'll help construct the new barn we're building this spring."

Josiah Birch stepped forward, his large hand resting on his son's shoulder. "I be there too, Mr. Rudger, sir. To help pay my son's debt."

Strangling the hat in his hands, Hank Bolden's struggle could not have been more evident. "And I'll come with Billy. We'll work until the barn is finished."

Billy looked up at his father, a wealth of meaning in his youthful face, and an unexpected swell of pride filled James's chest at what passed between the father and son.

He rose from his desk. "I'll accompany Angelo too, once the boy's able to work again." His offer wasn't even close to selfless. He wanted to make sure Angelo was treated right and that Rudger didn't try to overwork the boy, frail as Angelo was, and would be for a while.

Rudger gave a nod and took his leave. The Boldens and Birches followed, until only Davenport was left, with Willis and Molly standing off to the side. The pride in Molly's eyes touched a place inside James that he was fairly certain had never been disturbed, and he welcomed it. And her, liking how she looked at him now.

He had a question he was burning to ask her, and would—come Christmas. But there was something he needed to tell her first, before she could give her fair answer. He'd planned on telling her last night on a sleigh ride. Dark of night had appealed to him somehow. But maybe light of day was better, once she'd had some rest.

Davenport walked to the door, absent his normal measure of bravado. "Well, Sheriff, it seems you've had a busy night. I only wonder what our new governor in Denver would say if he knew of your decision today. You didn't exactly uphold the letter of the law, now did you?"

James heard the thinly veiled threat and knew what the mayor said was partially true. The governor would have wanted Billy to stand trial in Denver. But James knew the heart of that boy—Davenport's *own nephew*—and in his gut, he knew his decision had been the right one, despite it not fulfilling the "letter of the law." It had fulfilled the spirit of the law. Justice had ruled today, and it would rule again in Little Italy. James would make sure of it.

He shifted his weight and managed a shrug. "Next time you're there, Mayor, why don't you ask him what he thinks?"

Davenport pandered a grin, opening the door. "I might just do that."

"And be sure and let him know about what happened in Little Italy." James watched as Davenport's eyes narrowed. "I'm sure the governor's wife . . . Francesca, will be interested in hearing about that."

Molly followed Mary Willis from the sheriff's office, admiring the baby in the woman's arms. "Callie's beautiful, Mary. She's just beautiful."

Mary kissed her daughter's forehead, love evident in her eyes. "Dean and I still can't believe she's ours." Her eyes brightened. "Would you like to hold her?"

"Oh . . ." Molly's heart skipped a tender beat. "You wouldn't mind?"

"Mind?" Mary made a face as though the question were silly. "Here . . ."

Molly cradled the sleeping little girl in her arms, breathing in her sweet scent. "She's perfect," she whispered, not wanting to awaken her. She firmed her lips to stem the tears. It had been a long night, and promised to be an even longer day. But with the sun shining down as it was, it could have been an early day in spring instead of mid-December in the Rockies.

Angelo was holding his own, as Dr. Brookston had said earlier. He'd awakened only once and hadn't spoken yet, and was bruised in more places than not. She wouldn't have thought a boy that slight of build could take such a beating and live. Not for the first time, Angelo Giordano's tenacity had surprised her. And Dr. Brookston's skill continued to impress her. He'd insisted she get some rest during the night, and she was glad now that she had.

James and Deputy Willis joined them on the boardwalk, still discussing the outcome of the meeting with Davenport and Rudger. She was so proud of how James had handled the situation. Timber Ridge was fortunate to have him as sheriff. What LuEllen Spivey had said to her the evening before returned, and though she knew Mrs. Spivey had a spiteful side, she also knew that what the woman had said held bits and pieces of truth.

More than bits and pieces . . .

Molly caught James staring at little Callie, and his blue eyes mirrored the same longing she felt. Oh, how she wished things were different.

Deputy Willis fingered his daughter's bonnet. "Anybody up for breakfast? Miss Clara's open on Saturday mornings now."

They all laughed, but Molly saw James look in her direction. She gave a half shrug, thinking of the packing she had to do. But she was also famished, and not overly tired—yet. She nodded. "Then, maybe we can stop by Dr. Brookston's and check on Angelo?"

James smiled. "My thoughts exactly."

Miss Clara's was busy, but it didn't take long to get their food, and the more Molly ate, the more renewed she felt. Or perhaps it was the two cups of Miss Clara's stout coffee. Mary held Callie, and Molly reached over and brushed a finger against the silk of the little girl's cheek.

"Callie's extra special to us." Deputy Willis tucked his napkin beside his plate. "I'm not sure if Mary told you, ma'am, but we lost our first baby, a son, when Mary was right at seven months along—"

"Dean!" Mary threw him a look, her cheeks growing pink.

Molly's heart skipped a beat, but she forced a weak smile. Mary had lost a baby in her seventh month of pregnancy?

Deputy Willis sighed. "I-I'm sorry, ma'am. I didn't—" He shook his head. "I flat out wasn't thinking."

"No," Molly whispered. "That's all right, really." *Her seventh month?* "I . . . deeply sorry for your loss." That was so far along to lose a child, and similar to where she was in her own pregnancy.

Their parting with the couple moments later on the boardwalk was subdued and slightly awkward, but Molly held no ill will toward the deputy. He'd meant nothing by what he'd said, and she told herself it had no bearing on her situation.

She and James arrived at the clinic to find that Angelo hadn't awakened again. Dr. Brookston assured her that was best for now, to give the boy's body time to heal, and insisted she go on home. Molly retrieved the still-unopened gift Lori Beth had given her from the back room and met James outside.

She accepted his help onto the horse, riding sidesaddle, then leaned forward as he swung up behind her. The gentle plod of Winsome's unhurried gait and the warmth of the sun lulled her into shutting her eyes. When she opened them again, she saw the turnoff to her cabin. *Her* cabin. That wouldn't hold true much longer.

James paused. "We don't have the sleigh, but it sure is a pretty day for a ride. If you're up to it."

His hopeful tone was persuasive, as was thinking of the packing that awaited her if she went home. "A ride sounds nice."

He guided Winsome around the cabin and up a trail Molly had walked twice before, only she'd never gone past the large boulder where the path forked. The trail to the left looked as though it continued on around the ridge. The other way, more narrow and twisting, led higher into the mountains. James nudged the mare to the right.

The incline grew steep, and Molly leaned back

into him. His arms came around her and her unborn child, and she smiled, wondering if this closeness had figured into his choice of trail. A spasm tightened across her midsection, and she squeezed her eyes shut. It took every ounce of concentration to breathe normally until the discomfort passed. Finally, she exhaled deep. This was the strongest one so far. Dr. Brookston had told her she'd have mild contractions on occasion, but what had he meant by mild?

James leaned to one side. "Are you all right?"

She nodded. "I'm fine. I just think the baby's telling me we need some rest."

"We won't be long."

"No, no . . . I'm enjoying this." And she was, but another pain like that one and she would ask him to take her back.

The trail gradually leveled again and James reined in. They sat in silence for the longest time, staring out over the world below, and the world beyond. Wave after wave of mountain ranges rose majestic white against the cobalt sky, stacked one behind the other for as far as Molly could see. Ethereal beauty . . . The air was cooler up here than down in the valley, and she appreciated the warmth from both James and Winsome.

"There's something I need to speak to you about, Molly."

She closed her eyes, not having forgotten about this, and guessing what was coming. "James, perhaps . . . with everything else that's happened, it might be best to wait until later."

His arms tightened around her. "I don't think so. I think you need to know this . . . now."

She stole a glance behind her. His expression was noticeably more serious than before, as was his tone. "All right," she whispered, facing forward again, wondering if she'd guessed wrong.

"Molly, you and I have spoken about our homes, and our families . . . what it was like growing up. Your parents . . . your father and mother," he added quickly, as though needing to clarify the term *parents*. "They sound like they were fine people. Yours was a proper heritage, your family name well honored, well thought of."

She didn't follow what he was saying, but he seemed so intent on finding the right words, she kept silent, not wanting to make this any harder for him. At the same time, her imagination darted in all directions, coming back empty as to what he might say next.

He exhaled. "I'm not doing a very good job of this, am I?"

"I think you're doing fine." She turned so he could see her smile. "Of course, I have no idea what you're trying to tell me."

He touched the side of her face, then drew his hand away. "What I'm trying to tell you is this. . . . My family—the family I described to you before—

was my family. At least . . . it was how I saw it until I got older. Until I learned the truth."

She would have sworn from his tone that he'd winced.

"My father was a physician, as you already know. I was never close to him growing up, but didn't understand why until later in life."

Unhindered silence filled the passing seconds, and Molly settled her gaze on a mountain peak far in the distance. And waited.

"The reason I'm telling you all this is because"—his breath came out part laugh, part sigh—"is because I care for you . . . so much." His hand inched forward until it rested on the swell of her belly. "I care for you both," he whispered in her ear, his face closer now.

Molly closed her eyes and covered his hand.

"It hurt when you told me about the baby." His breath was warm against her cheek. "When I realized you'd lied to me, to us. But that's behind us now," he whispered. "I understand what it's like to be afraid that something will change people's opinions of you—if they knew the truth."

Never had she so wanted to know what someone would say next. She could scarcely hear over the pounding in her chest.

"When my father was on his deathbed, he told me the truth . . . about something he'd done." His voice went cold and hard. "My father was an excellent physician, but he was not a moral man.

He had . . . *relationships* with women outside of his and my mother's marriage. A woman he'd had an affair with . . . she came to be with child."

A sickening premonition welled up inside her, and Molly swallowed. She stared at his hand beneath hers. It began to tremble.

"That woman . . . she died giving birth to a son. When my father—" His voice caught. He cleared his throat. "When he brought the boy home," he said, his deep voice gravelly, "he gave him to my mother and told her that one of his patients had died that day, that the woman had no family and had left the boy orphaned. My mother, God bless her soul, had lost her first child to a stillbirth . . . only weeks earlier."

Tears choked Molly's throat. She squeezed his hand. "You . . ." she whispered, "were that baby."

He didn't answer for the longest time. "My mother didn't learn the truth until a year after he brought me home." He sniffed. "She said that by then it didn't matter where I'd come from—or from whom—that I was already hers."

Molly suppressed a sob. So that was it . . . the pain responsible for this man's discerning spirit. As what he'd told her became clearer, so did the reason he was telling her. He felt obliged that she be told of the inferiority of his birth. Of his lack of heritage in comparison to hers. Ever the Southern gentleman, no matter where the gentleman was.

The irony of the situation struck a dull and dissonant chord inside her. Sensing he was awaiting her response, she looked back, careful with what she said. Because she knew he would remember this once she told him *who* she really was. "You are the finest man I've ever known, James McPherson. Nothing you've told me changes that. Or ever will."

He kissed her, but it was different this time. There was a sweet shyness in the way he held her, in the way his mouth moved over hers, as though he wanted to drink her in, yet was reluctant to, wanting to savor it. Savor her. Just as she was him.

The ride down the mountain was quiet, and Molly felt a silent clock ticking inside her, the pendulum slicing off the seconds.

All his life, James had tried to forget who had given him birth. And since Molly had been in Timber Ridge, she'd been trying to forget who she was, and what she'd done. Two people on such diverse, yet similar, converging paths. But no matter what good she'd done since moving to Timber Ridge, no matter what lessons she'd learned or how much she regretted her choice, in James's eyes, once he knew, she would always be . . . *that woman.*

41

Back at the cabin, Molly held on to James's shoulders as he eased her down off the horse. She tried to quiet the question inside her, but it wouldn't be stifled. "Did you ever learn who she was? The woman who gave birth to you?"

James didn't meet her eyes. "No. I never had any desire to know who she was. Not after knowing *what* she was . . . and what she'd done."

Seeing the hardness in his expression, the lingering hurt, and this after so many years, she wished now that she hadn't asked the question. "Thank you . . . for the ride this afternoon. And for telling me." He'd been right. She had needed to know this about him, only not for the reasons he thought.

A wave of fatigue hit her, as did another spasm. Only not as hard as before, and it didn't last as long. Perhaps she shouldn't have taken that ride after all. Her back was aching and breakfast wasn't sitting too well. James walked her to the door, and she slipped the key from her pocket into the lock, eager to get to bed.

"You get some rest." He held out his arm and assisted her into the cabin. "I'll do the same and be back later this afternoon, to help you pack."

"And we'll go see Angelo?" she asked, already knowing the answer.

"You bet." He kissed the top of her head. "Sleep well, Molly."

Sunlight streamed in through the windows of the cabin, such an unusual day for winter. But she welcomed the warmth. After slipping into her gown, she used the chamber pot, then crawled beneath the covers. Another pain hit as she lay down, and she gripped the mattress until it passed. If this is what Dr. Brookston meant by mild, she had a new respect for women who'd borne numerous children, and a deeper dread of what giving birth would be like.

She felt the urge to use the chamber pot again and sighed. This was happening more often these days—this dire urge to relieve herself only to have so little a reward once she got there. She pushed back the covers and stood, and felt a warm gush flow down between her legs.

Startled, she stared, disbelieving.

She tried to stop it. And couldn't. She lifted her gown. It kept coming. *Oh, God . . .* She tried to get to the chamber pot, but a cramp doubled her over. Followed by another. And another. Fighting to get her breath, she grabbed the footboard of the bed to steady herself. Her legs shook uncontrollably.

She needed to lie down. But didn't have the strength to get back to the bed.

She sank down to the floor as another contraction hit. She cried out, cradling her abdomen. This shouldn't be happening. Not yet. It was too soon.

"We lost our first baby, a son, when Mary was right at seven months along. . . ."

Molly tried to block out the words, but what Deputy Willis had said played again and again in her mind. She had to get to Dr. Brookston's. She struggled to her feet and held on to the doorframe before managing a few more steps. Another pain hit, and she gripped the back of a kitchen chair, but it toppled beneath her weight. She went down and her knees made a dull crack on the wooden floor.

"Oh . . . God . . ." She curled onto her side and stared through the window at a snow-covered peak set against a patch of blue sky. She shivered, her gown wet and cold around her legs. "Help me, Lord . . . please." *Don't let my baby die. Please, don't let my baby die.*

The room started to spin seconds before everything went dark.

James stopped by his office on the way home, more from habit than anything else, and when he dismounted, he noticed a red ribbon peeking out from one of his saddlebags. Then he remembered. . . . He'd tucked Molly's reticule and sack inside.

He'd seen Miss Matthews give the cloth bag to Molly last night, then had overheard Molly asking the woman to tea the following week, as had a few other people. He'd toyed with saying something to Molly earlier but had decided to leave it alone, for now.

Molly had a tender heart, and she probably felt sorry for Lori Beth Matthews. Being mindful of those less fortunate was an admirable character trait, and something he cherished about Molly. But it was a fine line to walk, and she also needed to be mindful of her own reputation. Especially if she was going to be the sheriff's wife, which was looking more promising every day. A smile worked at the corners of his mouth.

He tucked the ribbon inside. He'd give Molly her things when he saw her later. He walked into the office, hat in hand, and Deputy Stanton looked up from his desk.

"Hey, Sheriff, I was just penning you a note. Brookston sent word that the boy woke up. Says he's asking for you and Mrs. Whitcomb. Doc said for y'all to come as soon as you could."

James was nearly to Brookston's office when he thought of having to tell Molly he'd visited Angelo without her. She wouldn't be pleased. Knowing better than to purposely rile the woman, he gave Winsome a good prod, and the mare took off down the road as if already knowing where to go.

James made it to Molly's in no time flat, out of breath from the hard ride. Winsome snorted, and James smoothed a hand down her forehead. "That felt good, girl."

He grabbed Molly's reticule and the ribboned sack from the saddlebag and knocked on the door. And waited. Chances were good she was already asleep. She'd looked a little tired. He felt a pinch of guilt for keeping her out when she needed to rest, but he'd needed to talk to her and was glad now that he had. He pictured her face again, after he'd told her. He'd seen it in her eyes. She didn't fault him for his inferior birth, or for his lack of honor in that regard. To say he was grateful was an understatement.

He knocked a second time. "Molly? You still up?"

Then he heard something. A moan? He tried the door. It was locked.

"Molly! Are you in there?"

He walked around to the side of the cabin and peered through a window—and his heart wrenched tight. She was curled up on the floor, holding her stomach, a kitchen chair overturned by her head. "Molly!" He banged on the window. She didn't acknowledge him.

He dropped the reticule and sack and ran back to the porch. He tried shouldering the door open, but it wouldn't budge. He gave it a hard kick. The wood splintered but held. He backed up and came at it again, putting his full weight behind his right shoulder, and the door flew open.

He raced in and knelt beside her. He brushed strands of hair from her face. "Molly, can you hear me?" She was pale, her skin cold and clammy.

She looked up at him, her eyes glazed over.

"Molly, what happened? Did you fall?"

She blinked, then cradled her belly, moaning. "It's . . . too soon."

He saw her wet gown clinging to her thighs and emotion choked him. *The baby* . . . Her face blurred in his vision. "I've got to get you into town." He grabbed a blanket from the bedroom and wrapped it around her. There wasn't time to ride for Brookston and he couldn't leave her here alone.

Her whole body shook. "It hurts. . . ."

"I know it does, and I'm sorry." He lifted her in his arms and she cried out. "I wish there was another way."

Her arms came around his neck and she squeezed tight, groaning. With effort, he got her onto the horse, but the ride into town was excruciatingly slow. In between pains, she panted for breath and cried.

"James . . ."

"I'm here, Molly. I'm right here. Just hold on." Five more minutes and they'd be to Brookston's.

"I don't want to die," she said in a rush, sobbing.

Tears he'd been fighting slipped past his defenses. "Y-you're not going to die."

"But you don't know. . . ."

He cradled her head against his chest, wishing he did know for sure. "Shhh," he whispered. "It's going to be all right." *God, please let it be all right.*

"I'm so sorry," she whispered, crying harder.

He scoffed. "You've got nothing to be sorry for.

I'm the one who's sorry. I had no business asking you to go for a ride today when—"

"No . . ." She shook her head. "You don't understand. James, I . . . I need you . . . to listen. I'm sorry for not—" A strangled noise rose from her throat and she bent forward, hugging herself tight.

James urged Winsome to a faster pace, feeling so helpless. If he could take her pain away, he would. He'd take it upon himself. *God, don't let her die. You can't let her die.*

A long minute passed, and Molly finally leaned back again, her breath uneven, her body limp against him. "I'm *her*, James," she whispered, moaning and rubbing the side of her belly. "I'm *that woman.*" She started crying again, and her words slurred.

He couldn't make sense of what she said. He saw Brookston's clinic ahead. "Molly, we're almost there. Just hold on."

She gripped the material of his pants and fisted it tight. Her body went rigid. *"Oh, dear God . . ."*

The boardwalk was dotted with Saturday shoppers, mostly women, some of whom were looking their way. James spotted Arlin Spivey in the crowd. "Spivey!"

The man turned, searching. Then headed for them at a full run.

James reined in at the clinic and, with Spivey's help, lowered Molly from the horse.

Her arms came around him in a vise grip, her face twisted in pain.

Spivey ran ahead and opened the door. "Doc!" he yelled inside, then turned back. "It's not her time yet, is it, Sheriff?"

James shook his head, careful as he stepped up to the boardwalk. "But the baby's coming." He looked down. Molly was still conscious. "It's going to be okay," he whispered, praying it would be.

Brookston appeared in the doorway. Concern darkened his features. "How long has she been like this?"

"I don't exactly know." James watched her head as he crossed the threshold.

Brookston motioned him to the back room.

James followed. "I left her cabin maybe an hour ago. Came into town, then rode back out to get her once I got your message about the boy. It's been ten minutes . . . maybe fifteen, since I found her. I had to take it slow coming into town."

Spivey came alongside him. "LuEllen's next door, Sheriff. I'll get her to come help, if you want."

James nodded and saw Angelo watching from the patient table, his dark eyes wide. "Would you ride for Rachel too, Spivey? Check the store first, then head out to the ranch. And tell her to hurry!"

"Good as done, Sheriff."

Brookston yanked the blankets from the bed, leaving only the sheet. "When you found her, was she conscious?"

"Don't take my baby," Molly whispered. *"Please . . . don't take my baby."*

But James got the feeling she wasn't talking to either of them. He gently laid her on the bed. "Yes, she was conscious, but barely."

She grabbed hold of his shirt. "Don't leave me!"

He leaned close. "Molly, I'm not leaving you, honey. I'm here, and I'm staying."

"But you don't know yet. And when you do—" She shook her head.

James cupped the side of her face, then looked at Brookston, who was standing at a table in the corner. "She's out of her mind with pain. Can't you give her something?"

"I'm already working on it." Brookston turned, syringe in hand. "Molly—" He bent close and indicated for James to hold her arm. "I need to examine you to ascertain your condition and that of your baby." He slipped the syringe into her arm, his voice calm and reassuring. "This is going to make you a little woozy, but I need you awake, at least for a little while. So you can answer some questions, all right?"

Molly nodded, her eyes stark with fear.

"And . . . though you've never asked . . ." He smiled, laying the syringe aside. "Babies are my specialty."

Molly's eyes watered again, and James found his doing the same.

"Now—" Brookston pulled the stethoscope from

around his neck. "Take some deep breaths for me. Nice and slow." He listened to her heart, then moved to her belly.

James looked down to where Molly gripped his shirtsleeve. He carefully pried her fingers loose and tucked her hand inside his. She looked up at him, and despite the comfort he tried to give, the fear in her expression wouldn't leave.

After a couple of minutes, her eyes fluttered, then closed.

"Can you hear me, Molly?" Brookston asked.

"Yes," she whispered.

"Do you still hurt?"

"Yes, but . . . not as bad as before."

"Good." Brookston sighed.

James gestured. "What was that you gave her?"

"Morphine. But only a little. Just enough to take the edge off the pain. It won't last long."

"I can still hear you both."

James smiled at the smartness in her tone. "Well, we'll have to really start talking about you then. Make up some good gossip." His smile died as tears slid down her temples.

She looked up at him. "I need to talk to you, James. I need to . . . tell you something."

James searched her eyes, wondering if this was the medicine talking, or if it really was her. The clarity in her expression answered his question, and he would've sworn he'd lived this moment with Molly before. And he hadn't liked it the first time.

Brookston straightened. "I'll get what I need from my storeroom. But I won't be long."

James pulled a chair from the corner over to the bedside, knowing Brookston was giving them privacy. "Molly, I don't—"

"No, James. Please, just listen." She took hold of his hand. "If I don't do this now—" She clenched her teeth and tightened her grip.

"Squeeze as hard as you need to," he said softly, praying her pain would pass.

Seconds ticked by, and she relaxed again. Her head sank farther into the pillow. "Then I may not get another chance to tell you."

He waited. Footsteps sounded in the outer office. They didn't have much time.

She took a deep breath and held it, then exhaled. "I am not a widow, James. And I have never been married."

James stared, feeling everything slowing around him. He'd heard what she'd said, he saw her say it, but somewhere in between the time when the words left her mouth and when they fell on his ear, they jumbled out of order and made no sense. And yet they did make sense. And yet they couldn't. Because he knew, all this time, *he knew*, she'd been married. She'd told him that. She'd worn a ring. She was a widow. A pregnant wid—

He spurned the thought forming in his mind.

"There's no excuse for what I've done, James. I had my reasons, but they were wrong. They were all

wrong. *I* was wrong. I convinced myself that—"
She inhaled quickly and, grimacing, pressed a hand to her abdomen. Gradually, her features smoothed. "I convinced myself that I was the only one who would pay the price for what I'd done. But as time went on, I realized that wasn't the case.

"I planned on telling you everything . . . the night of the sleigh ride. But aft—" Her voice broke as tears renewed. "But after I told you about the baby that night, I was too afraid that you would—" She shook her head. "That you would look at me . . . like you're looking at me now."

He tried, but he couldn't turn away. It felt as if someone had just told him that up was down, and down was up. He simply couldn't get what she'd said to make sense in his head. At the same time, every doubt he'd had about her returned. He'd known something wasn't right. He'd sensed it. But he'd put those doubts aside because he loved Molly Whitcomb with everything in him.

But right now, he felt as though he were looking at a stranger.

She squeezed his hand, and only then did he realize that his grip on hers had gone slack.

She slowly drew her hand away. "I came to be with child outside of wedlock, and I deserve to pay for that mistake. I have, and will, again. But you . . . you didn't do anything wrong, James. And yet my mistake—my sin—is costing you dearly. And I'm so, so very sorry."

James felt a wetness on his cheeks and wiped it away.

"Please," she whispered. "Say something."

He swallowed, doubting he could speak past the knot in his throat. He heard a creaking behind him and turned.

LuEllen Spivey stood in the doorway. Her gaze locked on Molly before slowly moving to him. "I've come to help, Sheriff. In any way I can."

Molly looked into LuEllen Spivey's eyes and felt the blood drain from her own face.

James rose and walked to the door. "Mrs. Spivey, I'd be obliged if you'd wait in the front area." He closed the door before the woman could respond, then held on to the metal latch. When he turned back, Molly couldn't bring herself to look directly at him.

He sat down beside her again, leaned forward, elbows on his knees, and put his face in his hands. "'I'm *her*,'" he whispered, his voice muffled. "'I'm *that woman*.' That's what you meant earlier."

"Yes."

He looked up at her, and his blue eyes were vacant and hollow. "I thought it was the pain talking."

Oh, how she wished . . .

She tried to think of something else to say that would make a difference, but there was nothing. She'd known that all along. That was why she'd put off her confession for as long as she had. Her body felt as if she'd been running for days and days without stopping, and she only wanted to sleep. But the low, steady drum of pain was returning, and she cringed, knowing she didn't have the strength to do this.

She tried to keep her voice steady. "Is Rachel coming?"

"Yes," he whispered, his own voice sounding weak and broken. "She should be on her way."

"Thank you, James." She summoned every ounce of courage. "You don't have to stay, if—"

Pain unlike anything she'd imagined ripped through her body and twisted her insides until she couldn't hold back the scream any longer. How could something so tiny inside her cause so much pain? She was sucked down into a dark hole, and no matter what she did, she couldn't claw her way out. She couldn't breathe. She couldn't speak. Her head pounded with every beat of her heart, and she begged for the pain to stop.

After an eternity, the wave that dragged her down thrust her back to the surface again, and the pain she thought unbearable only grew more so. She tried to open her eyes but couldn't. She heard voices, then felt a sharp prick in her arm.

"I have no choice, Sheriff. I can't stop her labor. Her body is trying to deliver the child. At the same time, it's refusing to allow the child to come."

"What are the chances that this will work?"

James . . .

"I'm sorry, James," she tried to say aloud, not knowing if her voice could be heard or if it was only in her head. *"Please forgive me. . . ."*

Warmth spread through her arms and legs, and her body began to relax. The voices became fluid, drifting close, then moving away again. A spasm tightened her belly, reminding her that pain crouched nearby, waiting.

"Dr. Brookston—she's pushing!"

At the split instant Molly recognized Rachel's voice, she also realized that what Rachel had said was true. She was obeying her body's directive to bear down hard and deliver her child.

"Molly, if you can hear me, *don't push!*"

She heard Dr. Brookston's voice but couldn't make her body stop. She bore down harder, tasting a copper tinge in her mouth.

A flurry of voices and noises. Someone took hold of her hand and pressed close against her on the bed.

"Molly, you *must* listen to me. I know what you're feeling right now. I know the sensation to push is overwhelming. You're hurting and you want the pain to stop. But if you keep pushing, your baby will die."

Rachel's words acted like a knife, severing mind from body, and Molly reached deep inside her for the will to refuse her body's command. *Oh . . . it hurts. . . .*

"That's very good, Molly. You're doing well."

Molly tried to speak, but the words caught in her parched throat. She swallowed and tried again. "Promise . . . me." She squeezed Rachel's hand and felt Rachel's response. "If I die . . . and my baby—"

"Molly, nothing's going to happen to you. So don't—"

Molly shook her head. "Please . . ." She felt a cloth come over her mouth and nose. But she pushed it away.

"Molly, I need to deliver your child." Brookston's voice was insistent. "We don't have much time."

"Rachel," Molly pleaded, fighting to maintain hold on the invisible tether that kept her from slipping back under.

"Yes," Rachel whispered into her ear. "I will, Molly. I promise. I will."

42

O ne more suture should do it."
Molly felt a sting on her tummy, followed by a sharp tug, but it was nothing compared to the pain from before—which was blissfully gone. She told her eyes to open, and they did. Partially. She blinked against the unaccustomed light.

"Molly . . . are you back with us?" Rachel appeared above, looking more like an angel than a rancher.

Molly nodded slowly, able to see Dr. Brookston in her peripheral view. She licked her parched lips, still experiencing a little of the floating sensation.

"Here—" Rachel reached for something. "You can have some water to drink now."

"Only in small increments, please, Mrs. Boyd."

"Thank you, Dr. Brookston. I'm aware of that."

Rachel lifted Molly's head and held the cup as Molly drank in tiny sips. Molly didn't think she imagined the subtle shake of Rachel's head.

Then she noticed it—the absence. The void. Her womb was empty.

Her pulse raced. She looked to the side. "My baby. Where's my baby?"

"Shhhh . . ." Rachel smiled. "If you're not careful, you'll wake her."

Her? Molly gave a soft gasp. "I had a girl?"

"A very little girl." Dr. Brookston moved closer as Rachel turned away. "But she's healthy, for being so early."

"So . . . there's nothing wrong with her? She's going to be all right?" Molly whispered.

Dr. Brookston cradled the side of her head as her father used to. "I'm going to do my best to make sure of that. But she's going to need special care for a good while, and so are you. Along with a lot of rest. Since your baby came so early, your body wasn't prepared to deliver the child. I made an incision on your abdomen and removed the baby from your womb. Your sutures will be tender for quite a while but should heal well."

Rachel moved back into view, and as soon as Molly saw the tiny bundle in her arms, she felt the tears coming again.

Rachel leaned close. "I'm a little jealous," she said, smiling as she placed the baby in Molly's arms. "I always wanted a little girl."

Molly cradled her daughter close and edged back the blanket, not sure what to expect. Though smaller than any baby Molly had ever seen, her daughter was more beautiful than she'd imagined. "She's perfect," she whispered.

"Isn't she?" Rachel pointed. "Ten fingers and ten toes. We've already counted. Twice! Have you chosen a name yet?"

"Yes," Molly said. "Josephine, a character from my favorite book."

Rachel's eyes lit. "Will you call her Jo, for short? Like in the story?"

Molly smiled. "Perhaps." She touched her daughter's delicate fist. "She's so tiny. And a little wrinkled."

They all laughed, and in the quiet that followed, the events that had led up to the birth caught up with the present. Molly looked at Rachel. "Do you know?"

Rachel held her smile, to her credit. But her eyes dimmed. "Yes. James told me."

One look at Dr. Brookston said he knew too.

"I know my apology makes entirely no difference now, and comes far too late. But please know how sorry I am that I made the choice to lie . . . to all of you." Molly looked into her daughter's precious face and saw, instead, the face of a newborn son. And James's noticeable absence became even more so.

"I won't presume to know what your plans are, Molly," Dr. Brookston said gently. "But it will be at least six weeks, maybe a little longer, before I'd advise travel of any kind for you or your daughter."

Molly understood what he was saying, and a while later, as she lay in bed, holding her sleeping daughter, she watched the daylight fade to evening and take with it any hope of leaving Timber Ridge before people discovered the truth. She could almost feel the rumor spreading across town even now. LuEllen Spivey was seeing to that, no doubt.

Molly shifted in the bed, careful of the sutures. Dr. Brookston had brought dinner from Miss Clara's for himself, her, and Angelo, who had somehow survived the earlier excitement in the clinic and who was already asleep in the other room. Molly could hear Dr. Brookston's quiet movements down the hall and saw the pale yellow light of his oil lamp. Rachel had left to pick up her boys from Ben and Lyda's and was likely home by now. With James. Who hadn't stopped by at all. Not that she'd expected him to. But she had hoped.

She had foolishly hoped.

Late afternoon the following day, Molly stirred from her sleep when she heard the telling creak of the clinic door. The doctor was out visiting other patients.

"Dr. Brookston isn't in right now," she called, keeping her voice soft so as not to awaken Angelo or Josephine.

Soft boot steps sounded on the wood plank floor and James walked around the corner, a hesitant look on his face. "Are you up for a visitor?" he asked softly.

She was so pleased, and surprised. "Yes, of course. Come in." Only then did she think about how she must look, and she leaned on her side and ran her fingers through her hair, trying to make an improvement. Then finally gave up. "Please, have a seat." She pointed to the chair in the corner.

He chose to remain standing. He had a wrapped package in one hand, and her reticule and the sack Lori Beth had given her in the other. "I started to come by last night, but . . ."

The awkwardness of the moment stretched on.

"That's all right, James. You don't need to offer an explanation."

He stared at her, and she saw the pain in his eyes, the disappointment, and felt a fresh wave of regret. He looked around the room, and she realized what—or whom—he was looking for.

"Would you like to see her?"

"Very much." He stepped closer and held out the package. "This is a little something for her."

"Thank you." Molly took the gift and laid it by her side on the bed.

He deposited her reticule and the sack on a table by the door. Molly painfully leaned down to the makeshift cradle—a shallow drawer from Dr. Brookston's chifforobe, lined with a blanket—and pulled back the cover to show him her sleeping daughter.

James took a step closer, a slow smile turning his mouth. "Oh . . . she's beautiful, Molly. Just beautiful." He looked up. "Can I touch her?"

She nodded, trying not to cry. "Of course."

He knelt down and stroked her daughter's cheek, his large hand making the baby seem even smaller. "Rachel said you named her Josephine."

"That's right."

"That's a real pretty name." A shy smile crept over his face. "I read the book," he said softly, his voice tender with admission.

It took Molly a second to make sense of that. "You read *Little Women*?"

He nodded. "But don't tell anybody." The gentle lines around his mouth and eyes crinkled when he smiled. "I saw it on your desk that first day. Then later Billy told me it was your favorite." He gave a slight shrug, looking more like a boy himself than a man. "It just seemed right to read it." The tip of his index finger dwarfed her baby's hand. "I liked Josephine March. She reminded me of you."

Molly couldn't have spoken right then for the world. That he would have done that . . . for her. She stared up at him, realizing how much she'd thrown away.

He cleared his throat and rose to his full height. "Rachel told me about what Brookston did during the delivery. That sounds like it was really something."

"Yes, I guess it was. I'm grateful for his skill."

"So am I," he whispered.

He held her gaze for the longest time, and Molly sensed a question coming. Not one spur of the moment, but one he'd been considering.

"Did you leave Franklin College of your own accord?"

She trembled at the look in his eyes and slowly shook her head, hoping her voice would hold. "When President Northrop found out about my . . . *indiscretion*," she said softly, "he 'strongly encouraged' me to resign. I was . . . reluctant, at first, especially knowing that the father of my child wasn't being given the same ultimatum."

James frowned. "He was a teacher there too?"

She nodded.

"And they allowed him to stay?"

She nodded again, tempted to tell him about Jeremy marrying, about the donation to the college, about everything. Yet she knew that, in the end, it didn't matter. Because it wouldn't change the decision she'd made that one night. "It was only after President Northrop told me what he intended to do if I *didn't* resign . . . that I realized I had no choice."

James stared, his expression unreadable, his silence asking the unvoiced question.

"My father dedicated his life to teaching at that college." Molly closed her eyes and pictured her father standing before her, proud and tall, her diploma in his hand. Tears slid down her temples into her hair. "Before he died . . . they named a scholarship after him, as well as a new building. He was so honored, and humbled," she whispered, her voice shaking. She firmed her lips, the weight in her chest making it difficult to breathe. "If I didn't agree to resign and come here, President Northrop told me"—she remembered his exact words—"that he would strip my father's memory from every brick, from every piece of paper, and that he would do everything he could to make it as if my father had never been there."

She choked back her emotions, determined to hold herself together.

For the longest time, James said nothing. Then he reached down and took hold of her hand. "I'm so sorry, Molly," he whispered.

She didn't know which was worse—the gentleness of his touch and knowing she'd never feel it again, or the pitying look of compassion she'd seen from him before, when he looked at Lori Beth.

The silence lengthened, and everything she thought of to say didn't fit the moment. When she was certain she couldn't take one more second, James took a step back, and let go of her hand.

"Well, I'd better go. Let you get some rest. I know you must be tired."

Hearing what he wasn't saying, perhaps what his decency wouldn't allow him to say, she nodded. "Yes, that would probably be best."

He didn't move. "We packed you up this morning. Josiah, Elijah, Ben, and me. The boys helped too. Kurt packed your bug board real well. So no need to worry about that."

She hiccupped a laugh, and another traitorous tear slipped past her defenses. "Thank you . . . for doing that."

"Ben's storing your trunks in his back room until you're ready to move into the hotel."

Her throat a vise, she smiled. "Please give them all my thanks." She'd never known civility could be so agonizing. "Thank you for coming by."

He walked to the door and turned back. "Maybe we can talk again, in a few days. If you're feeling up to it."

Not trusting her voice, she simply nodded again, praying he would leave before she broke down. But instead of leaving, he walked back to her and kissed the crown of her head. When he pulled away, she saw tears in his eyes.

And when she heard the clinic door close behind him, she sank back on the pillow and wept.

James swung the axe high and brought it down with such force the log severed clean in the middle and joined its predecessors in the heap of kindling and shards of bark littering the snow. The burnished glow from the lantern hanging on the barn cast a dingy halo in the dark, and James's breath came heavy.

"I'm sorry, James. Please . . . forgive me."

Every waking hour the memory of Molly's whispered voice cried softly inside him, over and over, just as she'd done as Brookston had prepared for her baby's birth. He forgave her. That wasn't a question. But forgiveness didn't mean things could just be put back the way they were. He scoffed in the darkness. Especially when things hadn't been right to begin with.

The crunch of footfalls sounded as he reached for another log.

"I'm still keeping your dinner warm, James. And the boys are already in bed."

"Thanks, Rachel. I'll be in later." He placed the log on the tree stump and gripped the axe.

"You said that over two hours ago. It's dark now. You need to come in and eat."

He clenched his jaw as he brought the axe down. The log separated and went flying. He exhaled, the air puffing white from his lungs. "I said I'd be in directly. I want to get this finished."

This time the axe sank deep into the stump, and it took three tries to get it out. His shoulders burned from overexertion and his chest muscles ached from the cold. But he welcomed it compared to the pain inside.

"Come inside, James. You've chopped enough wood for two winters."

He kept working.

"You're going to make yourself sick if you don't—"

"Not now, Rachel." He laid the axe aside and began stacking the wood against the barn, waiting to hear her retreating footsteps . . . that didn't come.

"I saw her today." Rachel's voice was quiet—and cut like a knife. "Jo too."

The ache inside him that he'd managed to dull over the past two hours rose again to a steady thrum.

"She's still at the clinic. She'll be there for a while, she said. At least until—"

"Rachel!" He turned, another load in his arms. "Please . . . don't do this."

"I'm just trying to tell you how she's—"

He threw the logs down. "No you're not. You're not just trying to tell me how she's doing. You're trying to fix things, like you always try to do. But this isn't something you can fix." He put his back into the work until his muscles screamed—anything to avoid seeing the hurt on his sister's face.

"I know what's going on inside you, James. I know you better than you think I do."

He swallowed, hearing the determination in her tone, and reached for patience beyond what he possessed. "You think you know me." His throat tightened, making it difficult to get the words out. "But you don't."

He went back to chopping wood, hoping she would give up. She didn't speak for the longest time, and he thought she'd gone. But when he looked back, she still stood there, staring at him.

He sank the axe into the stump, grabbed the lantern, and strode past her into the barn. But when he walked inside and saw the sleigh, he stopped cold. All this time, he'd *known* there was something Molly wasn't telling him. But he never, ever would have guessed the secret she hid from him— from the whole town.

The soft crunch of Rachel's boots on the hay told him she wasn't giving up easily.

"You told Kurt not long ago that no matter what he did, you would still love him. And that he couldn't do anything to change that."

Lantern in hand, James turned back. "And I meant every word of that." Rachel loved Molly— he knew that. But he also knew that Rachel needed to understand why this was especially hard for him to accept.

For years he'd told himself he hadn't shared his secret with her because he didn't want to burden her with the truth. But the truth was, he didn't want her knowing because he feared it would change the way she looked at him. He'd worked so hard, ever since his father had bequeathed his *legacy*, to be a man people respected. And not just respected, but a man who stood for what was right and who upheld it at all costs.

"Rachel, there are things you don't know about our family. About me. About our father." He took a breath. "When I was born, I—"

"I know," Rachel whispered.

He stared. Then a fire, white-hot, shot up inside him. "Molly told you."

A tender smile turned Rachel's mouth, reminding him so much of their mother. "Mama told me before she died."

He bowed his head and closed his eyes. "So . . . all these years . . . you've known."

Her soft sigh drew his gaze. "It doesn't matter where you came from, James. What matters is who you are. What you've made of yourself. What God has made in you. And—" Her smile faded, but the love in her eyes didn't. "Other than Thomas Boyd, you're the finest man I've ever known." She turned to go, then looked back. "Love like yours and Molly's, like mine and Thomas's—" her voice broke—"doesn't come along but every so often. Don't throw it away so easily, James."

He watched her walk back to the house, and all

he could hear was Molly's voice. *"I'm her,"* she'd whispered. *"I'm that woman. . . ."*

"Bring her trunks in here, please, Charlie." Lori Beth gestured. "Right over there beneath the window will be fine."

Molly nodded for Charlie to go on in, then followed with Jo nestled snug against her chest. "Are you sure this isn't going to be an intrusion, Lori Beth?"

"An intrusion?" Lori Beth put her hands on her hips. "Please tell me you're kidding. I couldn't be happier about this, Molly." Lori Beth fingered the white crocheted cap hugging Jo's little head. One of several she'd made in various colors, along with matching booties. The red-ribboned cloth bag had been stuffed full. "She's a doll, Molly. And you're welcome to stay here for as long as you like."

Charlie hefted the last of the trunks into the corner, which barely left enough space to walk. "Lori Beth's been talking of nothin' else for the past two days, Miss Molly. So she's tellin' the truth."

Lori Beth smiled. "See?"

Molly hugged her tight. "Thank you. Thank you both."

Charlie tipped his hat. "I'll be back tomorrow to check on things."

Lori Beth walked him outside while Molly stood and looked around the bedroom. She'd stayed the past three weeks at Dr. Brookston's clinic—largely for Jo's health, Dr. Brookston wanted her close so he could check on her often—and when the time came to move elsewhere, Molly had planned on moving to the hotel. But the agreement she'd had with the proprietor had somehow changed.

The rent was double what he'd quoted her the first time—since he'd learned, along with the rest of Timber Ridge, that she wasn't a widow and had never been married.

Molly hadn't put up an argument.

She'd delivered a face-to-face apology to the town council, reliving all over again the look on James's face as he'd sat, eyes downcast, listening. She'd visited the parents of each of her students. Most of the couples had been solemnly accepting, though a handful hadn't even allowed her entrance into their homes. It wasn't as if she hadn't realized what telling the truth would cost her. She'd had plenty of time to consider the consequences. The cost was exacting. But it still didn't equal the pain James had suffered over her betrayal.

Or did it outweigh the price of ultimate forgiveness for what she'd done.

Christmas had come and gone quietly. Ben and Lyda had invited her and Jo, Dr. Brookston, and Angelo and his family over for dinner. Afterward, the Mullinses had graciously offered her the use of a room above their mercantile, but that would have meant coming and going through the store. And the few times she'd visited the mercantile in past weeks she'd noticed that people hung back from her, and moved away from whatever aisle she was on. Two customers, when seeing her, had set their items down and left the store entirely. But it had been greeting former students and having their mothers gently usher them away—with false smiles and under the guise of being late—that had hurt the most.

No one openly cast stones or harangued her in the streets, but their silence delivered about as equal a blow. And the withdrawal of their acceptance was deafening.

So when Lori Beth had offered a bedroom in her cabin, Molly had gratefully accepted, knowing it was only temporary. As soon as Dr. Brookston gave her and Jo clearance to travel, she would leave Timber Ridge. The thought of leaving renewed the near constant ache in the pit of her stomach. As hard as facing some of the towns-people had been, it didn't compare to the ache she felt when she considered never seeing James again.

Yet the handful of times she had seen him in recent weeks had been heartbreaking. The ever-so-polite conversation, the distance, the reminder of what might have been.

At one time, she'd thought that maintaining a friendship with him would be possible, even if they couldn't mean more to each other. But that had been short-sighted on her part. It was impossible for her to be with him and not want more. She thought she'd glimpsed that same desire in his eyes too—once, when they'd met by chance on the street—which made her even more determined to leave town as soon as possible.

She couldn't allow him to sacrifice his life in Timber Ridge, his reputation, all the good he'd done in this town and would do in the future, for her. Because if she did, she would be destroying the very man she loved. Taking something just because she wanted it, no matter how badly, wasn't love. Being willing to do what was best for the other person—even if it meant sacrificing what she thought was best for herself—was. And her love for James wouldn't allow her to do any less.

A few days later, Charlie drove her and Lori Beth out to Little Italy. Molly had heard about the progress that had been made but could scarcely believe her eyes when she saw the rows of clapboard homes standing straight and tall and proud. Gone were the tents and the makeshift lean-tos. Someone had even constructed a seesaw and swing. It was a real community now.

People came out of their homes to greet her, and Mrs. Giordano met them on the street and kissed her cheeks. Angelo had returned home in recent days, his cuts and bruises all but healed. His right arm was out of the sling, and Miss Clara's cooking had put some meat on his bones, as the woman had promised it would.

"Dr. Brookston," Angelo said as they walked. "He teach me about medicine. He say I learn well."

Molly smiled. "You do learn well, Angelo. And you learn quickly. You're a very smart young man."

They stopped by the wagon, where Charlie and Lori Beth were already seated and waiting. "But I would not have this learning. *We* would not have this"—he looked around—"if not for you, and Sheriff McPherson. I am glad God brought you from this Georgia where you were, Dr. Whitcomb." He looked up at Lori Beth, who held Jo bundled in a blanket. "I miss your Jo. But not her crying at night."

Molly laughed and hugged him tight.

On the way back into town, she couldn't help thinking of the good that had been done in Little Italy and in Angelo's life, and this after so much bad. She stared across the fields covered with snow and listened to the rumble of the wagon wheels. The Scripture she'd read the other night was holding true—God really did work *all* things together for good for those who loved Him, and who were called according to His purpose.

His purpose though. Not hers.

Charlie drove through town on the way back to Lori Beth's, and Molly sat wedged beside Lori Beth on the bench seat, Jo having nursed and resting contentedly in her arms. She tried to keep her eyes straight ahead, but occasionally they would wander and she would brush the gaze of someone she knew. Some people looked away quickly, acting as if they hadn't seen her. Others met her gaze and gave a solemn nod. Still others simply stared, then looked away.

"Daggett! Slow up!"

Molly recognized the voice, and her heart leapt to her throat. She turned and saw James riding toward them.

He guided Winsome alongside the wagon, next to her. "Good day to you all."

"Good day, Sheriff." Charlie motioned behind them. "We just been out to Little Italy. I was showing the women what's been done."

James smiled. "It's really coming along. We've got a church to build yet, come spring, but we'll get it done." His gaze fell to Jo. "How's Miss Josephine?"

Molly swallowed before speaking. She seemed to have a perpetual catch in her throat every time she saw him. "She's doing well. Dr. Brookston says he's very pleased with her progress." She made a point of touching the pink blanket James had given her the day following Jo's birth. "Thank you again, for this. It's her favorite."

James smiled, keeping Winsome's pace with the wagon's. "Would you be willing to have dinner with me this weekend . . . Miss Whitcomb?"

The question caught her off guard, as did the way he addressed her, and Molly had trouble responding. A subtle nudge from Lori Beth helped that along. "I . . . um . . ." Molly knew she shouldn't. She needed to say no. But when she looked into his eyes . . . "Yes, I'd . . . like that very much."

"Good." One side of his mouth edged up. "I'll pick you up Saturday night, at seven."

Molly turned to watch him as he rode away.

Molly was ready by five o'clock on Saturday. She stood in front of the mirror, trying to decide whether she should wait until seven, when he arrived, or if she should ride out to Rachel's to tell James what a bad idea their having dinner was.

"Stop fidgeting, Molly. You look stunning."

Molly looked past her reflection in the mirror to see Lori Beth standing in the doorway. She gave a soft laugh. "What am I doing, Lori Beth?"

"You're going to dinner with a man who—telling by the way he looks at you—loves you very much."

That wasn't what Molly needed to hear, but it was exactly what she was thinking. "But that's just it. Nothing can come of this, so why am I acting as if it could? I can't stay here, Lori Beth. I've told you before . . . I'm not as strong as you are."

Lori Beth sat on the edge of the bed, mindful of Jo, who was nestled between pillows, making soft cooing noises. "I remember when you first said that to me—that you thought I was strong." Lori Beth's expression turned thoughtful. "I carried that around inside me for days, turning it over. And I realized that my staying here in Timber Ridge isn't because I'm stronger than you, Molly. I think it's because that, with time, and perspective, I've learned that we all have things we'd rather hide, that we'd prefer to keep locked away. Even from God, if we could. Mostly from Him, I guess." She stroked Jo's cheek. "But when you're made to stand before others, naked, so to speak," she said, her eyes widening, "with all your faults showing, like we have been . . . that changes a person.

"Seeing yourself for who you really are, without your Sunday-go-to-meetin'-clothes on, as Charlie might say . . ." She huffed softly, smiling. "It makes a person more grateful for having been for-given of so much." She stared outside into the fading light, her eyes glistening. "Because once you've seen yourself without Him, you realize you don't ever want to see yourself like that again." She blinked and slowly stood, smoothing her hands over her skirt. A surprisingly perky grin swept her face. "Most people never get the chance to see themselves so clearly. So I guess that makes you and me kind of lucky."

Molly smiled, marveling at the depth of humility in this woman, while also asking God to take the dross in her own life and bring good

594

from it. And to please, *please* shield her daughter from the repercussions of her mother's mistakes.

When James stopped the wagon across the street from Miss Clara's cafe, Molly wanted to grab the reins and head back in the direction from which they'd come. It was Saturday evening and the dining room was full. What was he thinking in bringing her here? And what had she been thinking to accept his invitation in the first place?

He'd been right on time, and conversation on the way had been superficially pleasant, nothing of great importance, and had kept the awkwardness at an almost bearable level.

James helped her down from the wagon and his hands lingered on her waist. She didn't dare look up at him. Her arms suddenly felt so empty without Jo, and an inexplicable longing to hold her daughter came over her, to stare into her pink-skinned face and kiss the reddish blond fuzz of hair crowning her head.

"I thought you might bring Jo along," he said quietly, sounding disappointed. He didn't move away.

"I wish now that I had. I was just thinking of how much I miss her." Molly waited for him to say, "Well, why don't I take you home, then," but he didn't. And she knew Lori Beth and Charlie would be disappointed if she returned too soon.

He offered her his arm, and she slipped her hand

through, not wanting to hurt his feelings, but removed it before he opened the door.

Just as it had the night she'd discovered Lori Beth eating there alone, conversation in the dining room dropped to a simmer and heads turned.

Molly glanced around, careful not to meet anyone's eye, and didn't see an open table. Still embarrassed, though relieved, she started to turn but then saw Miss Clara waving at them, motioning toward the front. There, by the window, sat an empty table for two in the corner, and Molly couldn't help wondering if James had prearranged the table, and if the man had taken leave of every last bit of good sense she knew he had.

She glanced back at him, barely vocalizing the words. "James, I really don't think—"

"There's a table free in the corner there." His eyes said he knew exactly what she meant, but his palm pressed gently, yet firmly, against the small of her back urged her forward.

Molly had no choice but to comply and kept her head down.

James greeted everyone they passed by name, and without exception, everyone reciprocated. But it wasn't the congenial, warmhearted response she'd witnessed so many times. *God, give me the courage to follow your lead, no matter where it takes me.*

How often had she prayed that in recent days. . . .

Responding to a silent inner warning, Molly

glanced up—and stopped abruptly. Directly ahead was LuEllen Spivey. But it wasn't only Mrs. Spivey's scathing stare that nailed her boots to the floor, it was LuEllen's husband, Arlin, and Mayor and Eliza Davenport—and Miss Judith Stafford, Mrs. Spivey's niece. The five occupied a table a few feet away, set directly in their path.

Molly prayed the floor would open wide and swallow her whole. Either that or perhaps this was what James needed for him to finally realize how foolish an idea this was, and he would take her home.

A possessive arm came about her waist. "One step at a time," James whispered feather-soft in her ear, and guided her toward certain doom.

43

Molly forced a pleasant countenance, unable to find anything within her resembling a believable smile. She tried to go left in the hope of avoiding LuEllen Spivey's table, but as if on cue, a gentleman pushed back his chair and stood. James's hand on her arm guided her forward, and Molly cringed inwardly.

James paused by Arlin Spivey's chair. "Arlin, Mayor . . . ladies. How are you this evening?"

Mayor Davenport didn't even look in Molly's direction. "We're fine . . . Sheriff. It's a bit crowded in here tonight, though."

"And getting more so by the minute." LuEllen Spivey's smile looked as if it might snap in two.

Molly felt James move closer to her, the underlying possessiveness of his gesture unmistakable.

"Molly"—James touched her arm, his personal manner of address not lost on her—"I'm sure you remember meeting Miss Stafford at the town celebration."

"W-why, of course I do." Molly met the young woman's eyes and wasn't surprised not to find a friend there. *What* was James doing? "It's nice to see you again, Miss Stafford."

"Likewise . . . I'm sure."

Tension layered the already thick air.

"Well, enjoy your evening, folks," James said, his tone genuine.

Feeling the onus on her to add something cordial, Molly glanced back at Judith Stafford. "I hope you enjoy your visit, Miss Stafford."

The entire table laughed. Too late, Molly realized she'd made a misstep, and that everyone around them was listening.

"Apparently you haven't heard, *Miss* Whitcomb." Mayor Davenport leaned forward. "Or perhaps you've been . . . indisposed recently. Miss Stafford is our new teacher."

Molly felt time stutter, and heard Lori Beth's words clearly in her memory. *"When you're made to stand before others, naked, with all your faults showing, like we have been . . . that changes a person.*" If there was one thing she wanted out of all this, it was to be changed. To be made new. For so long she'd wanted to make a difference in lives around her. But never before had she so wanted her own life, the woman she was, to be changed.

"Congratulations, Miss Stafford," she heard herself say. "I wish you all the best in your future here, both in school with the children and in Timber Ridge." And she meant every single word.

Molly waited until the store was about to close before she slipped inside.

"Dr. Whitcomb." Ben Mullins met her coming down the aisle. "I was just about to lock the doors, ma'am." He yawned. "But I'll stay open for you and that sweet little girl anytime." He lightly patted Jo's back. "Take your time shopping. I'm just going to start bringing the produce inside."

Molly smiled. "Thank you, but all I need to do is mail this letter." She handed it to him.

He took it from her and stuck it in his apron pocket. "Mail doesn't run tomorrow, of course. So it'll go out first thing Monday morning."

"That'll be just fine." She looked around the store one last time.

"You sure there's not anything else you need tonight?"

She glanced at the shelf on the far wall. "In fact, I think there is. I'd like a tin of sugar sticks, please."

• • •

Early the next morning, Molly boarded the stage, Jo in her arms and her stomach in knots. Leaving Timber Ridge was difficult enough, but dredging up the nerve to get back onto a stagecoach was nauseating. She chose the seat facing forward this time, and was glad when only two other passengers boarded after her. An elderly couple who sat together on the opposite bench seat. She didn't recognize them.

"You sure you're comfortable in there, Dr. Whitcomb?" Mr. Lewis poked his head inside the window and gave her a conspiratorial wink. "I promise, this'll be a good one this time."

Molly's pulse raced thinking about their "last one," and she held Jo closer, wondering if she was doing the right thing. Not in leaving Timber Ridge—she was convinced of that—but in her mode of transportation. Yet there was no other way to get down the mountain other than to ride a horse, and she couldn't exactly do that in freezing weather with a baby.

"Yes, I'm quite comfortable. Thank you."

"How long you plannin' on bein' gone, ma'am? You're not takin' much."

She'd only checked her satchel and a small trunk. She was sending the rest of her possessions by wagon, to be sent on a later train, not wanting to risk weighing down the coach. Not with what happened last time. "I haven't thought that completely through yet, Mr. Lewis." She shifted Jo in her arms to face him, hoping the baby would distract him from further questions.

"Well, would you look at her!" Grinning, he reached out and chucked her little chin. "I think she's my youngest passenger yet." His expression sobered a degree. "You rest assured, ma'am. I'll take care of her. I give you my word."

The coach shifted as he climbed up to the driver's seat. And when the horses surged forward, Molly's stomach did a little flip. She glanced at her traveling companions, but their eyes were already closed, their heads angled to the side. And she pushed away the unwelcome sense of déjà vu.

Thankfully there'd been no new snow in recent days and the roads were clear. The skies were gunmetal gray, and a fog, heavy and thick, hung low over the mountains, shrouding the highest peaks. But Molly didn't have to see them to remember what they looked like.

Some things, once you saw them, stayed with you forever.

Besides Lori Beth, Dr. Brookston was the only one who knew they were leaving this morning. At their last appointment, Dr. Brookston had declared Jo "fit as a feisty little fiddle" and had reluctantly given Molly the name of a physician near Athens, Georgia, who specialized in children's medicine, someone he'd attended school with and that he highly recommended. To say she dreaded going back to Athens was an understatement. She still had the family home there, but it wasn't her home any longer. She'd written to a school in Atlanta—a modest establishment dedicated to teaching teachers—and had received a favorable reply about her credentials and a current opening. Her chest ached as Timber Ridge disappeared from view.

Whatever she ended up doing—*God, give me the courage to follow your lead*—she knew it would be best done away from Timber Ridge. And away from James. *Lord, give him the courage too.*

Part of her felt like a coward for not saying goodbye to him face-to-face, but if he'd known she planned to leave, he would have tried to make her stay. That had become clear the night of their dinner at Miss Clara's over a month ago.

He'd held the back of her chair as she'd sat down, and he'd done everything he could that night to show her—and everyone else—that he wasn't ashamed of being in her company. But she was ashamed enough for both of them.

The ride home was quiet, a mirror image of dinner. And when they got back to the house, as soon as he stopped the wagon, she tried to climb down of her own accord. But he'd caught her arm and held her there. "I'd hoped we'd have a chance to talk tonight, Molly. I've missed you. I just need some time to sort things through. To gain my bearings again." He'd touched her face, and the summoned courage inside her had nearly puddled at her feet.

And that's when she'd known—

He would do it. He would give up everything for her—his reputation, his job, his standing in this town, his entire life here—if she'd let him. But just as she hadn't known what would come from that one hasty decision she'd made after stepping from the train in Sulfur Falls, he had no idea what he was giving up and what repercussions would follow.

But she did.

And she wouldn't do that to him, now knowing how it felt. Not having lived with it. And every time she'd seen him in the past month, her conviction had strengthened.

The coach jostled over the winter-rutted road, and Molly stared out the window, watching the sun burn away the morning fog. The day promised to be a brilliant one.

Jo began to fuss. Molly usually tried gently bouncing her in her arms to distract her, but the stage was already doing that. Nursing her was out of the question with an audience sitting directly across from them—regardless of the couple dozing—so Molly withdrew a rattle from the satchel and tried to interest her. It didn't work.

Jo's disgruntled whimpers grew louder, and Molly cradled her close, patting her back. It was going to be a long ride down the mountain.

This coach was considerably nicer than Mr. Lewis's previous one, but all Molly could think about was how close the wheels would come to the cliff when they rounded the corners. She did relatively well suppressing her mounting anxiety until the terrain outside began to change. And became disturbingly familiar.

The drop-off grew steeper, the road narrower, and her nerves tauter. The boulders in the ravine below resembled teeth, waiting to chew her alive. Again. She scooted toward the opposite side of the seat, as far away from the window, and Devil's Gulch, as she could get. Images from that day last summer flashed in her mind.

The coach made a sudden jerk and expelled the air from her lungs. Jo cried louder.

Molly tightened her hold on her daughter as the stage slowed. Or was it sliding? The elderly couple had awakened and were staring out the window, their expressions inquisitive.

Mr. Lewis called out, whether to the horses or to his passengers, Molly didn't know. She couldn't understand him. But when the stage came to a stop, she froze. The coach tilted to one side, and she braced her feet on the opposite bench, drawing a curious stare from the older woman.

"Sorry, folks." Mr. Lewis appeared in the window, rubbing his whiskered jaw. "But I . . . ah . . ." He cleared his throat. "I need to check the harnesses on the horses." He seemed hesitant to look his passengers in the eye. "We'll be back on the road before you know it."

He hurried away, and the elderly couple settled back in their seat. Molly let out a breath. *Check the harnesses? Check the harnesses!* Heart pounding, she grabbed her reticule. No way was she was staying on this stage. Not with Jo. Not again.

Securing her daughter in her arms, she unlatched the door and climbed out. She would walk the rest of the way down. The sun was out. It was warming up, and she could get an extra blanket for Jo from the trunk. It wouldn't be that bad, and—

That's when she saw him. Standing there on the edge of the cliff in his rain-slicked duster and weathered Stetson. She stared, numb inside. Partly from being back in this spot again, but mostly from seeing him here, now. The certainty of her decision began to sway inside her, but looking at him, loving him the way she did, she determined to follow through.

James walked toward her. Handsome hardly began to describe him, especially with that half grin slowly edging up one side of his mouth. "Beg your pardon, ma'am. But do you need some help getting your luggage down?"

"What are you doing here? How did you—"

He pulled an envelope from his pocket. She recognized her handwriting. It was the envelope she'd mailed last night. Or thought she'd mailed. *Ben Mullins . . .*

"I got a special delivery around midnight." He stepped closer, the blue of his eyes turning more so in the sunlight. "Ben had a pretty good tussle with his conscience, but he finally decided this was something I might need to see before Monday." He gave her a scolding look. "He was right."

Molly found it difficult to hold his gaze. "James . . . it's best this way. You don't realize that now. But you will, given time."

"I told you once that I'd take you down the mountain . . . if and when you ever needed to go."

Emotion wavered his voice and touched a place inside her. Molly shook her head. "But you wouldn't have. Not if I'd asked. You would have tried to talk me into staying. And I can't stay, James. We both know that."

A gleam lit his eyes. "What I know, Molly, is that you belong with me. Both you and Jo do. Deep down, you know that."

"Deep down, I know that if I were to stay in Timber Ridge, everything would change for you. And not in a good way. You can no more stop being the sheriff, James, than you can stop breathing. Leading people, protecting people, it's in your blood. I won't be the one to take that future away from you."

He laughed softly and cradled her cheek. "*You* are my future, Molly Whitcomb. You and this sweet little girl. I'm a better man, and I'll be a better sheriff, with you beside me." He leaned down and placed a tender kiss on Jo's forehead.

When he raised his head, Molly read the intimacy in his expression and took a backward step. "What if, come spring, the people of Timber Ridge don't agree with that assessment?"

"The people of Timber Ridge don't hold my future. Or yours. God does, and He'll bring what He wants to bring, and He'll take what He wants to take. And I'll do my best to accept whatever comes from His hand. Whether that means being sheriff, or doing something else with my life. But whatever I'm doing"—he moved closer and slipped his arms around her waist—"I want you and this sweet little girl beside me, for as long as God sees fit."

Emotion welled up in Molly's throat. He seemed so sure, and was so convincing. She found herself wanting to trust his certainty, and the quality of rightness and goodness in his heart that always pointed true north.

He kissed her cheek, his breath warm against her skin. "The toast you made that night, on our sleigh ride . . . I've prayed that every day since then, for myself and for you. For us. I don't know how all the pieces of our lives fit together, Molly, but I do know, without a doubt, that God led you here. Of all the places you could have gone, He brought you to Timber Ridge. And to me." A twinkle lit his eyes. "And I'll tell you this, my bonny lass, I'm not of a mind to let you go either. Not without a good fight."

She smiled at his brogue and at the mischievous gleam in his expression.

"But if it's a fight you're wantin' "—he winked— "then you've come to the right man, my lady. Because I won't be lettin' you go without one."

She laughed, and with a trembling hand she touched his face. "I don't want to fight you. Not anymore," she whispered. "And I don't want to leave you, James McPherson."

The humor in his expression faded and was replaced by something far more powerful. "Molly, I've got something I've been meaning to give you for a while now. This isn't quite the setting I imagined, but . . ." He laughed, glancing at the ravine. "In a way, it seems fitting."

Wordlessly, she waited, hoping it was what she thought it would be.

"I found this"—he pulled something from his pocket—"when we were packing up your stuff. After Jo was born." He held out the ring she'd bought in Sulfur Falls all those months ago.

And her heart fell. She couldn't bring herself to look at him.

He fingered the ring, all dull metal now, no sheen. "I didn't know if you'd want to keep it. But it didn't seem right to pack it up with your stuff— not when I'd already bought this one to replace it."

He opened his other hand to reveal a small white box, and Molly wanted to slap him and kiss him at the very same time.

"I'd be honored, Miss Molly Whitcomb, if you'd take me to be your husband. And if you'd allow me to be this sweet little girl's papa." He brushed a finger against Jo's tiny fist. Jo latched on to him and didn't let go.

Molly looked up, tears in her eyes, seeing the same in his, and words wouldn't come. She didn't deserve this man, or this second chance.

James opened the box, and every shred of remaining doubt inside Molly fled. It couldn't be . . .

The ring was lovely—shiny gold with delicate etchings that gave the finish a brushed look. It was the ring she'd first chosen all those months ago, pure gold, refined by fire. But it had been too costly—and too pure—for what the ring she'd bought that day would represent.

The distinct clearing of a throat drew their attention. Mr. Lewis stood watching, along with the older couple.

Mr. Lewis motioned. "I don't mean to hurry you young folks along, but I've got a stage to run." Humor punctuated his grin. "And I'm just wondering how much longer you might be."

James tossed him a smile. "Well, that all depends"—he turned back—"on what Miss Whitcomb's answer is."

Molly smiled up at him. God seemed determined to give her what she did not deserve, and she determined to spend the rest of her life making sure He knew she was grateful. "You already know what my answer is."

He cradled her face. "Yes, ma'am, I do. But I'd like to hear it, just the same."

"Yes," she whispered. "For both me and Jo, for as long as God sees fit." She stood on tiptoe and kissed him, without reservation and without holding back. Just as she'd wanted to do ever since he'd told her he'd read *Little Women*.

A Note From Tamera

Dear Friends,

If you've made it this far, you've invested quite a bit of time in James and Molly's journey. Thank you for choosing to travel this road with them, and with me. While I hope you've been entertained and have experienced some laughs and maybe even some tears along the way (I don't feel as if I've gotten my "money's worth" unless I experience both), my sincerest desire is that you've taken a step closer to Christ. After all, it's all about Him.

To say that teachers have made a difference in my life would be a great understatement. They have shaped my eternity. I was thrilled to watch Molly's relationships with her students grow and flourish in ways she couldn't have imagined (and that I didn't either, when first plotting this story). I think of teachers I've been blessed to know in my life—Mrs. Putnam and Miss Deborah Ackey (Idlewood Elementary School), Jimmy Jones, David Fincher, John Clovis, and Dwight Smith (Greater Atlanta Christian School), Jimmy Allen and Jim Woodroof (Harding University), and many others—and I still treasure all they taught me. And will forever. Thank you, dear friends, for investing in me.

I don't know if you've ever been in a situation

when you, quite literally, couldn't wait to be "beyond this moment," regardless of whether your circumstances stemmed from your own poor choices or rather simply from living in a fallen world. But at certain points in Molly's journey, I identified with her situation far more than I wanted to, and the discomfort in those moments was palpable. Regret over things I've done in my life returned a hundredfold, and I relived that gut-wrenching sourness one feels in the pit of their stomach when wishing they could have a "do over" on certain decisions. But can't.

Some decisions, once made, have unavoidable consequences that cannot be removed, much like Molly's. However, even in those darkest of times, when we feel the overwhelming weight of our sin, God is always—*always*—yearning to forgive. He's not simply *willing* to forgive, mind you, He's eager to extend pardon. So if you've wandered from Him, know that He's standing on the porch even now, watching for you, waiting for you to come home. Or if you need to come to Him for the very first time, don't delay. Run for Him with all you've got. His arms are open wide, ready to catch you. Doesn't the Cross of Jesus Christ say that?

Until next time,
Tamera Alexander

ACKNOWLEDGMENTS

My thanks . . .

First and always, to Jesus—who searches me and knows my heart, and is leading me in the way everlasting.

To Joe, Kelsey, and Kurt—without you . . . Well, I don't even want to go there.

To Natasha Kern, my agent—your insights, not only into this industry but into writing, amaze me. I'm glad we're together.

To Karen Schurrer, Helen Motter, Charlene Patterson, Julie Klassen, Sharon Asmus, and Ann Parrish, my editors at Bethany House, and to Raela Schoenherr, an early reader—your comments and feedback as this story grew and took shape added such richness and depth, and helped me keep my sanity.

To Francesca Muccini—for sharing your love of your native tongue, and for translating the necessary phrases into Italian. *Molte grazie.* And any mistakes are mine.

To my readers—your notes and letters are blessings I treasure, and that you grow to love these characters as much as I do is an unexpected joy. I look forward to more journeys together.

Join me again in Fall 2009 for *Within My Heart,* the next book in the Timber Ridge Reflections series.

TAMERA ALEXANDER is a bestselling novelist whose deeply drawn characters, thought-provoking plots, and poignant prose resonate with readers. Having lived in Colorado for seventeen years, she and her husband now make their home in Tennessee, where they enjoy life with their two college-age children and a silky terrier named Jack.

Tamera invites you to visit her Web site at
www.tameraalexander.com
or write her at the following postal address:

Tamera Alexander
P.O. Box 362
Thompson's Station, TN 37179

Center Point Publishing
600 Brooks Road ● PO Box 1
Thorndike ME 04986-0001 USA

(207) 568-3717

**US & Canada:
1 800 929-9108**
www.centerpointlargeprint.com